A
Garland Series

VICTORIAN
FICTION

NOVELS OF FAITH
AND DOUBT

*A collection of 121 novels
in 92 volumes, selected by
Professor Robert Lee Wolff,
Harvard University,
with a separate introductory volume
written by him
especially for this series.*

FOXGLOVE MANOR

Robert Buchanan

Three volumes in one

Garland Publishing, Inc., New York & London

1975

Bibliographical note:

this facsimile has been made from a copy in the
Yale University Library
(Ip.B851.884K)

Library of Congress Cataloging in Publication Data

Buchanan, Robert Williams, 1841-1901.
   Foxglove manor.

   (Victorian fiction : Novels of faith and doubt ;
v. 36)
   Reprint of the 1884 ed. published by Chatto and
Windus, London.
   I. Title. II. Series.
PZ3.B852Fo15 ₍PR4262₎   823'.8   75-483
ISBN 0-8240-1560-6

82-1256

Printed in the United States of America

FOXGLOVE MANOR

FOXGLOVE MANOR

A Novel

BY

ROBERT BUCHANAN

AUTHOR OF

"GOD AND THE MAN," "THE SHADOW OF THE SWORD,"
"THE NEW ABELARD," ETC.

IN THREE VOLUMES
VOL. I.

London
CHATTO AND WINDUS, PICCADILLY
1884

PREFATORY NOTE.

THE following attempt at a tragedy in fiction (a tragedy, however, without a tragic ending) must not be construed into an attack on the English priesthood generally. I have simply pictured, in the Rev. Charles Santley, a type of man which exists, and of which I have had personal experience. Fortunately, such men are uncommon; still more fortunately, the clergymen of the English Establishment are for the most part sane and healthy men, too unimaginative for morbid deviations.

ROBERT BUCHANAN.

CONTENTS OF VOL. I.

FOXGLOVE MANOR.

CHAPTER I.

ST. CUTHBERT'S.

As the sweet, clear voices of the sur-
pliced choristers rose in the closing
verse of the hymn, and the vicar, in
his white robe and violet hood, ascended
the pulpit steps, old Gabriel Ware,
sexton and doorkeeper of St. Cuthbert's,
limped across the pavement and slipped
into the porch, as his custom was at
sermon-time on Sunday afternoons.

He waited till the singing had ceased
and the congregation had settled in

their pews ; and while he listened to
the vicar announcing his text—" For in
Him we live, and move, and have our
being "—he fumbled in the pockets
beneath his black gown of office, and
then limped noiselessly out into the
sunshine, where, after a glance round
him, he pulled out a short clay pipe,
well seasoned, filled it with twist, and
began his usual after-dinner smoke.

It was a hot, shimmering July afternoon, and it was much pleasanter to sit
out of doors on a tombstone, listening
to the vicar's voice as it came though
the dark lancets like a sound of running
water.

Half a mile or so away, nestled in
trees, was the village of Omberley, with
its glimpses of white walls and tiled or
slated roofs. Then there were soft,
hazy stretches of pasture, with idyllic

groupings of cattle and sheep and trees.
The fields of wheat and barley, turnips
and potatoes, lay out idle and warm,
growing and taking no care, and apparently causing none. The sight and
smell of the land filled Gabriel with a
stolid satisfaction at the order of nature
and the providential gift of tobacco.

There was but the faintest breeze
stirring, and it wafted all manner of
sweet odours and lulling whispers about
the graveyard. Everywhere there was
evidence of a fervent throbbing vitality
and joyousness. The soft green turf
which spread all round the church to
the limits of the churchyard, here
billowing over a nameless grave, here
crusting with moss the base of a tombstone or a marble cross or a pillared
urn, here edging round an oblong plot
brilliant with flowers and hothouse

plants,—the very turf seemed stirred by
glad impulses, and quivering with a
crush of hurrying insect life. Daisies
and buttercups and little blue and
pink eyed flowers danced among the
restless spears of grass with a merry
hardihood. Laburnums and sycamores
stood drowsing in the hot shining air,
but they were not asleep, and were not
silent. A persistent undertone came
from among their shadowy boughs, as
if the sap were buzzing through every
leaf and stalk. Up their trunks, toiling
through the rugged ravines of the rough
bark, travelling along the branches,
flitting from one cool leaf to another,
myriads of nameless winged and creeping things went to and fro, and added
their murmurs to the vast, vague reso-
nance of life. A soft, ceaseless whispering was diffused from the tall green

spires of a row of poplars which went along the iron railing that separated the enclosure from the high-road. Blue and yellow butterflies fluttered from one flowery grave to another; the big booming humble-bee went blundering among the blossoms; a grasshopper was singing shrilly in the bushes near the railing; a laborious caravan of ants was crossing the stony wilderness of the gravel path; a dragon-fly hawked to and fro beneath the sycamores; small birds dropped twittering on cross or urn for an instant, flashed away up into a tree, and then darted off into the fields, as though too full of excitement and gamesomeness to rest more than a moment anywhere. Soft fleecy masses of luminous cloud slumbered in the hot blue sky overhead, and only in its remote deeps did there seem to be unimpassioned quietude and a sabbath stillness—only there and in the church.

Notwithstanding the dazzling sunshine and the heat, the church was cool and dim and fragrant. The black and red tiles of the pavement, the brown massive pillars and airy arches of sandstone, the oaken pews, the spacious sanctuary with its wide stone steps, affected one with a refreshing sense of coolness and comfort. The light entered soft and subdued through richly stained glass, for the windows looked, not on familiar breadths of English landscape glowing and ripening in the July sun, but seemed rather to open into the strangely coloured world of nineteen centuries ago. The blessing of the little children, the raising of Lazarus, the interview at the well with the woman of Samaria, the minstrel rout about the house of the ruler whose little maid lay not dead but sleeping, took the place of the mundane scenes beheld through unhallowed windows. Even the unpictured lancets were filled with leaded panes of crimson and blue and gold. Then there was a faint, pleasant odour of incense about the building, emphasizing the contrast between the mood of nature and the mood of man. St. Cuthbert's was floridly ritualistic, and the vicar was one of those who felt that, in an age of spiritual disquiet and unbelief, a man cannot cling with too many hands to the great Revelation which appeared to be daily growing more elusive, and who believed that if the soul may be lost, it may also be, in a measure, saved through the senses. Feigned devotions and the absence of any appeal to the physical nature of man had, he was convinced, drawn innumerable souls into indifference on the one hand, and into Catholicism on the other. If there was a resurrection of the body as well as of the soul, surely the body ought not to be abandoned as a thing accursed, from which no good can come. The vicar encountered no difficulty in realizing his views of the dignity of flesh and blood at St. Cuthbert's.

A thick, softly toned carpet lay on the broad stone steps which led up to the communion table. Behind the communion table, and for some distance to right and left, the sanctuary walls were hung with richly coloured tapestry. The table itself—or the altar, as it was usually called—was draped with violet silk, embroidered with amber crosses, and upon it stood a large crucifix of brass, with vases of flowers, and massive brazen candlesticks on either side. In the

centre a large brass gasalier was suspended from a large ring, containing an
enamelled cross, and beneath it hung an
oil-lamp, which was kept perpetually
burning. Amid all the coolness and
fragrance and mystical flush of colour,
that little leaf of flame floating in its
glass cup attracted the attention of the
stranger most singularly. It piqued the
imagination, and added an indescribable
feeling of hallowed sorcery to the general
effect, which was that of an influence too
spiritual not to excite reverence, but too
sensuous to be considered sacred. Stepping out of the churchyard, with its
throbbing warmth and glad undertones
of commotion, into the cool, soft-lighted,
artificially coloured atmosphere of the
church, one might have felt as if dropped
into the Middle Ages, but for the modern
appearance of the congregation.

St. Cuthbert's was the fashionable
place of worship at Omberley, and its
afternoon service was always well attended, though at a glance one perceived,
from the chromatic effect of the pews,
that the large majority of the congregation were of the more emotional sex.
As the vicar gave out his text, his taste
for the bright and beautiful must have
been gratified by the flowers and feathers
and dainty dresses, and still more by the
rows of young and pretty faces which
were raised towards the pulpit with such
varied expression of interest, affection,
and admiration.

The Rev. Charles Santley had been
Vicar of St. Cuthbert's for little less than
a year. He was unmarried, just turned
thirty, a little over the middle height,
and remarkably handsome. It was not
to be wondered at that, with such recom-

mendations, the new vicar had at the very outset fascinated the maids and matrons of his congregation. A bright shapely face, with soft dark eyes, a complexion almost feminine in its clear flush, a broad scholarly forehead, black hair slightly thinned with study on the brow and at the temples, black moustache and short curling black beard,—such was the face of the vicar as he stood uncovered before you. His voice was musical and sympathetic ; the pressure of his hand invited confidence and trust ; his soft dark eyes not only looked into your heart, but conveyed the warmth and eagerness of his own ; you felt instinctively that here you might turn for help which would never be found wanting, and seek advice that would never lead you astray, appeal for sympathy with a certainty that you would be understood, obey the prompting to transfer the burthen of spiritual distress with a sure knowledge that your self-esteem would never be wounded. Of course there were ladies of a critical and censorious disposition among his flock, but even these were forced to acknowledge the charm of his presence and the kindliness of his disposition. Among the men he was less enthusiastically popular, as was natural enough ; but he was still greatly liked for his frankness and cordiality, and his keen intellect and sterling common sense commanded their respect.

On one thing you might always reckon at St. Cuthbert's—a thoughtful, eloquent sermon, delivered in a voice full of exquisite modulations. It happened often enough that the preacher forgot the capacities of his hearers, and became dreamy and mystical; but, though you failed to comprehend, you were conscious that the fault lay less with him than with your own smaller spiritual nature. This, too, happened only in certain passages, and never throughout an entire discourse. He began on the grass, as the lark does, and gradually rose higher and higher in the brightening heavens till your vision failed; but, if you waited patiently, he descended again to earth, still singing.

On this Sunday afternoon, preaching from the text in the Acts, he held his hearers spell-bound at the outset. Referring to the memorable discourse in which the text occurs, he conjured up before them Athens—glittering, garrulous, luxurious, profligate—the Athens St. Paul had seen. The vivid picture was crowded with magnificent temples, countless altars, innumerable shapes of mortal loveliness. Here was the Agora, with its altar of the Twelve Gods, and its painted cloisters, and its plane trees, beneath whose shade were disputing groups of philosophers, in the garb of their various sects. Gods and goddesses, in shining marble, in gold and ivory, caught the eye wherever it fell. There were altars to Fame and Health and Energy, to Modesty and Persuasion, to Pity and to Oblivion. On the ledges of the precipitous Acropolis glittered the shrines of Bacchus and Æsculapius, Venus, Earth, and Ceres. Over all towered the splendid statue of Pallas, cast from the brazen spoils of Marathon, visible, as it flashed in the sun, to the sailor doubling the distant promontory of Sunium. Every divinity that it had entered into the imagination of man to

conceive or the heart of man to yearn
for, every deified attribute of human
nature, had here its shrine or its
voluptuous image. "Ye men of Athens,
all things which I behold bear witness
to your carefulness in religion." It was
easier, said the Roman satirist, to find
a god than a man in Athens. And
yet these men, with all their civilization,
with all their art and poetry and philosophy, had not found God, and, notwithstanding all the statues and altars
they had erected, were aware that they
had not found Him; for St. Paul, as
he traversed their resplendent city, and
beheld their devotions, had found an
altar with this inscription, "To THE
UNKNOWN GOD." Referring then to
those "certain philosophers of the
Epicureans and of the Stoics," who
encountered the apostle, he briefly

sketched the two great systems of Greek speculation, and their influence on the morality of the age: the pantheism of the Stoics, who recognized in the universe a rational, organizing soul which produced all things and absorbed all things,—who perceived in pleasure no good, in pain no evil,—who judged virtue to be virtue and vice vice, according as they conformed to reason; the materialism of the Epicureans, who perceived in creation a fortuitous concourse of atoms, acknowledged no Godhead, or, at best, an unknowable, irresponsible Godhead, throned in happy indifference far beyond human impetration,—taught that the soul perished as the body perished, and was dissipated like a streak of morning cloud into the infinite azure of the inane. Following Paul as the philosophers " took him and brought him unto Areopagus," where from immemorial time the judges, seated on benches hewn out of the rock, had sat under the witnessing heavens, passing sentence on the greatest criminals and deciding the most solemn questions of religion, he glanced down once more at the city glittering with temples and thronged with gods and goddesses, and bringing into broad contrast the radiant Apollo and the voluptuous Aphrodite, with the scourged and thorn-crowned figure on the cross, he read the message of the apostle to the pagan world. On how many altars to-day might not the words "To the Unknown God" be fittingly inscribed! "In Him we live, and move, and have our being;" but how few of us have "felt after" and found Him! In a strain of impassioned eloquence the preacher spoke of that unseen sustaining presence, which brooded over and encompassed us ; of the yearning of the human heart for communion with the Creator ; of the cry of anguish which rose from the depths of our being, when our eyes ached with straining into the night and saw nothing, when our quivering hands were reached out into the infinite and clasped but darkness ; of the intense need we felt for a personal, tangible, sympathetic Being, for an incarnation of the divinity ; of those ecstatic ascensions of the soul, in which man "felt after" and actually touched God ; and, as he spoke, his glowing words gradually ceased to convey any definite meaning to the great majority of his hearers : but one face, flushed with joyous intelligence, one young beautiful face, with large, liquid blue eyes of worship, and with eager

tremulous lips, was all the while turned
fixedly up to his.

Seated in a little curtained nook near
the organ, a slim, fair girl of two and
twenty watched the preacher with almost
breathless earnestness. She was a
bright little fragile-looking blossom of
a being, who seemed scarcely to have
yet slipped out of her girlhood. Her
face was of that delicate white, tinged
with a spot of pink, which so often
indicates a consumptive constitution, but
in her case this delicacy of complexion
was owing rather to the fineness of the
material of which nature had moulded
her. Light fine hair, in silky confusion
rather than curls, clustered about her
forehead and temples. Her little hands
still clasped the music-book from which
she had been playing the accompani-
ment of the hymn—for Edith Dove was

the organist of St. Cuthbert's—as though
from the outset she had been too absorbed to remember that she was
holding it.

Occasionally the vicar turned towards
the aisle in which she sat, and his glance
rested on her for a moment, and each
time their eyes met Edith's heart beat
more rapidly, and a deeper tinge of
rose-colour brightened her cheeks. But
Mr. Santley showed no sign of kindred
emotion ; he was wholly absorbed in
the fervid thoughts which flowed from
his lips in such strains of exaltation.
As his eyes wandered over the congregation, however, he suddenly saw
another face which was turned attentively towards him, and which made
him pause abruptly. He stopped in
the midst of a sentence. He felt the
action of his heart cease, and he knew

that the blood was driven from his cheeks. He looked dazedly down at his manuscript, but was unable to find the place where his memory had failed him. For a few seconds there was dead silence in the church, and the eyes of the congregation were turned inquiringly towards the pulpit. Then, stammering and flushing, he resumed almost at haphazard. But the enthusiasm of the preacher had deserted him ; his attention was distracted by a rush of recollections and feelings which he could not banish ; the words he had written seemed to him foreign and purposeless, and it was only with a resolute effort that he constrained himself to read the parallel he had drawn between the pantheism and materialism of the days of St. Paul and those of our own time. To the close of his sermon he never once

ventured to turn his eyes again in the
direction of that face, but kept them
fixed resolutely upon his manuscript.
Not till he had descended the pulpit
steps and was crossing the chancel, did
he hazard a glance across the church
towards that disquieting apparition.

When the service was ended, and the
choristers, headed by the cross-bearer,
had passed in procession down the nave
to the vestry, the vicar hastily disrobed
and issued into the churchyard. As
with a strange fluttering hopefulness
he had half anticipated, he was being
waited for. A lady was moving slowly
about among the graves, pausing now
and again to read an inscription on a
stone, but keeping a constant observation on the church doors. As he came
out of the porch, she advanced to meet
him, with a smile upon the face which

had so terribly disconcerted him. She was a most beautiful, starry-looking creature—a tall, graceful, supple figure, with the exquisitely moulded head of a Greek statue ; a ripe rich complexion suffused with a blush-rose tint ; large lovely black eyes full of fire and softness ; long, curved, black eyelashes ; a profusion of silky black hair parted in little waves on a broad, bright forehead ; and a pair of sweet, red lips.

She held out a little white hand to him, and, as he took it, their first words were uttered simultaneously.

" Ellen ! "

" Mr. Santley ! "

" I never dreamed," said the vicar, excitedly, " I never dared to hope, to see you again ! "

" Oh, the world is very small," she replied gaily, " and people keep crossing

each other at the most unexpected times
and in the oddest of places. But I am
so glad to see you. Are you doing
well? You can scarcely imagine how
curious it was when I recognized you
to-day. Of course I had heard your
name as our vicar, but I had no idea
it could be *you.*"

"I am sure you are not more glad
than I am," rejoined the vicar. "Are
you staying at Omberley? Have you
friends here?"

She regarded him for a moment with
a mixed expression of surprise and
amusement.

"Do you not know that I am one
of your parishioners now?" she asked,
with a pleasant laugh.

He looked wonderingly into her dark,
joyous eyes, and felt a sudden sense of
chill and darkness within him, as a quick

intelligence of who and what she now was flashed into his mind.

"Are you at the Manor?" he asked, in a low, agitated voice.

"Yes," she answered, without noticing his emotion. "We arrived only yester-day, and have hardly had time yet to feel that we are at home; but I could not resist the inclination to see what sort of a church, and what sort of a vicar," she added, with a glance of sly candour, "we had at St. Cuthbert's. I am really so glad I came. Of course you will call and see us as soon and as often as you can, will you not? Mr. Haldane will be delighted, I know."

"You are very kind," said the vicar, scarcely aware of what he was saying.

"Indeed, I wish to be so," she replied, smiling. "Of course you know Mr. Haldane?"

" No; I have not yet had the pleasure
of meeting him. He—you had gone
abroad before I came to Omberley."

" Then you have not been here
long ? "

" Not quite a year yet."

" And do you like the place—and the
people ? "

" Both, very much indeed ! "

" You are not married yet, I think
Mr. Haldane said ? "

The vicar looked at her with a sadness that was almost reproachful as he
answered, " No; I have my sister living
with me."

" How pleasant ! You *must* bring
Miss Santley with you when you come,
will you not ? "

As she spoke she moved slowly
towards the gateway opening on to the
road, where a little basket-carriage was

awaiting her. He accompanied her, and for a few seconds there was silence between them. Then they shook hands again before she got into the carriage, and she repeated her assurance—

" I am so glad to have met you, Mr. Santley ! "

She took the reins, and, lightly flicking the ponies with the whip, flashed upon him a farewell smile from those dark, spiritual eyes and laughing lips.

The vicar turned back into the church-yard, and following a narrow path that led across the sward through a wicket and a small beech plantation, entered the Vicarage with a pale, troubled face.

CHAPTER II.

AT THE VICARAGE.

WHEN he reached the house he found that his presence was needed at the bedside of a labourer, who had met with a serious accident a day or two before, and who was now sinking rapidly. Mr. Santley was a man who never begrudged time or trouble in the interests of his parishioners; and, though he had yet another service to attend, and was already fatigued by the work of the day, he readily signified his willingness to comply with the request of the dying man, and at once started for the village.

He felt at the moment that the duty placed before him would be a relief from the thronging recollections and the wild promptings which had set his heart and brain in a turmoil. As he went down the road, however, the face of the dying man who had sent to seek his priestly aid, and the face of the beautiful wife of the owner of Foxglove Manor, seemed to be striving for mastery over him ; he was unable to concentrate his attention on any subject. His will was in abeyance, and he appeared to himself to be in a sort of waking nightmare, in which the most distorted thoughts of marriage and death, of a lost love and of a lost God, of the mockery of life, the mockery of youth, the mockery of religion, presented themselves before him in a hideous masquerade, till the function he was about to fulfil appeared to him at one moment a sacrilege and at another a degrading folly.

To understand in some degree the vicar's mental condition, it is necessary to glance back on his past life. In early manhood Charles Santley had been seriously impressed with the sense of a special vocation to a religious life. He was the son of a wealthy merchant, whose entire fortune had perished in one of our great commercial crises, and whose death had followed close upon his ruin. Up to that period Charles had been undecided as to his choice of a pursuit; but the necessity of making an immediate selection resulted in his devoting himself to the Church. Barely sufficient had been saved from the wreck of their property to support his widowed mother and his sister. For himself, he was endowed with a splendid physique, a keen intellect, and indomitable energy; and he at once flung himself into his new career. He supported himself by teaching until he was admitted to orders, when he obtained a curacy, and eventually, through the interest of some old friends of his father, he was presented with the living of St. Cuthbert's. In the course of these years of struggle, however, there was gradually developing within the man a spirit which threatened to render his success worse than useless to him. Ardent, emotional, profoundly convinced of the eternal truths of revelation and of the glorious mission of the Church, the young clergyman was at the same time boldly speculative and keenly alive to the grandiose developments of the modern schools of thought. It was not till he stood on the extreme verge of science and looked beyond that he fully realized his position. He then perceived with horror that it was no longer impossible—that it was even no longer difficult—to regard the great message of redemption as a dream of the world, the glorious faith of Christendom as a purely ethnic mythology, morality as a merely natural growth of a natural instinct of self-preservation. Indeed, the difficulty consisted in believing otherwise. The Fatherhood of a personal God was slipping away from his soul; the Sonship of a Saviour was melting into a fantastic unreality; the conviction of a personal immortality was dissipating into mental mist and darkness. The mystery of evil was growing into a fiendish enigma; virtue passed him, and showed herself to be a hollow mask.

His whole nature rose in revolt against this horrible scientific travesty of God's universe. He shrank back alike from the new truths and from the theories evolved from them. His faith could not stand the test of the wider knowledge. If God were indeed a myth, immortality but a dream, virtue an unprofitable delusion, man simply a beast gifted with speech, better the old faith concerning all these—accepted though it were in despite of reason and in outrage of immortal truth—than the hideous simulacra of the new philosophy. He cast himself back upon the bosom of the Church; he clung to her as to the garment of God; but he was powerless to exorcise the spirit of scepticism. It rose before him in sacred places, it scoffed at his most earnest and impassioned utterances; he seemed to hear within himself cynical laughter as he stood at the bedside of the dying; when he knelt to pray it stood at his ear and suggested blasphemy; it converted the solemn light of the Church into a motley atmosphere of superstition; it stimulated his strong animal nature to the very bounds of self-restraint. Still, if he was unable to exorcise it, he had yet the strength to contend with and to master it. Precisely because he was sceptical he was rigid in outward doctrine, zealous for forms, and indefatigable in the discharge of his clerical functions. In his passionate endeavour to convince himself, he convinced his hearers and confirmed them in the faith in which he was himself unable to trust.

To-day the old conflict between the sacerdotal and the sceptical was complicated by new elements of spiritual discord. After seven years of hopeless separation, Charles Santley had once more stood face to face with the embodied dream and inspiration of his early manhood, and had found her, in the full lustre of her peerless womanhood, another man's wife. During those years he had, it was true, reconciled himself to what then had been forced upon him as the inevitable, and he had sternly set himself to master the problem of his existence, without any secret hope that in the coming years his success might bring her within his reach ; but he had never forgotten her. She was to him the starry poetry of his youth. He looked back to the time when he had first known and loved her, as a sadder and a wiser world looks back to the Golden Age. The memory of her was the ghost of an ancient worship, flitting in a dim rosy twilight about the Elysian fields of memory, and, it being twilight, the fields were touched with a hallowed feeling of loss and a divine sentiment of regret. And now—oh, bitter irony of time and fortune!—now that he had achieved success, now that all the old gulfs which had separated them were spanned with golden bridges, now that he might have claimed her and she might have been proud to acknowledge the claim, she once more crossed his life—a vision of beauty, a star of inspiration—and once more he knew that she was hopelessly, infinitely more hopelessly than ever, raised beyond his seeking.

He was detained so long at the bed-side of the dying man that, by the time he had again reached the Vicarage, the bells were ringing for evening service and the western sky was ablaze with sunset. In the church the light streamed through the lancets and the painted casements, filling the air with motley breadths of glowing colour, and painting pillar and arch and the brown sandstone with glorious blazonry. Even in the curtained nook near the organ the space was flooded with enchanted lights, and Edith Dove sat beside the tall gilded instrument like a picture of St. Cecilia in an illuminated missal. In the pulpit the vicar stood as if transfigured. He spoke, too, as though he felt that this was the splendour of a new heaven opening upon a new earth, and the glad rustle of the trees in the cool breeze outside was the murmur of paradise.

" We shall not all sleep, but we shall all

be changed," were the words of his text, and throughout the fervid exposition of the apostle's faith in the resurrection the sweet, blue eyes and the eager lips of the organist were turned towards the preacher. He seemed this evening, however, to be unconscious of her presence. He addressed himself entirely to the listeners in the pews in front of him, and never cast even a solitary glance towards the aisle where she sat.

At the close of the service Edith found Miss Santley waiting for her at the entrance. It had now been customary for several weeks past for Miss Dove to go over to the Vicarage on Sunday evening and remain to supper with Mr. Santley and his sister. They went slowly through the churchyard together, and took the little path which led to the house. They remained chatting at the wicket for a few moments, expecting the appearance of the vicar. When Mr. Santley issued from the church, however, he passed quickly down the gravelled walk to the high-road. He had thrown a rapid look towards the plantation, and had seen the young women, but he gave no indication of having observed them.

"Why, Charles is not coming!" exclaimed Miss Santley, with surprise, as she saw her brother; "he surely cannot be going down to Omberley again."

"He is not going to Omberley, dear," said Edith, who had been watching for the vicar, and had been keen enough to notice the hasty glance he had cast in their direction; "he is going up the road."

"Then wherever can he be going

to ? And he had not had tea yet, poor fellow ! "

Miss Santley stepped a few paces back into the churchyard, and stood on tiptoe to catch a glimpse of him over the hedge ; but the vicar had already passed out of sight.

" Never mind, dear," she said to Edith. " Shall we go in and have a little chat by ourselves ? He may have some sick call or other, and he is sure to be back soon, or he would have told me where he was going. Come, you needn't look so sad," Miss Santley continued, as she observed the expression of her companion's face.

" I didn't think I was looking sad," replied Edith, blushing.

" Oh yes, you were ; dreadfully," said Miss Santley, laughing in a bantering manner.

" You don't think Mr. Santley is—is not quite well ? " asked Edith, timidly.

" Oh no ; Charles is quite well, I am sure."

" Perhaps he is displeased with something," said Edith, as if speaking to herself rather than to Miss Santley.

" What a little fidget you are ! " said her companion, taking the girl's arm. " I know what you are thinking of. I am sure he has no cause to be displeased with *you*, at any rate."

" I hope not," replied Miss Dove, brightening a little. " Only I felt a misgiving. You do feel misgivings about all sorts of things, don't you, Mary, without knowing why—a sort of presentiment and an uneasy feeling that something is going to happen ? "

" Young people in love, I believe, experience feelings of that kind," said

Miss Santley, with mock gravity.
" Come in, you dear little goose, and
don't vex your poor wee heart like that.
He will be back before we have got
half our talk over."

The vicar strode rapidly along the
road until he reached the summit of a
rising ground, from which he could see
two counties spread out before him in
fruitful undulations of field and meadow
and woodland. The sunset was burning
down in front of him. Far away in the
distant landscape were soft mists of blue
smoke rising from half-hidden villages,
and here and there flashed points of
brightness where the sun struck on the
windows of a farmstead. On either hand
were great expanses of yellowing corn
swaying in the cool breeze and red-
dening in the low crimson light. He
left the road, and passed through a gate

into one of the fields. Following a footpath, he went along the hedge till he reached a stile. Here he was alone and concealed in a vast sea of rustling corn. He sat down on the top of the stile, and resting his elbows on his knees and his chin in his hands, gazed abstractedly into the glowing west.

A single word which escaped him betrayed the workings of his mind : " Married ! "

Seven years ago, when Charles Santley began his struggle in life, he obtained through a clerical friend a position as teacher of classics in a seminary for young ladies in a small sea-side town in a southern county. He found his new labour especially congenial. A handsome young professor, whose attention was fixed on the Church, and who purposed to devote himself to her service, was cordially welcomed by the devout ladies who conducted the establishment. They were three sisters who had been overlooked in the wide yearning crowd of unloved womanhood, and who had turned for consolation to the mystical passions of religion. Under their care a bevy of bright young creatures were brought up as in the chaste seclusion of a convent. Their impressionable natures were surrounded by a strange artificial atmosphere of spiritual emotion; life shone in upon them, as it were, through the lancets of a mediæval ecclesiasticism, and their young hearts, breaking into blossom, were coloured once and for ever with those deep glowing tints.

It was here that the young man, in the first dawn of the romance of manhood, met the beautiful girl who was now the wife of the owner of Foxglove Manor. She was then turned of seventeen, and had become aware of the first shy longings and sweet impulses of her nature. She was his favourite pupil, and sat at his right hand at the long table when he gave his lessons. He used her pen and pencil, referred to her books, touched her hand with his in the ordinary work of the lesson. Her clothes touched his clothes beneath the table. At times their feet met accidentally. She regularly put a flower in a glass of water before his place. All these trifles were the thrilling incidents of a delicious romance which the school-girl was making in her flurried little heart. He, too, was not insensible to the trifles which affected his passionate pupil. Her great dark eyes sent electric flashes through him. Her breath reached him sweeter than roses. Her beautiful dark hair rubbed against his shoulder or his cheek, and he tried to prevent the hot blood from flushing into his face. When their hands touched he could have snatched hers and kissed it.

Ellen Derwent was happily not a boarder at the establishment, but resided with her aunt. Her family were wealthy country people, and Ellen, who had been ailing for a little while, had been ordered to the sea-side for change of air. Early in the bright mornings, and after the day's schooling was over, Ellen wandered about the sea-shore or took long walks along the cliffs. Santley met her first by accident, and after that, though the meetings might still be called accidental, each knew that to-morrow and to-morrow and yet again to-morrow the same instinctive feeling—call it a divine chance or love's premonition—would bring them together.

Ah ! happy, radiant days by that glad sea and in the wild loveliness of those romantic cliffs! Oh,vision of flushed cheek and shining eyes, and sweet red lips and throbbing bosom ! Oh, dim heavenly summer dawns, when the sea mists were just brightening, and the little birds were singing, and the sea-side town was still half asleep, and only two lovers were walking hand in hand along the green brow of the cliffs ! Oh, sweet autumn twilights which the shining eyes seemed to fill with dark burning lustre ! Oh, kisses, sweeter than ever pressed by woman's lips before or since ! Oh, thrill of clasped hands and mad palpitations of loving bosoms !

The swaying corn sounded like the

sea as the breeze passed over it, and the murmur broke the vicar's reverie.

" Married ! "

Married ? yes, married ! The sweet secret could not be kept for ever, and when Miss Lilburn, Ellen's aunt, discovered it, she at once spoke to Mr. Santley. She did not oppose his suit—indeed, she liked him greatly, but love, after all, was no mere school-girl's dream. Was he in a position to make Ellen his wife ? In any case, they must know about it at home. If Mr. Derwent approved, she would be most happy that Mr. Santley should visit her; but, in the meantime, it was only prudent that Ellen should discontinue these pleasant rambles.

He had never seen Ellen since, until her face made his heart stand still in the midst of his sermon.

The vicar rose from the stile with clenched hands and set teeth.

" Bitter, bitter ! " he said, raising his face to the sky and shaking his head as though he saw above him an invisible face, and spoke half in exquisite pain, half in stoical endurance.

CHAPTER III.

"THERE IS A CHANGE!"

WHEN Edith and Miss Santley reached
the Vicarage, they went into the parlour,
which, besides having a western exposure, commanded to a considerable
distance a view of the high-road along
which the vicar had passed.

"I always think this is the pleasantest
room in the house," said Miss Santley,
as she drew an armchair into the recess
of the open window, and Edith seated
herself on the couch. "Charles prefers
an eastern frontage, for the sake of the
early morning, he says ; but I am always

busy in the morning, so I suppose I like the afternoon light best, when I have a little time to sit and bask."

"Isn't it natural, too," suggested Edith, "that men should prefer sunrise and women sunset ? Men are so active and sanguine, and have so many interests to engage their attention, and women—well, as a rule—are such dreamers! Is it not almost constitutional ? "

"And when did you ever see me dreaming, may I ask ? " inquired Miss Santley.

"Oh no; you are not one of the dreamers," replied Edith, quickly. "You should have been called Martha instead of Mary."

"Insinuating that I am a bit of a busybody, eh ? " said Miss Santley, with a sly twinkle of humour.

" You know I did not mean to insinuate that."

" Or that you had yourself chosen the better part, eh ? " she continued gaily.

Edith coloured deeply, and cast her eyes on the floor, while an expression of pain passed across her face.

" Nay, my dear, do not look hurt. You know that was only said in jest."

" You cannot tell how such jests hurt me," replied the girl, her lips beginning to tremble.

" Even between our two selves ? " asked Miss Santley, taking Edith's hand gently and stroking it with both of hers. " You know, my dear little girl, how I love you, and how pleased I was when I discovered the way in which that poor little heart of yours was beating. You know that there is no one in the world whom I would more gladly—ay, or a thousandth part so gladly—take for a sister. Don't you, Edith ? Answer me, dear."

"Yes," replied the girl, letting her head hang upon her bosom, and feeling her face on flame.

"And have I not tried to help you ? I know Charles is fond of you—I am sure of that. I have eyes in my head, my dear, though they are not so young and pretty as yours. And I know, too, that a little while ago he was anxious to know what I would say if he should propose to take a wife. I shall be only too pleased when he makes up his mind. It will relieve me of a great deal of care and anxiety. And he could not in the wide world choose a better or a dearer little girl."

Miss Santley was not ordinarily of a demonstrative disposition, but as she uttered those last words she drew Edith towards her and kissed her on the forehead.

The vicar's sister was some twelve years his senior. A stout, homely, motherly little woman, with plain but pleasing features, brown hair, a shrewd but kindly expression, clear grey eyes, and a firm mouth and chin, she was as unlike the Vicar in personal appearance as she was unlike him in character and temperament. This family unlikeness, however, had had no prejudicial effect on their mutual affection, though in Miss Santley's case it was the source of much secret uneasiness on her brother's account. As unimaginative as she was practical, she was at a loss to understand her brother's emotional mysticism and dreamy idealism; but her knowledge of human nature made her timorously

aware of the dangers which beset the combination of a splendid physique with a glowing temperament which was almost febrile in its sensuous impulsiveness. She was spared the torture of sharing that darker secret of unbelief; but she was sufficiently conscious of the strong fervid nature of the vicar, to feel thankful that Edith had made a deep impression on him, and that when he did marry it would be a bright and congenial young creature who would be worthy of him and attached to herself.

"So why should it hurt you, if I do jest a little?" asked Miss Santley, as she kissed Edith. "Love cannot always be transcendental, otherwise two people will never come closely together. The best gift a couple of lovers can possess in common, is a capacity for a little fun and affectionate wit. Your solemn lovers are always misunderstanding each other, and quarrelling and making it up again."

"But we are not lovers yet, Mary;" said Edith in a timid whisper.

"Not yet, perhaps; but you will be soon, if I am capable of forming any opinion."

"I don't know, I don't know," Edith replied with a sigh; and her soft blue eyes filled with tears. Then raising her eyes imploringly to Miss Santley, and nervously taking her hand, she continued : "Oh, Mary, do not think me too forward and eager and unwomanly. Do not judge me too hardly. I know a girl should not give her heart away till she is asked for it. But I cannot help it—I love him—I love him so! I have done all I could to prevent myself from loving him, but it is no use—oh! it is no use."

She burst into a paroxysm of passionate sobbing, and Miss Santley, without saying a word, put her arms about her and softly caressed her soft flaxen hair.

The outburst was gradually subdued, and Edith, with a hot glowing face hidden on her friend's shoulder, was too ashamed to change her position.

"Do you feel better now, dear?" asked Miss Santley in a kindly voice.

"Oh, Mary, are you not ashamed of me—disgusted?"

Miss Santley replied in a woman's way with another kiss, and again fondled the girl's head.

After a pause of a few moments, she gently raised her face and regarded it affectionately.

"You must come upstairs and wash away those tell-tales before he returns. And "—she added a little hesitatingly—

" will you not trust me with the cause of all this trouble ? "

" I am afraid you will laugh at me, dear, it must seem such a foolish cause to you. And I know you will say it was all simply my fancy."

" What was it ? "

" You know, dear, where I sit in church?" Edith began, nervously playing with the lace on Miss Santley's dress. " Well, he always used to turn twice or thrice in my direction during the sermon. I used to think he did it because he knew I was there. And he did it this afternoon. But in the evening he never looked once during the whole time."

Miss Santley began to smile in spite of herself.

" Then when he came out of the church he saw you and me waiting for him—I saw him give one single sharp look—and then he went on as if he had not perceived us. He would not have gone away like that, Mary, if I had not been with you."

"And is that all?" inquired Mary as Edith paused.

"I think it is quite enough," the latter replied sorrowfully. "It means that he is tired of me; he was displeased that I was with you; he did not want to speak to me."

"My dear girl, all this is simply silly fancy; you will make your whole life miserable if you imagine things in this way."

"I knew you would say that; but you do not understand. I hardly understand myself; but I know what I say is true. You remember old Harry Wilson down in the village—he has a wooden leg, you know, but when there is going

to be a bad change of weather, he says
he can feel it in the foot he has lost ;
and he is always right. I think I am
like him, dear ; I have lost something,
and it makes me feel when there is a
change, long before the storm breaks."

" All this is nothing but nonsense, my
little woman ! " said Miss Santley re-
assuringly. " Come with me upstairs,
and let us make ourselves presentable."

When Edith had bathed her face, the
two came downstairs again, but instead
of returning to the parlour they went
into the library. This was specially the
vicar's room, and, more than any other,
it indicated the tastes and character of
its occupant. The whole house, indeed,
was tinged with the mediæval colouring
of the church, and in all parts of it you
came upon indications of the ecclesiastical spirit of the owner ; but here the

vicar had given fullest expression to his fancy, and the room had as much the appearance of an oratory as of a library. At one end a small alcove jutted out into the plantation, and the windows were filled with stained glass. On the walls hung several of Raphael's cartoons ; on the mantelpiece stood, under glass, a marble group of The Dead Christ ; the furniture, which was of carved oak, suggested the stalls in the chancel ; the brass gasalier and brackets were of ecclesiastical design ; and, lastly, the library shelves were solemnly weighted with long rows of theology, sermons, and Biblical literature in several languages. In a separate bookcase, which was kept locked, were gathered together a number of scientific works and volumes of modern specu- lative philosophy. A third bookcase was devoted to history, poetry, travels, and miscellaneous works. The great bulk of the library, however, was clerical, and the vicar had within arm's reach a fair epitome of all that the good men of all ages and many countries had discovered regarding the mystery of the world and the relationship of man.

In one corner of the room stood a tall richly carved triangular cupboard of black oak, and it too, like the bookcase of science, was kept perpetually locked.

As Edith entered the room her eyes fell upon it, and turning to her companion she asked—

"Oh, Mary, have you discovered the skeleton yet?"

"No," replied Miss Santley, with a laugh. "Charles is forgetful enough in some things, but he has never yet left the key in that lock. I once asked him

what it was he concealed so carefully,
but he refused to satisfy my curiosity ; so
I resolved to trust to chance and his
carelessness. I have waited so long,
however, that my curiosity has at last
been tired out. I don't suppose, after all,
it is anything worth knowing."

"And why does he always keep this
bookcase locked too ? The books all
look so fresh and new, and they are
much more attractive than those dusty
old fellows any one can look into. I
should like to read several of those, one
hears so much about them. There is
Darwin, ' The Descent of Man '—I
have read articles about that book in
the magazines, and I know he believes
Adam and Eve were apes in Paradise
or something like that."

"Oh, my dear, Charles would never
allow you to read those books on any

account.   They are all dreadfully wicked and blasphemous.   He only reads them himself to refute them and to be able to show how false and dangerous they are."

Edith, who had approached the window, now suddenly started back, and a bright flush rose to her face.

"Here is Mr. Santley, Mary!   How pale and wearied he looks!"

A moment or two later the vicar entered the library.   At the sight of Miss Dove he paused for an instant, and then advancing, held out his hand to her.

"You here, Miss Edith!" he said coldly.   "How are you, and how is your aunt?"

He did not wait for an answer, but went to his writing-table and sat down.

The two women exchanged glances of

surprise, and Edith's face grew sad and white.

"Are you not well, Charles?" his sister asked, going up to him and looking solicitously into his face.

"I am not very well this evening," replied the vicar; "it is the weather, I think. If Miss Edith will excuse me, I think I will leave you and lie down. I feel tired."

He rose again abruptly, and Edith stood regarding him with large, wistful eyes. He moved towards the door, and then suddenly stopped and turned to her.

"Good evening," he said once more, holding out his hand and speaking in a cold, distant manner. "Present my compliments to your aunt."

"I hope you will be well in the morning," said Edith, timidly.

"Thanks. Yes; I expect I shall be all right again after a little rest."

He turned and left her, and Miss Santley, glancing at her significantly, followed him to his room.

"He has over-exerted himself to-day," said Mary a little later, as she accompanied Miss Dove to the garden gate. "He had a sick call in the afternoon, and was unable to take his usual rest. You will excuse my not accompanying you home, will you not?"

"Oh certainly," said Edith. "I hope it is nothing serious. Would you not like to see Dr. Spruce? I can call, you know."

"He says he does not need the doctor; he knows what is the matter with him, and only requires rest. Good night, dear! I am so sorry I cannot go part of the way with you."

"Do not think of that," said Edith, shaking hands. "It is not late, and you must not leave him."

The sunset had lowered down to its last red embers, but it was still quite light as Edith turned away from the Vicarage gate. She proceeded slowly down the road towards the village for a few moments, and then paused and looked back. No one was on the road. Retracing her steps, she passed the Vicarage at a quick pace, and took the direction which the vicar had taken an hour before. Strangely enough, she stopped at the top of the rising ground where he had stopped; went through the same gate, into the same field, and, following the same path, reached the stile on which he had sat. Here she sat down, with the great sea of corn whispering and murmuring about her, and the distant landscape growing gradually more and more indistinct in the bluish vapour of the twilight. Alone and hidden from observation, she sat on the step with her arms on the cross-bar of the stile and her head laid on them, weeping bitterly.

" I have lost something, and it makes me feel when there is a change !"

CHAPTER IV.

GEORGE HALDANE.

THE low-lying landscape had vanished in the twilight, and the stars were twinkling in the clear blue sky before Edith rose, dried her eyes, and began to return homeward. The moon had risen, but had yet scarcely freed itself from the tops of the dark woods, through which it shone round and ruddy. As she passed the Vicarage, she paused and looked up at the windows. She felt prompted to steal quietly up to the door and inquire whether Mr. Santley was any better, but a fear arising from many causes held her back. Besides, the house was in darkness, and every one seemed to have retired to rest.

Since Edith had been in the habit of visiting the Vicarage, this was the first occasion on which she had returned home alone. Unreasonable as she acknowledged the suspicion to be, she could not rid herself of the belief that Mr. Santley's indisposition had been assumed as an excuse for avoiding her. She strove to convince herself that she was foolishly sensitive and jealous, to hope that the change in the vicar's manner was but an illusion of her excited fancy, to feel confident that when she saw him to-morrow she would recognize how childish she had been.

Miss Dove was exceedingly fond of music, and during the week she was accustomed to spend hours alone in the church, giving utterance to her thoughts and feelings in dreamy voluntaries, which were the fugitive inspiration of the moment, or filling the cool, richly lighted aisles with the impassioned strains of Mozart, Haydn, and Mendelssohn. The sound of the organ could be heard at the Vicarage, and Mr. Santley had been in the habit of going into the church, and conversing with her while she played. It was with the hope that one of his favourite pieces would again bring him to her that, during the afternoon of the following day, Edith took her seat at the organ. With nervous, eager fingers she swept the key-board, and sent her troubled heart into the yearning anguish and clamorous impetration of the *Agnus Dei* of Haydn's No. 2. When she had finished she rested for a little, and glanced expectantly down the aisle ; but no footstep disturbed the quiet of the place. She then turned to another of the vicar's favourites—a *Gloria* of Mozart's. The volumes of throbbing sound vibrated through the stained windows, and floated across the bright churchyard to the Vicarage ; but Edith's hope was not realized. She played till she felt wearied, rather with the hopelessness of her task than with the physical exertion ; but the schoolboy who blew the organ for her was exhausted, and when she saw how red and hot he looked, she closed the instrument and dismissed him. Every day that week she repeated her experiment, but her music had apparently lost its magical influence. The vicar never came. She called thrice to see Miss Santley, but each time he was away from home. Once she saw him in the village, and her heart began to beat violently as he approached; but they were on different sides of the street, and instead of crossing over to her, as he had always done hitherto, he merely smiled, raised his hat, and passed on. Sunday came round at length, and she looked forward with a sad, painful wonder to the customary visit in the evening.

It was a bright, breezy sabbath morning, and the great limes and syca-mores which buried Foxglove Manor in a wilderness of billowy verdure, rolled gladsomely in the sun, and filled the world with a vast sealike *susurrus*. On the stone terrace which ran along the front of the mansion the master of the Manor was lounging, with a cigar in his mouth, and a huge deer-hound basking at his feet; while in the shadow of the room his wife stood at an open French window, conversing with him.

Mr. Haldane was a tall, broad-shouldered, powerful man of about forty years of age. His face, especially in repose, was by no means handsome. His grave, large, strongly marked features expressed decision, daring, and indomitable force. His forehead was broad, and deeply marked with the perpendicular lines of long mental labour. The poise of his head suggested a habit of boldly confronting an opponent. His short hair and closely trimmed beard were touched with gray, and gave a certain keenness and frostiness to his appearance. A grim, self-sufficing, iron-natured man, one would have said, until one had looked into his bright blue-gray eyes, which lit up his strong, rugged face with an expression of frankness and dry humour.

"My dear Nell," he said at length, in answer to the persistent persuasion of his wife, "do not be cross. There are two things in the world which I abhor beyond all others : a damp church and a dry sermon. Invite your vicar as often as you please. I will do my best to entertain him ; but do not press me to sit out an interminable farrago of irritating platitudes in a chilly, straight-backed pew."

"I assure you, George, you will be charmed with him, if you will only let me prevail on you to come."

"Why cannot you Christians dispense with incense, and allow smoking instead —at least during the sermon ? "

Mrs. Haldane made a little grimace of horror.

"You would then have whole burnt offerings dedicated with a devout and cheerful heart."

"George, you are shockingly profane ! I see it is no use urging you any further; but I did think you would have put yourself to even some little inconvenience for my sake."

"For your sake, Nell !" replied Mr. Haldane, laughing. "Why did you not say so sooner ? You know I would do anything on those terms. Have I not often told you the married philosopher has but one moral law—to do his wife's will in all things."

"Then you will accompany me ?"

"Certainly I will."

"You are a dear, good old bear," exclaimed Mrs. Haldane, slipping on to the terrace and caressing his head with both hands. "But you know you *are* a

bear, and you will try for once to be nice
and good-natured, will you not? And
you will not be cold and cynical with
him because he is ideal and enthusiastic?
And if you do not acknowledge that he
is a delightful preacher, and that the
dear little church is charming—— "

" You will not ask me to go again ? "

" I was going to say that, but it will
be wiser to make no promises. You
know, dear, you should go to church, if
it were only for the sake of giving a
good example ; and it is my duty to try
and persuade you to go. And oh, George,
seriously I do wish you could feel that it
drew you nearer to God ; that where two
or three are gathered together, He is in
the midst of them. Now, do not smile
in that hard, derisive way. I know I
cannot argue with you, but if I cannot
reply to your reasoning, you cannot con-

vince my heart. I do believe, in spite
of all logic, that I have a heavenly
Father who loves and watches over me
and you too, dear; and I should be
wretched—— "

"My dear little woman," said Mr.
Haldane, taking both her hands in one of
his, "you have no cause to be wretched.
I have no wish to deprive you of your
belief in a heavenly Father. With
women the illusions of the heart last
longer than with men; and perhaps, in
these days of change and innovation, it
is as well that women have still a creed
to find comfort in. For my part, I confess I hardly understand what it is
attracts you in your religion. The
civilized world, so far as I can see, has
outgrown the golden age of worship, and
latria is one of the lost arts."

The presence of the master of Fox-

glove Manor created considerable surprise and curiosity among the congregation at St. Cuthbert's. Though he had
lived in the neighbourhood for the last
twelve years, this was the first time he
had been seen inside a church. Much
more attention was paid during the service to the beautiful lady of the Manor,
and the grim, powerful man who sat
beside her, than was in keeping with the
sacred character of the occasion. Mr.
Haldane, on his part, though he did his
best by imitating the example of his wife
to conform to the ritual, was keenly
critical of the whole service. The dim
religious light of the painted windows
pleased his eye, but failed to exercise
any influence on his feelings. The
decorations of the church seemed to
him insincere and artificial. He missed
in the atmosphere that sense of reverence

which he had experienced in the old cathedrals in Spain and Italy. The ceremonies appeared dry, joyless, and uninteresting, and as he watched the congregation bowing, kneeling, praying, singing, pageants of the jubilant mythic worship of the ancient world crowded upon his imagination.

"What are you thinking of?" his wife once whispered, as she caught a sidelong glance at his abstracted face.

"Diana at Ephesus!" he replied, with a curious twinkle in his keen gray eyes.

Once or twice during the sermon a saturnine smile passed across his face, and Mrs. Haldane pressed his foot by way of warning; but otherwise he listened gravely throughout, with his large, strongly marked features turned to the preacher.

"Well, have you been interested,

dear?" asked Mrs. Haldane, when the service was over, and they were waiting in the churchyard for the vicar.

"Yes," he replied drily; "your vicar is interesting."

"Now, what do you mean by that?"

"He will repay study, my dear."

Mrs. Haldane looked sharply into her husband's face, but was dissatisfied with her scrutiny.

"You don't like him?"

"I have no reason yet to like or dislike him. In a general way, I should prefer to say that I do like him."

"But what do you mean by your remark that he will repay study?"

"Perhaps you will not understand me," he answered thoughtfully. "Your vicar has a soul, Nell."

"So have we all, I suppose."

"At least he believes he has one,"

said Mr. Haldane, with a slight shrug of his shoulders.

" Well ! "

" And he is trying to save it."

" We all are, I hope."

" I beg your pardon, Nell; the pheno-menon in these days is a psychological rarity, and, being rare, is naturally interesting. It is one of the obscure problems of cerebration. Ah ! here comes your vicar."

With a bright smile Mrs. Haldane advanced to meet him, and cordially shook hands with him. " You must allow me to introduce you to my hus-band. George, Mr. Santley."

" My wife tells me," said Mr. Haldane, as they shook hands, " that she was an old pupil of yours."

" Yes," said the vicar, with an uneasy glance towards her, " many years ago."

"It is a little curious," continued Mr. Haldane, "how people lose sight of each other for years, and then are unexpectedly thrown together into the same small social circle, after they have quite forgotten each other's existence."

The vicar winced at the last words, but replied with a faint smile, "The great world is, after all, a very little world."

"Ah, my dear sir, I see I have started a familiar train of thought—the littleness of the world," said Mr. Haldane, with a dry light in his eyes.

"And you fear I may improve the occasion?" asked the vicar a little coldly.

"Pray do not misunderstand my husband," interposed Mrs. Haldane. "He was delighted with your sermon to-day; and I do not wonder, for you have the power of appealing to the heart and raising the mind beyond earthly things. It was only a few moments ago that he told me he was deeply interested."

"I perceived that he was amused once or twice," replied the vicar, with a smile.

"I confess that I may have smiled at one or two points in your discourse."

"Excuse my interrupting you," said Mrs. Haldane; "will you not walk? You can spare time to accompany us a little way?"

Mr. Santley bowed, and Mrs. Haldane signed to the coachman to drive on slowly towards the village.

"For example," resumed Mr. Haldane, "I see you still stick to the old chronology and the mythic Eden."

"Certainly I do."

"And yet you should be aware that at least a thousand years before the date you fix for the creation of Adam, tribes of savage hunters and fishers peopled the old fir-woods of Denmark, and set their nets in the German Ocean."

"It may eventually prove necessary to revise the chronology of the Bible," replied the vicar; "but there is at present too much conflict of opinion among your archæologists to decide on the absolute age of these tribes. After all, the question is one of minor importance."

"Granted. But you cannot say the same of the efficacy of prayer."

Mrs. Haldane laid her hand on her husband's arm, and stopped abruptly. "Ask Mr. Santley to dinner, George, and then you can discuss as long and as profoundly as you like; but I will

not allow you to argue now. Besides,
I want to talk to Mr. Santley."

Mr. Haldane laughed good-naturedly.
" Just as you please, my dear. If
Mr. Santley will favour us with his
company, I shall be very glad. Your
predecessor was a frequent visitor at
our house. A jovial, rubicund fellow,
whose troubles in this life were less of
the world and the devil than of the
flesh ! A fat, ponderous man and a
Tory, as all fat men are ; a sort of
Falstaff *in pontificalibus ;* a man with
a wit and a shrewd palate for old port.
Poor fellow ! he was snuffed out like
a candle. One could have better spared
a better man."

" Will you come to-morrow ? " asked
Mrs. Haldane ; " and, if your sister can
accompany you, will you bring her ?
You will excuse our informality and so
short a notice."

" I shall be very happy to call to-morrow."

" Then, if you can spare me a few moments I will have a better opportunity of speaking to you. I must learn all about the parish, and I have a whole catechism of questions to ask you. You will come to-morrow, then ? " she concluded, with one of those flashing looks from her great dark eyes.

He watched them drive away with that look burning in his brain and the pressure of her hand tingling through every nerve. He stood gazing after her with a passionate light in his eyes and an eager, yearning expression on his pale, agitated face. This was the woman he had lost, and now they were again thrown together in the same small social circle, after she had completely forgotten his existence ! Those words of her husband had cut him to the quick. Could she so soon, so easily, so completely have forgotten him? It seemed incredible. If she had used any such expression to her husband, was it not rather to forestall any jealous suspicion on his part? Clearly she had not divulged the secret of those school-girl days. *He* knew not the story of that sweet, imperishable romance; those burning kisses and unforgotten vows had been hidden from him; and in that concealment the vicar found a strange, subtle pleasure. It was at least one tie between him and her; one secret in common in which her husband had no share.

CHAPTER V.

THE LAMB AND THE SHEPHERD.

THE vicar was standing close beside the village school, and as he turned to go back home he saw the schoolmistress in the doorway of her little cottage. He started as though she had been looking into his heart, instead of watching the carriage as it bowled along towards the village. Without a moment's hesitation, however, he opened the schoolyard gate and went up to her.

"Well, Miss Greatheart, how are you to-day?"

Dora, a bright, merry-looking woman

of about thirty, dropped a curtsy, and invited the vicar into the house.

"Thank you, no; I must not stay. I have just been speaking, as you have seen, to my new parishioners. I call them new, though I suppose they are older in the parish than I am myself."

"Old as they are, this is the first time I ever set eyes on Mr. Haldane in our church, sir. His pretty wife must have converted him."

"Then they have not been long married?"

"Somewhere about two years, I should think. All last year they were away in Egypt and Palestine; and perhaps now that he's seen the Land, he believes in the Book."

"Indeed!"

"Seeing's believing, you know, sir; and if all tales be true, he used not to believe in anything from the roof upward. Oh, you may well look shocked, sir, but he was quite an atheist and an infidel; but you see he was so rich that the gentry round about didn't care to give him the go-by. I suppose you haven't been to the Manor yet, sir? The old vicar, Mr. Hart, was always there. People did say he paid more court to the people at the Manor than he should have done, considering the need for him in the parish; and when Mr. Hart got his second stroke, there were those that said it was a judgment on him for high living, and the company he kept. But you know, sir, how folks' tongues will wag."

"Is the Manor far from here? Of course I have heard of the place, but I have never been near it."

"It's about four miles, sir, and a lonely place it is, and dismal it must be in winter, with miles of wood about it. In summer it is not so bad, but it is awfully wild and solitary. I went over the grounds once, years ago. I became acquainted with one of the housemaids, you see, sir—quite a nice young person— and she invited me to tea. I remember it was getting dusk when I left, and she took me through the woods. Dear me, what a fright I got! I happened to look up, and there was a man, quite a giant, standing among the trees. I screamed, and would have run had not Jane—that was the maid, sir—laughed, and said it was only a statue. And so it was, for we went right up to it. All the woods are full of statues—quite improper and rude, and rather frightening to meet in the dusk. But now he is converted, Mrs. Haldane will have them all taken away, I should think. I don't believe the place is haunted, though there are some strange stories told about it; but I do know that the chapel—there is an old chapel close by the house—is shut up, and no one goes near it but Mr. Haldane and his valet—a dark foreign person, with such eyes! Queer tales are told about lights being seen in it at all hours of the night, and some of the old folk believe that if any one could look in they would see that the foreign valet had horns and a cloven foot, and that his master was worshipping him. I think that's all nonsense myself; but there's no doubt Mr. Haldane used to be dreadfully wicked, and an atheist."

"If he was so very bad," said the vicar, smiling, "surely it was strange that Mr. Hart used to associate with him so much."

"Well, you see, sir, he was always

liberal, and kept a good table, and Mr. Hart was a cheerful liver. Then Mr. Haldane was always ready with his purse when there was a hard winter, or the crops were bad, or any poor person was ill."

" I see, I see," said the vicar.

" But his charity could not do him any good, people said, when he didn't believe there was a God, or that he had a soul."

"So they didn't consider it worth while to be thankful ? "

" I don't think they did, sir."

" And was Mrs. Haldane staying at the Manor the first year of their marriage ? "

" Yes ; he brought her back with him after the honeymoon."

" And do they speak as kindly of her in the village as they do of her husband ? "

" Oh, indeed, sir, they worship her. Even old Mother Grimsoll, who said she wanted to make a charity woman of her when you bought her that scarlet cloak last winter, has a good word for Mrs. Haldane. She isn't the least bit conceited, and she knows that poor people have their proper pride ; and when she helps any one she makes them feel that they are doing her a favour. When Mr. Hart was alive she used to go round with him, devising and dispensing charities. It's only a pity she is married to—to—" — and Miss Greatheart beat impatiently on the ground with her foot in the effort to recall the word—" to an agnostic. Mr. Hart said he wasn't an atheist, but an agnostic, though I dare say if the truth were known one is worse than the other."

" You are not very charitable, Miss

Greatheart ; come, now, confess," said the vicar, good-humouredly.

"Perhaps not, sir ; but I have no patience with atheists and agnostics."

"An atheist," continued the vicar, " is a person who does not believe in a God ; an agnostic is one who merely says he does not know whether there is a God or not."

"Doesn't know!" exclaimed Dora, indignantly. "Wherever was the man brought up ? "

That evening, as Miss Santley and Edith went across from the church to the Vicarage together, the vicar joined them, and Miss Dove remained to supper as usual. The time passed pleasantly enough ; but Edith was conscious of a certain restraint in the conversation, a curious chilliness in the atmosphere. When at length she rose to go home, the vicar went to the window, and looked out for a few seconds.

"I think, Mary, you might accompany us; and when we have seen Miss Edith home, we could take a turn round together. It is a beautiful night."

Mary nodded assent, and Edith felt her heart sink within her. She was certain now that he was avoiding her. As she followed Miss Santley upstairs to put on her things, a sudden thought flashed upon her.

"I shall be with you in a moment, Mary," she said; "I have dropped my handkerchief, I think."

She ran back to the parlour, and met the vicar face to face as he paced the room.

She stood still, and looked at him silently for a moment. She had taken him by surprise, and he too stood motionless.

"Well," he said at last, with a faint smile.

"Do you hate me, Charles?" she asked in a low, steady voice.

"Hate you! Why should I hate you, my dear Edith? What should put such thoughts—— "

"I have only a few seconds to speak to you," Miss Dove continued hastily. "Answer me truly and directly. You do not hate me?"

"I shall never hate you, dear."

"'Why do you avoid me?"

"Have I avoided you?"

"You know you have. Why?"

"I have not avoided you, Edith."

"Do you still love me?"

"You know I do."

"As much as ever you did?"

" As much as ever."

" Can I see you to-morrow—alone ? "

" You know I am going to the Manor."

" I know," said Edith, with a slight tone of bitterness. " You will return in the evening, I suppose ?   I shall wait for you on the road till nine o'clock."

" I may be detained, you know, Edith."

" Then I shall be practising in the church on Tuesday afternoon as usual."

" Very well," he assented.

" Am I still to trust you, Charles ? " she asked, raising her soft blue eyes earnestly to his face.

" Yes."

" Yes ? "   She dwelt upon the word, still looking fondly up to him. He understood her, and bent over and kissed her.

"You will try to return home to-
morrow before nine? I have been
miserable all this week, and I have so
much to say to you."

"I will try to see you," said the vicar.

"I must run now; Mary will wonder
what has kept me."

The great woods about Foxglove
Manor were certainly lovely, and in the
winter, with the snow on their black
branches, and snow on the fallen leaves
and the open spaces between the clumps
of forestry, the place might have seemed
dreary and dismal; but on this July
afternoon the vicar experienced an indescribable sense of buoyancy and en-
largement among these vast tossing
masses of foliage. Their incessant
murmur filled the air with an inarticulate
music, which recalled to his memory the
singing pines of Theocritus and the voices

of the firs of the Hèbrew prophets. A spirit of romance for ever haunts the woodland, as though the olden traditions of dryad and sylvan maiden had not yet been wholly superseded by the more accurate report of science. In the skirts of the great clusters of timber, cattle were grazing in groups of white and red ; in the open spaces of pasture land between wood and wood, deer were visible among the patches of bracken. In the depths of the forest ways he came upon the colossal statues copied from the old masters ; and at length, at a turn of the shadowy road, he found himself in view of the mansion—an ancient, square mass of brown sandstone, stained with weather and incrustations of moss and lichens, and covered all along the southern exposure with a dense growth of ivy. The grounds immediately in front were laid out in formal plots for flowers and breadths of turf traversed by gravelled pathways. A little withdrawn from the house stood the ruined chapel of which the school-mistress had spoken. The ivy had invaded it, and scaled every wall to the very eaves, while patches of stonecrop and houseleek, which had established themselves on the slated roof, gave it a singular aspect of complete abandon-ment.

As Mr. Santley entered one of the walks which led to the terraced entrance, Mrs. Haldane, who had observed his approach, appeared on the stone steps, and descended to meet him.

" How good of you to come so early !" she exclaimed. " George will be de-lighted. He is in his laboratory, ex-perimenting as usual. We shall join

him, after you have had some refreshment."

" No refreshment for me, thank you."

" Are you quite sure ? You must
require something after so long a walk."

" Nothing really, I assure you."

" Well, I shall not press you, as we
shall have dinner soon. Shall we go
to Mr. Haldane ? Have you visited
the Manor before—not in our absence ?
How do you like it ? "

" I envy you your magnificent woods.

" Yes ; are they not charming ? And
you will like the house, too, when you
have seen it."

" Do you not find it dull, however ? "
asked the vicar, looking into her face
with an expression of keen scrutiny.
" You are still young—in the blossom
of your youth—and society must still
have its attractions for you."

"One enjoys society all the more after a little seclusion."

"No doubt."

"And we have just returned, you must recollect, from a whole year of wandering and sight-seeing, so that it is a positive relief to awaken morning after morning and find the same peaceful landscape, the same quiet woods about one."

"That is very natural; but the heart does not long remain content with the unchanging face of nature, however beautiful it may be. Even the best and strongest require sympathy, and when once we become conscious of that want——"

"Have you begun to feel it?" she asked suddenly, as he paused.

"I suppose it is the inevitable experience of a clergyman in a country parish," he replied, with a smile.

" Yes, I suppose it is. So few can take an interest in your tastes, and aspirations, and intellectual pleasures, and pursuits. Is not that so ? "

" It may seem vanity to think so."

" Oh no ; I think not. The people you meet every day are mostly concerned in their turnips or the wheat or their cattle, and their talk is the merest village gossip. It must indeed be very depressing to listen day after day to nothing but that. One has, of course, a refuge in books."

" But books are not life. The daydreams of the library are a poor substitute for the real action of a man's own heart and brain."

" Then one has also the great fields of natural science to explore. I think you will find the work of my husband interesting, and if you could turn your mind in the same direction, you would find in him inexhaustible sympathy."

As she spoke, they reached the low-arched portal of the chapel. The thick oaken door, studded with big iron nails, was open, and before them stood a man who bowed profoundly to Mrs. Haldane, and then darted a swift, penetrating glance at the vicar.

"Mr. Haldane is within, Baptisto?" she asked.

"Yes, señora."

He stood aside to allow them to pass, and as Mr. Santley entered he regarded the man with an eye which photographed every feature of his dark Spanish face. It was a face which, once seen, stamped itself in haunting lineaments on the memory. A dusky olive complexion; a fierce, handsome mouth and chin; a broad, intelligent forehead ; short, crisp black hair sprinkled with grey ; a thin, black moustache, twisted and pointed at the ends ; and a pair of big, black, unfathomable eyes, filled with liquid fire. It was the man's eyes that arrested the attention first, gave character not only to the face but to the man himself, and indeed served to identify him. In the village, " the foreign gentleman with the eyes " was the popular and sufficient description of Baptisto.

CHAPTER VI.

THE UNKNOWN GOD.

As the vicar entered the chapel, he stopped short, struck with astonishment at the singular appearance of the interior.

The sunlight streaming through the leaded diamond panes of the casements, instead of falling on the familiar pews, flagged nave, and solemn walls, shone with a startling effect on the heterogeneous contents of a museum and laboratory. Along one side of the building were ranged several glass cases containing collections of fossils, arctic and tropical shells, antique implements of flint, stone, and bronze, and geological specimens. The walls were decorated with savage curiosities—shields of skin, carved clubs and paddles, spears and arrows tipped with flint or fishbone, mats of grass, strings of wampum, and dresses of skins and feathers. On a couple of small shelves grinned two rows of hideous crania, gathered as ethnic types from all quarters of the barbarian world, and beside them lay a plaster cast of a famous paleolithic skull. On the various stands and tables in different parts of the room were retorts and crucibles, curious tubes, glasses and flasks, electric jars and batteries, balances, microscopes, prisms, strange instruments of brass and glass, and a bewildering litter of odds and ends, for which only a student of science could find a name or a use. At the

further end of the room, under the
coloured east window, stood an escritoire
covered with a confused mass of paper,
and beside it stood a small table piled
with books.

As Mrs. Haldane and the vicar
entered, the master of Foxglove Manor,
who had been writing, rose, laid down
his pipe, buttoned his old velvet shoot-
ing-jacket, and hastened forward to
welcome his visitor.

Baptisto gravely set a couple of chairs,
and, at a sign from his master, bowed
profoundly, and retired to the further
end of the apartment.

"Do you smoke, Mr. Santley?"
Mr. Haldane asked, glancing at a box of
new clay pipes.

"No, thank you; but I do not dislike
the smell of tobacco. I find, however,
that smoking disagrees with me—irri-

tates instead of soothing, as professors of the weed tell me it should do."

" Touches the solar plexus, eh ? Then beware of it ! The value of the solar system is often determined by the condition of the solar plexus."

" That does seem to be frequently the case," replied Mr. Santley, smiling.

" Invariably, my dear sir, as the ancients were well aware when they formulated that comprehensive, but little comprehended, proverb of the sound mind in the sound body. It is curious how frequently modern science finds herself demonstrating the truth of the guesses of the old philosophers ! "

" I perceive you are devoted to science," said Mr. Santley, waving his hand towards the evidences of his host's taste.

" Oh yes, he is perpetually experimenting in some direction or other," said Mrs. Haldane, with a laugh. "I believe he and Baptisto would pass the night here, boiling germs or mounting all manner of invisible little monsters for the microscope, if I allowed them. You must know, Mr. Santley, that Mr. Haldane is writing a *magnum opus*— 'The History of Morals,' I believe, is to be the title—and what with his experiments and his chapters, he can scarcely find time to dine."

"You have been happy in your subject," said the vicar, turning to the master of the Manor. "The history of morals must be an enthralling book. I can scarcely imagine any subject affording larger scope for literary genius than this of the development of that divine law written on the heart of Adam. Why do you smile, may I ask?"

" Pardon me ; I was not conscious that I did smile, except mentally. You will excuse me, however, if I frankly say that I was smiling at your conception of the genesis of morality. What you term the divine law written on the heart of Adam represents to me a very advanced stage in the development of the moral sense. We must begin far beyond Adam, my dear sir, if we would arrive at a philosophic appreciation of the subject. We must explore as far as possible into that misty and enigmatic period which precedes historical record ; approach as nearly as may be to the time when in the savage, possibly semi-simian, brain of the earliest of our predecessors experience had begun to reiterate her proofs that what was good was to his personal advantage, and that what was bad entailed loss and suffering. It has hitherto

been the habit to believe that the Deca-
logue was revealed from Sinai in thunder
and lightning and clouds of darkness.
As a dramatic image or allegory only
should that be accepted. Clouds of
darkness do indeed surround the genesis
of the moral in man, and the law has
been revealed by the deadly lightnings
of disease and war and famine and
misery, through unknown and innumerable generations. No divine law was
written on the heart of the first man, or
society would not be where it is to-day.
No; unhappily, one might say, morality
has been like everything else human—
like everything else, human or not,—like
the coloured flower to the plant, the gay
plumage to the bird a dearly bought
conquest, a painfully laboured evolution.

Once or twice during Mr. Haldane s
remarks, the vicar had raised his hand

in disclaimer, but waited till he had finished before speaking.

" I was about to protest," he now said, "against several of your expressions, but I fear controversy is of little good when the disputants argue from different premises. I perceive that you have accepted a theory of life which completely shuts out God from His creation."

" Pardon me ; like the old Greek, I can still raise an altar to the unknown God."

" To a cold, remote, indifferent abstraction, then," replied Mr. Santley, impulsively ; " to a God unknowing as unknown—a vague, unrealizable, impersonal Power."

" Impersonal, I grant you, and therefore more logical, even according to human reason, than the huge, passionate anthropomorphism of Jew and Christian.

Consciousness and personality imply the notion of limits and conditions; and which is the grander idea—a limited, conditioned Power, however great, or an absolute transcendent Godhead, free from all the limits which govern our finite being? God cannot be conscious as we understand consciousness, nor personal as we understand personality. If He were, then indeed we might well believe that we were made after His image and likeness."

"And can you find comfort in such a creed? Can you turn for strength, or grace, or consolation to such a power as you describe?"

"Why should I?" asked Mr. Haldane, smiling. "If I need any of these things, my need is the result of some law violated or unobserved. The world is ruled by law, and every breach of law entails an inescapable penalty. If I suffer I must endure."

"That is cold comfort for all the sum of misery in the world."

"It is the only true comfort. The rest is delusion. Preach that every violated law avenges itself, not in some half mythical hell at the close of a life that seems illimitable—for men never do realize that they will one day die—but avenges itself here and now ; preach that no crucified Redeemer can interfere between the violater of the law and its penalty; preach that if men sin they will infallibly suffer, and you will really do something to regenerate mankind. Christianity, with its doctrines of atonement and vicarious suffering and redemption, has done as much to fill the world with vice, crime, and disease as the most degraded creed of pagan or savage. The groaning and **travail of** creation are clamant proofs **that vicarious** suffering and redemption are **the veriest** dreams."

"Either purposely or **inadvertently** you mix up the physical and **the moral** law," interposed the vicar.

"The physical and the **moral are but** one law, articles of the **one universal** code of nature."

"True," said the vicar. **"I forgot** that you denied man his **immortal soul,** as you deny him his divine **sonship.** And so you are content to **believe that** man is born to live, labour, **suffer, and** perish."

Concede that God is **content that** such should be man's **destiny," replied** Mr. Haldane, "what **then?"**

"What then?" echoed **the vicar,** rising from his chair with **flashing eyes** and agitated face; "why, then life is a fiendish mockery!"

Mr. Haldane's face wore a grim smile as he heard the bitter emphasis of the vicar's reply.

"Ah, my worthy friend," he said, "you illustrate how necessary it is that when one has his hand full of truth he should only open it one finger at a time. If you revolt thus angrily against the new gospel, what can be expected from the ignorant and the vicious? The meaning and purpose of life does not depend on whether the individual man shall perish or shall be immortal. If perish he must, he may at least perish heroically. Annihilation or immortality does not affect the validity of religion, whose paramount aim is not to prepare for another world, but to make the best of this—to realize its ideal greatness and nobility. If life should suddenly appear a mockery, contrast the present with that remote past of the naked savage of the stone age, or the brutal condition of his more remote sylvan ancestor, learning to walk erect and to articulate; and then summon up a vision of the possible future, when superstition shall have ceased to embitter man's life, when a knowledge of natural law shall have made men virtuous, when disease shall have vanished from the world, and the nations shall, in a golden age of peace and perfected arts, have learnt the method of a patriarchal longevity. Millions of individuals have wept and toiled and perished to secure for us the present; we and millions shall weep and toil and perish to secure the future for them."

"And that you take to be the significance of life, the progress of the race?"

" And is not that at least as noble a significance as a heaven peopled with the penitent thief, the drunkard, the gallow's-bird, the harlot, the thousand bestial types of humanity redeemed by vicarious agony—the thousand brutes of civilization who, in this age, are not fit for life even on this earth, to say nothing of an enlarged immortality ? "

" But with ever-rising grades of immortality before them, even those bestial types might ascend to a perfect manhood, and shall they perish ? "

" Have they not been ascending ever since the Miocene ? " asked Mr. Haldane, with a scornful laugh. " However, it is little use discussing the matter. As you have said, we cannot agree upon first principles. Let me show you, instead, some of my curiosities. Did you ever see the Mentone skull ? Here is a plaster cast of it."

"And do you accept this dark and comfortless creed of your husband?" asked Mr. Santley, turning to Mrs. Haldane as he took the cast in his hand.

"Oh no," she replied, raising her soft dark eyes to him earnestly; "the progress of humanity does not satisfy me as an explanation of the enigma of life in man or woman. I cannot abandon my old faith and trust in the God-Man for an unknown power who does not care for my suffering and cannot hear my prayers. What to me can such a god be? And what can life be but a mockery if my soul, with its yearnings and aspirations and ideals, ceases to exist after death—has no other world but this, in which I know its infinite wants can never be satisfied?"

The vicar's face brightened, and his

heart beat with a strange, impulsive ardour as he listened to her. Why had this woman, whose enthusiasm and sympathy might have enabled him to realize his own high ideal of the spiritual, been denied him? What evil destiny had bound her for ever to a man whose paralyzing creed must make a perpetual division between them — a man who could look into her sweet face and yet think of her as merely a beautiful animal; who could fold her in his arms, and yet tranquilly accept the teaching that at death that pure, radiant soul of hers would be for ever extinguished? These thoughts and feelings went through the vicar's consciousness swiftly as sunshine and shadow over a landscape.

His eyes dropped on the plaster cast in his hand.

"This is very old?" he asked musingly.

"One of the oldest skulls in the world," replied Mr. Haldane. "It was discovered by Dr. Rivière in a cave at Mentone, in a cliff overlooking the sea. The man belonged to the ancient stone age, and was contemporary with the mammoth and woolly rhinoceros of the Post-pliocene. The cave was a place of burial, and on the head of the skeleton was a thickly plaited network of sea-shells, with a fringe of deers' teeth around the edge; the limbs were adorned with bracelets and anklets of shells also; and in front of the face was placed a little oxide of iron, used as war-paint, no doubt."

"Even in the Post-pliocene, then," said the vicar, "it would appear that man believed in a hereafter."

" Ah, yes ; it is an antique superstition, and even yet we have not outgrown it. Human progress is slow."

"And this face was raised to the blue sky ages ago, looking for God !"

Mr. Haldane shrugged his shoulders and smiled grimly.

" How is it possible that you, who must share the weaknesses and sorrows of the human heart, can so stoically accept the horrible prospect of annihilation ? " asked the vicar, half angrily.

" I accept truths. Do you imagine I prefer annihilation ? I could wish that life were ordered otherwise, but wishing cannot change an eternal system. Immortality cannot be achieved by defying annihilation."

" Have you realized death ? " exclaimed the vicar, passionately. " Can you, dare you, look forward to a time when, say, your wife shall lie cold and lifeless,—and hold to the doctrine that you have lost her for ever, that never again shall your spirit mingle with hers, that you and she are for all eternity divorced ? "

" You appeal to the passions, and not to the reason," replied Mr. Haldane, coldly. " What holds good for the beast which perishes, holds good for all of us, and will hold good for those who come after us, and who will be greater and nobler than we."

" Be it so," replied the vicar, in an undertone. As he spoke he bit his lip, and his cheek coloured. The thought was not meant for utterance, but it slipped into words before he was aware. For the full significance of that thought was a singular exemplification of the conflicting spiritual and animal natures of the man. That divorce of death which had been pronounced inevitable opened before him, in a dreamy vista of the future, a new world of ecstatic beatitude, where his soul and the radiant spirit of the woman who stood beside him should be mingled together in indissoluble communion.

CHAPTER VII.

CELESTIAL AFFINITIES.

SHORTLY afterwards Mrs. Haldane suggested that they should take a turn about the grounds, instead of wasting the sunshine indoors. As they left the chapel the vicar paused and looked back at the ivy-draped building, with its half-hidden lancets.

"You have turned a sacred edifice to a strange use," he said. "Here, within the walls where past generations have dwelt and worshipped, you have set up your apparatus for the destruction of man's holiest heritage. Pardon me if I speak warmly, but to me this appears to be sacrilege."

"The Church has always been intolerant of science and research," replied Mr. Haldane, good-humouredly, "and it is the fortune of conflict if sometimes we are able to make reprisals. But, seriously, I see no desecration here."

"No desecration in converting God's house into a laboratory to analyze soul and spirit into function and force!"

"No desecration, *I* should say, in converting the shrine of a narrow, selfish superstition into a schoolroom where one may learn a truer and a grander theology, and a less presumptuous and illusive theory of life. It is, however, impossible for us to be at one on these matters; let us at least agree to differ amicably. Your predecesor and I found much of common interest. He was of the old school, but life had taught him a kindly tolerance of opinion. To you, as I gleaned from your sermon yesterday, the new philosophy and modern criticism are familiar. You must surely concede that the old theological ground must be immeasurably widened, if you are still resolved to occupy it. Why should you fear truth, if God has indeed revealed Himself to the Church ? "

" The Church does not fear truth," replied the vicar ; " but she does fear the wild speculations and guesses at truth which unsettle the faith of the world. For myself I have looked into some of these fantastic theories of science, and I repudiate them as at once blasphemous and hopeless. It is easy to destroy the old trust in the beneficence of Providence, in the redemption and destiny of man ; but when you have accomplished that, you can go no further. Tyndall proves to you that all life in the world is the outcome of antecedent life ; Haeckel contends that science must in the long run accept spontaneous genera- tion. Your leading men are at logger- heads ; and it signifies little which is right, for in either case the *causa causans* is only removed one link further back in the chain of causation. Some of you hold that there is only matter and force in the universe, but on others it is begin- ning to dawn that possibly matter and force are in the ultimate one and the same. And again, it signifies little which is right, for both, being conditioned, must have had a beginning. A God, a creative Power, is needed in the long run —' a power behind humanity, and behind all other things,' as Herbert Spencer describes it ; a God of whom science can predicate nothing, of whom science declares it to be beyond her province to speak, but of whom every heart is at some time vividly conscious and has been from the beginning—demonstrably from the Paleolithic period — until now."

"Oh, Mr. Santley, I am so pleased you have said that. I have often wished that I were able to answer my husband, but I have no power of argument," said Mrs. Haldane, looking gratefully at the vicar. "You must not think he is not a good, a real practical Christian, in spite of his opinions."

Mr. Haldane laughed quietly as his wife slipped her hand into his.

"As to the God of the Paleolithic man, Mr. Santley forgets that it was at best a personification of some of the great natural powers—wind, rain, thunder, sunshine, and moonlight; and as to Christianity, my dear, there is much in the teaching of Christ, and even of the Church, which I reverence and hold sacred. Morality, and the consequent civilization of the world, owes more to Christianity than to any other creed. It has done much evil, but I think it has done more good. Purified from its mythic delusions, it has still a splendid future before it."

"And *à propos* of practical Christianity, Mr. Santley," continued Mrs. Haldane, " I want to talk to you about the parish. I am eager to begin with my poor people again ; and, by-the-bye, the children have, I understand, had no school treat yet this year. Now, sit down here and tell me all about your sick, in the first place."

Mr. Haldane stood listening to the

woes and illnesses of the village for a few minutes, and then left them together in deep discussions over flannels and medicines and nourishing food. Dinner passed pleasantly enough. The vicar had satisfied his conscience by protesting against the desecration of the chapel and the disastrous results of scientific research. Clearly it was useless, and worse than useless, to contend with this large-natured, clear-headed unbeliever. It was infinitely more agreeable to feel the soft dark light of Mrs. Haldane's eyes dwelling on his face, and to listen to the music of her voice as she told him of their travels abroad. In his imagination the scenes she described rose before him, and he and she were the central figures in the clear, new landscape. He thought of their walks on the cliffs and on the sea-shore, in the golden days that had gone by. How easily it might have been!

The sun had gone down when he parted from his host and hostess at the great gate at the end of the avenue. He had declined their offer to drive him over to Omberley. He preferred walking in the cool of the evening, and the distance was, he professed, not at all too great. As he shook hands with her, that wild, etherial fancy of a world to come, in which her husband would have no claim to her, brightened his eyes and flushed his cheek. There was a strange nervous pressure in the touch of his hand, and an expression of surprise started into her face. He noticed it at once, and was warned. Mr. Haldane's farewell was bluffly cordial, and he warmly pressed the vicar to call on them at any time that best suited his convenience.

They were pretty sure to be always at home, and they were not likely to have too much company.

As he walked along the high-road, bordered on one side with the green murmuring masses of foliage, and on the other with waving breadths of corn, his mind was absorbed in that new dream of transcendent love. There was nothing earthly or gross in this dawning glow of spiritual passion ; indeed, it raised him in delicious exaltation beyond the coarseness of the physical, till, as it suddenly occurred to him that somewhere on his way Edith was waiting for him, his heart rose in revulsion at the recollection of her. At the same time there was a large element of the sensuous beauty of transient humanity in that celestial forecast. The pure, radiant spirit of the woman he loved still wore the sweet lineaments of her earthly loveliness. Death had not destroyed that magical face; those dark, luminous, loving eyes; that sweet shape of womanhood. The spiritual body was cast in the mould of the physical, and the chief difference lay in a shining mistiness of colour, which floated in a sort of elusive drapery about the glorified woman, and replaced the worldly silks and satins of the living wife. This spiritual being was no intangible abstraction, of which only the intellect could take cognizance. As in its temporal condition, it could still kiss and thrill with a touch. Clearly, however unconscious he might be of the fact, the vicar's conception of the divine was intensely human, and his spiritual idealizations were the immediate growth and delicate blossom of the senses.

A great stillness was growing over the

land as he pursued his way. The wood-
lands had been left behind him, and their
incessant murmur was now inaudible.
Sleep and quietude had fallen on the
level fields; not an ear of wheat stirred,
no leaf rustled. The birds had all gone
to nest, except a solitary string of belated
crows, flying low down in black dots
against the distant silvery green horizon.
The moon was rising through a low-
lying haze, which had begun to spread
over the landscape. The vicar looked
at his watch. It was after nine o'clock.
He began to hope that Edith had grown
tired of waiting for him, and had returned
home. He had a sickening feeling of
repugnance and vague dread of meeting
her.

Little more than a month after Mr.
Santley had settled in Omberley, Miss
Dove had come to live with her aunt.

Her father and mother had died within a year of each other, and the girl gladly accepted the offer of Mrs. Russell to consider her house as a home until she had had time to look about her. Edith had been left sufficiently well provided for, and her aunt, the widow of a banker, was in a position of independence, so that the disinterested offer was accepted without any sense of dependence or humiliation. The bright, innocent face of the girl instantly caught the eye of the vicar. He saw her frequently at her aunt's house, and gradually learned to esteem, not only her excellent qualities, but to find a use for her accomplishments. She was especially fond of music, and when the vicar suggested that she might add to the beauty of the service at St. Cuthbert's by interesting herself in the choir and presiding at the organ, she eagerly acquiesced. The church was one of Edith's favourite haunts; and when the vicar, who was himself a lover of music, heard the soul-stirring vibrations of some masterpiece of the great composers, his steps were drawn by an easily explicable fatality to the side of the pretty performer. Still, it was a fatality. Slowly, and imperceptibly at first, the sense of pleasure at meeting grew up between the two; then swiftly and imperceptibly they found that there was something in the presence of each other that satisfied a vague, indefinable craving; and lastly, with a sudden access of self-consciousness, they looked into each other's eyes, and each became gladly and tremulously aware of the other's love. Edith was still young, almost too young yet to assume the station of the wife of the spiritual head of the parish;

and Mr. Santley was not sure as to the manner in which his sister would receive the intimation that there was, even in the remote future, to be a new mistress brought to the Vicarage. The girl was, however, still too happy in the knowledge that she was beloved to look forward to marriage. With a strange, feminine inconsistency, she regarded their union with a certain dread and shamefacedness. It seemed such a dreadful exposure that all the village should know that they loved each other. "Oh no, no; it must not be for a long, long time yet!" she once exclaimed nervously. "Is it not sufficient happiness to know that I am yours and you are mine? I cannot bear to think that every one must know our secret." To have those long, pleasant chats under cover of the music; to be invited to the Vicarage, and to sit and talk with him there; to receive those haphazard glances, as it were, while he was preaching; to be escorted home by him in the evening when it was dark, and no one could see that her hand was on his arm; to receive those almost stolen kisses; to feel his arm about her waist;—what more could maiden desire to dream over for weeks and months— for years, if need were?

Edith was endowed with the intense feminine faith and fervid ideality of the worshipper. To sit at her lover's feet and to look up adoringly to him, was at once her favourite mental and physical attitude. On her side, she exercised a curious spiritual influence over him. There was such an aerial brightness and lightness about her, such sweet fragile loveliness in her form and figure, such tender abandonment of self in her disposition, that he felt he had not only a woman to love, but a beautiful child-like soul to keep unspotted from the world, to guide through the dark ways of life to the arms of the great loving Fatherhood of God. The presence of Edith helped him to banish the dark doubts and evil promptings of the spirit of unbelief. When she spoke to him of her spiritual experiences, he felt joyous ascensions of the heart which raised him nearer to heaven. She created in him the unspeakable holy longings and vague wants that give the lives of the mystic saints of Roman Catholicism so singular a blending of divine illumination and voluptuous colour. Unconsciously the vicar was realizing in his own nature Swedenborg's doctrine of celestial affinities. This love restored to him the innocence and ardour of the days of

Eden; he had found at once his Eve
and his Paradise, and he felt that, as of
old, God still walked in the garden in
the cool of the day. Some such glamour
surrounds the first developments of
every sincere attachment. It is the
first rosy tingling flush of dawn, dim
and sweet and dreamy, and, like the
dawn, it glows and brightens into the
fierce clear heat of broad day, burning
the dew from the petal and withering
the blossom.

As Mr. Santley's thoughts turned to
Edith, the recollection of these things
came vividly upon him. Only a week
ago, and she was the one woman in the
world he believed he could have chosen
for his wife. In an instant, at the sight
of a face, all had been changed. His
love had become a burthen, a shame,
a dread to him. Edith had grown

hateful to him. At the same time, he could not deaden the sting of remorse as he reflected on his broken vows. The passionate protestations he had uttered sounded again in his ears in accents of bitter mockery; the pledges he had given seemed now to him hideous blasphemies.

At a bend of the road he suddenly came in sight of a figure moving before him in the dusk. He knew at a glance it was she, and he prepared himself for the meeting. Although he earnestly wished to disembarrass himself of her, he found himself unable to do so at once and brutally. He would try to estrange her, and free himself little by little.

As they approached each other he saw that Edith's face was grave and sad. She was trying to learn from his look in what manner she ought to speak to him.

His assurances on the previous evening had not tranquillized her, and she had still a terrible misgiving that a chasm was widening between them.

The vicar was the first to speak.

" I am a little later than I expected," he said, as he held out his hand to her.

" It does not signify *now*. I was only afraid that you might be so late I should have to go home without seeing you."

He made no reply, and they walked on side by side in silence for a few seconds. At last she stopped abruptly and looked at him.

" Charles," she said, " you know what you said to me last night ? "

" Yes."

" Was it true ? "

"Why should you ask such a question ? Why should you doubt its truth ? "

" I try not to doubt it, but I cannot

help it. Oh, tell me again that you do not hate and contemn me! Tell me you still love me."

"My dear Edith," replied the vicar, laying his hand on her arm, "you are not well. You have been overtaxing your strength and exciting yourself.'

Edith did not answer, but the tears rose to her eyes and began to run down her cheeks. She did not sob or make any sound of weeping, but her hand was pressed against her throat.

"Come, don't cry like that; you know I cannot bear to see you cry."

He stopped as he spoke, and took her hand in his. They stood still a little while, and she at length was able to speak.

"Do you remember," she asked in a low, broken voice, "that I once told you you were my conscience?"

He regarded her uneasily before he replied.

"Yes; you once said that, I know. But why return to that now?"

"And have you not been?"

He was silent.

"Your word," she continued, "has been my law; what you have said I have believed. Have I done wrong?"

"Why are you letting these things trouble you now?" he asked impatiently.

"Because I know that when a woman gives herself wholly to the man she loves, it is common for her to lose him, and I have begun to feel that I am losing you."

"I do not think I have given you any reason to feel that."

She did not speak again immediately, but stood with her innocent blue eyes raised beseechingly to his face. Suddenly she took hold of his hands, and said—

"You told me that in the eyes of God we were man and wife, that no marriage ceremony could ever join us together more truly, that marriage really consisted in the union of heart and soul, not in the words of any priest—did you not? Was that true? Am I still your little wife?"

He hesitated. The blood had vanished from his cheek, leaving it haggard and pale; she felt his hands trembling in hers. Then, with a sudden impulse, he took her face between his hands and drew her towards him, as he answered—

"You are, darling. I will not do you any wrong."

CHAPTER VIII.

A SICK-CALL.

MR. Santley's reply was as sincere at the moment it was spoken as it was impulsive. The saner and better part of him rose in sudden sympathy towards this young, confiding girl who had laid her whole being in his hands, to be his treasure or his plaything. He resolved to be faithful to the solemn pledge he had given her, and to cast from him for ever all thought of Mrs. Haldane, and all memory of that passionate episode of the past. He drew Edith's hand under his arm and held it

there. That warm little bit of responsive
flesh and blood had still, he felt, a
power to thrill through his nature. He
bent down and kissed it. For some
time their conversation was embarrassed,
but gradually all sense of doubt and
estrangement vanished, and he was telling her about his visit to the Manor.
A pressure was laid upon him to make
her such amends as he was able for his
coldness during the past week, and he
determined to break the spell which
Mrs. Haldane's beauty threw over him
by revealing their old friendship to
Edith. It was not wise, but under the
stress of remorse and a reviving passion
men seldom act wisely. Except in the
case of a jealous disposition, a woman
is always pleased to hear of her lover's
old vaguely cherished love affairs, when
there is no possibility of their ever

coming to life again. She knows instinctively, even when she is not told so
adoringly, that she supersedes all her
predecessors and combines all their
virtues and charms. He loved this one
for her beauty and sweetness, that one
for her clear bright intelligence; each
in a different way; but her he loves in
both the old ways, and in a new way
also which she alone could inspire.

"Mrs. Haldane was an old pupil of
mine—indeed, a favourite pupil—many
years ago; so, naturally, I am much
interested in her," said the vicar in a
tentative manner.

The words were a revelation to
Edith; they explained to her all her
uneasiness and all his change of manner.

"And you find that you still love
her a little?" Edith ventured to say in
a sad, faltering tone.

"I never said I loved her, my dear," replied the vicar, with a forced laugh.

"But you did, did you not? She was your favourite pupil."

How uncomfortably keen-sighted this young person seemed to be, in spite of her soft, endearing ways!

"Would you be a little jealous if I said I did?" he asked, regarding her with a scrutinizing look.

"Jealous! Oh no. Why should I? Is she not married? And am I not really and truly your little wife?"

He pressed her hand gently for answer.

"And when you saw her again last Sunday, and saw how beautiful she was," Edith continued, "you felt sorry that you had lost her—just a little regretful, did you not?"

The vicar hesitated, and then did the

most foolish thing a man can do in such circumstances—confessed the truth.

"You will not be vexed, darling, if I say that I did feel regret?"

"You loved her very much?"

"She was my first love," replied the vicar. "But you must remember it was years ago. Long before I knew you; when I was quite a young man."

"And was she very fond of you?" Edith went on quietly.

"I used to think she was."

"But she was not true to you?"

"I do not blame her. I do not think it was her fault. Her people were wealthy, and I was poor, a poor teacher."

"And it was this made you so cold and hard to me all last week?"

Mr. Santley did not answer at once. It would be brutal to say yes, and he dared not hazard a denial.

"Oh, Charles, she never loved you as I have."

"Never, never," replied the vicar hurriedly; and a flush rose to his face.

"When you meet her, when you see her again," said Edith, grasping his arm with earnest emphasis, "will you remember that? Promise me."

"I will never forget it," said the vicar in a low voice.

He did not see Mrs. Haldane again, however, during the week. On the following Sunday his eyes wandered only for a moment towards the Manor pew, and he perceived that she was alone. When he met her after the service his manner was constrained, but she appeared not to notice it. She spoke again of the parish work, and told him that in a day or two she would drive over and accompany him on some of his calls. He looked forward with un-easiness and self-distrust to her co-operation in his daily work. There was an irresistible something, a magical atmosphere, an invisible radiation of the enticing about this woman. Her large glowing black eyes seemed to fasten upon his soul and draw it beyond his control. Her starry smile intoxicated and maddened him. Beside her, Edith was but a weak, delicate child, with a child's clinging attachment, a child's credulity and trust, a child's little gusts of passion. His lost love was a woman —such a woman as men in old times would have perished for as a queen, would have worshipped as a goddess— such a woman, he fancied, as that Naomi whose beauty has been the mysterious tradition of five thousand years.

Early one afternoon, about the middle of the week, the vicar was just about to set out on his customary round of visitation, when Mrs. Haldane's pony-carriage drove up to the gate. He assisted her to alight, and returned with her to the house.

Miss Santley, who had been as sensitive to the change in her brother as Edith herself, regarded Mrs. Haldane with little favour. She was ready to acknowledge that it was very good and kind of the mistress of Foxglove Manor to interest herself in the wants and suffering of the parish, but she entertained grave misgivings as to the prudence of her brother and this old pupil of his being thrown too frequently together. She was just a little formal and reserved with her visitor, who announced her intention of

going with the vicar to this sick-call he
had spoken of.

"You will have to walk, however,"
said Mr. Santley, "as the cottage is
some little distance across the fields."

"I came prepared for walking," she
replied, with a laugh. "James can put
up at the village till our return."

"Will you do us the favour of taking
tea with us?" asked Miss Santley. "You
will require it, if my brother takes you
his usual round."

"Thank you, I shall be very glad. If
James calls for me at—what time shall
I say?—six, will that be soon enough?"

The coachman received his instructions, and Mr. Santley and Mrs. Haldane set out on their first combined
mission. They traversed half a dozen
fields, and came in sight of a small
cluster of cottages lying low in a green

hollow. A narrow lane ran past them to Omberley in one direction and to the high-road in another. Half a dozen poplars grew in a line along the lane, and the cottages were surrounded by small gardens, filled with fruit trees.

" What a picturesque little spot ! " exclaimed Mrs. Haldane. " I think nothing looks so pretty as an English cottage with its white walls and tiled roof peering out from a cluster of apple and pear trees."

" Pretty enough, but damp ! " replied the vicar. " In wet weather they are in a perfect quagmire. Ah, listen ! "

They were now very near the houses, and the sound to which Mr. Santley called her attention was the voice of a man crying out in great pain.

" What can it be ? " asked Mrs. Haldane, with a look of alarm.

" It is the poor fellow we are going to see. He was knocked down and run over by a cart about two years ago. His spine has been injured, and the doctors can do nothing for him. He is quite helpless, and has been bed-ridden all that time."

" Poor creature! what a dreadful thing it must be to suffer like that!"

" Sometimes for weeks together he feels no pain. Then he is suddenly seized by the most fearful torture, and you can hear his cries for a great distance."

As they approached the cottage the man's voice grew louder, and they could distinguish his words : " Oh, what shall I do? Oh, who'll tell me what to do?"

Mrs. Haldane shuddered. In that green, peaceful, picturesque spot that persistent reiteration of the man's agony was horrible.

" Will you come in ? " asked the vicar, doubtfully.

His companion signed her assent, and Mr. Santley knocked gently at the door. In a few seconds some one was heard coming down the staircase, and a little gray-haired, gray-faced woman, dressed in black, came to the door and curtsied to her visitors.

" Mansfield is very bad again to-day ? " said the vicar.

" Ay, this be one of his bad days, sir. He have been that bad since Sunday, I haven't known what to do with him."

The voice of the sick man suddenly ceased, and he appeared to be listening.

" Who's there ? " he shrieked out, after a pause. " Jennie, blast you ! who's there ? "

"He be raving mad, ma'am!" said Mrs. Mansfield, apologetically. "He don't know what he is saying."

"Jennie, you damned little varmint——"

"Hush, John, it be the parson!" his wife called up the staircase.

"To hell with the parson! Oh, what shall I do? Oh, who'll tell me what to do?"

"I'll go up to him, sir, and tell him you're here. He be very bad to-day, poor soul! Will it please you to walk in, ma'am?"

The little woman went upstairs, and her entrance to the sick-room was greeted with a volley of foul curses screamed out in furious rage. Gradually, however, the access of passion was exhausted, and the man was again heard repeating his hopeless appeal for relief.

"How do they live?" asked Mrs.

Haldane, glancing about the small but scrupulously clean room in which she stood. " Have they any grown-up children ? "

" No, only their two selves. She is the bread-winner. She does knitting and sewing, and the neighbours, who are very kind to her, assist her with her garden and do her many little kindnesses."

"Poor woman ! And she has endured this horrible infliction for two years ! "

" If you please, sir, you can come up now," said Mrs. Mansfield from the top of the stairs.

The vicar went up, and Mrs. Haldane followed him. They entered a pretty large whitewashed bedroom, with raftered roof and a four-post bedstead in the centre of the room. Though meagrely furnished, everything was spotlessly clean and tidy. On the bed lay a great gaunt man, panting and moaning, with his large filmy blue eyes turned up to the roof. He was far above the common stature, and his huge wasted frame, only half hidden by the bedclothes, was piteous to look at. His large venerable head, covered with thin, long white hair, filled one with surprise and regretful admiration. His face was thin and colourless, and a fringe of white beard gave it a still more deathly appearance. One could scarcely believe that the wreck before him was a common labourer. It seemed rather such a spectacle as Beatrice Cenci might have looked on had her father died cursing on his bed.

" Here's parson come to see thee, and a lady wi' him," said Mrs. Mansfield, raising her husband's head.

He looked at them with his glazed blue eyes, made prominent with pain, and his moaning grew louder, till they could again distinguish the constant cry for release from pain: "Oh, what shall I do? Oh, who'll tell me what to do?"

"Try to think of God, and pray to Him for help," said the vicar, bending over the suffering man.

"Oh, I have prayed and prayed and prayed," he replied querulously; "but it does no good."

"He were praying all day yesterday and singing hymns," said Mrs. Mansfield. "I don't know what's gotten hold of him to-day, but he have been dreadful. And he were ever such a pious, God-fearing man. It fair breaks my heart to hear him swearing like that. But God will not count it against him, for he's been clean beside himself."

"Well, let me hear you pray now, Mansfield," said the vicar. "Turn your heart and your mind to God, and He will comfort you."

"O God," said the sick man, with the obedient simplicity of a child, "I turn my heart and my mind to Thee; do Thou comfort me and take me to Thyself. O Lord Jesus Christ, Son of God and Saviour of mankind, do Thou remember me in Thy paradise. Look down upon me, O Lord, a miserable offender, and spare Thou them which confess their faults and are truly penitent."

With a strange light on his white, wasted face, with his gaunt hands folded on the counterpane before him, the old man sat up in bed and prayed in the same loud voice of pain and semi-delirium. A wild, inconceivable, interminable prayer; for long after they had left the house, old Mansfield could be heard some hundreds of yards away, screaming to God for mercy and consolation.

"We had better leave him praying," said the vicar softly; "and when he begins cursing and swearing again, Mrs. Mansfield, just kneel down and pray in a loud voice beside him. It will suggest a new current to his thoughts."

"God won't count his cursing against him, sir, will he?" asked the little woman. "He were ever a sober Christian man till this misery came on him."

"No, no," said the vicar; "God judges the heart, not the tongue of delirium."

"How old is your husband?" inquired Mrs. Haldane.

"He be eighty-one come Martinmas, ma'am."

" Poor old man !   And you do sewing and knitting, do you not ? "

" Yes, ma'am, what he lets me do.   He be main fractious whiles."

" And have you plenty to go on with at present ? "

" I have what 'll keep me busy for a fortnight yet."

" I will see you again before then.   I hope your husband will soon be better."

" There be no hope of that, ma'am. The only betterness for him 'll be when God takes him."

" I know you will be able to find a use for this," said Mrs. Haldane in a whisper, as they went out of the house.   " Good-bye for the present."

" Oh, ma'am !   God bless you ! " said Mrs. Mansfield, the tears springing into her eyes as she looked at the gold coin in her hand.

CHAPTER IX.

A SUMMER SHOWER.

AFTER that first round of visitation Mrs. Haldane and the vicar met very frequently.

She found that she could be of use to a great number of poor people, and the occupation afforded her by her self-imposed duties was novel and interesting. It is pleasant to take the place of Providence, and mete out help and gladness to afflicted humanity. She was actuated by no petty spirit of vanity or ostentation ; and though she soon learned that the poorer and more necessitous people are, the more thankless they are as a rule, these disagreeable experiences did not disillusion her. Very often she would leave her carriage at the village inn and accompany Mr. Santley on foot across the fields and down the deep green lanes to the different houses at which he was to call. Their conversations on these occasions were very interesting to her; and more than once as she drove back home in the evening she fell a-thinking of that distant school-girl past which had so nearly faded away from her memory, and began to wonder whether, if her family had not so promptly extinguished that little romance of hers, she would now have been the wife of the vicar of Omberley. No word had yet passed between them of that old time, and occasionally she felt just the least curiosity to know how he regarded it. She knew he had not forgotten it, and she smiled to herself as she called to mind the way in which he had addressed her as "Ellen" that first Sunday. She had ever since been only Mrs. Haldane to him. There was a singular fascination about him which she was unable to explain to herself. She remembered his words, his looks, his gestures with a curious distinctness. She was conscious that, notwithstanding his reticence, he still entertained a warm attachment to her. She could see it in his eyes, could hear it in the tones of his voice, could feel it in the pressure of his hand. There is no incentive to affection so powerful and subtle as the knowledge that one is beloved. Without any analysis of her feelings or any misgiving whatever, Mrs. Haldane knew that the vicar's friendship was very dear to her, that his sympathy and counsel were rapidly growing indispensable. Many things troubled her in connection with her husband—his indifference to any form of religion, his stern acceptance of the conclusions of science, however destructive they might be of all that the world had clung to as essential to goodness and happiness, his utter disbelief of the truths of revelation, his rejection of the only God in whom she could place trust and confidence. Diffidently at first, and with pain and doubt, she spoke to Mr. Santley of these troubles, and of the waverings of her own convictions. Her husband was so good, so upright and noble a man, that she could not despair of his some day returning to the faith and the Church of his boyhood. Could the vicar not aid her in winning him back to God? Then, too, at times her husband's words appealed to her reason so irresistibly that she began to question whether after all she had not spent her life in the worship of a delusion. That did not happen often, but it terrified her that it should be possible for her at any time or in any circumstance to call in question the fatherhood of God or the divinity of Christ.

It was only natural that these matters should draw the vicar and his fair parishioner very close to each other ; and that intimate relationship of soul with soul by subtle degrees widened and widened till each became deeply interested in everything that could in any way affect the other. In spite of his strongest resolve to be true to Edith, Mr. Santley felt himself irresistibly drawn to her beautiful rival. He struggled with the enchantment till further resistance seemed useless, and then he sought refuge in self-deception. His nature, he fancied, was wide enough to include the love of both. To Edith he could give the affection of a husband, to Ellen the anticipative passion of a disfranchised spirit. One was a temporal, the other an eternal sentiment.

One afternoon, as they were returning from a visit, being on the edge of the moss about a couple of miles from the village, they were overtaken by a storm. There was a clump of trees hard by, and they entered it for shelter. Mrs. Haldane had her waterproof with her; but the rain drove in such drenching showers, that the vicar insisted on her standing under his umbrella and sheltering her person with her own. Side by side, with the large trunk of a beech-tree behind them and its tossing branches overhead, they stood there for nearly half an hour. He held his umbrella over her so that his arm almost touched her further shoulder. They were very close together, and while she watched the flying volleys of rain he was gazing on the beautiful complexion of her face and neck, on the rich dark masses of her hair, her sweet arched eyebrows and long curving eyelashes. For years he had not been able to regard her so closely. She did not notice his scrutiny at first, but, when she did, little sunny flushes of colour made her loveliness still more electrical. They were talking of the storm at first, but now there was an interval of silence. She felt his eyes upon her face—they seemed to touch her, and the contract made her cheeks glow. At last she turned and looked straight at him.

" I was thinking of long ago," he said
in answer to her look; "do you remember how once we were caught by a
thunderstorm at Seacombe, and we
stood together under a tree just as we
are now ? "

"What an excellent memory you
have!" she said with a smile, while her
colour again rose.

" I never forget anything," rejoined
Mr. Santley with emphasis.   " But
surely you too recollect that ? "

"Oh yes; I have not forgotten it,"
she said lightly.   "We were very foolish
people in those days."

"We were very happy people, were
we not ? "

"Yes, I think we were; it was a
childish happiness."

" Manhood, then, has brought me no
greater.   Ah, Ellen, you seem to have

easily let the past slip away from you. With me it is as vivid to-day as if it were only yesterday that you and I walked on the cliffs together. Do you remember we went to the gipsy's camp in the sand-hills, and had our fortunes told?"

Mrs. Haldane blushed and laughed.

"We were foolish enough to do anything, I think, at that time."

"That pretty gipsy girl with the dark almond eyes and red-and-amber head-dress was sadly out in her reading of our destinies."

Mrs. Haldane made no reply. These reminiscences, and especially the tone in which the vicar dwelt on them, disquieted her.

"I think the worst of the shower is over now," she said, stepping from under his umbrella. As she spoke, however, a fresh gust of wind and rain contradicted her, and she stepped further into the shelter of the tree.   Mr. Santley clearly understood the significance of her words and action.

" It is raining far too heavily to go yet," he said gently.   " Let me hold my umbrella over you."

She consented a little uneasily, but he laid his hand upon her arm and said—

" I have displeased you by referring to the past, have I not ?   Come, be frank with me.   Surely we are good enough friends by this to speak candidly to each other."

She raised her great dark eyes to his face and replied gravely,

" I do not like you to speak of the past in that way.   I do not think it is right.   I hope we *are* good enough friends to speak candidly.   I have trusted you as a friend, as a very dear and true friend. I wish to keep you always my friend; but when you spoke just now of our childish liking for each other, I do not think you spoke as a—friend."

The vicar was silent, and his eyes were cast on the ground.

" Have I done you an injustice ? " she asked in a low tone, after a little pause. " Then, pray, do forgive me."

The vicar regarded her with a look of sadness, and took the little gloved hand she held out to him.

" You do me injustice in thinking that I have forgotten your position."

Mrs. Haldane coloured deeply.

" No," continued the vicar, " I have not forgotten that. I *cannot* forget it. And if I still love you with the old love of those vanished years, if I love you with a love which will colour my whole life, do not imagine that it is with any hope of a response in this world. I do your husband no injustice; I do you no dishonour. I loved you long before he knew you; I shall love you still in that after life in which he has deliberately abandoned all claim to you, in the very existence of which he places no belief. Between this and then let me be your friend—your brother; let me be as one in whom you will ever find sympathy and devotedness; one who can share and understand all your doubts and distress, all your temptations and trials. I do not ask you to love me; I only ask you to let me love you."

This gust of passion was so sudden, so unexpected, so overwhelming, that almost before she was aware, he had spoken and she had listened. And now as she thought of what he said a strangely mixed sensation of doubt and pleasure awoke within her. All that he wished to be he was indeed already in her eyes—her adviser, sympathiser, friend. Only this secret unexpectant love which lived on the past and the future agitated her. And yet surely it was a pure spiritual love which asked for no return on this side of the grave. These thoughts occurred to her before she took the sober common-sense view of what he had said.

"You are taking too visionary, too feverish a view of life when you speak in that way," she said gently. "We cannot live on dreams. Our duties, our work, our disappointments and cares are too real for us to be satisfied with any love less real. You will some day meet some one worthy of your affection, capable of sympathising with you and aiding you in your life-work—some one who will be a fitting helpmeet to you. For my part, I think that whenever we have missed what we are apt to consider a great happiness it is a sure sign that God intends some better thing for us."

The vicar shook his head silently.

"Oh, you must have more faith!" she continued brightly. "And it ought to be very easy for you to have faith in this matter. You have all the advantages on your side. And, if I may be frank with you, I will say that I think you would be happier if you *were* married. You need some responsive heart, and nowhere could one more need close companionship than in such a place as Omberley."

The rain had ceased, and as she spoke the last words she glanced up at the clouds breaking away from the sunny blue of the sky.

" I think we may safely start now. How bright and sweet everything looks after the rain ; and what a fragrance the fields have ! "

Mr. Santley did not attempt to renew the conversation. Clearly she was not in the mood, and he believed that what he had said had fallen as seed in a generous soil, and would germinate in the warmth of her fervid temperament. It was enough that she knew he still loved her.

Such a knowledge is ever dangerous to an imaginative woman. For several days after that incident Mrs. Haldane never thought of the vicar, never heard his name mentioned without at the same time unconsciously recalling—or rather without having flashed upon her a mental picture not only of that little wood near the moss, but of the romantic shore at Seacombe. She felt a strange tender interest in the man who had loved her so long, and still loved her so hopelessly, so unselfishly. Hitherto in their relationship she had only thought of herself, of her own needs and her own happiness. She had looked up to him. But that avowal had changed their position towards one another in a singular way. He to whom every one felt entitled to appeal to for advice, assistance, consolation, was evidently himself in need of human affection. She had hitherto regarded the priest rather than the man, but now the man chiefly engaged her attention, and attracted her sympathy while he excited and perplexed her imagination. What could she do to be of service to him? She set her woman's wit to work in a woman's way, and speedily arrived at one means of serving him.

"George," she said to her husband one morning at breakfast, " I have been thinking of asking an old schoolfellow of mine, Hettie Taylor, to come and spend a few weeks with us. She lives in London, and she will be delighted with the change to the country, I know. What do you say ? "

" Beginning to feel lonely already ? " he asked, glancing up at her.

" Oh no, not at all. Only I have been thinking of her, and should like to have her with me again for a little while. I am sure you will like her. She is very pretty—such beautiful brown hair and eyes—and decidedly intellectual."

" Ask her by all means, then."

"Thanks. I will write to her to-day. No, not to-day—I shall be busy seeing after the children's picnic. Will you not come, dear? You know you love children."

"To a picnic, my dear girl!" cried Mr. Haldane aghast.

"Yes, in Barton Wood. The children are all going in a couple of waggons. And there will be some of the old people there if the weather is fine. Do come."

"A picnic, my dear Nell, is pure atavism—it is one of those lapses into savagery which betray the aboriginal arboreal blood," said Mr. Haldane, laughing. "No, no; I have too much respect for the civilization of the century and for my personal comfort to willingly retrograde to the Drift Period."

CHAPTER X.

THE KISS.

THE artist in search of a pretty rural subject could not do better than paint a village holiday—a holiday from which the men and women are all but excluded, and the village school-children and the old people are gathered together for a voyage through the leafy lanes to the picturesque playground of a neighbouring wood. Such an enjoyable spectacle as that presented on the day of the Omberley school-treat deserved to be immortalized by art, if only for the sake of filling a city parlour with a

sense of eternal summer. It was a
glorious August morning that laughed
out over Omberley on the day of the
great picnic. The young people were
astir early, for it had been impossible to
sleep from the excitement they felt after
the first glimmer of dawn. About ten
o'clock the streets were gay with troops
of children, clean, rosy-cheeked, and
dressed in their Sunday clothes, who
went singing to the rendezvous at the
schoolhouse. There they were received
by Miss Dora Greatheart, who inspected
them all, and expressed her approbation
at finding them so neat and prim. In
twos and threes the old people, the
men in tall hats and swallow-tailed coats
for the most part, and the women in
their best black gowns and church
bonnets, came slowly along the road,
gossiping and laughing and breathing

hard with the weakness of old age. Then came the musicians—old Gabriel Ware, the sexton, with his fiddle, and two younger men, one of whom played the concertina and the other the cornopean, each with a huge nosegay in his breast and wearing the jauntiest air conceivable. There was a happy buzz of excitement about the schoolhouse as the people assembled ; a joyous babble of the clear treble voices of little lads and lasses, and the piping notes of garrulous patriarchs and ancient dames ; a strange picture, as pathetic as it was pretty, of bright young faces and dancing little figures mingling among gray wrinkled visages and frail stooping shapes.

"Well, Dora, we are to have a fine day," said Edith, as she entered the garden and shook hands with the schoolmistress.

" Splendid ; only we shall be a little late in starting. We should have been off at ten, and the waggons have not come yet. Why, here is old Daddy coming ! "

She had stepped out to the road to look for the waggons, and now she went to welcome the new arrival whom she called Daddy. He was a very old, very wiry little man, with a funny little face full of wrinkles, a pair of little grey eyes, and a perfectly bald head. This was the oldest inhabitant of Omberley ; and though he was in his ninety-second year, he was as brisk and hearty as many who were twenty years his juniors.

" Well, Daddy, you have actually come ! " said Dora, shaking hands with him. " I am very glad. And how do you feel to-day ? Pretty strong and hearty ? '

"Strong as Samson, mistress, and hearty as—hearty as anything," replied the old man, with a chuckle.

"Please, miss," said a young woman who accompanied him, "mother sends her duty, and will you kindly take care of him and see as he doesn't go a-thinking."

Daddy's only symptom of senility was an aptitude to fall into a state of unconsciousness, and in these cases, which sometimes lasted for hours together, he would sit down wherever he was, and consequently ran considerable risks when he went out-of-doors alone. Though the old fellow was quite unable to give any account of himself during these lapses into oblivion, he always stoutly declared that he had been only thinking.

"And please, miss, you'll find his bacca-box and his pipe in his tail pocket, and his hankercher, and the matches is in his vest pocket. He do forget where he puts his things."

Daddy laughed scornfully.

"I never forgets nothing, I don't," he said boastingly. "I can mind o' the great beech as was blown down on the green in the whirlywind of '92; ay, I mind——"

A loud cheer from the school children interrupted the flow of Daddy's reminiscences. The greeting was intended for the vicar and the patroness of the festival, Mrs. Haldane, who now drove up to the school-house. She was already acquainted with Dora, but she had not yet met either Edith or the oldest inhabitant. Mr. Santley introduced both as the waggons came in sight, and at once the cheering was renewed, and the children streamed out into the road.

What a fine sight those waggons were

—the long, curved, wheeled ships of the inland farmer, painted yellow and red, and drawn by big horses, with huge collars and bright iron chains! The semicircular canvas awning had been removed, but the wooden arches which supported it were wreathed with leaves and flowers, and festoons hung overhead between arch and arch. The horses, too, were gaily decked out, each having a nosegay between its ears, and its mane and tail tied up with ribbons. The bottom of the waggons were covered with trusses of straw, to make comfortable seats for the old folk. The more daring of the lads were already clambering up the wheels, and securing seats on the flakes which went along the sides of the rustic ship like a sort of outrigger.

Before allowing Daddy to be helped

on board, Miss Greatheart beckoned to her a little pale-faced girl who was obliged to use crutches.

"Nannie dear, I want you to look after Daddy as much as you can. When you are tired of him you must come and tell me. Don't let him go away by himself, and wake him up if he sleeps too long."

This was said in a whisper to the child, who smiled and nodded.

"Now, Daddy, here's little Nannie Swales," said Dora ; "I want you to take care of her. You're the only person I can trust to look after her properly. And she likes to talk to you and see you smoke."

The little old man smiled and chuckled complacently.

"Put her aside of me, mistress, and I'll see as no ill comes to her."

What could have been more charmingly idyllic than those two great waggons, crowded with little shining-eyed tots, merry lads and lasses, withered old men and women, all happy and contented? The blue sky laughed down on them; the green leaves and flowers embowered them; and as a start was made, one of the musicians struck up "For we'll a-hunting go" on the concertina, and a score of clear, fresh voices joined in the jovial song.

Through the village, which turned out to wave hands to them as they passed singing and cheering, away through gold-green stretches of ripening harvest, past empty fields where the hay had all been cut and carted, between level expanses of root crops lying green in the hot sun, till at last the dark embankment of Barton Wood rises above

the distant sky.   How cool and refreshing it is, after the glare of the midday
sun, to get into the green shadowland
of these grand old beeches and syca-
mores !

The road winds leisurely as if to seek
out the coolest recesses of the wood,
and beneath the great bunches of heavy
foliage, what quiet, dim distances one
sees between the trunks, strewn thick
with withered leaves, through which
the moss and grass and a thousand
moist plants thrust their emerald way,
and blue and pink and yellow flowers are
clustered in cushions of velvet colour !
A few yards away from the road the air
seems brown and transparent.   That
must be the reason why the leaves of
the mountain ash are so darkly green,
and the berries so brilliantly crimson.
If you pluck a bunch and take it out of

the wood, you will find it has become disenchanted; the colour is no longer the same.

The road is not a highway, but leads to an old quarry of brown sandstone. There has been no work done here for a few years, but many generations of stonemasons have plied hammer and chisel in this picturesque workshop. It is a tradition that the stone of Foxglove Manor, old as it is, was got here. The old church was built from these brown walls of stone; so was the Vicarage, and so were the windowsills and facings of all the houses in Omberley. It is an unusually large quarry, for a great deal of stone has been taken away during these two hundred odd years. A great deal of half-shaped stone lies about in large square and oblong blocks, both on the floor of the quarry, and among the trees at its entrance. The trees must have sprung up since many of these blocks were cut, otherwise it is not easy to see why they should have been put where you now find them. On two sides the walls of rock are high and precipitous, but on the others the grass and ferns and beeches are carried into the quarry as on the swell of a green wave. A stone shed and hut, roofed with red tiles, stand at the foot of one of these slopes, and here the commissariat department has established itself. A romantic, green, cosy, convenient spot for a picnic and a dance !

The waggons were driven right into the quarry, and the horses were hobbled and allowed to graze beneath the trees. The hour before dinner was spent in wandering through the woods gathering flowers and berries, in rolling about on the soft grass, or in smoking and chatting among the blocks of sandstone. When the cornopean sounded the signal for the feast, the youngsters came trooping in, dancing and eager to begin, for the excitement had prevented most of them from taking breakfast.

And what a luxurious feast it was! The vicar, Mrs. Haldane, Edith, and Miss Greatheart, went about the various groups seeing that every one was well supplied with what they liked best. After the cold meats, pies, and pastry, came a liberal distribution of fruit and milk to the children, and a glass of wine to the old people; and at this point Daddy was made the object of so much nudging and whispering and signalling, that at last he got upon his feet and made a wonderful little speech on behalf of the company, keeping his wine-glass in his hand all the time, and every now and then holding it up between his eye and the light with the shrewd air of a connoisseur. Then there were three cheers for Mrs. Haldane, and three cheers for the vicar, three for Dora and for Edith, and happily some young rascal, whose milk had been too strong for him, proposed in a frightened scream three cheers for Daddy, which were very heartily given by all the school children, though the seniors looked much shocked and surprised at so daring a demonstration.

In about an hour the racing and games were to begin, and meanwhile Mrs. Haldane, the vicar, and the two young ladies were to have lunch together. It is not necessary to enter into any detail of the various sports which

took place, or to linger over the dancing
and merrymaking that followed. When
the fun was at its height, and Daddy
was capering gaily to the jigging of the
small orchestra, Edith, who felt only
half interested, slipped quietly away into
the wood. She was not surprised or
aggrieved that Mr. Santley paid so much
attention to the lady of the Manor,
but she felt hurt that he seemed so
completely to forget and overlook herself. She wished now to be a little
alone in Arden, for Edith loved the
woods, and in every glade she could
imagine in her fanciful moments that
Jaques, or Rosalind, or Touchstone
had just gone by, so closely had she
associated the dramatic idyl with every
piece of English forest-land.

She followed at haphazard a foot-track
that went through the trees until she

reached a brook, which she found she could cross by means of three slippery-looking stepping-stones, against which the water bickered and gurgled as it raced along. All the steep banks were knee-deep in beautiful ferns close by the water's edge, and higher up the slope grew luxurious tufts of wild flowers. The sound of the water was very pleasant to hear, and when she had nimbly jumped across it, instead of following the path, she went up the side of the stream to where a mountain ash leaned its dense clusters of blood-bright berries right across. At the foot of the tree was a large boulder, and, after a glance round her, she sat down and drew off her shoes and stockings. The weather was warm, and the clear, sun-flecked water was irresistibly inviting. There she sat for some time, dreamily paddling with her little white feet, like a pretty dryad whose tree grew in too dry a soil.

She had finished playing with the cool stream, and was letting her feet dry in the patches of sunlight that pierced through the branches above her, when she heard a sound of voices. She hastily tried to draw on her stockings, but her skin was still too moist ; and so, gathering her feet under her skirt, she concealed herself as much as possible from the observation of the intruders. As they approached she recognized the voices with a start, and crouched down behind the boulder more closely than before.

We can go no further this way," said Mrs. Haldane.

" Oh yes, we can. I will assist you over the stones," the vicar rejoined.

" They look very treacherous and

slippery, and the water makes one nervous, running so fast."

"Look, it is quite safe!" said the vicar; and Edith, peeping from the side of the boulder, saw him step quickly across the brook. "It is a pity you should miss the old Roman camp, when you are so near it."

"If you will come back and assist me from this side, I will try them," said Mrs. Haldane.

The vicar returned across the brook, and Edith saw the lady gather her dress and prepare to step on to the first stone.

"Now, you must be ready to reach me your hand in case I need it."

"Oh, you will find it quite easy when you try. Don't stop, but go right across without hesitation."

Mrs. Haldane jumped fairly enough on to the first boulder, but, instead of allowing the forward impetus to carry her on, she tried to stop and steady herself on the narrow footing among the rushing water. She lost at once her balance and her courage, and turning to him with outstretched arms, she cried out, "Quick! quick! I shall fall!"

She threw herself back to the side as she spoke, and he caught her in his arms. Her arms were about his neck, her face close to his; he felt her breath upon his cheek. It was only for an instant, and as she tried to recover herself, their eyes met with a flash of self-consciousness. In the passionate excitement of that supreme moment he strained her to his breast, and pressed his lips to her in a long, violent kiss.

Edith sprang to her feet as though she had been stung; but instantly she recollected herself, and sank down into her hiding-place.

Mrs. Haldane tore herself from the arms that encircled her, and fronted the vicar with a flushed, angry face.

"Are you mad, Mr. Santley?" she asked indignantly. "Allow me to pass at once."

He stood aside trembling, white, and speechless; and she swept by him and hurried back through the wood.

The vicar looked after her, but stood as if rooted to the spot; while Edith, heedless of the hard stones and her naked feet, ran down wildly to the stepping-stones.

He turned as she approached, and there, with the water whirling between them, she confronted him like his outraged conscience.

CHAPTER XI.

EDITH.

" Is this your fidelity ? is this your love ?" she asked bitterly.

The deadly pallor of the vicar's face had given place to a flush of guilt and shame. He crossed the brook and stood beside her.

" Edith, I have done wrong. Can you forgive me ? " he asked, attempting to take her hand.

" Do not touch me, Mr. Santley ! " she exclaimed, stepping back from him. " Do not speak to me."

" Will you not forgive me, Edith ? "

"Ask God to forgive you.   It matters little now whether I forgive or not. Please go away and leave me."

"I cannot leave you in this manner. Say you forgive.   I confess I have done wrong, but it was in the heat of passion, it was not premeditated."

"The heat of passion!   Was it only in the heat of passion that you—— Oh, go at once, Mr. Santley!   Go before I say what had better be left unspoken!"

The vicar paused and looked at her anxiously; but Edith, throwing her shoes and stockings on the ground, sat down on a stone, and resting her pale, unhappy face on her hands, gazed with a hard, fixed expression at the water.

"Dearest Edith, try to believe that what I did was only an act of momentary madness; blame me if you will, for I cannot too severely blame myself, but do not look so relentless and unfor-giving."

She never stirred or gave any indica-tion that she had heard him, but sat staring at the water.

" You will be sorry for your unkind-ness afterwards," he continued.

She paid no heed to him, and he saw it was hopeless to try to effect a recon-ciliation at the present moment.

" Since you command me to go, I will go."

Still she appeared not to have heard him. He went back across the brook, and, glancing back once or twice, dis-appeared in the wood. A minute or two later he stole back again, and saw that she was still sitting by the brook in the same stony attitude. A vague sense of uneasiness took possession of him. He knew that even the meekest, frailest, and gentlest of women are capable of the most tragic extremities when under the sway of passion. Yet what could he do ? She would not speak to him, and was deaf to all he could say in extenuation of his conduct. Trusting to the effect of a little quiet reflection, and to the love which he knew she felt for him, he resolved at length to leave her to herself. After all he had, it seemed to him, more to fear from Mrs. Haldane than from Edith. To what frightful consequences he had exposed himself by that act of folly ! Would she tell her husband ? Would the story leak out and become the scandal of the country side ? With a sickening dread of what the future had in store for him, he retraced his steps to the quarry.

Mrs. Haldane's first impulse was to order her carriage and at once drive home, but her hurried walk through the wood gradually became slower as she reflected on the strange interpretation that would be put upon so sudden a departure. She had brought the vicar, and if she now hastened away without him, evil tongues would soon be busied with both her name and his. For the sake of the office he held, and for her own sake as well, she resolved to be silent on what had happened. She felt sure that the vicar would be sufficiently punished by the stings of his own conscience, and if any future chastisement were required he should find it in her distance and frigid treatment of him. Consequently, when Mrs. Haldane reached the quarry she assumed a cheerful, friendly air, stopped to say a few kind words to the old people, and interested herself in the amusements of the children. It was now drawing near tea-time, and the sun was westering.

Mr. Santley felt relieved when he found that Mrs. Haldane had not abruptly left, as he dreaded she would do, but he made no attempt to speak to her or attract her attention. At tea-time she took a cup in her hand and joined a group of little girls, instead of taking her place at the table set aside for her.

The vicar's eye glanced restlessly about for Edith, but she had not obeyed the summons of the cornopean, and in the bustle and excitement, her absence was not noticed. It was only when the horses had been put into the shafts, and the children, after being counted, were taking their places in the waggons, that Miss Greatheart missed her.

" Have you seen Miss Dove, Mr. Santley ? " she asked, after she had searched in vain through the little crowd for Edith. " I don't think she was at tea."

" She went in the direction of the old camp," replied the vicar, hurriedly ; " she cannot have heard the signal. Do not say anything. I think I shall be easily able to find her. If Mrs. Haldane asks for me, will you say I have gone to look for her ? You can start as soon as you are ready ; we shall easily overtake you."

So saying, Mr. Santley plunged into the wood, and hurried to the brook. Edith was still sitting where he had left her, but she had in the meanwhile put on her shoes and stockings. Instead of the fixed, determined expression, her face now wore a look of intense wretchedness, and evidently she had been crying. She looked up at the sound of his footsteps.

"Edith, we are going home," he said, as he reached the edge of the stream.

"You can go," was the answer.

"But not without you."

"Yes, without me. I am not going home. I am never going home any more. I have no home. Oh! mother, mother!"

The last words were uttered in a low, sobbing voice.

"Come, come, you must not speak like that. You must go home. What would your poor aunt say if you did anything so foolish?"

"Oh, what would she say if she knew how I have disgraced her and myself? No, I cannot go home any more."

"But you cannot stay here all night," said the vicar, with a chill, sinking tremor at the heart.

She gave no answer.

" Edith, my dear girl, for God's sake do not say you are thinking of doing anything rash ! "

" What else can I do ? What else am I fit for but disgrace and a miserable end ? Oh, Mr. Santley, you swore to me that before God I was your true wife. I believed you then. I did not think you were only acting in a moment of passion. But now I see that it was a dreadful sin. I was not your wife ; and oh ! what have you made me instead ? "

He was very pale, and he trembled from head to foot as he listened to her words.

" Do not speak so loud," he said in a hoarse whisper.

" What ! do you feel ashamed ? Are you afraid of any one knowing ? But God knows it now, and my poor, poor mother knows it—God help me!—and all the world will know it some day."

"Edith, you will not ruin me?"

"Have you not ruined me? Have you not cast me off for a woman who does not even care for you—for another man's wife? Oh no, do not be afraid. I will take my shame with me in silence. No one shall be able to say a word against you now, but all the world will know at the last."

"Edith, listen to me. I will tell you everything; I will hide nothing from you; but do not condemn me unheard. All that I said to you was true, and is still true. Till *she* came, I did really and most truly love you with all my heart and soul. You were my very wife, in God's eyes, if love and truth be, as they are, what makes the validity of marriage. I did not deceive you; I did not speak in a moment of passion. Before Heaven I took you for my wife, and before Heaven I believed myself your husband."

" And then she came !" interposed Edith, bitterly.

" And then she came. I have told you all she was to me once, all I hoped she would one day be. But I have not told you how I have struggled to be true to you in every word and thought. It has been a hard and a bitter struggle—all the more hard and bitter that I have failed. I confess, Edith, that I have not been true. But are we all sinless ? are we perfect ? "

" We can at least be honourable. Your love of her is a crime."

" Her beauty maddens me. She is my evil angel. To see her is to love her and long for her. And instead of helping me to conquer temptation, instead of trying to save me from myself, you cast me from you, you upbraid my weakness, you taunt me with your unhappiness. When she is not near, my better nature turns to you. You help me to believe in God, in goodness; she drives me to unbelief and atheism. Did you fancy I was a saint? Have not I my passions and temptations as well as other men? Even the just man falls seven times a day; if you indeed loved me as a true wife, you would find it in your heart to forgive even unto seventy times seven."

"You know how I have loved!"

"*Have* loved! Ay, and how easily you have ceased to love!"

"No, no; I have never ceased to love you. It is because I must still love and love you that I am so wretched."

"Then how can you be so unforgiving?"

"Oh, I am not unforgiving. I can forgive you anything, so long as I know that I am dear to you. Seven and seventy-seven times."

"And you forgive me now?"

"I do. But you will never any more—— "

"You must help me not to; you must pray for me, and assist me to be ever faithful to you."

"I will, I will."

He drew her to him, and kissed her on the lips.

"And you will come home now?"

"Yes, with you."

"The waggons have started, and we must walk quickly to overtake them."

"Oh, I don't care now how far we have to walk."

"Mrs. Haldane, however, may have waited for us."

Edith stopped short.

"I couldn't go near her."

"Consider a moment, darling. She knows nothing about you, and she does not know that you know anything about her. It might look strange if she drove home without me, after bringing me here. I feared at first that she would have left instantly, but she did not. She may not wish to give people any reason for talking about any sudden coolness between us. Do you understand me?"

"Yes. I will go."

The vicar had correctly divined the course Mrs. Haldane had pursued. When she learned that Mr. Santley had gone in search of Edith, she drove very leisurely along, so that they might overtake her. She had just got clear of the wood when, on looking round, she observed them coming through the trees. She drew up till they reached her; and when they had got in, she started a brisk conversation with Edith on all manner of topics. She was in her liveliest mood, and to Edith it seemed almost incredible that the scene she had witnessed at the brook was a very serious fact, and not an hallucination. Edith noticed, however, that the vicar seldom spoke, and that, though Mrs. Haldane listened and answered when he made any remark, the conversation was between Mrs. Haldane and herself.

At parting Mrs. Haldane gave him her finger-tips, and was apparently paying more attention to Edith when she said good-bye to him.

CHAPTER XII.

CONSCIENCE.

MRS. HALDANE came no more to the Vicarage that week, and on Sunday she did not remain, as she had hitherto done, for the communion at the close of the morning service. She was evidently deeply offended, and was doing all she could to avoid meeting the vicar. With him that week had been one of terrible conflict. Tortured with remorse and shame, he was still mad with passion. That kiss was still burning on his lips. He still could feel that voluptuous form in his arms. It seemed, indeed, as though Mrs. Haldane were his evil genius, driving him on to destruction. He was unable to pray ; and when he sat down to prepare his sermon, her face rose between him and the paper, and, starting up, he rushed from the house and walked rapidly away into the country. This was in the forenoon, and he walked on and on at a quick pace for several hours. He passed little hamlets and farmsteads which he did not notice, for his mind was absorbed in a wretchedness so intense that he scarcely was conscious of what he was doing. In the afternoon he came to a wood, and, worn out with fatigue and agitation, he entered it and flung himself beneath the shadow of a tree.

There he lay, a prey to conscience, till the sun went down. He had had no food since morning, and he was now weak and nervous. He returned from the wood to the high-road and retraced his steps homeward. As he passed by the wayside cottages, he was tempted once or twice to stop and ask for bread and milk, but after a mental contest he each time conquered the pangs of hunger and thirst, and went on again. The fathers of the desert had subdued the lusts of the flesh by hunger and stripes and physical suffering, and if mortification could exorcise the evil spirit within him, he would have no mercy on himself. He was a great distance from home, and, notwithstanding his resolution to suffer and endure, he was several times forced to sit down and rest on heaps of broken stones by the wayside ; and on one of these occasions a spray of bramble-berries

hanging over the hedge caught his eye,
and looked so rich and sweet that he
plucked one and raised it to his mouth.
The next moment, however, he had
flung it away from him. On another
occasion he was startled to his feet by
the sound of wheels, and as he walked
on he was overtaken by a neighbouring
farmer in his gig, who drew up as he
was passing, and touched his hat.

"Making for home, Mr. Santley?"
he asked, as he shook up the cushion
on the vacant seat beside him. "I can
put you down at your own door, sir."

"Thank you, Mr. Henderson; I prefer
walking, and I have some business to
attend to."

"All right, sir. It's a fine evening
for a walk. Good-bye."

"Good-bye."

The vicar watched the gig diminish

on the distant road till at length the hedgerows concealed it, with a certain sense of stoical satisfaction. He felt he was not all weakness; there was yet left some power of self-denial, some fortitude to endure self-inflicted chastisement.

It was nearly dark when he arrived again in Omberley. The windows were ruddy with fire and gaslight; there were no children playing in the streets; several of the small shopkeepers who kept open late, were now at last putting up their shutters. There was a genial glow from the red-curtained window of the village inn, and a sound of singing and merriment.

"Why should I not go in and join them?" he thought to himself. "What an effect it would have, if I stepped into the sanded taproom and called for a pipe and a quart of beer! The vicar smoking a long clay, with his frothing pewter on the deal table beside him! Why not? Has not the vicar his gross appetites as well as you? Why should you be scandalized, friends, if he should indulge in the same merry way as yourselves? Is he not a mere man like you, with the same animal needs and cravings? Fools, who shrink with horror from the humanity of a man because he wears a black coat and talks to you of duty and sacrifice and godliness! How little you know the poor wretch to whom you look for counsel and comfort and mediation with Heaven!"

He was turning away, when the tap-room door was flung open, and half a dozen tipsy men, cursing and quarrelling, staggered out into the street.

Among them was a handsome, swarthy girl of two and twenty, gaily dressed in colours, with a coloured handkerchief bound over her black hair, and a guitar in her hand. They were evidently quarrelling about the girl, who was doing her best to make peace among them.

"You does me no good by your fighting and kicking up a row, masters. Decent folks won't let a wench into the house when there's always a fight got up about her. You spoils my market, and gets me an ill name, masters."

"Any way, Jack Haywood shan't lay a finger on thee, Sal!" cried a burly young fellow, deep in his cups, as he clenched his horny fist and shook it at Jack.

"What is't to you what Jack does?" returned the girl, saucily. "Neither

Jack nor thee shall lay a finger on me against my will. I reckon I can take care o' myself, masters."

"Ay, ay, thou canst that!" assented several voices.

The vicar, who had stood to witness this scene, now stepped in among the group. The men recognized him, and, touching their forelocks, slunk away in sheepish silence. He uttered not a word, but his pale face sobered them like a dash of cold water. Only the girl was left, and she stood, red and frightened, while her hands were nervously busied with the guitar.

"You are back again, Sal, and at your old ways," said the vicar, in a low voice. "I see, all good advice and all encouragement are wasted on you."

"I can't help it, sir," said the girl, sullenly. "I was born bad; I'm of a bad lot. It's no use trying any more. It's in the blood and the bone, and it'll come out, in spite of everything."

"Have you made much to-day?" asked the vicar.

"A shilling."

"Where are you going to stop to-night?"

"At old Mary Henson's, in Barn Street."

"Then, go home at once, Sal," said the vicar, giving her a half-crown. "Will you promise me?"

"Yes."

"And you will speak to no man to-night? You promise?"

"Yes," said the girl, taking the money, with a strange look of inquiry at the vicar.

"And try to say your prayers before you go to sleep."

The girl dropped a curtsy, and went slowly down the street. With a bitter laugh, the vicar pursued his way homeward.

" In the blood and the bone! In the blood and the bone!" he repeated to himself. "You are right, girl; we are born bad—born bad. The bestial madness of ages and æons, the lust and lasciviousness of countless generations, are still in our blood, and our instincts are still the instincts of the beast and the savage. Hypocrite and blasphemer that I am! Whited sepulchre, reeking with corruption! Living lie and mask of holiness! O God, what a wretch am I, who dare to speak of purity and repentance to this woman!"

When he reached the Vicarage, his sister was anxiously awaiting him, and supper was ready

"Where have you been so long?" she asked, a little impatiently. "I think you might leave word when you expect to be detained beyond your usual time. It is eleven o'clock."

"I could not say how long I should be," replied the vicar, with a weary look, which touched his sister and changed her ill-temper to solicitude.

"You are quite tired out, poor fellow," she said, laying her hand on his shoulder. "Well, come to supper. It is ready."

"I cannot take anything at present," replied Mr. Santley. "I will go and do a little of my sermon."

"Shall I leave something out for you, then?"

"Yes, please. Good night."

He went into the study, lit the gas, and, locking the door, flung himself into an armchair.

"In the blood! in the blood!" he bitterly communed with himself. "And, with all our wild dreams and aspirations, we are but what science says we are, the conqueror of the lascivious ape, the offspring of some common ancestral bestiality, which transmitted to the simian its animalism free and unfettered except by appetite, and to man the germs of a moral law which must be for ever at variance with his sensual instincts. God! we are worse than apes— we the immortals, with our ideals of spirit and purity!"

He rose, and going across the room to the tall, carved oak cupboard, whose contents were a secret to all but himself, he unlocked it and opened the folding doors. The light fell on a large, beautiful statue of the Madonna, with the Infant Christ in her arms. The figure was in plaster, exquisitely coloured, and of a rare loveliness. He looked at it abstractedly for a long while.

" Mother of God!" he exclaimed at length, with passionate fervour. "Spotless virgin, woman above all women glorified, the solitary boast of our tainted nature—oh, dream and desire of men striving for their lost innocence, how vainly have I worshipped and prayed to thee! How ardently have I believed in thy immaculate motherhood! How yearningly I have cried to thee for thy aid and intercession! And no answer has been granted to my supplications. My feverish exaltation has passed from me, leaving me weak and at the mercy of my senses. Art thou, too, but a poetic myth of a later superstition—an idealization more beautiful, more divine than the frail goddesses of Greece and

Rome ? The art and poetry of the world have turned to thee for inspiration, the ascetic has filled the cold cell with the shining vision of thee, altars have been raised to thee over half the globe, the prayers of nations ascend to thee, and art thou but a beautiful conception of the heart, powerless to aid or to hear thy suppliants ? "

He paused, as if, indeed, he expected some sign or word in answer to his wild appeal. Then, closing the doors again and locking them, he went towards his desk. On it lay the manuscript of the sermon he had preached on the Unknown God.

" The Unknown God !" he exclaimed. " What if her husband is right ! What if, indeed, there be no God, no God for us, no God of whom we shall ever be conscious ! All science points that way. When the man is dead, his soul is dead too. We deny it; but what is our denial worth? It is our interest to deny it. All phenomena contradict our denial. No man has ever risen from the grave to give us assurance of our immortality. Ah, truly, 'if there be no resurrection of the dead, then is Christ not risen; and if Christ be not risen, then is our preaching vain, and your faith is also vain!'"

He paced the room excitedly.

"Why act the knave and the hypocrite longer? Why delude the world with a false hope of a future that can never be? Why preach prayer and sacrifice, and suffering and patience, when this life is all? If Christ is not risen, our preaching is vain, and your faith is also vain."

He again paced the room; and then,

going to a drawer where the keys of the church were kept, he took them, and stole noiselessly out of the house. All was very still outside. The stars were shining, and it was duskily clear. He traversed the churchyard, and reaching the porch he unlocked the door and entered. It was quite dark, except that the tall, narrow windows looked grey against the blackness of the rest of the building, and a little bead of flame burned in the sanctuary lamp. He closed the door after him, and went up the echoing nave to the chancel. Thence he groped his way to the pulpit, and ascending he looked down into the darkness before him.

He stood there in silence, straining his eyes into the gloom, and gradually there came out of the darkness faint, spectral rows of faces, turned up to his

with a horrified and bewildered aspect.
He uttered no word, but in his brain he
was preaching from the text of Paul,
and proving that Christ, indeed, had
never risen, and that their faith was
vain. This world was all, and there was
nothing beyond it. Vice and virtue
were but social and physical distinctions,
implying that the consequences of the
one were destructive of happiness, of the
other were conducive to happiness. Sin
was a fiction, and the sense of sinfulness
a morbid development of the imagination. Every man was a law unto himself, and that law must be obeyed. A
man's actions were the outcome of his
constitution. He was not morally responsible for them. Indeed, moral
responsibility was a philosophical error.
In dumb show was that long, phrenzied
sermon preached to a phantom congre-

gation. At the close the vicar, omitting the usual form of benediction, descended from the pulpit, staggered across the chancel, and fell in a swoon at the foot of the steps which led to the altar.

CHAPTER XIII.

IN THE LABORATORY.

THE grey dawn was glimmering through the chancel when Mr. Santley regained consciousness. He looked wonderingly about him, and at first was unable to understand how he came to be in his present position. That physical collapse had been a merciful relief from a state of mental tension which had become intolerable. He felt faint but calm, and the horrible excitement of the last few hours presented itself to his memory as a sort of ghastly nightmare from which he had been providentially awakened.

He rose and went out into the church-yard. The air was moist and cool. A strange white mist lay in fantastic pools and streaks on the bare hayfields. The corn was full of an indistinct white gauzy vapour. So were the trees. There was not much of it in the open air. It had a spectral look, and, like spirits, it seemed to require some material thing to interpenetrate and rest upon. The grass was heavy with dew, and the gravelled walk as dark coloured as though there had been rain. From the corn came the sound of innumerable chirpings and twitterings. The fields seemed to be swarming with sweet, sharp musical notes. In the trees, too, though there was no stir of wings, there was a very tumult of bird-song—not the full, joyous outpouring, but a ceaseless orchestral tuning up and rehearsing as it were. The familiar graveyard in this unusual misty light, and alive with this strange music, seemed a place in which ne had never been before. The effect was as novel as the first appearance of a well-known landscape buried in snow.

The newness of what was so familiar excited an indefinable interest in him. He felt somehow as though he had passed through the valley of the shadow, and this was the day after death—that death by which we shall not all die, but by which we and all things shall be changed. He lingered in that mental state in which thought expands beyond the bounds of consciousness, and it was not till a low, faint flush of red began to colour the east that he returned to the Vicarage, and, throwing himself on his bed, fell into the deep, dreamless sleep of exhaustion.

"When may I come again ? "

"When you have anything really parochial to say to me. Please go now."

Their eyes met, and hers sank beneath his own.

As he crossed towards the door it opened, and Baptisto appeared upon the threshold.

" Did you ring, señora ? "

At the sight of the Spaniard's dull impressive face Mrs. Haldane started violently, and went a little pale. She had heard nothing of his return, and he came like an apparition.

" Baptisto ! What are you doing here ? I thought——"

She paused in wonder, while the Spaniard inclined his head and bowed profoundly.

" I was taken with a vertigo at the

station, and the señor permitted me to return."

" Then your master has gone alone ? "

" Yes, señora."

" Very well. Order the carriage at once.   I am going out."

Baptisto bowed and retired, quickly closing the door.

Santley, who had stood listening during the above conversation, now prepared to follow, but, glancing at Ellen, saw that she was unusually agitated.

" That is a sinister-looking fellow," he remarked. "I am afraid he has frightened you."

" Indeed, no," she replied ; " though I confess I was startled at his unexpected return.   Good-bye."

" Good-bye," he said, again taking her hand and holding it up a moment in his own.

Passing from the drawing-room, he again came face to face with Baptisto, who was lurking in the lobby, but who drew aside with a respectful bow, to allow the clergyman to pass.

He crossed the hall, descended the stone steps of the portico, and walked slowly towards the lodge. As he passed the ruined chapel, its shadows seemed to fall upon his spirit and leave it in ominous darkness. He shivered slightly, and drew his cloak about him, then with his eyes cast down he thoughtfully walked on.

He did not glance back. Had he done so, he would have seen Baptisto standing on the steps of the Manor house, watching him with a sinister smile.

CHAPTER XV.

CONJURATION.

It was a chill day in early autumn, and as Charles Santley passed along the dark avenue of the Manor his path was strewn here and there with freshly fallen leaves. Dark shadows lay on every side, and the heaven above was full of a sullen, cheerless light. It was just the day for a modern Faust, in the course of his noonday walk, to encounter, in some fancied guise, canine or human, the evil one of old superstition.

Be that as it may, Santley knew at last that the hour of his temptation was over, and that the evil one was not far away. He knew it, by the sullen acquiescence of evil of his own soul; by the deliberate and despairing precision with which he had chosen the easy and downward path; by the sense of darkness which already obliterated the bright moral instincts in his essentially religious mind. He had spoken the truth when he said he would follow Ellen Haldane anywhere, even to the eternal pit itself. Her beauty possessed him and disturbed him with the joy of impure thoughts; and now that he perceived his own power to trouble her peace of mind, he rejoiced at the strength of his passion with a truly diabolic perversity.

As he came out of the lodge gate he saw, far away over the fields, the spire of his own church.

He laughed to himself.

But the man's faith in spiritual things, so far from being shaken, was as strong as ever. His own sense of moral dete-rioration, of spiritual backsliding, only made him believe all the more fervently in the heaven from which he had fallen, or might choose to fall. For it is surely a mistake to picture, as so many poets have pictured, the evil spirit as one ignorant of or insensible to good. Far wiser is the theology which describes Satan as the highest of angelic spirits— the spirit which, above all others, had beheld and contemplated the Godhead, and had then, in sheer revolt and nega-tion, deliberately and advisedly decided its own knowledge and rejected its own truthright. Santley was, in his basest moods, essentially a godly man—a man strangely curious of the beauty of goodness, and capable of infinite celestial dreams. If, like many another, he confused the flesh and the spirit, he did no more than many sons of Eve have done.

As he walked slowly along he mused, somewhat to this effect—

" I love this woman. In her heart she loves me. Her superior spiritual endowments are mystically alive to those I myself possess. Her husband is a clod, an unbeliever, with no spiritual promptings. In his sardonic presence, her aspirations are chilled, frozen at the very fountain-head ; whereas, in mine, all the sweetness and the power of her nature are aroused, though with a certain irritation. If I persist, she must yield to the slow moral mesmerism of my passion, and eventually fall. Is this necessarily evil ? Am I of set purpose sinning ? Is it not possible that even a breach of the moral law might, under certain conditions, lead us both to a higher religious place—yes, even to a deeper and intenser consciousness of God ? "

And again—

" What *is* sin ? Surely it is better than moral stagnation, which is death. There are certain deflections from duty which, like the side stroke of a bird's wing, may waft us higher. In the arms of this woman, I should surely be nearer God than crawling alone on the bare path of duty, loving nothing, hoping nothing, becoming nothing. What is it that Goethe says of the Eternal Feminine which lead us ever upward and onward ? Which was the highest, Faust before he loved Marguerite, or Faust after he passed out of the shadow of his sin into the sphere of imperial and daring passion ? I believe in God, I love this woman. Out of that belief, and that love, shall I not become a living soul ? "

Was this the man's own musing, or rather the very devil whispering in his ear ? From such fragmentary glimpses of his mind as have been given, we can at least guess the extent of his intellectual degradation.

As he walked along the country road, his pale countenance became seraphic ; just so may the face of Lucifer have looked when he plumed his wings for deliberate flight from heaven.

He stepped into a roadside farm and had a glass of milk, which the good woman of the place handed to him with a sentiment of adoration ; he looked so gentle, so at peace with all living things. His white hand rested for a moment on the head of her little girl, in gentle benediction. He had never felt more tenderly disposed to all creation than at that moment, when he was prepared to dip a pen into his own heart's blood, and sign the little promissory note which Mephistopheles carries, always ready, in his pocket. He had hated his congregation before ; now he loved them exceedingly—and all the world.

CHAPTER XVI.

AT THE OPERA.

ON arriving in London, George Haldane was driven straight to the house of an old friend at Chelsea, where he always stayed during his visits to the Metropolis. This friend was Lovell Blakiston, as eccentric a being in his own way as Haldane himself was in his. He had been, since boyhood, in the India Office, where he still put in an appearance several hours a day, and whence he still drew a large income, with the immediate right to a retiring pension whenever he choose to take it. He was a great student, especially of the pagan poets and philosophers; and the greater part of his days and nights were spent in his old-fashioned library, opening with folding doors on to a quiet lawn, which led in its turn to the very river-side. He had two pet aversions—modern progress, in the shape of railroads, electricity, geology; all the new business of science and modern religion, especially in its connection with Christian theology. He was, in short, a pagan pure and simple, fond of old books, old wine, old meditations, and old gods. However he might differ with Haldane on such subjects as the nebular hypothesis, which he hated with all his heart, he agreed with him sufficiently on the subject of Christianity. Both had a cordial dislike for church ceremonies and church bells.

The two gentlemen had another taste in common. This was the opera, which both enjoyed hugely, though Blakiston never ceased to regret the disappearance of that old operatic institution, the ballet, which, like a rich dessert wine, used to bring the feast of music to a delightfully sensuous conclusion. Haldane was too young a man to remember such visions of loveliness as Cerito, whom his old friend had often gone to see in company with Horne Took.

So it happened that two or three days after his arrival, Haldane accompanied his host to the opera house, where Patti was to appear in " Traviata."

Seated comfortably in the stalls, he was glancing quietly round the house between the acts, when his attention was attracted to a face in one of the private boxes. A pale, Madonna-like, yet girlish face, set in golden hair, with soft blue eyes, and an expression so forlorn, so wistful, so ill at ease, that it was almost painful to behold.

Haldane started in surprise.

"What is the matter?" said his friend. "Have you recognized anybody?"

"I am not certain," returned Haldane, raising his opera-glass and surveying the face through them. Then, after a long look, he added as if to himself, "I am almost sure it is the same."

"Do you mean that young lady in black, seated in the second tier?"

"Yes. Oblige me by looking at her, and tell me what you think of her."

Blakiston raised his opera-glass, and took a long look.

"Well?" asked Haldane.

"She reminds me of one of your detestable pre-Raphaelistic drawings, shockheaded and vacuous. She is pretty, I grant you, but she has no expression."

" I should say, on the contrary, a very marked expression of deep pain."

" Tight lacing," grunted Blakiston. " Your modern women have no shape, since Cerito."

Here Haldane rose from his seat. Looking up again, he had met the young lady's eyes, and had perceived at once that she recognized him.

" I am going to speak to her," he explained. " She is a neighbour of ours, and a friend of my wife."

He made his way to the second tier, and finding the door of the box open, he looked in, and saw the person he sought, seated in company with an elderly lady and a young man.

" Miss Dove !" he said, advancing into

the box. " Although we have only met twice, I thought I could not be mistaken."

Edith (for it was she) turned quickly and took his outstretched hand.

" How strange to find you here ! " she exclaimed. " Is Mrs. Haldane with you ? "

" No, indeed. I left her to the pious duties of the parish, which she is fulfilling daily, I expect, in company with your seraphic friend the minister."

Edith looked at him with strange surprise, but said nothing.

" When did you come to town ? " he asked. " I thought you were quite a country young lady, and never ventured into the giddy world of London."

" I was not very well," replied Edith, " and my aunt invited me to stop with her a few weeks. This is my aunt, Mrs. Hetherington ; and this gentleman is my

cousin Walter." Here Edith went somewhat nervously through the ceremony of
introduction. She added, with a slight
flush, " My cousin insisted on bringing us
here to-night. I did not wish to come."

"Why not ? " demanded Haldane,
noticing her uneasiness.

" Because I did not think it right; and
I have been thinking all the evening
what the vicar will say when I tell him
I have been to such a place."

Here the old lady shook her head
ominously, and gave a slight groan.

" Is the place so terrible," asked Haldane, smiling, " now you have seen it ? "

" No, it is very pretty ; and of course
the singing is beautiful. But Mr.
Santley does not approve of the theatre,
and I am sorry I came."

" Nonsense, Edith," said young
Hetherington, with a laugh. " You

know you wanted to see the 'Traviata.' The fact is," he continued, turning to Haldane, "my mother and my cousin are both terribly old-fashioned. My mother here is Scotch, and believes in the kirk, the whole kirk, and nothing but the kirk; and as for Edith, she is entirely, as they say in Scotland, under the minister's 'thoomb.' I thought they would have enjoyed themselves, but they have been doing penance all the evening."

Without paying attention to her cousin's remarks, Edith was looking thoughtfully at Haldane.

"When do you return to Omberley?" she asked.

"I am not sure—in a fortnight, at the latest. I am going on to France."

"And Mrs. Haldane will remain all that time alone?"

"Of course," he replied. "Oh, she

will not miss me. She has her household duties, her parish, her garden—to
say nothing of her clergyman. And you,
do *you* stay long in London ? "

" I am not sure ; I think not. I am
tired of it already."

Again that weary, wistful look, which
sat so strangely on the young, almost
childish face. She sighed, and gazed
sadly around the crowded house. A
minute later, Haldane took his leave,
and rejoined his friend in the stalls.
Looking up at the end of the next act,
he saw that the box was empty.

The women had yielded to their con-
sciences, and departed before the end of
the performance.

That night, when Haldane went home
to Chelsea, he found a letter from his
wife. It was a long letter, but contained
no news whatever, being chiefly occupied

with self-reproaches that the writer had
not accompanied her husband in his
pilgrimage. This struck Haldane as
rather peculiar, as in former communications Ellen had expressed no such
dissatisfaction; but he was by nature and
of set habit unsuspicious, and he set it
down to some momentary *ennui*. The
letter contained no mention whatever
of Mr. Santley, but in the postscript,
where ladies often put the most interesting part of their correspondence,
there was a reference to the Spanish
valet, Baptisto.

"As I told you," wrote Ellen, "Baptisto seems in excellent health, though he
is mysterious and unpleasant as usual.
He comes and goes like a ghost, but if
he made you believe that he was ill, he
was imposing upon you. I do so wish
you had taken him with you."

Haldane folded up the letter with a smile.

" Poor Baptisto ! " he thought, " I suppose it is as I suspected, and the little widow at the lodge is at the bottom of it all."

After a few days' sojourn at Chelsea, during which time he was much interested in certain spiritualistic investigations which were just then being conducted by the London *savants*, to the manifest confusion of the spirits and indignation of true believers, Haldane went to Paris, where he read his paper before the French Society to which he belonged. There we shall leave him for a little time, returning to the company of Miss Dove, with whom we have more immediate concern.

Mother and son lived in a pleasant

house overlooking Clapham Common, a district famous for its religious edification, its young ladies' seminaries, and its dissenting chapels. Mrs. Hetherington was the wealthy widow of a Glasgow merchant, long settled in London, and she set her face rigidly against modern thought, ecclesiastical vestments, and cooking on the sabbath. Curiously enough, her son Walter, who inherited a handsome competence, was a painter, and followed his heathen occupation with much talent, and more youthful euthusiasm. His landscapes, chiefly of Highland scenes, had been exhibited in the Royal Scottish Academy. His mother, whose highest ideas of art were founded on a superficial acquaintance with the Scripture pieces of Noel Paton, and an occasional contemplation of biblical masterpieces in the Doré Gallery, would have preferred to have seen him following in his father's footsteps, and even entering the true kirk as a preacher ; but his sympathies were pagan, and a gloomy childish experience had not fitted him with the requisite enthusiasm for John Calvin and the sabbath.

Walter Hetherington was a fine fresh young fellow of three and twenty, and belonged to the clever set of Scotch painters, headed by Messrs. Pettie, Richardson, and Peter Graham. He was "cannie" painstaking, and rather sceptical, and, putting aside his art, which he really loved, he felt true enthusiasm for only one thing in the world—his cousin Edith, whom he hoped and longed to make his wife.

As a very young girl, Edith had seemed rather attached to him ; but of late years,

during which they saw each other only
at long intervals, she seemed colder
and colder to his advances. He noticed
her indifference, and set it down somewhat angrily to girlish fanaticism, for
he had little or no suspicion whatever
that another man's image might be
filling her thoughts. Once or twice, it
is true, when she sounded the praises
of her Omberley pastor, his zeal, his
goodness, his beauty of discourse, he
asked himself if he could possibly have
a rival *there ;* but knowing something of
the relinquent fancies of young vestals,
he rejected the idea. To tell the truth,
he rather pitied the Rev. Mr. Santley,
whom he had never seen, as a hard-
headed, dogmatic, elderly creature of
the type greatly approved by his mother,
and abundant even in Clapham. He
had no idea of an Adonis in a clerical

frock coat, with a beautiful profile, white hands, and a voice gentle and low—the latter an excellent thing in woman, but a dangerous thing in an unmarried preacher of the Word.

CHAPTER XVII.

WALTER HETHERINGTON.

WHEN the party got home from the opera, it was only half-past ten. They sat down to a frugal supper in the dining-room.

"I am sorry you did not wait till the last act," said the young man, after an awkward silence. "Patti's death scene is magnificent."

"I'm thinking we heard enough," his mother replied. "I never cared much for play-acting, and I see little sense in screeching about in a foreign tongue. I'd rather have half an hour of the

Reverend Mr. Mactavish's discourses than a night of fooling like yon."

"What do *you* say, Edith? I'm sure the music was very pretty."

"Yes, it was beautiful; but not knowing much of Italian, I could not gather what it was all about."

"It is an operatic version of a story of the younger Dumas," explained Walter, with an uncomfortable sense of treading on dangerous ground. "The story is that of a beautiful woman who has lived an evil life, and is reformed through her affection for a young Frenchman. His friends think he is degrading himself by offering to marry her, and to cure him she pretends to be false and wicked. In the end, she dies in his arms, broken-hearted. It is a very touching subject, I think, though some people consider it immoral."

Here the matron broke in with quiet severity.

" I wonder yon woman—Patti, you call her—doesn't think shame to appear in such dresses. One of them was scarcely decent, and I was almost ashamed to look at her—the creature!"

" But her singing, mother, her singing; was it not divine?"

" It was meeddling loud; but I've heard far finer in the kirk. Edith, my bairn, you're tired, I'm thinking. We'll just read a chapter, and get to bed."

So the chapter was read, and the ladies retired, while Walter walked off to his studio to have a quiet pipe. He was too used to his mother's peculiarities to be much surprised at the failure of the evening's entertainment; but he felt really amazed that Edith had not been more impressed.

The next morning, when they met at breakfast, Edith astonished both her aunt and cousin by expressing her wish to return to Omberley as soon as possible.

" Go away already ! " cried the young man. "'Why, you've hardly been here a week, and you've seen nothing of town, and we've all the picture-galleries to visit yet."

" And you have not heard Mr. Mactavish discoorse," cried his mother. " No, no ; you must bide awhile."

But Edith shook her head, and they saw her mind was made up.

" I can come again at Christmas, but I would rather go now," she said.

" But why have you changed your mind ? " inquired her cousin eagerly.

" I think they want me at home ; and there is a great deal of church work to be done in the village.

Walter was not deceived by this excuse, and tried persuasion, but it was of no avail. The girl was determined to return home immediately. He little knew the real cause of her determination. Haldane's presence in London had filled her, in spite of herself, with jealous alarm. Ellen Haldane was alone at the Manor, with no husband's eyes to trouble her; and, despite the clergyman's oath of fidelity, Edith could not trust him.

Yes, she would go home. It was time to put an end to it all, to remind Santley of his broken promises, and to claim their fulfilment. If he refused to do her justice, she would part from him for ever; not, however, without letting the other woman, her rival, know his true character.

It was arranged that she should leave

by an early train next morning. For the greater part of the day she kept her room, engaged in preparations for the journey; but towards evening Walter found her alone in the drawing-room. The old lady, his mother, who earnestly wished him to marry his cousin, had contrived to be out of the way.

"I am so sorry you are going," the young man said. "We see so little of each other now."

Edith was seated with her back to the window, her face in deep shade. She knew by her cousin's manner that he was more than usually agitated, and she dreaded what was coming—what had come, indeed, on several occasions before. She did not answer, but almost unconsciously heaved a deep sigh.

"Does that mean that you are sorry too?" asked Walter, leaning towards her to see her face.

"Of course I am sorry," she replied, with a certain constraint.

"I wish I could believe that. Somehow or other, Edith, it seems to me that you would rather be anywhere than here. Well, you have some cause; for the house is dreary enough, and we are all dull people. But you and I used to be such friends! More like brother and sister than mere cousins. Is that all over? Are we to drift farther and farther apart as the years pass on? It seems to me as if it might come to that."

"How absurd you are!" said Edith, trying to force a laugh, but failing lamentably. "You know I was always fond of you and—and—of your mother."

Walter winced under the sting of the last sentence, so unconsciously given.

"I don't mean that at all," he exclaimed. "Of course you liked us, as relations like each other; but am I never to be more to you than a mere cousin? You know I love you, that I have loved you ever since we were boy and girl; and once—ah, yes, I thought you cared for me a little. Edith, what does it mean? Why are you so changed?"

Edith was more deeply changed than ever her cousin could guess. Had he been able to see her face, he would have been wonderstricken at its expression of mingled shame and despair. She tried to reply; but before she could do so her voice was choked, and her tears began to fall. In a moment he was close beside her, and bending over her, with one hand outstretched to clasp her.

"Now, you are crying. Edith, my darling, what is it?"

"Don't touch me," she sobbed, shrinking from him. "I can't bear it."

"Forgive me, if I have said anything to pain you; and oh, my darling! remember it is my love that carries me away. I do love you, Edith. I wish to God I could prove to you how much!"

He took her hand in his; but she drew it forcibly from him, and, shrinking still further away, entirely losing her self-control, sobbed silently.

"Don't!" she exclaimed. "For pity's sake, be silent. You do not know what you are saying. I am not fit to become your wife."

He moved a few steps from her, and waited until her wild, hysterical sobbing should have ceased. She commanded herself quickly, as it the wild outburst which she had not been able to control had terrified her.   Then she rose, and would have left the room, but the young man stopped her.

" Edith," he said, " surely you did not mean what you said just now, that you are not fit to become my wife ? "

" Yes," she replied quickly ; " I did mean it."

She was glad that her face was turned from him, and that the room was in partial darkness.   She was glad that she was able to steady her voice, and to give a direct reply.

He did not answer ; she felt he was waiting for her to speak on.

" Even if two people love each other," she said, trembling, " or only think they do, which is too often the case, they have no right to thoughtlessly contract that holy tie.   There cannot be perfect happiness in this world without perfect spiritual communion. I know—I feel sure—that this does not exist between you and me."

The young man flushed, and his brow contracted somewhat angrily.

" Take time to think it over," he said quickly ; " this is not your own heart that is speaking now. The seeds which that man, your clergyman, has been sowing in your heart have borne fruit. Religion is changing your whole nature. It is alienating you hopelessly from all to whom you are so dear ; it is making you unjust, cruelly unkind, to yourself, but doubly so to others, under the shallow pretence that you are serving God."

She did not interrupt him ; but when he ceased, she put out her hand and said, quickly but firmly—

" Good night."

"Good night," he repeated. "It is so early, surely you are not going to your room already? This is our last night together, remember."

"I am so tired," returned the girl, wearily. "I must get a good night's rest, since I am to start early in the morning."

"And you will not say another word?"

"I don't know that there is anything more that I can say."

"You are angry with me, Edith. Before you go, say at least that you forgive me."

"I am not angry; indeed, I am glad you have spoken. I know now I should never have come here. I know I must never come again."

So, without another word, they parted. Edith went up to her room. Walter sought his, and there he remained all the evening, sitting in the darkness, pondering over the unaccountable change which had taken place in the girl.

Yes, she was changed; but was it hopeless, and altogether unexpected? Might she not, with gentle care, be freed from this hateful influence of the Church? Walter believed that might be so. Already he seemed to see light through the cloud, and to trace the secret of this man's influence over her. Edith was imaginative and highly fanatical; he had appealed to her imagination. Being a High Church clergyman, he had employed two powerful agents—colour and form. He had scattered the shrine at which she worshipped with soft and durable perfumes, and had set up sacred symbols; and he had said, "Kneel before these; cast down all your worldly wishes and earthly affections." She, being intoxicated, as it were, had yielded to the spell. It was part of his plan, thought Walter, that she must neither marry nor form any other earthly tie; for was it not through her, and such as her, that his beloved Church was able to sustain its full prestige? The Church must reign supreme in her heart, as it had done in that of many another vestal; it was at the altar alone that her gifts of love and devotion must be burned. She must be sacrificed, as many others had been before her, and the Church would stand.

This was the young man's true view of the case. He believed it, for he had learnt in his home to hate other worldliness; but though he fancied he saw the nature of the discord, he could not as yet perceive the directest means of cure.

The next morning, when Edith, looking very pale and weary, but still very pretty in her simple travelling costume, came down to breakfast, she was a little surprised to find Walter already there. His manner was kind and considerate, as it had always been, and he made no reference whatever to what had passed between them on the previous night. They sat and carried on a constrained but polite conversation; but both were glad when it was interrupted by the entrance of Mrs. Hetherington. The old lady was filled with genuine regret at her niece's sudden departure, and, while presiding at the breakfast-table, was so busy laying down plans for her speedy return that she did not notice that every morsel on Edith's plate remained untouched, and that, while sipping her tea, her eyes wandered continually towards the window, as if anxiously watching for the cab which was to take her away. Walter noticed it with pain, and remained discreetly silent.

As soon as the cab arrived, he left the room, ostensibly to superintend the removal of Edith's luggage, but in reality to be absent at the leave-taking between his mother and his cousin.

He accompanied Edith to the station. It was merely an act of common courtesy, to which she could make no possible objection. On the way there was very little said on either side. She was silent from preoccupation, and he feared to tread on dangerous ground. But when they were near their parting, when Edith was comfortably seated in the train, and he stood by the open carriage door, he ventured in a covert manner to refer to what had passed.

" The house will be brighter in winter-time," he said, "and we shall have more means of amusing you. You will come back at Christmas, Edith ? "

She started, dropped his hand, and drew herself from him.

" No, I think not," she said ; "it is always a busy time with us at Christmas. There is much to be done in the church."

This was their good-bye ; for before he could say more the guard noisily closed the carriage doors, and whistled shrilly. Mechanically Walter took off his hat, and stood sadly watching the train as it moved away.

CHAPTER XVIII.

CHURCH BELLS—AND A DISCORD.

EDITH was glad that the next day was Sunday.

She rose early, dressed hurriedly, and went for a walk in the fresh morning air. She felt instinctively that she had a battle to fight, and that all her resources must be brought into play to gain her the victory. If her influence over the man was to continue, she knew there was one way by which she could regain it. With such pale cheeks and lacklustre eyes as she had brought with her from London, where, she asked,

would her chances be against Ellen
Haldane's fresh country charms? She
must banish all painful thoughts for the
present, and try to win back the roses
which he had caused to fade.

She walked for above an hour; and
when she returned home, she went
straight into the garden to gather a
little bouquet of flowers. Then she
went up to her room to dress for church.
When she came down to breakfast, she
wore her prettiest costume, and the
bunch of flowers was fastened at her
throat.

Her aunt had a headache, she said,
and could not go to church. Edith was
not sorry; indeed, when the time came
for her to set out, she was glad she was
alone.

She arrived at the church rather
earlier than usual, nevertheless she

walked straight in, and no sooner had she crossed the threshold than she obeyed a sudden impulse which seized her, and determined for that day at least not to occupy her usual seat. She selected one which was some distance from the pulpit, but from which she could command an excellent view of the pew belonging to Foxglove Manor.

The congregation gathered, but the Haldane's pew was empty. Edith watched it with feverish impatience. Presently, just as the tolling bell was about to cease, she saw Mrs. Haldane enter and take her seat.

Two minutes later, Mr. Santley, clothed in his white, priestly robes, ascended the steps of the reading-desk, and bent his beautiful head in prayer. As he rose to his feet, Edith, who had been watching him in extreme fascination, saw his gaze wandering round the church, and finally fix upon the face of the mistress of Foxglove Manor. She saw, or thought she saw, the lady's eyelids quiver and finally droop beneath that glance; while the clergyman arose, like a sick man suddenly restored to health, and began to read the lessons for the day.

How that morning passed Edith scarcely knew. She remained like one in a dream, mechanically going though the religious forms, but feeling as if her heart's blood was slowly ebbing away. Of one thing only she was conscious— that of all those upturned faces before him the clergyman seemed to see but one, but that from this one face seemed to draw his inspiration, as the earth draws life and light from the shining rays of the sun.

At length the service was over, the congregation dispersed, and Edith found herself walking up and down the quiet lanes alone, panting for air, feeling sick at heart, and shivering through and through, though she stood in the warm rays of sunlight. Go home she could not. She must see Mr. Santley before she could face another human soul.

She turned, intending to go to the Vicarage, but when she was yet within some distance of the house, she saw coming towards her the very man she sought.

She paused, not knowing whether to feel glad or sorry. It was certainly better than having to go to the Vicarage, yet now that the meeting was so near, she shrank from it. She made a desperate effort to compose herself, and paused, waiting for him. The clergyman was evidently lost in deep thought, his head was bent, his eyes were fixed on the ground, and he was quite close to Edith before he saw her.

When their eyes met he paused, almost involuntarily, a momentary flush of mingled annoyance and surprise passed over his face, then he recovered himself, walked forward, and quietly extended his hand.

" Miss Dove!" he said, glancing nervously round. " I had no idea you were at home.   How do you do?"

It had been agreed between them, long before, that so long as their secret remained a secret, no warmer greeting than this must be exchanged between them in public.   When the proposition had been made, Edith had quietly assented.   What was it to her that Santley should bow his head with a politeness even more frigid than he bestowed upon any one of his flock. Had she not seen the burning light of love in his half-lowered eyes ? and had she not known that a few hours later she would feel his caressing arms about her, and hear his rich, mellow voice whispering tenderly in her ear ?

But now all was changed. The frigid bow which had formerly been the prologue, had rapidly developed into the play. There were no stolen meetings now ; no consoling whisperings. The clergyman had latterly become alive to the risk of such indulgences, and had gradually allowed them to cease ; and Edith, receiving as her portion the cold bow and cold handshake that every eye might have seen, had watched the love light gradually fade from her hero's eyes.

But she had never seen him so cold as to-day. When their eyes had met, she had noticed the look of positive annoyance which had passed across his face. It had soon fled, but when he spoke and extended his hand, his face had assumed a look of cold severity.

Edith did not speak; the painful beating of her heart almost stifled her, and her tongue clove to the roof of her mouth. She extended her hand; the cold, listless touch of his fingers throbbed through her like ice. The clergyman saw her trouble, and again that look of impatient annoyance passed across his face; then he raised his brows in calm surprise.

"What is the matter?" he asked quickly. "Has some domestic trouble caused your sudden return home?"

She withdrew her hand from his cold, lax fingers, and answered, "No."

Then she turned and walked along in silence by his side.

The good man was annoyed, seriously annoyed. First at her sudden appearance in the village, when he believed she was safely bestowed in London for several weeks to come ; next at the *rôle* she thought fit to assume. He hated scenes at any time ; just now he particularly wished to avoid one. So he walked on in silence, until he could command his voice to speak quietly ; then he said, in the most careless manner possible—

" *When* did you return home ? "

" Last night. I attended church this morning."

She looked at him quickly, to see what effect her words produced. Apparently they produced none. The clergyman's face remained as coldly impassive as before ; he raised his brows slightly as he replied.

"Indeed! I did not see you there." Then, after a pause, he added, " Your return was very sudden, was it not ? I thought you intended staying away for some time."

" I changed my mind. I thought you would have been glad to have me back again."

Then, swept on by a wild impulse, which she could not possibly restrain, she added slowly, but tremulously—

"Charles, are you *sorry* I have come ? "

The clergyman started, flushed, then quickly recovered himself, as he added—

" Sorry, my dear Edith ? What a question ! Why of course I am not sorry."

Then, why not say that you are glad ?

Why not let me know it? Don't you see you are breaking my heart?"

Santley paused, and looked at her. He did not flush this time, his face grew white as marble, his eyes quite steel-like in their coldness. He had dreaded a scene, but this was so very much worse than he had expected; for by this time Edith had lost all self-control, and was sobbing violently. His face hardened terribly. He must put an end once and for ever to such unpleasant encounters.

" Edith, have you lost your senses?" he said; and the bitterness of his tone was like putting a knife into the girl's heart. " If you wish to perform in such scenes as this, you could surely find some other time and place than the public road and the broad daylight. If you have anything to say to me, you must come to me again in private. At present I have no more time which I can place at your service. I have business with Mrs. Haldane, who is waiting for me at the Vicarage; and my duties at the church will soon begin again."

He raised his hat, and would have moved away, but Edith laid her hand upon his arm and forcibly detained him.

"Stop!" she cried. "One word! You shall not go. I must speak."

He turned upon her almost angrily; he attempted, but in vain, to shake off her detaining hand.

"Tell me," she cried; "why are you going to meet Mrs. Haldane?" Then, before he could recover from his astonishment sufficiently to speak, she added, "You need not tell me, for I *know*. It is this woman who has come between you and me. Oh, do you think

I don't know that since she came to the village you have been a changed man ? What did I come home for ? Because I knew it was not right that you and she should be in the village *alone.*"

This time the clergyman succeeded in shaking off her hand. The face which he turned towards hers was almost livid in its pallor.

" You forget yourself," he said, with a sternness which was even harder to bear than bitter reproach. " Well, I suppose you think you have a right to insult me ; but permit me to remind you that your right does not extend to religious affairs, or to a lady who is the most esteemed member of my congregation."

" I have not insulted you, Charles ; I am only warning you."

"You are very kind," he interposed, with a sneer, "but I am in no greater need of your warning than is the lady. Until you can learn how to control your own words and actions, it would be better for *you* that we should not meet."

Again he moved, as if about to leave her; again she put forth her hand, and held him fast. The scene had become more violent than she had intended. It was now too late to pause.

"One more word," she sobbed. "Promise me that you will not see her, then I will promise never to mention this subject again."

"Promise you what? To discontinue all communications with Mrs. Haldane?"

"Yes, yes; that is all. It is not much to ask you."

"It is much more than you have any

right to ask. You have chosen to connect my name dishonourably with a lady whom I esteem. Enough! I cannot control your actions, but I mean to regulate my own. Good morning, Edith. Since you have nothing more important to say to me, I suppose I am at liberty to go ? "

He raised his hat and walked away, pausing a minute later to raise it again, and to address some pleasant remark to a member of his congregation, who happened at that moment to be coming along the road. It was the sight of this stranger which prevented Edith from following, which made her turn and walk with rapid steps towards her home. She felt cold and sick and heart-broken, and she shrank from the sight of any human face.

When she reached her home, she

found her aunt, who had been surprised at her protracted absence, gazing
uneasily up and down the road. The
sight of the girl's pale, tear-stained face
alarmed her, but Edith silenced her
inquiries by declaring that she had not
been very well.

" It was foolish of me, but I could not
help crying at the service," she said.
" Dear aunt, do not be anxious. I
am better now, and only want rest."

" Shall I send you up some dinner,
darling ? "

" No ; nothing. I want to be alone
—quite alone."

So, with a weary, listless look upon
her, the girl went up to her room, and,
having locked the door, she threw herself upon the bed, and cried as if her
heart were broken.

Meanwhile Mr. Santley went on his

way, almost as much disturbed as Edith herself. He was angry, terribly angry ; for if scenes similar to the one through which he had passed were allowed to continue, he anticipated a storm of troubles in the future. But how to avoid them ? What would be the best and safest course to adopt ? The good man was terribly perplexed. To openly defy the girl might cause her, in her bitterness and pain, to expose herself and him ; which would certainly be awkward, since he wished, above all things, to stand well with his congregation. And yet to adopt any other course, he must at least pretend to subscribe to her conditions. He must be content to renounce, or pretend to renounce, his intimacy with Mrs. Haldane. The man of God was justly indignant.

Such a course, he knew, must not be thought of, and he resolved with pious determination to continue Ellen Haldane's conversion, for which he was so zealous, and to leave matters between himself and Edith exactly as they were.

He knew the girl's disposition. She would soon acknowledge her folly, and make the first advances towards reconciliation. Well, then he would be inclined to meet her half-way, but she must be the first to move. If, on the other hand, she chose to take the unpleasant course of exposing him, why, he would have but one alternative : he would simply deny her statements, and who would believe her ? It would be an unpleasant phase of experience to have to pass through, and it would compel him to sacrifice a fellow-creature.

Nevertheless, he acknowledged to himself, with the air of a Christian martyr, that if she pushed him to extremities it would be necessary.

After all, he hoped that Edith, shut up with her own grief, in the solitude of her own room, would soon be brought to see the error of her ways, and would make that first advance towards reconciliation which was necessary for the peace of mind of both.

But, whatever might happen in the future, Edith had succeeded for that day at least in completely destroying the good man's peace of mind. His agitation was so great that he was compelled to walk about the quiet lanes until his tranquillity was somewhat restored. Then he returned to the Vicarage, where Mrs. Haldane was comfortably seated with his sister, and enjoyed her society until the hour of his labours returned.

When he entered the church that afternoon, all the congregation thought he was looking more seraphic than ever. Many a young heart fluttered with holiness, and many an eyelid drooped reverently, before the calm serenity of his gaze. As he stood facing his people, he cast his eyes around the church. Edith was not there.

He turned the leaves of his gold-clasped volume, and as his rich voice filled the church, and the congregation rose, he gazed once more about him. This time his cheek flushed slightly, and a soft sigh of relief and happiness escaped his parted lips. Mrs. Haldane was again in her place, calmly joining in the prayers.

That afternoon the clergyman preached

like one inspired ; all were impressed, but none were cognizant of the cause. Though the clergyman's eyes wandered continually around the church, he saw only one face, was conscious only of one presence. So engrossed was he, and so wrapped up in his fervour of admiration, that he did not notice what was going on around him. Had he done so, he would have seen that there was another member of the congregation besides Mrs. Haldane who attracted a certain amount of interest. Seated in the gallery, calmly joining in the service and watching the minister, was the foreign " gentleman with the eyes."

CHAPTER XIX.

"HE IS BUT A LANDSCAPE PAINTER."

AFTER Edith's departure from London, Walter Hetherington thought long and deeply over the mysterious change in his cousin. The more he thought, the more uneasy he grew. Of one thing he felt tolerably sure—that the girl had got into the hands of a religious fanatic, who either consciously or unconsciously was completely destroying himself, his happiness—in this world at least. She was fairly possessed by the fever of other worldliness, he said to himself, and if left alone she would, like many others before her, probably end her days in a mad house.

Having arrived at this enlightened conclusion, which was chiefly based on what Edith had herself told him, Walter determined that she should not be left alone. What would be more rational, he said to himself, than that he should pack up his sketching paraphernalia and pay a short visit to the picturesque little village where his aunt and cousin lived ? Surely Edith would be glad to see him, and while he remained to watch over her, his time would not be entirely lost.

When he told his mother of his determination to revisit the country, the old lady was unfeignedly glad. She suspected, from the unaccountable sudden departure of the girl, that the two young people had had a quarrel, and she was glad to see her son was magnanimous enough to make the first advances towards reconciliation. So she helped him to put a few things together, and on the spur of the moment he started off.

He had written neither to his cousin nor aunt to tell them of his coming. He had intended sending a telegram from the station, but at the last moment he changed his mind, and as he sat in the train which was rapidly whirling him onward, he began to ask himself whether it would be judicious of him to go to his aunt's house at all. To be sure, he had always made it his head-quarters; but now things were changed. Edith had left his mother's house to avoid *him;* would it be fair to either of them that he should become his aunt's guest? By living in the house he would force from her a communication which might be very grudgingly given, and at the same time

his lips must be inevitably sealed. He
finally decided that, during the visit at
least, it would be better for every one
that he should stay at the inn.

So on arriving at the station he drove
to the inn, secured at a cheap price a
couple of cosy rooms, and determined to
delay calling upon his relations until the
following day.

The next day was fine, a fit day for
an artist to lounge, dream, perhaps work.
Walter hung about the inn till midday ;
then he took his sketch-book under his
arm, and strolled forth in the direction
of his aunt's cottage. When he reached
the door, and was about to knock, it was
suddenly opened by Edith, dressed in
walking costume.

On coming thus unexpectedly face to
face with her cousin, she looked mani-
festly angry.

"Walter, you here?" she said coldly; then she added quickly, "Is anything the matter at home?"

"Nothing whatever," said Walter, quietly giving his hand, and taking no notice whatever of the irritation so plainly visible on her face. "I got tired of London, that was all, and thought a few days in the country might do me good. I am not going to bore *you*. I have brought my working tools down with me, and mean to take some sketches back."

"But where is your luggage?"

"Down at the inn."

"At the inn?"

"Yes; I had it taken direct there last night. I was fortunate enough, too, to secure rooms—a capital little parlour fit for a studio, and a bedroom leading out of it. I shall be able to do the host, and entertain you, if you'll come."

"You are going to stay at the inn?" said Edith. "You always stayed with *us* before!"

"Of course I did; but I am not going to be so inconsiderate as to plant myself upon you *now*."

He laid the slightest possible stress upon the "now," and Edith understood; nevertheless, she deemed it prudent to affect ignorance and read a different meaning in his words. She murmured something about being very much occupied, and having little time to attend to visitors; then led the way across the hall to their sitting-room, and brought him into the presence of his aunt.

Mrs. Russell welcomed him cordially, but when she heard of his domestic arrangements, her face went very blank indeed. She used every argument in her power to persuade the young man to change his mind, and to have his luggage brought up to the cottage. Walter, eager to accept her kindness, was listening for one word from Edith. It never came, and he expressed his intention to remain at the inn.

But, although he abided by his former decision and remained *en garçon* at the inn, a very great part of his time was spent at the cottage. The old lady, anxious to atone for the inhospitable behaviour of her niece, altered all her household arrangements to suit the erratic habits of the young painter. The heavy midday meal was replaced by a light luncheon ; while for the light supper at six was substituted a substantial dinner, to which Walter was always bidden. On the afternoon of that day, when the young man had first made his appearance at the cottage, a rather unpleasant interview had taken place between the aunt and niece, almost the first which had come to ruffle the peaceful course of their evenly flowing lines. The old lady had been indignant at the coolness of Edith's reception, and had accused the girl of inhospitality and ingratitude ; while Edith had coolly given it as her opinion that the young man was much better located elsewhere.

" It is a tax to have a visitor always in the house, aunt," said Edith, quietly ; " and—and I haven't the strength to bear it, I think."

Mrs. Russell looked up, and was surprised to find that the girl, after bearing her reproaches so mildly, was now actually crying. She noted again, too, with a start of shocked surprise how sadly she had changed. The fresh, bright beauty which had once charmed every eye had gone, leaving scarcely a trace behind it, and the face was pale, careworn, and sad. She got up and kissed her, and that silent caress did more than a dozen reproaches. It made Edith hurriedly leave the room, to cast herself, crying bitterly, upon the bed, while Mrs. Russell sat down and wrote a note to Walter.

"You shall have your own way about staying at the inn," she wrote, "and you shall also have every possible hour of the day that you can make use of for your work; but surely you can spare your evenings for us. I have arranged to dine every day at six, and I beg of you, for Edith's sake, to make one of the party. Dear Edith is far from well, and sadly changing. She sees so few people, and the house is dull. Dear Walter, come often, for her sake if not for mine."

Thus it happened that every night, when the little dining-room was laid out for dinner, Walter made his appearance at the cottage door, and that during those evening hours the family party was increased to three. Sometimes they left the dinner-table to lounge in the pretty little drawing-room, where Walter was permitted to smoke his cigar, while the old lady worked at wool-work, and Edith played to them in the slowly gathering darkness. Sometimes they strolled out on to the lawn, and had the tea brought out, and laughed and chatted while they watched the stars appear one by one in the heavens. Was it fancy, or since these social evenings commenced was Edith really changed for the better? Walter fancied that her eye was brighter, her cheek less pale, and that her manner towards himself was sometimes very tender, as if she wished in a measure to atone for her past coldness. This was particularly noticeable one night when the two sat alone in the drawing-room.

Mrs. Russell, murmuring something about household affairs, had left them together. Walter was reclining in an armchair, smoking his cigar and watching his cousin, who was busily engaged embroidering crosses upon a handsome altar-cloth, intended for the decoration of the church.

" These have been pleasant evenings," he said—" pleasant for me, that is. I shall be sorry enough when they come to an end."

Edith looked up and smiled sadly.

" If we always had pleasure it would become a pain," she said. " Though we rebel against pain and suffering, it is, after all, a very great boon to the world."

"Humph! Perhaps so, if it were better distributed. What about the poor creatures whose portion is only pain? — who, to put it vulgarly, get all the kicks, and none of the halfpence?"

"In this world, you should have said, Walter. Let us hope their measure of happiness will be greater in the world that is to come."

Walter was silent. The conversation had taken precisely the turn which he would have avoided, and he was wondering how to bring it to the subject which was for ever uppermost in his mind. For a time he remained in a brown study. Edith stitched on. Then he rose, took a few turns about the room, and stopped near to her chair.

"Edith," he said quietly, "do you know why I came down here?"

Something in his tone rather than his words made her start and flush painfully. She did not raise her eyes or cease her work. Before she could answer, he had taken her hand.

"I came for *you*, Edith," he continued passionately. "Listen to me, my darling. Do not answer hastily, if you cannot give me a decided answer. At least let me hope."

Decidedly yet tremblingly the girl put his hands from her, and half rose from her seat. His words had frozen her to ice again.

"Why *did* you come here?" she said. "Do you call it manly or kind to persecute me? I tell you I shall never marry."

As she spoke her eye fell upon the

altar-cloth, which she held in her hand.
Walter saw the look, and as he was
walking back to the inn that night it
recurred to his mind again. The altar-
cloth! There was the symbol of the
thing which had come between them—
which was blighting his life and hers.
Edith was changing; but she was not
utterly changed. He resolved to do the
only thing which now remained to be
done. He determined to appeal to her
spiritual adviser.

All night his mind was filled with this
idea; it troubled his sleeping as well as
his waking moments, and when he rose
in the morning it was the one thing
which possessed him. Now, he had
never seen the clergyman, but he had
pictured him as a middle-aged, benevo-
lent-looking man, perhaps with spec-
tacles; a gentle fanatic in religion,

willing, through the very bigotry of his
nature, to sacrifice everything for the
good of the Church, but still, perhaps,
amiable. He might be open to reason,
and an appeal made directly to him
might be the means of putting an end
to all the trouble.

Breakfast over, the young man issued
from the inn, and strolled deliberately
through the village in the direction of
the Vicarage. It was early in the day
to make a call, so he walked very slowly,
meditating as he went on the nature of
his errand ; and the course he was about
to take, after what had passed between
him and his cousin, was, perhaps, a little
unwarrantable, and Edith might be inclined to resent it if she knew. But
then, he reflected, she need never know.
Mr. Santley would surely grant him the
favour of keeping the matter a secret ;

and afterwards, when the shadow of the
Church had ceased to darken her life,
and she was happy with him in her
married home, she would be glad to
hear that it was he who had saved her.

These were the kind of rose-coloured
visions which filled his brain as he
walked on towards the Vicarage, and
by the time he had reached the hall
door and pulled the bell, he had even
converted Mr. Santley into the good
fairy of the tale, or rather a sort of
Father Christmas, in a surplice, smiling
benevolently upon them and pairing
their hands. A trim little servant came
to the door, and, in answer to his inquiries, informed him that Mr. Santley
was not at home. He was expected in
immediately, however, if the gentleman
would like to wait. Yes; Walter would
wait. So he followed the little maid

across the hall, into a somewhat chilly but sufficiently gorgeous room, which was reserved solely for the comfort and convenience of Mr. Santley's guests. As Walter sank down into an easy-chair, the arms of which seemed to enfold him in a close embrace, and looked about the room, he acknowledged that Mr. Santley at least did not give all his substance to the poor. Here at least there was no appearance of penury, or of sackcloth and ashes ; all was comfortable and luxurious in the extreme. He walked about the room ; examined the books upon the tables, which were all works of education, elegantly bound ; noticed the engravings on the walls—one or two of Raphael's Madonnas (coloured copies), and an old engraving after Andrea del Sarto. Mr. Santley did not come. He rang the bell, gave the little maid his card, told her he would call again, and left the Vicarage.

This time he walked in the direction of the schoolhouse. He had his sketch-book under his arm, and in it a half-finished sketch of the schoolmistress's picturesque home. He would fill up his spare time by adding a few touches to the sketch before he returned to the Vicarage.

In this matter fortune favoured him. It being Saturday afternoon, there was no school, and the schoolmistress was leaning in a listless attitude upon the low trellised gate. She welcomed the young painter with a nod and a bright smile, and readily assented to his proposition that she should stand for the figure in the picture. He took out his book and set to work.

Dora meanwhile chatted and laughed

to make the time pass pleasantly, and
sometimes, in answer to an invitation
from him, she would run round the easel
to take a peep at the figure of herself,
which was gradually growing under his
hand. At last their pleasant interview
was brought to an end. Walter remembered the appointment which this
chattering lady had made him forget.
He put up his sketching materials, and
prepared to take his leave. Then
Dora stopped him.

"Surely, Mr. Hetherington, you will
do me one favour," she said : "you will
honour me by stepping for a moment
into the cottage which you have trans-
ferred so beautifully to paper. I have
some cream and milk, some fresh strawberries from our garden, if that is any
inducement to you."

The invitation was tempting. Nevertheless, Walter, while wishing to accept, was about to refuse, pleading an engagement at the Vicarage when another voice broke in—

"Good day, Miss Greatheart!" it said.

The schoolmistress smiled, made a prim curtsey, and answered, "Good day, sir!" Then she waited to see if her visitor had anything more to say.

The new arrival was a man, and Walter, who was looking at him, thought he was the handsomest man he had ever seen in his life. He was dressed as a clergyman, but the cut of his garments was elegant and eminently becoming. As his eye fell upon Walter he raised his hat, and discovered a head beautifully shaped and slightly thinning at the temples. Walter remained fascinated, staring at the man, who moved here and there with easy grace, and whose face grew singularly handsome with every varying expression which flitted across it.

He had not much to say to the school-mistress ; and as he moved away his hat was again swept off to Walter, and the clergyman's eyes rested upon him for a moment with a look one might love to paint in the eyes of a saint.

Walter turned to Miss Greatheart.

" A handsome fellow," he said—" a very handsome fellow ; and a clergyman, I see, by his dress. Who is he ? One of Mr. Santley's curates, I suppose ?"

The schoolmistress stared at him for a moment in amazement.

"One of Mr. Santley's curates !" she said. " Why, my dear sir, that is our vicar himself!"

CHAPTER XX.

IN THE GLOAMING.

It was now Walter's turn to look amazed.

"That Mr. Santley!" he said. "Why, he is quite a young man!"

"Of course he is—and handsome as good, and good as handsome. But won't you come in, Mr. Hetherington, and have some refreshment? It is two hours quite since you opened out your sketch-book at the gate!"

This time Walter accepted her invitation, and followed her into the quaint little parlour, where most of her days were spent. The little maid who attended to the house had got a holiday with the children, and Dora was left to attend to herself that day. Walter was glad of it, since he was left free to sit by the window and follow the train of his thoughts, while Dora busied herself spreading the snowy cloth upon the table, and setting forth her simple fare. When it was ready, he came to the table and ate some strawberries and drank some milk, thinking all the while of Mr. Santley. Presently he spoke of him.

" You have known Mr. Santley some time, Miss Greatheart ? " he said.

" I was schoolmistress here when he came."

" He is a very good man, you said ? "

" Yes, indeed. But it stands to reason that a man with Mr. Santley's gifts must be very good indeed not to get spoiled.

In justice to at least half of his congregation, he ought to marry."

" Why, pray ? "

" Why ? If he had arrived here with a wife, many a young girl in the village would have been saved a severe heartache. He is a prize in the matrimonial lottery well worth striving for. He is idolized by every female in the village. Now, it is certain he cannot marry them all, and on the day when the happy one is chosen, fancy the hearts that will break ! "

" Yours amongst the number ? "

" No, sir ; I am happy to say I am free. But I take no credit to myself on that account. If I had been idle like some of the young ladies here, there might have been another victim added to the list; but I have so much to do in the school, I have no time to think about the vicar," she added. " Have you heard him preach, Mr. Hetherington?"

" No, not yet."

"Ah, you must go to the church to-morrow. He speaks magnificently, and looks a picture in his robes; besides, his sister, Miss Santley, told me he will wear for the first time to-morrow a new surplice and a magnificent embroidered band, which has been worked for him by Miss Dove!"

At the mention of his cousin's name Walter felt his face flush and his heart leap; but he made no direct reply. He went on eating his strawberries, and turned his face to the open window, as he said—

" What have you made for him, Miss Greatheart?"

" I? Oh, nothing! He has so many beautiful presents from the young ladies in the village that he has no need of them from me, even if I had the time to make them, which I have not ; all day I am teaching in the school, and all the evening I am busy preparing lessons for the following day."

" Have you always lived here ? "

" Not always. My mother was a prison matron at Preston, and we lived together until she died, several years ago ; then, through the influence of some friends, I got this place, and have lived here ever since ! "

" Working and striving," added Walter ; " finding pleasure in things which to some would mean only trouble and irritation. During the holidays do you ever come to London, Miss Greatheart ? "

" No ; I generally remain here."

" From choice ? "

" Not at all. I should like a change ; but then, to go alone to a city where you have no friends, and to parade crowded streets alone, is a holiday which I should not enjoy."

Walter rose to go.

" You will come back and finish the sketch on Monday, perhaps?" said Dora.

" I shall be glad to ; I should like, above all, to finish the figure leaning on the gate."

" Then you must come in the evening. I promise to give you an hour after school hours."

Then Walter shook hands with her and left, taking the way to the inn instead of to the Vicarage. He would make no appeal to the clergyman. The sight of Mr. Santley, so different to the benevolent, elderly gentleman of his imagination, had decided him on that point ; it had also brought with it other trouble, for it threw an entirely new light on Edith's religious fervour.

Was it, then, the man or the church, infatuation or fanaticism ? He asked himself the question for the first time. Was Edith among the mass of simple girls who were breaking their hearts for his sake ? Probably. It remained now for him to watch her, and ascertain the truth.

He went up to the cottage that evening, and regarded Edith with quite a new light in his eyes. She also seemed changed. Her manner was restless and ill at ease ; her cheek was flushed. All through the dinner she scarcely touched any food, but glanced furtively at her aunt and cousin.

When the dinner was over, they all retired to the drawing-room as usual.

Here Edith's restlessness asserted itself more strongly. Instead of sitting quietly to her work, as was her usual custom, she flitted restlessly about the room. Presently she declared that she had a terrible headache, and wished her cousin "good night."

"I have been trying to bear it," she said, "but it gets worse instead of better. You will excuse me for to-night, Walter, will you not?"

As he took her hand and held it for a moment in his, he felt that it was trembling and very hot. He scarcely believed in the headache, but he deemed silence the most prudent course; so he wished her "good night" without more ado.

Her aunt rose to go with her to her room, but permission to do so was firmly refused.

"You will stay and keep Walter

company, or else you will make me regret I did not bear the pain without a word. Indeed, dear aunt, all I want is rest and quietness. I shall be quite well to-morrow."

So she went. Mrs. Russell sat down again to her wool-work, and Walter subsided into his chair.

There was not much talking done after that, and Walter, as soon as his cigar was finished, rose to take his leave. The old lady looked at him tenderly and sadly, but she said nothing. Instinct had told her the true state of things between the cousins ; she was sorry, but helpless. It would be better, she thought to herself, if the poor boy would resign a useless courtship, since Edith had evidently no affection to give, and take to himself some pretty little wife who would make his home happy.

He did not return directly to the inn, but with head bent in deep thought he strolled on, he knew not whither. He was wondering whether or not this hopeless quest should end. If Edith had deceived him—if, indeed, it was the man, and not religion, which held the girl so entranced—why, then his task of regeneration would surely be a very difficult one. It was strange, he thought, that Edith, knowing his mistake, should have allowed it to remain. He had repeatedly spoken to her of Mr. Santley as an elderly man ; and, although she knew the truth, she had never corrected him. It looked black, very black ; the more he thought over it, the more complicated matters became.

He had been so engrossed in his own thoughts, that he had been almost unaware of his own actions. He was only conscious of strolling idly on and on, he knew not in what direction. Suddenly he paused, looked helplessly about him ; then took a few stealthy steps forward, and paused again. Where he was he did not know. The night had grown quite dark and chilly, for heavy, rain-charged clouds were covering both stars and moon. But his quick ear had detected what his eyes could not at first perceive—the close neighbourhood of two figures in earnest conversation —a man and a woman. The darkness shrouded their figures, but the breeze brought to him the sound of their voices. Walter hated to play the spy, yet for once in his life his feet refused to move. For he had recognized one of the voices as belonging to his cousin Edith.

Yes, the voice was Edith's.

Having wished her aunt and cousin

"good night," she had hastened to her room and locked the door ; but instead of throwing herself on the bed, she had lit the candles, sat down near the dressing-table, drawn forth a letter from her pocket, and begun to read.

The letter was as follows :—

" MY DEAR MISS DOVE,

" I am very sorry to hear that you have been suffering. You will find what you require at Dr. Spruce's surgery. You are right about the time—nine o'clock will do very well.

" Yours faithfully,

" CHARLES SANTLEY."

This letter had come through the post in the ordinary way. It had been handed to Edith in the morning ; and the very sight of it had sent the hot blood coursing through her veins, and kept her in a state of feverish excitement the whole day. It was the knowledge of this piece of paper in her pocket which had rendered her so uneasy during the dinner; it was the knowledge of this letter also which had caused her excitement after dinner, and which finally had made her wish her cousin a hasty "good night." And now, as she read it again, the flush remounted to her cheeks and her heart beat pleasantly. She had not seen Santley alone since that Sunday morning, nearly a week past, when the two had parted in anger—an anger which to Edith meant utter misery and prostration. And now, at the eleventh hour, he had written to her appointing a meeting, and she was ready to fly to him with open arms.

She sat for some time looking at the letter, reading it over and over until she knew every word of it by heart; then she kissed it, returned it to her pocket, opened the window, and looked out. It was a cloudy but fine night, and the welcome darkness was gathering quickly.

If it would only rain, she thought, they would be sure to have the road to themselves in that case; and for herself, why, what did it matter so long as she felt her lover's arms about her again, and knew that he was true? But now her first care was to effect her escape stealthily from the house. She had decided upon her course of action; the great difficulty which remained was to carry it through. She hastily put on her walking boots, took up a cloak of sombre colour, fastened it round her, drew the hood over her head, and stood ready to set forth to the place of meeting—which she knew, by old experience, well.

She opened her bedroom door and listened. She could hear nothing. Perhaps her cousin was gone, perhaps he was still sitting in the drawing-room, quietly smoking his cigar. In any case, it seemed, she need not fear interruption ; the way was clear. She hastily blew out her candles, locked her door, and slipped the key into her pocket ; then noiselessly descending the stairs, she left the house unseen.

In the garden she hesitated, curious to know what they could all be doing ; so she crept round the house and peeped in at the drawing-room window. Walter was still there, but he stood near the door, holding his aunt's hand,

and evidently taking his leave. Edith turned, and without more ado fled quickly in the darkness.

Even as Edith was leaving the cottage, Santley was already at the meeting-place, walking with impatient strides up and down the lonely lane selected for their interview, and wondering as every minute passed away why Edith did not come.

A week's reflection, and the frequent sight of Edith's pale, careworn face when they met in public, had brought him to this pass. He saw that she was suffering, and for the sake of what she had been to him he felt really sorry. Besides, he looked at the matter philosophically, and he asked himself, why *should* they quarrel ? After all, she had been very patient and forbearing ; and for that little fit of jealousy about

Mrs. Haldane she had been sufficiently punished.

But perhaps there was another and a stronger motive for this sudden wish for a meeting and a reconciliation. So long as this absurd quarrel continued, it was evident Edith had no intention of visiting the Vicarage; and this fact alone subjected him to a series of unpleasant questions from his sister. Santley therefore decided that it would be better for him in every possible way to send the letter, which would be certain to effect a reconciliation.

"Is it you, Edith? Quick! Is it you?"

His quick ear had caught the rustle of her dress on the grass. Even as the words left his lips came the eager answer.

"Yes, Charles; I have come!" And

the girl, forgetting all their quarrels, leapt with a glad cry into his arms.

For a time no words were spoken. After that one cry of joy, Edith had laid her head upon his shoulder and sobbed as if her heart would break. At this manifestation of hysteria, Santley was not altogether pleased ; but he could say nothing, so he clasped his arms firmly about her, and tried to soothe her sorrow. When at last Edith lifted her head from his shoulder he kissed her lips, and whispered to her so gently that the girl's heart beat as gladly as it had done the first day that words like these had been spoken.

" There, there," said the good man, kissing her again, and patting her head like that of a spoilt child.   " You are better now, my darling ; and remember you must not quarrel with me again.

You were breaking your little heart for nothing at all."

Part of the girl's emotion had communicated itself to him ; and for the time being, while he stood there holding her to him, feeling her breath upon her cheek, her clinging arms about his neck, he felt almost as passionately disposed as he had done the first day that he told her of his love. As for Edith, a serene happiness and peace seemed to enter into her soul. They stood thus for some time, exchanging whispered words and fond embraces ; then the clergyman told her she had better go. A spot or two of rain had fallen, and the sky was clouding over as if for a storm.

" Will you play the organ to-morrow, Edith ? " he asked, as they moved away together.

" Yes, if you wish it."

"I do wish it, Edith; for when you are playing, it seems as if you were helping me with my work."

Sweet words! She said nothing, but the hand which lay in his pressed his fondly, and he knew that she was pleased.

"And will you come to the Vicarage to-morrow afternoon, and have tea with us? I shall be so glad if you will!"

He did not add that his sister, wondering all the week at Edith's non-appearance, had threatened repeatedly to call at the cottage, when she would doubtless have elicited something of the truth.

"No, I cannot come!" she said; "my cousin, Walter Hetherington, is staying in the village, and so long as he remains here he is to spend the evenings with us. As to-morrow is Sunday, and no work can be done, my aunt has invited him up for the day."

Santley was relieved, very much relieved indeed. He could now give his sister a tangible reason for Edith's absence from the Vicarage, while he himself would be perfectly free to spend the afternoon with Mrs. Haldane. He tried to suppress the delight which he could not help feeling, and said quietly, " Let us hope the young man will make a speedy departure, if he means to monopolize you so much. But that reminds me, Edith, a young man, a Mr. Walter Hetherington, called upon me to-day and left his card. I suppose it is the same ? "

"Of course it is," returned Edith. " But what could he want with *you ?* "

" I don't in the least know. Nothing of very great importance, I suppose, since he promised to call again, and never reappeared."

The clergyman paused.

They had come now to within a short distance of Edith's home. Again, after a furtive look round, he clasped her fondly to him, pressed her lips, and murmured, " Good night, my Edith ! "

" Good night," returned the girl, withdrawing herself reluctantly from his embrace. " Oh, I am so happy now ! You were quite right, dear ; another week like the last would have broken my heart ! "

Thus they parted—Edith, happy as a child, creeping quickly to the cottage : the good man smiling celestially, and well pleased to have made everything comfortable at little personal inconvenience, walking back to his holy hearth, and thinking of his Sunday sermon.

CHAPTER XXI.

IN THE VICARAGE PARLOUR.

NEARLY the whole of this interview had been witnessed by Walter Hetherington.

He had heard, yet he had not heard; for, though instinct told him that the voice was Edith's, he could only catch fragments of what she said. Nevertheless, as he remained crouched in the shadow of the trees, he was conscious of sobs and tears, of stolen kisses and softly murmured words. He remained until the interview was over; then, when the two walked together back towards the

village, he still very stealthily followed
them. When they stopped again, he heard
the passionate words of parting. His
suspicions were, in his own despite, fast
becoming certainties; they were soon
established certainties beyond a doubt.
He followed the girl after she had left
her lover, and saw her stealthily open
the door and disappear across the threshold of Edith's home.

Then Walter turned, and feeling like
one who has had a terrible nightmare,
he walked back to his lodgings at the
inn. He was sorry he had not had
time to follow the man, for he remained
completely in the dark as to who he
might be. He got little sleep that night.
The next morning he awoke sadly un-
refreshed. After breakfast he strolled
out among the meadows; and when he
heard the bells ring, calling the villagers

to prayer, he entered the church with the rest.

When the congregation had assembled and the clergyman was in his place, Walter looked about for Edith. He felt almost a sense of relief when he saw that she was present ; it repulsed him to think of her calmly joining in the service after the events of last night. He looked at the gallery where the school children bestowed themselves, and saw Dora, quiet, unobtrusive, and happy, sitting serenely amongst her flaxen-haired flock. How cosy, how comfortable she was ! but the very bitterness of his heart compelled him to ask himself the question : was she as bad as the rest ? At one time, yes, even so late as the preceding night, he had possessed so much blind faith in genuine human nature as to

believe that the face indicated the soul.
Now, however, he felt that such a belief
was puerile and false. No woman on
earth could possess a more spiritual
countenance than his cousin Edith—yet
his eyes had assured him of the blackness and impurity of her soul. Disappointment was turning his heart to
gall.

At last the service was ended : the
congregation streamed forth, Walter
amongst the rest. The crush was so
great he could hardly get along—for
Mr. Santley was a popular preacher.
Once outside the edifice, Walter paused
to draw his breath and look about him.
He started, turned first hot, then cold,
for not many yards from him was Edith
herself, calmly leaving the church with
the rest. Almost before he could recover himself she saw him, and ad-

vanced with a bright smile and out-stretched hand.

"I saw you in church," she said, "and thought you looked dreadfully pale. Are you not well, Walter?"

He murmured something about late hours and a sleepless night; then he had to confess he had been looking about for her, for he added—

"I did not see *you* in church."

"No, you would not. I was in the organ-room. It is my Sunday for playing, you remember!"

To this he made no reply. He was wondering how it was that Edith could manage so effectually to play such a double part. He expected at least a downcast eye, and a blush of guilt upon her cheek; with this he might have been tolerably satisfied. But Edith's face looked brighter than it had done for many a day.

"I forgot to ask you," he said suddenly, "if your headache was better."

"My headache?" she replied. She had been so engrossed with happy thoughts at the reconciliation, that the question took her completely by surprise. "Ah yes," she added, suddenly recollecting herself; "it is so much better, that I had quite forgotten it. You see what a good night's rest will do!"

Walter uttered an impatient sigh, and turned on his heel; while Edith added—

"You are coming up to dine with us to-day, you know. Shall we walk together?"

"I am not coming!"

"Not coming? I thought——"

"Yes, I did accept your aunt's invitation; but I feel upset to-day, and am not fit company for any one. Will you make my excuses at home ? "

" Yes, certainly I will; and I hope that to-morrow you will be so much better. Good-bye."

She shook hands with him, and tripped away.

For a time Walter made no attempt to move, but gazed after her with eyes full of sadness and despair. Although he said to himself that henceforth Edith must be nothing to him, he felt pained at the curtness with which she could dismiss him. He had noticed that she had never once attempted to persuade him to alter his decision; indeed, she had not been able to hide from him her delight at hearing it, and he felt very bitter.

He turned from the church, walked away, and, after strolling about for some

time he knew not whither, he raised his
head and found himself quite close to
the schoolmistress's cottage. Dora stood
in the doorway, surrounded by her
flowers.

She came forward when she saw him,
and, after giving him a bright smile and
a warm handshake, stood by the gate
and continued to talk. She was a wise
little woman, and knew exactly what to
say and what to leave unsaid; she had
been a witness of the interview between
the cousins in the churchyard that morning, and her woman's instinct had divined
something of the true state of things.
So she chatted pleasantly to the young
man, and took no notice whatever of his
pale cheek and peculiarity of manner;
and when he said suddenly, "Are
you not going to ask me in to-day,
Miss Greatheart?" she threw open

the gate at once, and said that she was sadly neglectful and inhospitable, and that if Mr. Hetherington would like to come in, he would be more than welcome. So he followed her again into the quaint little parlour, and again took his seat by the open window, to gaze with strange, meditative eyes upon the little garden where the sun was shining. It was a ragged little garden enough, and by no means well cared for, since Dora was not rich enough to pay for labour, like her more fortunate neighbours in the village.

During her leisure hours she worked among the flower-beds until her plump hands ached again ; but, after all, her leisure hours were very few, and the grass and weeds grew so quickly. Walter saw that the grass was many inches too long, and that it was scattered thickly with withered rose-leaves ; that here and there a rose tree was sadly in want of the pruning knife. But that did not make the scent of the flowers any the less delicious ; nor did it take from the quiet beauty of their place. There was plenty of light and colour everywhere, and there was beauty.

While looking at the garden, Walter began to think of the garden's mistress—quiet little Dora, living so contented among her children ; and in the winter still living here alone, when the flowers had faded, when withered rose-leaves were scattered profusely on the grass, and the leafless branches of the trees bent before the biting breath of the bitter winter wind. It was a pretty picture of Dora—he loved it as we love the creatures of our imagination ; it seemed to make Dora belong to him, artistically, as it were, and bring him consolation. Then his reflections took another turn, and he began, for the first time, to think it strange that the little woman should be so much alone.

He said something of this to Dora ; and she laughed and blushed, and answered frankly enough.

" Yes, I am a good deal alone. You see, I am in an equivocal position. I am too good for the servants, and not good enough for their mistresses. I am only the governess ! "

"At any rate," said Walter, " you have contrived to brighten up what would otherwise have been a very cheerless visit. As a token of my gratitude, will you accept a little present from me ? "

" I want no present, sir ; your friendly words are quite enough."

"Nonsense! I should like to give you some of the sketches I have made of the village."

"To me! give them to me?" said Dora, with wide-open eyes. "Why, Mr. Hetherington, I thought you wanted them to—to—— "

"To—what?"

"Well, to remind you of this visit!"

"Perhaps when I began them I had some notion of that kind in my head; we are all fools sometimes, you know. But I have changed my mind; I don't want to be reminded of this visit. Yes, I shall give you the sketches—that is to say, if you will accept them; and when I have taken my departure—and I shall do so soon—I shall try to forget that such a village as Omberley ever existed at all."

"And the people," said Dora; "of course you will try to forget the people?"

"That is the first thing I shall try to do!"

We are most of us selfish in our grief, and Walter was no exception to the rule. Mortified and suffering himself, it never once entered his head that he might be unpolite, and even rude, to another. But the knife entered Dora's little heart, and made her wince. She had been happy in the knowledge that she had met a fellow-creature who could treat her exactly as an equal—a man whom she could call a friend; and lo! when her interest is strongest, when she has been telling herself that the memory of the few days which he has brightened for ever will linger in her memory and never die, he came to tell her that his

first effort would be to forget the place—
and *her*.

"I will take the pictures, if you like,
Mr. Hetherington, but merely as a
loan. You will change your mind again.
I am convinced that some day you will
ask me for them back again, and when
you do they shall certainly be yours.
But the sketch of the cottage—is it
finished already?"

"The sketch of the cottage? Oh, I
should like to keep *that*. It contains
the picture of a lady whom I should
certainly not like to forget."

Then, while the glad light danced in
Dora's eyes again, he rose and took her
hand, as he said—

"Good-bye, Miss Greatheart. When
I said I should forget the village and
the people I was wrong. Your kindness and hospitality I shall always remember."

So he crossed the threshold of the happy little schoolhouse, to stroll out again into the sunshine ; and again he thought very bitterly of the woman who had effectually taken all the sunshine from his life.

He need not have thought so bitterly of her. If she had wounded him she was receiving her punishment.

Having left Walter in the churchyard, Edith flew home like one walking on air. She had accepted his decision gleefully, never attempting to alter it by word or look, for she was thinking all the time of the invitation she had received from Mr. Santley, and which had cost her such a pang to refuse. Walter's sudden determination left her free—free to spend a few hours in the company of the man who was more to her than the whole world. Lighthearted and happy, she hurried home, gave Walter's message to her aunt, and then sat down and made a very hearty meal. After it was over, and a reasonable time had elapsed, she again put on her hat, and told her aunt she was going down to the Vicarage.

"I shan't be back till late, aunt," she added, "for, as I have to go to the Vicarage, I may as well walk to evening service with Miss Santley. If Walter changes his mind and comes, you will look after him well, won't you?"

And Mrs. Russell, promising implicit obedience, kissed her niece fondly, and watched her go down the road. On reaching the Vicarage, Edith was admitted at once. There was no necessity to take her card and keep her waiting while she ascertained if master or mistress was at home. She was known to the servants as a visitor who was always welcome—at any rate to the mistress of the house. So, without any preamble at all, she was shown into the sitting-room, and into the presence of Miss Santley.

The room was as luxuriously furnished as any in the Vicarage, and charmingly decorated with the choicest of hothouse flowers. The lady sat in a low wicker chair, with a book in her hand, and at her elbow a little gipsy table, holding a tea-service of Dresden china. The opening of the door disturbed the lady. She let her book fall upon her knee, and looked up dreamily; but the moment her eye fell upon Edith she rose, smiling brightly, gave the girl both her hands, and kissed her fondly.

" My dear Edith, I am so glad!" she exclaimed; and there was a ring of genuine welcome in her voice. "Why, you are a perfect stranger.—Jane, bring a cup for Miss Dove.—Now, dear, select your chair, take off your hat, and make yourself comfortable."

Edith did as she was bidden. She placed her hat on one of the many little tables with which the room abounded, stood before one of the glasses for a moment to rectify any disarrangement of hair and costume ; then she drew forth a little wicker chair similar to that occupied by her hostess, and sat down. By this time the teapot was brought in, and the tea poured, so Edith sat and sipped it, talking and laughing meanwhile like a happy child.

"Well, dear," said Miss Santley, "and what have you been doing with yourself all the week ? Charles tells me you have a cousin in the village, who completely monopolizes you. By the way, he told me that he had tried to persuade you to come to tea to-day, but that you had positively refused. That could not have been true."

"Yes, it was true," returned Edith. "I did refuse when he asked me, because I thought I could not come. I thought my cousin would dine with us as usual ; but I met him at church this morning, and he said he was rather unwell and could not come. So I thought it would not matter if I came after all."

"Matter ! My dear, I am delighted."

And so, having thus satisfactorily arranged matters, the two sat chatting to their hearts' content.

It was very pleasant, exceedingly pleasant—at any other time Edith would have enjoyed it hugely ; but as the hands of the bronze clock on the chimneypiece travelled so quickly round, she began to grow uneasy, and to wonder at the protracted absence of her lover. Miss Santley was a very pleasant person indeed, and Edith was very fond of her; but it had been a stronger inducement than Miss Santley that had brought her to the Vicarage that afternoon. Santley must know she was in the house, thought Edith; it was strange he did not come.

Suddenly Miss Santley glanced at the clock. In a moment she was on her feet.

" My dear," she exclaimed, " how the time has flown ! Do you play again to-night ? "

" Yes."

The lady nodded.

" We'll walk to church together, dear," she said. " Amuse yourself by looking at the books, while I run away to get my bonnet and mantle on."

Ere the lady had reached the door of the room, Edith spoke. Prolonged disappointment had given her courage.

" Mr. Santley is busy, I suppose ? " she said.

" Mr. Santley—Charles ? Oh, my dear, he's not at home ! "

" Not at home ? "

" No. If he had been, do you suppose for a moment, my dear, he would have allowed you to be all this time in the house without coming out to say ' How do you do ' ? If he had known you had been coming, of course he would have stayed in ; but he didn't know, so immediately after afternoon service he went to Foxglove Manor. He wanted to see Mrs. Haldane, and he said he should go straight from there to the church."

Miss Santley was near the door. The moment she had finished speaking she passed out of the room, and left Edith alone.

It was not a pleasant task to her, this mentioning of Mrs. Haldane. She knew that people had already begun to speak somewhat unkindly of the relations between that lady and her brother. But since this was so, it was well that she should show to the world that she, his sister, thought nothing of it. Therefore she had made up her mind that, whenever it was necessary for her to mention that lady's name, she would do so without reserve of any kind. It was the only way, she thought, to prevent such absurd rumours from taking root.

A very few minutes sufficed to make her toilet. At the end of that time she returned to the room where she had left

Edith, to get her Prayer-book and the handkerchief which had fallen from her hand, and lay beside her chair.

"Ready, dear?" she asked brightly; then she paused, amazed.

There sat Edith, pale as a ghost, reclining in an easy-chair, with her head thrown back, and her forehead covered by a handkerchief soaked with eau-de-cologne.

"Why, my dear!" exclaimed Miss Santley. "Whatever is the matter? Has anything happened?"

"No, nothing," said Edith, faintly. "I have got a very bad headache, that is all; and—and—I cannot go to church again to-day, Miss Santley."

"Go to church," echoed Miss Santley. "Why, my dearest girl, of course you can't go to church! I will send Jane with a message to Charles, and stay and take care of you."

But this Edith would not allow. She pulled the handkerchief from her forehead, and declared her intention of going home.

Miss Santley kissed her kindly. At this exhibition of tenderness Edith fairly broke down. She threw her arms around the lady's neck, and burst into tears.

"I—I am so sorry," she said at last, when her sobs had somewhat subsided; "but I could not help it. I—I am such a coward when I am ill!"

Miss Santley said nothing; she knew she could do nothing. There was some mystery here which she could not fathom, so she yielded to the girl's solicitations and allowed her to go home.

CHAPTER XXII.

AT THE VICARAGE.

ONE evening about the middle of the week, as the Rev. Mr. Santley sat alone in his study a card was brought to him, on which was printed—

Mr. Walter Hetherington.

The clergyman raised his brows as he read, and asked the maid, who waited respectfully at the door, if the gentleman had not called upon him before.

" Once before, sir ! "

" Did he state his business ? "

" He did not, sir ; he only said he would not detain you long."

"Well, ask the gentleman to be good enough to walk this way."

The maid retired, and a moment afterwards Walter entered the room.

The two men bowed to each other. One glance had assured Santley that any attempt at a warmer greeting would be injudicious; the other might not respond, and it would never do for the vicar of the parish to be snubbed by an itinerant painter whom nobody knew—besides, under the circumstances, a bow was ample greeting. He infused into it as much politeness as possible, welcomed his young friend to the Vicarage, and, pointing to a chair which he had drawn forward, begged him to be seated. Decidedly the clergyman was the most self-possessed of the two. For Walter took his seat in nervous silence; while Santley, wondering greatly in his own mind what could possibly have procured him the honour of that visit, kept the scene from flagging by that wonderful gift of small talk with which he was possessed.

He was very pleased indeed to meet Mr. Hetherington. He had done him the honour to call upon him once before he thought—yes, he was sure of it; and he had also had the pleasure of meeting him once before, when he had not had the honour of his acquaintance. Was Mr. Hetherington thinking of making a long stay amongst them?

" Not very long," said Walter.

" I suppose you have made some charming sketches?" continued the clergyman. " There are pretty little spots about the village, spots well worthy of a painter's brush. I used to do a little in that way myself when I was a youngster at college; but the vicar of a parish has onerous duties. I suppose at the present moment I should hardly know how to handle a brush. Are you thinking of leaving us soon, Mr. Hetherington?"

"I am not quite sure!"

"Ah! well, if you stay and would like to make use of my library, I should feel greatly honoured. It is the only thing I have to offer you, I fear; but I shall be very pleased indeed to put it at your service. It contains a few books on your own art, which might interest you."

"You are very kind, Mr. Santley."

"Not at all, my dear sir; I am merely neighbourly. Life would be dreary indeed if one could not be neighbourly in a place like this!"

"Mr. Santley, I have come to you for your advice."

The clergyman, nervously dreading what was to follow, looked at his visitor with a calm smile, and answered pleasantly enough.

"My advice? My dear sir, I place it freely at your service, and myself also if I can be of the slightest use to you."

"You can be of very great use to me."

The clergyman merely bowed this time and waited, so Walter continued—

"You know my cousin, Miss Edith Dove?"

As he spoke he fixed his eyes keenly upon the clergyman's face, but the latter made no sign; he neither winced nor changed colour, but answered calmly enough.

"I have the pleasure of the lady's acquaintance. She is one of the most esteemed members of my congregation."

"It is about Miss Dove I wished to speak to you."

Again the clergyman bowed; again he found it unnecessary to make a reply.

Walter, growing somewhat ill at ease, continued—

"I don't mind confessing to you, Mr. Santley, that at one period of my career I hoped most earnestly, and indeed confidently believed, that at no very remote date I should have the happiness of making her my wife. I was sincerely attached to her; I believe she was attached to me. But recently all has changed. She is wasting her life; throwing aside all chance of happiness, through some mad infatuation about the Church."

"Some mad infatuation about the Church!" returned the clergyman, methodically. " Really, my dear sir, I am afraid you forget you are speaking to a clergyman of the Church. As to Miss Dove, she is a lady whose conduct is without reproach; she is one of the Church's staunchest supporters!"

"Then you approve her present mode of life; you uphold it? You will not advise her to shake her morbid fancies away? to accept an honest affection and a happy home?"

Santley seemed to reflect.

"As a clergyman of the Church, I should advise her the other way, I think. Surely the fulfilment of religious duties points to a more elevated mode of existence than mere marrying and giving in marriage. I am sorry for you, since I believe that any man possessed of that lady's esteem might deem himself fortunate ; still, I could not advise her to act against her conscience and the promptings of religion."

"And me, what do you advise me to do?"

The clergyman shrugged his shoulders.

"It seems to me that there is only one thing that you can do. If the lady finds your attentions disagreeable, surely the most honourable course for you to adopt would be to leave her—in peace."

Walter rose, and the clergyman breathed more freely, believing that the interview had come to a satisfactory end. Neither of them spoke for a minute or so, till the clergyman looked up, and said quietly—

"You have something more to say, Mr. Hetherington?"

"Yes," answered Walter; "I have something more to say." Then, going a few steps nearer to the clergyman, he added, "You are a hypocrite, Mr. Santley!"

The clergyman's face grew pale. He rose hastily from his seat; but before he could speak Walter continued, vehemently—

"Do you think I don't know you? Do you think I haven't discovered that it is you, and not the Church, who has taken my cousin from me? You talk to me of religion, of religious duties, and yet you know that you are playing the hypocrite to her, as you have done to me, and that you are breaking her heart."

He paused, flushed, excited, and angry. The clergyman stood calm and very pale.

"You do well to seek this interview in my house, sir," he said. "Now you have insulted me with impunity, perhaps you will take your leave."

But Walter made no attempt to move.

" Before I go," he said, " I wish to know what are your plans regarding my cousin ? "

" And I should like to ask you, sir," returned the clergyman, " what authority you have for interfering in my private affairs ? "

" I have no authority ; your private affairs are nothing to me. I speak in the interest of my cousin ! "

" Really ! I should fancy your inter- ference would be hardly likely to do her much good."

" Mr. Santley, I shall ask you one more question. Do you, or do you not, mean to marry my cousin ? "

" And if I refuse to answer ? "

" I shall make it my duty, before to- morrow night, to expose you."

" Really !" returned the clergyman,

with an exasperating smile. "You will draw your cousin's good name through the mire in order to throw a little mud at me. I should think, young man, you must be a treasure to your family. Good evening. I will ring for the servant to show you out."

And he did ring—at the most opportune moment too ; for Walter, staggered by that last thrust, perceived that his enemy was on the side of power. So, when in answer to her master's summons the servant appeared, Walter followed her ; he was afraid to utter another word, for Edith's sake.

When he was gone, all Santley's calmness deserted him, and he walked up and down the room in a fit of uncontrollable rage. When he had grown calmer, he sat down and wrote one of his neatly worded epistles to Edith, making an appointment for the following day.

He half believed that Walter had come to him, as Edith's authorized messenger, to attempt to force upon him those bonds which he was so very reluctant to wear. The clergyman could not in any other way account for his knowledge of the relations existing between the two. It was well for Edith that at that moment she was not near her lover—well for her, also, that no meeting could take place between them until the following day.

The next day Santley was very much more composed, and when he walked towards the trysting-place none would have known, from his outward appearance, that anything was materially wrong. He had made the appointment in daylight this time; since embraces could be dispensed with, so also could darkness and night. There was really nothing in this meeting after all ; nothing but what might have been witnessed by a dozen pair of eyes.. Those who did see it would see only an event of ordinary everyday life.

Miss Edith Dove, walking leisurely towards the village, was overtaken by the clergyman, who paused to shake hands with her, and to walk with her a part of the way. Had any one looked closely at these two, he would have seen that the clergyman, though calm, was very pale ; that Edith, pale too, had a weary, listless look about her face ; that after she had shaken hands with her pastor, she quickly turned away her head, for her eyes grew dim with tears.

If Santley saw the tears he did not care to notice them. He had found.

directly they met, that she was suffering from one of those deplorable fits of temper which had more than once caused trouble between them; but that could not be taken any notice of now. If she chose to wear herself to a shadow, it was her own affair; he had something more important on hand. The interview could not be a long one, therefore he must reach the heart of the matter at once.

So he began abruptly—

" Edith, this new course you have adopted is a dangerous one, and had better be abandoned without loss of time."

The girl raised her eyes to his face, and asked wearily—

" What do you mean? What have I done?"

" I suppose you are responsible for

your cousin's visit to my house ; you must have instigated it, if you did not actually advise him ! "

Again she raised her troubled eyes to his face, and said sadly —

" I don't know what you mean."

" Then I will tell you, Edith. Your cousin, a hot-headed, ill-mannered youth, has thought fit to take upon himself the part of protector, or guardian, of your happiness. In this capacity he paid me a domiciliary visit yesterday, and treated me to some most violent abuse. He threatened to make known to the public the relations between us. I advised him to think it over, for your sake ! "

" My cousin — Walter Hetherington, do you mean ? "

" Most certainly."

" But how does he know ? how has he learned ? "

"From you, I suppose."

"No; it is not from me," returned Edith, whose listlessness was fast disappearing. "I have said nothing; I have never even mentioned your name to him. It must be known; it must be talked of in the village. Oh, Charles, spare me! Keep your promise to me, for God's sake! Any open disgrace would be more than I could bear. I should die."

The girl, overcome by her emotion, had forgotten for the moment that their present interview was a perfectly public one. The clergyman coldly reminded her of the fact. Then, after she had forced upon herself a composure which she was far from feeling, he continued—

"You had better understand, Edith, once and for ever, that whatever my conduct may be, I do not choose to have it questioned by this exceedingly officious young man. A repetition of the scene of yesterday I will not bear. And as it is evident to me that my actions are under surveillance, I must refuse either to see or hear from you again, until that young man has removed himself from the village."

" Charles, you surely don't mean that ? " exclaimed the girl.

But he certainly did mean it, and though she pleaded and argued, he remained firm. At last she resolved that she would speak to Walter, resent his interference, and, if possible, induce him to return home.

Then the two shook hands and parted.

That evening Walter dined at the cottage. During the dinner Edith scarcely looked at him ; while he himself was silent and distrait. But after dinner, when they had all retired to the drawing-room, when the old lady had settled down to her wool-work, and Walter had lit his cigar, Edith threw a light shawl over her head, and asked him if he would come with her into the garden.

Wondering very much at the request, Walter rose at once, and offered her his arm. She took it; but the moment they were alone she withdrew her hand and turned angrily upon him. Walter listened, and he found that he had some chance of being heard. He acknowledged that she had spoken the truth; he *had* interfered; he had deemed it quite right that he should do so for her sake.

"For my sake!" returned Edith. "It seems to me there is more of selfishness than benevolence in what you have done. What is it to you if I am engaged to Mr. Santley ? and if we choose to keep our engagement a secret, what is that to you ? I am my own mistress ; I can act just as I think fit, without the fear of coercion from any one. *You*, at any rate, have no right to regulate my actions or to dictate them. I suppose you think I have no right to marry any one, simply because I refuse to be coerced into marrying you ! "

It was a cruel thing to say ; but Edith was simply dealing him, secondhand, some of the stabs which she herself had received from her beloved pastor in the morning. The stabs went deep into his heart, and the wounds remained for many a day. When Edith had uttered a few more truisms with the characteristic selfishness of love and hatred, Walter coldly suggested that their pleasant stroll in the garden might be brought to a termination.

They returned together to the house.

As the old lady, beaming with delight at what she believed to be the sudden and happy reconciliation of the cousins, had prepared the tea, Walter pleased her by sitting down to take some before he said good night."

But the next day he returned to town.

CHAPTER XXIII.

DR. DUPRÉ'S ELIXIR.

GEORGE HALDANE returned home in the
best of spirits. His paper had been
received with enthusiasm by the *savants*
of France, and his life in Paris had been
one pleasant succession of visits, learned
conversaziones, and private entertain-
ments. Thanks to his happy pre-occu-
pation, he scarcely noticed that his wife's
manner was constrained, nervous, yet
deeply solicitous; that she looked pale
and worn, as if with constant watching;
and that, in answer to his careless
questioning as to affairs at home, she
made only fragmentary replies.

On entering his dressing-room to change his apparel, he found Baptisto, who was quietly undoing his portmanteau and selecting the necessary things with a calm air, as if his services had never been interrupted.

"So, my Baptisto," he said, clapping that worthy on the shoulder, "you are not dead or buried, I see? Ah, you may smile, but I am quite aware of the trick you played me. Well, you have been the loser. You would have had a pleasant time of it in Paris, the best of entertainment, and nothing whatever to do."

"I am glad you have returned, señor," replied Baptisto, with his customary solemnity.

"I hope you have given satisfaction to your mistress during my absence?"

"I hope so, señor."

" Humph ! we shall see what report she has to make concerning you, and if that is favourable, I may forgive your freak of laziness."

" I have not been lazy, señor," said Baptisto, quietly preparing the toilette.

" Indeed ! Pray, how have you been employing yourself ? "

Baptisto did not reply, but smiled again.

" How is your inamerata and her family ? I saw the little woman curtsying as I passed through the lodge-gates."

Baptisto shook his head solemnly.

" Ah, señor," he said, " you are mistaken. The woman of the lodge is a stupid person ; and for the rest, I put no faith in women. *Cuerpo di Baccho*, no ! They smile upon us when we are near ; but no sooner do we turn our backs, than they smile upon some other man."

"Pretty philosophy," returned Haldane, with a laugh. "Why, you are a downright misogynist, my Baptisto. But I don't believe one word you say, for all that. Men who talk like you are generally very easy conquests, and I would bet twenty to one on the little widow still."

"Ah, señor, if all women were like your signora, it would be different. She is so good, so pure, so faithful at her devotions. It is a great thing to have religion."

As Baptisto spoke his back was turned to his master, so that the extraordinary expression of his face was unnoticed, and there was no indication in his tone that he spoke satirically. Haldane shrugged his shoulders and said nothing, not caring to discuss his wife's virtues with a servant, however familiar. Presently he went downstairs to dinner. All that evening he was very affectionate and merry, talking volubly of his adventures in Paris, of his scientific acquaintances, and of such new discoveries as they had brought under his notice. In the course of his happy chat he spoke frequently of a new acquaintance, one Dr. Dupré, whom he had met in the French capital.

"The French, however far behind the Germans in speculative affairs," he observed, "are far their superiors, and ours, in physiology. Take this Dupré, for example. He is a wonderful fellow! His dissections and vivisections have brought him to such a point of mastery that he is almost certain that he has discovered the problem poor Lewes broke his heart over—how and by what mechanism we can't think. I don't quite believe he has succeeded in that great discovery, but some of his minor discoveries are extraordinary. Did you read the account in the papers of his elixir of death ? "

Ellen shook her head. The very name seemed horrible.

" His elixir of death ? " she repeated.

" Yes. A chemical preparation, the fundamental principle of which is morphine. By its agency he can so produce in a living organism the ordinary phenomena of death, that even *rigor mortis* is simulated. I saw the experiment tried on two rabbits, a Newfoundland dog, and, to crown all, on the human subject. They were all, to every appearance, dead ; the rabbits for twenty-four hours, the dog for half a day, and the woman for an hour and a half."

"Horrible!" exclaimed Ellen, with a shudder. "Do you actually mean he experimented on a living woman?"

"Yes; on a strapping wench, the daughter of his housekeeper; and a very fine thing she made of it. We subscribed together, and presented her with a purse of a thousand francs."

"I think such things are wicked," cried Ellen, with some warmth. "Mere mortals have no right to play, in that way, with the mystery of life and death."

"My dear Nell," cried Haldane, laughing, "it is in the interests of science!"

"But I am sure it is not right. Life is given and taken by God alone."

"Your argument, if accepted, would

make all mankind accept the religion
of the Peculiar People, who will cure no
diseases by human intervention.   As to
this business of suspended animation, it
is merely a part of our discoveries in
anodynes.   Dupré's experiment, I know,
is perfectly safe."

"But that is not the question."

"How so, my dear?"

"What I mean is, that death is too
solemn and awful a thing to imitate as
you describe.   Such experiments are
simply blasphemous, in my opinion."

"Come, come," cried the philosopher.
"There is no blasphemy where there is
no irreverence.   According to your
religious people, your priests of the
churches, there was blasphemy in cir-
cumnavigating the globe; in discovering
the circulation of the blood; in ascertain-
ing the age of the earth; and, still later,

in using chloroform to lessen the pangs of parturition."

" But what purpose can be served by such experiments as *that ?* "

" A good many," was the reply. " For example, it may help us to the discovery of the nature of life itself, which has puzzled everybody, from Parmenides down to Haeckel. If we can by a simple anodyne . suspend the vital mechanism for a period, and then by a vegetable antidote restore it again to action, the resurrection of Lazarus will cease to be a miracle, and the pretensions of Christianity———"

Ellen rose impatiently, with an expression of sincere pain.

" My dear Nell, what is the matter ? " cried her husband.

" I cannot bear to hear you discuss such a thing. Oh, George, if you would leave such wicked speculations alone, and try to believe in the mystery and sovereignty of God!"

"You mean, burn my books, and go to hear your seraphic friend every Sunday?"

Had he not touched, unconsciously, on another painful chord? Why, otherwise, did his wife flush scarlet and partially avert her face? Conquering herself with an effort, she went over to him, and bending over him, looked fondly into his face.

"You are so much cleverer than I, so much wiser, and do you think I am not proud of your wisdom? But, all the same, dear, I wish you did not think as you do. When life becomes a mere experiment, a mere thing of mechanism, what will be left? If we knew everything, even what we are, and why we exist, the world would be a tomb—with no place in it for the Living God."

Touched by her manner, Haldane drew her down by his side and kissed her; then, with more earnestness than he had yet exhibited, he answered her, holding her hand in his own and pressing it softly.

" My dear Nell, do me the justice to believe that I am not quite a materialist; simple agnosticism is the very converse of materialism. There is not living a scientific philosopher of any eminence who does not, in his calculations, postulate a mystery which can never be solved by the finest intellect. Even if we had fully completed, with the poet—

' The new creed of science, which showeth to man
   How he darkly began,
How he grew from a cell to a soul, without plan ;
How he breaks like a wave of the ocean, and goes
   To eternal repose—
A tone that must fade, tho' the great Music grows ! '

even then, we should know nothing of the First Cause. That must for ever remain inscrutable."

" But how horrible it would be to believe in annhilation ? *Can* you believe in it ? "

" Certainly not," replied the philosopher.

Ellen's face brightened.

" Oh, I am so glad to hear you say that ! "

" My dear Nell, annihilation is absurd."

" Now, isn't it ? " she cried triumphantly.

" It is refuted, on the face of it, by the doctrine of the conservation of force. Life is eternal, in one shape or another ; no force can be destroyed, be sure of that ! "

" I wish Mr. Santley could hear

you! He wouldn't call you an atheist then!"

Haldane's face darkened angrily.

"What? Does the man actually——"

"Don't misunderstand," cried Ellen, flushing scarlet. "I do not mean that he really calls you an atheist, but he is so sorry, so deeply sorry, that you do not believe. He does not know you, dear, and takes all my bear's satirical growling for solemn earnest. Now, when I tell him——"

"You will tell him nothing," exclaimed Haldane, with sudden sternness. "I will have no priest coming between my wife and me!"

"Mr. Santley would never do that," she returned, now trembling violently.

"Mr. Santley is like all his tribe, I suppose—a meddler and a mischief-maker. That is the worst of other-worldliness; it gives these traders in the Godhead, these peddlers who would give us in exchange for belief in their superstitions a *bonus* in paradise, an excuse for making this world unbearable. Well, my atheism, if you choose to call it so, against his theism. Mine at least keeps me a man among men, while his keeps him a twaddler among women."

Haldane spoke with heat, for the word "atheist" had somehow stung him to the quick. This man, who rejected all outward forms of belief, and whose conversation was habitually ironical, was in his inmost nature deeply and sincerely religious; humbly reverent before the forces of nature; spiritually conscious of that Power beyond ourselves which makes for righteousness. True, he rejected the ordinary forms of theism; but he had, on the other hand, a deep though dumb reverence for the character of Christ, and he had no sympathy with such out-and-out materialists as Haeckel and *hoc genus omne.* For the rest, he was liberal-minded, and had no desire to interfere with his wife's convictions; could smile a little at her simplicity, and would see no harm in her clerical predispositions, so long as the clergyman didn't encroach tòo far on the domain of married life and domestic privacy.

His indignation did not last. Seeing his wife greatly agitated, and fearing that he had caused her pain, he drew her forehead down and kissed it; then, patting her cheek, he said—

" Forgive me, Nell. I did not mean to scold; but one does not like hard names. When any one calls me 'atheist,' I am like the old woman whom Cobbett called a ' parallelogram ; ' it is not the significance of the epithet, but its opprobrium, that rouses me. Besides, I do not like any man to abuse me—to my own wife."

"No one does that," she cried. "You know I would not listen."

"I hope not, my dear." He added after a little, looking at her thoughtfully and sadly, "Man and wife have fallen asunder before now, on this very question of religion. Well, rather than that should happen, I will let you convert me. Will that satisfy you?"

"I shall never be quite satisfied till I know that you believe as *I* do."

"What is that, pray?"

"That there is a just God, who made and cherishes us; and that, through the blood of His Son we shall live again although we die!"

"Well, it is a beautiful creed, my dear."

" And true ? "

" Why not ? I will go with you thus far. I believe that, if there is a God, He is just, and that we shall certainly live again, if it is for our good."

The emphasis with which he spoke the last words attracted her attention.

" For our good ?" she queried.

" I am quoting the saddest words ever written, by the saddest and best man I ever knew.* He, too, believed that a God might spare us, and give us eternal life, if—mark the proviso—eternal life were indeed *for our good*. But suppose the contrary—suppose God knew better, and that it would be an evil and unhappy gift ? Alas ! who knows ? "

He rose from his chair, still encircling

* J. S. Mill.

his wife's waist, and moved towards the door.

"Come to the drawing-room," he cried gaily. "After so much offhand theology, a little music will be delightful. Ah, Nell, one breath of Beethoven is worth all the prosings of your parsons. Play to me, and, while the music lasts, I will believe what you will."

CHAPTER XXIV.

THE EXPERIMENT.

THE next morning Haldane was busy in his laboratory. When he came in to lunch, looking disreputable enough in his old coat, and smelling strongly of tobacco, he said to his wife—

" By-the-by, Nell, do you remember what I told you last night about Dupré's wonderful elixir ? I forgot to tell you that I have brought some of it with me, for purposes of private experiment."

Ellen looked horrified.

" Don't be afraid," he continued, laughing ; " your cats and dogs are safe from me. I have found a better subject, and mean to operate on him this very afternoon."

" Whom do you mean ? "

" As a sort of penance for his shamming illness, I shall kill Baptisto."

She uttered a cry, and raised her hands in protest.

" For heaven's sake, George, be warned ! If you have any of that horrible stuff, throw it away."

" Now, my dear Nell," said the philosopher, " be reasonable ; there is not the slightest cause for alarm. You will see this experiment, and it will, I hope, treble your faith in miracles."

" I will *not* see it. I beseech you, abandon the idea. As for Baptisto—— "

At this moment the Spaniard entered the room, carrying certain dishes.

" I have been telling your mistress,

Baptisto, that you are ready to be a martyr to science. At four o'clock precisely, you will be a dead man."

Baptisto bowed solemnly.

" I am quite ready, señor."

But here Ellen interposed.

" It is ridiculous ; your master is only joking. He would not do anything so foolish, so wicked. As for you, I forbid you to encourage him."

Baptisto bowed again, with a curious smile.

" It is for the señor to command. As he knows, he has saved my life, and he may take it whenever he pleases."

Haldane nodded, in the act of drinking a glass of wine.

" Don't be afraid, Baptisto. After death, there is the resurrection."

" That, señor, is your affair," returned the Spaniard, phlegmatically, shrugging his shoulders. "You will do with me as you please."

And so saying, he glided from the room.

Ellen again and again entreated her husband not to proceed in his experiment; but he had long made up his mind that it was perfectly safe, and he could not be persuaded. To her gentle spirit, the whole idea seemed horrible in the extreme; but her greatest dread was that it might be attended with danger to the subject. Haldane, however, assured her that this was impossible.

All the afternoon Haldane and Baptisto were together in the laboratory. A little after four o'clock, as Ellen was walking on the terrace, Haldane came to her, smiling and holding up a small vial.

"It is all over," he said, "and the

experiment is quite successful. Come and see."

Not quite understanding him, she suffered him to lead her into the laboratory; but, on crossing the threshold, she uttered a cry of horror. Stretched on a sofa, lay Baptisto, moveless, and, to all seeming, without one breath of life. His eyes were wide open, but rayless; his jaw fixed, his face pale as grey marble; a peaceful smile, as of death itself, upon his handsome face. The light of the sun, just sinking towards the west, streamed in through the high window upon the apparently lifeless form. In the chamber itself there was a sickly smell, like that of some suffocating vapour. The whole scene would have startled and appalled even a strong man.

" Oh, George ! " cried the lady, clasping her hands. " What have you done ? "

"' Don't be alarmed," was the reply. " It's all right ! "

" But you said the experiment——

" Was successful ? Perfectly. There lies our poor friend, comfortably finished."

" But are you sure, quite sure, that he is not dead ? He is not breathing."

" Of course not. The simulation is perfect. Place your hand on his wrist— you will detect no pulse. Turn his pupils to the light—you see, they do not contract. The case would deceive a whole college of physicians."

As he spoke, he suited the action to the word—placed his finger upon the pulse, gazed at the glazing pupils ; raised one of the lifeless arms, which, on being released, fell heavily as lead.

" Horrible, horrible ! For God's sake. recover him ! "

"All in good time. He has only been dead a quarter of an hour; in half an hour precisely I shall say, 'Arise and walk.' Feel his forehead, Nell; it is as cold as marble."

But Ellen drew back, shuddering, and could not be persuaded to touch the sleeper.

"Well, go back to your promenade. I will call you when he is awakened."

Sick and terrified, Ellen obeyed her husband. Standing on the terrace, she waited for his summons; and at last it came. Haldane appeared, and beckoned; she followed him to the laboratory, and there, seated in an armchair, comfortably sipping a glass of wine, was the Spaniard—a little pale still, but otherwise not the worse for his state of coma.

"Thank God!" cried Ellen. "I

thought he would never recover. But it must have been a horrible experience."

Baptisto smiled.

" Tell the signora all about it," said his master. " Did you feel any pain ? "

" None, señor."

" What were your sensations ? Pleasant or otherwise ? "

" Quite pleasant, señor. It was like sinking into an agreeable sleep. If death is like that, it is a bagatelle."

" Were you at all conscious ? "

" Not of this world, señor, but I had bright dreams of another. I thought I was in paradise, walking in the sunshine—ah, so bright ! I was sorry, señor, when I came back to this world."

" You hear !" cried Haldane, turning to his wife. " After all, death itself

may be a glorious experience ; for 'in
that sleep of death what dreams may
come !.' It is quite clear at least that
all the phenomena of death, such as we
shrink from and shudder at, may be
accompanied by some kind of pleasant
psychic consciousness. Bravo, Baptisto !
After this, we shall call you Lazarus the
second. You have passed beyond the
shadow of the sepulchre, and returned
to tell the tale."

Despite the resuscitation, Ellen still
revolted from the whole proceeding.

" Now you are satisfied," she said,
" promise me never to use that dreadful
elixir again."

" I think you may make your mind
easy. The experiment is an ugly one,
I admit, and I am not anxious to repeat
it—at least, not on the human organism.
For the same reason, my dear Nell,

pray keep the affair to yourself, and make no confidences, even to your confessor—I should say, your clergyman. Will you promise ? "

" Most certainly. I should not like any one to know you did such things. As for Mr. Santley, he would be shocked beyond measure."

So saying, she left the two men together. In the mean time, Baptisto had finished his wine and risen to his feet. While his master regarded him with an approving smile, he walked over to the door, softly closed it, and returning noiselessly across the room, said in a low voice—

" There is something, señor, I did not tell you. I had dreams."

"So you said, my Baptisto."

" Ah yes, but not all. While I was lying there, I thought that *you* were the dead man, and that the señora, your widow, had married."

" Married ? "

" The English priest."

Haldane started, and looked in amazement at the speaker.

"What the devil do you mean?"

"Ah, señor, it was only my dream; a foolish dream. You were lying in your winding-sheet, and they were kneeling at the altar—smiling, señor. I did not like to speak of it to the señora; but it was very strange."

Haldane forced a laugh, while, with a mysterious look, Baptisto crept from the chamber. Was it in sheer simplicity or in deep cunning that the Spaniard had spoken, touching so delicate a chord ? Left alone, Haldane paced up and down the laboratory in agitation. He was not by temperament a jealous or a suspicious man, but he was troubled in spite of himself. The words sounded like a warning, almost an insinuation.

"What could the fellow mean?" he asked himself again and again. "Could he possibly have dreamed *that?* No; it is preposterous. There was malice in his eye, and mischief. . . . Ellen married to Santley! Bah! what am I thinking about? The fellow is not a *prophet!*"

In this manner, whether in innocence or for some set purpose of his own, Baptisto contrived to poison all the sweetness of that successful experiment. When Haldane again joined his wife that evening, he was taciturn, distraught, nervous, and irritable. All his buoyancy had departed. Ellen saw the change, and puzzled herself to account for it.

She played to him, sang to him, but failed to drive the cloud from his brow.

When she had retired for the night, he still sat pondering over Baptisto's words.

CHAPTER XXV.

"BEWARE, MY LORD, OF JEALOUSY!"

IF Baptisto's object in describing a
dream so ominous was to attract his
master's attention to the intimate relations between Mrs. Haldane ·and the
clergyman, he certainly succeeded.
Once assured in this direction, Haldane's
perceptions were keen enough. He
noticed that the mere mention of
Santley's name filled Ellen with a sort
of nervous constraint; that, although the
clergyman's visits were frequent, they
were generally made at times when
Haldane himself was busy and pre-
occupied—that is to say, during his well-

known hours of work; and that, moreover, Santley, however much he liked
the society of the lady, invariably avoided
the husband, or, if they met, contrived to
frame some excuse for speedy parting.
Now, Haldane trusted his wife implicitly,
and believed her incapable of any in-
fidelity, even in thought. Still, he did
not quite like the aspect of affairs. Much
as he trusted his wife, he had a strong
moral distrust for anything in the shape
of a priest; and he determined, therefore,
to keep his eyes upon the clergyman.

A few days after that curious physio-
logical experiment, he had the following
conversation with Baptisto. It was the
first day of the week.

"Baptisto, I thought you were a good
Catholic?"

"So I am, señor," returned the
Spaniard, smiling.

"Yet you went to an English church yesterday, I hear?"

"Yes, señor.   I go there very often."

"Why, pray?"

"Simply out of curiosity.   Mr. Santley is a beautiful preacher, and has a silvery voice.   While you were away, I went once, twice, three times.   There is a young señora there who plays sweetly upon the great organ; I like to listen, to watch the congregation."

"Humph!   By-the-bye, Baptisto, I have been thinking over that dream of yours, when—when you were lying there."

"Yes, señor?"

"Pray, what put such a foolish idea in your head?"

"I cannot tell, señor; all I know is, it came.   A foolish dream, do you say?   I suppose it is because the clergyman was here so often, when you were away. And madame is so devout! I trust, señor, my dream has not given you offence ; perhaps I was wrong to speak of it at all."

Haldane's face had gone black as a thunder-cloud. Placing his hand on the other's shoulder, and looking firmly into his face, he said—

" Listen to me, Baptisto."

" I am listening, señor."

" If I thought you would come back to life to tell lies about your mistress, I would have let you lie the other day and rot like a dead dog, rather than have recovered you at all. You hear ? Take care ! I know you do not love your mistress, but if you dare to whisper one word against her, I will drive you for ever from my door."

Baptisto bowed his head respectfully

before the storm, but retained his usual composure.

"Señor, may I speak?"

"Yes; but again, take care!"

"You should not blame me if I am jealous for your honour!"

Haldane started, and uttered an expletive.

"My honour, you dog? What do you mean?"

"This, señor. I would rather die than give you offence; and as for the señora, I love her also, for is she not your wife? But will you be angry still, when I tell you, when I warn you, to beware of that man, that priest? He is a bad man, very bad. Ah, I have watched—and seen!"

"What have you seen?" cried Haldane, clutching him by the arm. "Come, out with it!'

" Enough to show me that he is not your friend—that he is dangerous."

" Bah! is that all ? Now, listen to me, and be sure I mean what I say. I will have no servant of mine spying upon my wife. I will have no servant of mine insinuating that my honour is in danger. If I hear another word of this, if you convey to me by one look the fact that you are still prying, spying, and suspecting, I shall take you by the collar and send you flying out of my house. Now, go ! "

Baptisto, who knew his master's temper perfectly, bowed and withdrew. He had no wish to say one word more. He had thrown out a dark hint, a black seed of suspicion, and he knew that he might safely let it work. It did work, rapidly and terribly. Left alone, Haldane became a prey to the wildest fears and suspicions. He remembered now that his wife had been acquainted with this man in her girlhood ; that there had even been some passage of love between them. He remembered how eagerly she had renewed the acquaintance, and with what admiring zeal the clergyman had responded. He pictured to himself the sympathetic companionship, the zealous meetings, the daily religious intercourse, of these two young people, each full of the fervour of a blind superstition. Could it be possible that they loved each other ? Questioning his memory, he recalled looks, words, tones, which, although scarcely noticed at the time, seemed now of painful significance. The mere thought was sickening. Already he realized the terrible phrase of the poet Young—" the jealous are the damned. '

Haldane was not habitually a violent man. Though passionate and headstrong by temperament, he had schooled himself to gentleness after a stormy youth, and the chilly waters of philosophy, at which he drank daily, kept his head cool and his pulses calm. But the stormy spirit, though hushed, was not altogether dead within him, and under his habitual reticence and good-humoured cynicism, there lay the most passionate idolatry for his beautiful wife. He had set her up in his heart of hearts, with a faith too perfect for much expression; and it had not occurred to him, in his remotest dreams, that any other man could ever come between them.

And now, suddenly as a lightning flash illumining a dark landscape, the fear came upon him that perhaps he had been unwary and unwise. Was it possible, he asked himself, that he had been too studious and too book-loving, too reticent also in all those little attentions which by women, who always love sweetmeats, are so tenderly prized? Moreover, he was ten years his wife's elder—was that disparity of years also a barrier between their souls? No; he was sure it was not. He was sure that she was not hypocritical, and that she loved him. Wherever the blame might be, if blame there were, it was certainly not hers. She had been in all respects a tender and a sympathetic wife; encouraging his deep study of science, even when she most distrusted its results; proud of his attainments, and eager for his success; in short, a perfect helpmate, but for her old-fashioned prejudices in the sphere of religion. Ah, *religion!* There was the one word which solved

the enigma, and aroused in our philosopher's bosom that fierce indignation
which long ago led Lucretius into such
passionate hate against the Phantom,

" Which with horrid head
   Leered hideously from all the gates of heaven ! "

It needed only this to complete his
loathing for the popular theology, for all
its teachers. Yes, he reflected, religion
only was to blame. In its name, his
wife's sympathies had been tampered
with, her spirit more or less turned
against himself ; in its name, his house
had been secretly invaded, his domestic
happiness poisoned, his peace of mind
destroyed. It was the old story !
Wherever this shadow of superstition
crawled, craft and dissimulation began.
Now, as in the beginning, it came
between father and child, sister and
brother, man and wife.

It so happened that when George Haldane came forth from having his dark hour alone, he rather avoided meeting his wife at once, and, taking his hat, stepped out from the laboratory on to the shrubbery path. He had scarcely done so, when his eye fell upon two figures standing together in the distance, upon the terrace of the house. One was Mrs. Haldane, wearing her garden hat and a loose shawl thrown over her shoulders. The other was the clergyman of the parish.

Haldane drew back, and watched. In that moment he knew the extent of his humiliation; for never before had he been a spy upon his wife's actions.

Their backs were towards him. Santley was talking eagerly; Ellen was looking down. Presently they began to move slowly along the terrace, side by side.

Haldane watched them gloomily. The sunlight fell brightly upon them, and on the old Manor house, with its brilliant creepers and glittering panes, while the old chapel, with the watcher in its ruined porch, remained in shadow. It seemed like an omen. In the darkness of his hiding-place, Haldane felt satanic. Yes, there they walked—children of God, as they called themselves—in God's sunlight ; and he, the searcher for light, the unbeliever, was forgotten.

Presently Santley paused again, and, with an impassioned gesture, pointed upward. Ellen raised her head, and looked upward too, listening eagerly to his words. Haldane laughed fiercely to himself, with all the ugliness of his jealousy upon him.

Presently they disappeared into the house. A little afterwards Santley emerged from the front door, and came walking rapidly down the avenue. His manner was eager and happy, almost jubilant, and Haldane saw, when he approached, that his face looked positively radiant.

He was passing, when Haldane stepped out and confronted him. He started, paused, and a shadow fell instantaneously upon his handsome face. Recovering himself, he held out his hand. Haldane did not seem to see the gesture, but, nodding a careless greeting, said, with his habitual *sang froid*—

" Well met, Mr. Santley. Here I am again, you see, hard at work. Have you come from the house ? "

" Yes," answered Santley.

" On some new message of Christian charity and beneficence, I suppose ? Ah, my dear sir, you are indefatigable,

and the old women of the parish must
indeed find you a Good Shepherd. Did
you find my wife at home?"

"Yes."

"And zealous, as usual, I suppose?
Ah, what a thing it is to be pious! But
let me beg you not to encourage her too
much. Charity begins at home; and
what with soup-kitchens, offertories, sub-
scriptions for church repairs, and societies
for the gratuitous distribution of flannel
waistcoats, I am in a fair way of being
ruined."

Santley forced a laugh.

"Don't be afraid. My errand to-day
was not a begging one, I assure you."

"I am glad to hear it."

"I was merely bringing Mrs. Haldane
a book I promised to lend her. To tell
the truth, she finds your library rather
destitute of works of a religious nature."

"Do you really think so?" exclaimed Haldane, drily. "Why, I thought it unusually well provided in that respect. Let me see! There are Volney's 'Ruins of Empire,' Monboddo's 'Dissertations,' Drummond's 'Academical Questions,' excellent translations of Schopenhauer and Hartmann, not to speak of thirty-six volumes of Diderot, and fifty of Arouet."

Santley opened his eyes in horror and astonishment.

"Arouet!" he ejaculated. "Do you actually mean to call Voltaire a religious writer?"

"Highly so. There is religion even in 'La Pucelle,' but it reaches its culmination in the 'Philosophical Dictionary.'"

"And you would actually let Mrs. Haldane read such works as those?"

"Certainly; though, I am sorry to say,

she prefers 'The Old Helmet' and the 'Heir of Redclyffe.' May I ask the name of the work you have been good enough to lend her ? "

" It is a book from which I myself have received great benefit — Père Hyacinthe's 'Sermons.'"

" Père Hyacinthe ? " repeated Haldane. " Ah ! the jolly priest who reverenced celibacy, and proclaimed himself the father of a strapping boy. Well, the man was at least honest. I think all clergymen should marry, and at as early an age as possible. What is your opinion ? "

Santley flushed to the temples, while Haldane watched him with a gloomy smile.

" I think—I am sure," he stammered, "that the married state is the happiest —perhaps the holiest."

"With these sentiments, of which I cordially approve, why the deuce are you a bachelor?"

The clergyman winced at the question, and his colour deepened; then, as if musing, he glanced round towards the house—a look which was observed and fully appreciated by his tormentor.

"I am sure my wife would encourage you to change your condition. Like most women, she is by instinct a match-maker."

Santley did not seem to hear; at any rate, he made no reply, but, holding out his hand quickly, exclaimed—

"I must go now. I am rather in haste."

Haldane did not take the hand, but put his arm upon the clergyman's shoulder.

"Well, good day," he said. "Take

my advice, though, and get a sensible wife as soon as possible."

Santley tried to smile, but only suc-ceeded in looking more pale and nervous than usual. With a few murmured words of adieu, he moved rapidly away.

Haldane watched him thoughtfully until he disappeared down the avenue.

"I wonder if that man can smile?" he said to himself. "No; I am afraid he is too horribly in earnest. I suppose the women would call him handsome—*spiritual;* but I hate such pallid, waxen-featured, handsome dolls. A pretty shepherd, that, for a Christian flock to follow; a fellow who makes his very ignorance of this world constitute his claim to act as cicerone to the next. Fancy being jealous, actually *jealous*, of such a thing as that!"

He turned back into his laboratory

and tried to dismiss Baptisto's suggestion from his mind ; but it was impossible. He could not disguise from himself that Santley, with his seraphic face and sad, earnest eyes, was the kind of creature whom the weaker sex adore, and that he was rendered doubly dangerous to women by the radiant mesmerism of a fascinating and voluptuous celestial superstition.

CHAPTER XXVI.

FIRST LEAVES FROM A PHILOSOPHER'S NOTE-BOOK.

I AM about to set down, in as concise a manner as possible, and at present solely for my private edification (some day, perhaps, another eye may read the lines, but not yet), certain events which have lately influenced my domestic life. Were it not that even a professed scientist might decline to publish experiments affecting his own private happiness, the description of the events to which I allude might almost form a chapter in my slowly progressing "Physiology of Ethics," and the description would be at least as interesting as many of Ferrier's accounts of vivisection on dumb animals. But, unfortunately, I am unable, in this case, to apply the dissecting knife to my neighbour's heart, without laying bare the ugly wound in my own.

To begin then, I, George Haldane, recluse, pessimist, moral physiologist, and would-be moral philosopher, have discovered, at forty years of age, that I am capable of the most miserable of all human passions; worse, that this said ignoble passion of jealousy has a certain rational foundation. For ten years I have been happy with a wife who seemed the perfection of human gentleness and beauty; who, although unfortunately we have been blest with no offspring, has shown the tenderest solicitude and sympathy for the children of my brain ; and who, in her wifely faith and sanctity, seemed to be the sole link still holding me to a church whose history has always filled me with abhorrence, and a religion whose infantine theology I despise. Well, *nous avons changé tout cela.* My mind is no longer peaceful, my hearth no longer sacred ; and the woman I love seems slowly drifting from me on a stream of sensuous spiritualism—another name for a religious rehabilitation of the flesh.

If any other man were the victim, I should think the situation highly absurd. Here, on the one hand, is a fanatical Protestant priest, with the face of a seraphic monk, the experience of a schoolgirl, and the *gaucherie* of a country chorister who has never grown a beard ; a fellow whose sole claims to notice are his white hands, his clean

linen, and his function as a silly shepherd; a man fresh from college, ignorant
of the world.   Here, on the other hand,
am I, physically and intellectually his
master, knowing almost every creed
beneath the sun, and the slave of none;
indifferent to vulgar human passions,
and disposed to disintegrate them one
and all with the electric current of a
negative philosophy.   Between us both,
trembling this way and that, is that fair
thing of flesh and blood, my wife, zealous
to save her own soul alive, and fearful
at times, I fancy, that I have sold mine
to the Prince of Darkness.   It is
another version of science against superstition, common sense against a lie;
and Ellen Haldane is the prize.   A
fiery Spaniard, like Baptisto yonder,
would end the affair with a stiletto-
thrust; but I, of colder blood, am not

likely to do anything so courageous or so foolish, but am content to watch and watch, and to feel the sick contamination of my suspicion creeping over me like an unwholesome mildew. A stiletto thrust ? Why, the mere tongue, a less fatal weapon, would do it all. If I could only summon up the courage to say to my wife, " I know your secret ; choose between this man and me, between his creed and mine, between your duty as a wife and your zeal as a Christian," I fancy there would be an end to it all. But I am too timorous ; I suppose, too ashamed of my suspicions, too proud to acknowledge so contemptible a rival. As a Spaniard covers his face with his mantle, I veil my soul with my pride ; and, under the mantle of unsuspicion, rest irresolute, while the thing grows.

Once or twice, I have thought of another way—of taking my wife by the hand and saying, "To-morrow, my dear, we shall leave this place, and return to Spain or Italy—some quiet place abroad." I could easily find an excuse for the migration, which, once effected, would make an end of the affair. But that, in my opinion, would be too cowardly. It would, indeed, be an admission that the danger was real and imminent; that, in other words, the fight for honour could only be saved by an ignominious retreat. No; Ellen Haldane must take her chance. If she is not strong enough to hold out against evil, then let her go—*au bon Dieu* or *au bon diable*, as either leads.

Yet what am I saying? It is precisely because I have the utmost faith in her purity of heart that I watch the struggle with a certain patience. I believe there will be a victim, but not my Ellen. Surely, if there is a good woman in the world, she is that woman. As for the other, every day, every hour, brings the cackling creature further and further into my decoy. Even if he tried to turn back now, I do not think I should let him. No ; let him swim in and on, and in and on, till he reaches the place where I, like the decoy man, can catch him fluttering, and—wring his neck ? Perhaps.

It is quite clear that the man takes me for an idiot. At first he used precautions, invented subterfuges ; latterly, certain of my stupidity or indifference, he comes and goes without disguise. When I meet him driving side by side of my wife in the phaeton, on some pretended errand of mercy, he gives me

a careless bow, a nod. As he goes by my
den, on his way to invite her out to visit
his sister or his church, he makes no
excuse, but passes jauntily, with a con-
versational pat for the stupid watch-dog:
that is all. It would be amusing, I say,
if it were not almost insufferable.

This afternoon, as Ellen was going
out, I blankly suggested that she should
stay at home.

" But you are busy," she said—"always
busy with your books and experiments."

" Not too busy, my dear Nell, for a
tête-à-tête with you. Where are you
going? To the Vicarage?"

" Yes."

" To see the parson, or his sister?"

" Both. We have a great deal to
discuss, about the designs for the new
stained-glass windows, which have just
come from London."

" Very interesting ; but they will keep for a day. I fancy I could show you something quite as interesting, in my laboratory."

" I hate the laboratory," she cried, " and those horrible experiments."

" My dear, you should not hate what your husband loves."

" I don't mean that I hate them, quite; but I think them so useless ! "

" More useless than stained-glass windows ? "

" It is certainly not useless to beautify the House of God. Oh, I do so wish you could feel as I do about these things ! What is the world without them ? "

" Without stained-glass windows ? " I suggested sarcastically.

She flushed impatiently.

" George, why have you such a dislike

for religion ?   Why do you hate everything I love ? "

" Pardon me, my dear Nell, it was
you, not I, that spoke of hating.   Philosophers never hate."

" But you do worse ; you despise it.
Thank God we have no children.   It
would be horrible to tell them that
their father forbade them to go to
church, or pray !"

It was like a stab into my heart of
hearts, that cry of thanks to God.
Despite myself, I lost my composure.
She saw it instantly, and in the manner
of her sex, encroached.

" Oh, George, do try to think
sometimes of these things, for my
sake !   You would be so much
happier, you surely would have so
much more blessing, if you sometimes
prayed."

" How do you know that I do not pray ? "

" Because you do not believe."

" I do not believe precisely as your priest believes, that is all."

She looked at me eagerly ; then, after a moment's hesitation, cried—

" George, if I asked a favour, would you grant it ? "

" Try."

" Let Mr. Santley come sometimes, and speak with you about God ! "

This was too much, almost, for even me to bear with equanimity. I am afraid I did not look particularly amiable as I answered, sharp and short, turning from her—

" After all, I think you had better go and look at those designs."

" There, you are angry again ! " she cried ; and I knew by the sound of her voice that her throat was choked with tears. " You are always angry when I touch upon religion."

" You were not talking of religion,' I retorted ; " you were talking of that man."

" Why do you dislike him so ? Because he is a preacher of the Word ? "

" Because he is a canting hypocrite, like all his tribe," I cried.

She saw that I had lost my temper, as was inevitable, and, sighing deeply, moved to the door. I followed her with my eyes. I would have given the world to call her back; to clasp her in my arms; to tell her my aching fears ; to promise her I would worship any God she choose, in any place, in any way, so long as she would only be true, and answer my eager impulse with a little love. But I was too proud for that.

" Then you are going ? " I said.

She turned, looking at me very sadly.

" Yes, if you do not mind."

I shrugged my shoulders, and after another sad, reproachful look, she left the room. A minute afterwards, she drove her ponies past the window, without looking up.

Thursday, September 15.—A golden autumn day, so warm and still that it reminded me of the Indian summer. Not a leaf stirred, but the insects in the air were like floating blossoms, and seemed to sleep upon their wings. Even all round my den the shadows were sultry, and intertangled with slumberous shafts of light.

This fine weather rather disappointed me, for I had arranged for a day's recreation. In my youth, before I was caught myself in the tedious snares of speculation, I used to be an ardent fisherman, and I still retain sufficient knowledge of the gentle craft to cast a fly tolerably. So, tired of work, and a little weary of my own thoughts, I determined, for the first time, to take advantage of the permission my neighbour, Lord ———, has given me, and spend a day upon the river banks.

Despite the sunshine, and the absence of even a breath of wind, I shouldered my basket, lifted my rod, and set off. Ellen was already out and about; so I did not see her before I started. Taking a short cut through the shrubberies, I soon came to the banks of the Emmet—as pretty a little stream as ever rippled over golden sands, or reached out an azure arm to turn some merry watermill. Arrived there, I soon saw that it would be useless to try a cast till there was a little wind ; so, without putting my rod together, I strolled on along the river-side, till I was several miles away from the Manor house.

The stream was rather low, but here and there were good deep pools, but so calm, so sunny, that every overhanging tree, every finger of fern, every blade of grass, was reflected in them as in a mirror. Still, as the time was, the waters were full of life. Over the pools hung clusters of flies like glittering spiders' webs, scarcely moving in the sunshine ; and when, from time to time, a trout rose, he leaped a full foot into the golden air above him, and sank back to coolness beneath an ever-widening ring of light. Sometimes from the grassy edge of the bank a water-rat would slip, swimming rapidly across, with his nose just lifted above the water, and his tail leaving a thin, bright trail. Water-ouzels rose at every curve, following swiftly the winding of the stream; and twice past my feet flashed a kingfisher, like an azure ray.

The way lay sometimes through deep grassy meadows, sometimes by the sides of corn-fields where the sheaves were already slanted, oftentimes through thick shrubberies and woods already yellow with the withering leaf. From time to time I passed a farm, with orchards sloping down to the very water's edge, or pastures slanting down to shallows where the cattle waded, breaking the water to silver streaks and whisking their tails against the clustering swarms of gnats. It was very pleasant and very still, but, from a fishing point of view, exceedingly absurd.

By-and-by, however, a faint breeze

began to touch the pools, and putting my rod together, and selecting my finest casting-line and two tiny flies, I tried a cast. Fortunately the wind was blowing sunward, and as I faced the light, the shadow fell behind me ; but, nevertheless, the shadow of my rod flitted about at every cast, and threatened to spoil my sport. My first catch was an innocent baby-fish as big as my thumb, who came at the fly with a rush, and fought desperately when hooked. When I had disengaged him, and put him back into the water, he simply gave a flip of his little tail, and sailed contemptuously and quite leisurely out of sight, making me call to mind, with unusual humiliation, the well-known definition which Dr. Johnson gave of angling—"a fish at one end of the line, and a fool at the other."

I had tried a good many casts before

I took my first respectable fish—a trout of about half a pound. I caught him in a nice broken bit of water, just below a quaint old water-mill; and just as I put him into the basket, the portly miller came out to the granary door, and looked at me with a dusty smile. He evidently thought me a lunatic, to be out with a fishing-rod on such a day.

Half a mile further on I landed another glittering picture of at least a quarter of a pound; after that, another of half a pound; then my luck ceased, the wind fell, and it was full sunshine. By this time I had wandered a good many miles from home, and reached the spot where the river plunges into the Great Omberley woods. Here the stream was so rapid and the boughs so thick, that it was useless to think of casting; so I put up my rod, and, leaping over a fence, rambled away into the woods.

How strange and dark and still it was, passing out of the sunshine into those shadows, deep and cool as the bottom of the sea! The oak trees stretched their gnarled boughs into the air, and all around them were the lesser trees of the wood-willow, elder, black-thorn, ash, and hazel. The ground beneath was carpeted with moss and grass as thick and soft as velvet, with thick clusters of fern and blue-bells round the tree roots, and creepers dangling from every bough. And the wood, like the river, was all alive! Conies tumbled across the patches of light, and flitted in the shadow, like very elves of the woodland; squirrels ran up the gnarled tree trunks; harmless silver snakes glided along the moss; but here and there, swift and ominous, ran a weazel, darting its head this way and that, and fiercely scenting the air, in one eternal glutter and hurry of bloodthirsty emotion. Thrush, blackbird, finch, birds without number, sang overhead; save when the shadow of the wind-hover or the sparrow-hawk passed across the topmost branches, when there was a sudden and respectful silence, to be followed by a precipitate hurry of exultation, as the enemy passed away.

If I had been a moralist, I might have seen in this wood a microcosm of the world, with its abundant happiness, its beauty, and its dark spots of moral ugliness and cruelty. In you, Signor Weazel (who came so near that I touched you with my rod, which you snapped at ferociously, before bolting swiftly into the deep grass), I might have seen the likeness of a certain sleek creature of my own sex and species, who dwells not very far away. Nevertheless, I let you go in peace ; which was no mercy to the conies, I suppose.

So I entered the Forest Primæval—or such it seemed to me, as the blaze of sunshine faded, the boughs thickened, the air became full of dark shadows and ·ominous silence. My steps were now deep in grass and fern, and the scent of flowers and weeds was thick in my nostrils, but I chose a path where the boughs were thinnest, and quietly pushed through. While thus I rambled, I suppose that I fell, philosopher like, into a dream ; at any rate, I seemed to lose all count of time.

> " The world, the life of men, dissolved away
> Into a sense of dimness,"

as some poet sings. I felt primæval—

archetypal so to speak, till a sudden
shifting of the vegetable kaleidoscope
recalled from thoughts of Plato and the
Archetype to a cruel consciousness of
self.

I was moving slowly on, when I heard
the sound of voices quite close to me.
I paused, listening, and only just in time,
for in another moment I should have
been visible to the speakers. Well
shrouded in deep foliage, I looked out to
discover what sylvan creatures were dis-
porting themselves in that lonely place;
and I saw—what shall I say? A
nymph and a satyr? a dryad and a goat-
footed Faun?

Just beyond me, there was a broad
green road through the woodland, deeply
carpeted with soft grass, but marked
here and there with the broad track of
a wood-waggon; and on the side of this

solitary road, on a rude seat fashioned of two oaken stumps and a rough plank, the nymph was sitting. She wore a light dress of some soft material, a straw hat, a country cloak, and gloves of Paris kid—a civilized nymph, as you perceive! To complete her modern appearance, she carried a closed parasol, and a roll which looked like music.

How pretty she looked, with the warm light playing upon her delicate features, and suffusing her form in its delicate drapery; with the semi-transparent branches behind her, and flowers of the woodland at her feet!

CHAPTER XXVII.

THE NOTE-BOOK CONTINUED—NYMPH
AND SATYR.

AND the satyr ?   Ah ! I knew him at a
glance, despite the elegant modern **boots**
used to disguise the **cloven foot.**

He wore black broadcloth **and snowy**
linen, too, and a broad-brimmed **clerical**
hat.   His face was seraphically **pale,**
but I saw (or fancied I saw) **the twinkle**
of the hairy ears of the ignoble, sensual, nymph-compelling, naiad-pursuing
breed.

He was talking earnestly, with gestures of eager entreaty ; for the **nymph**

was crying, and he was offering her some kind of consolation.

Presently he sat down by her side, and threw his arms around her. She disengaged herself from his embrace, and rose trembling to her feet.

" Don't touch me ! " she cried. " That is all over now. I cannot bear it ! "

He rose also, and stood regarding her, not with the rapturous eyes of a lover, but with a dark and gloomy gaze. Then he said, in a low voice, something which I could not catch. But I heard her passionate reply.

" No, it is all over," she cried ; " and I shall never be at peace again. Even if you kept your word, it would be the same. You do not love me ; you never loved me—never ! "

I crept a little closer, for I was anxious to hear his answer.

"I do love you, Edith; and after what has passed between us——"

She shrank away with a faint, despairing cry, and put her hand to her face.

"After what has passed between us, do you think that my love can change? But you are unjust to me, to yourself; too violent and too hard to please. I do not like to be suspected, to be watched; and it is painful to me, very painful, to be constantly called to an account by you. It is not reasonable. Even as your husband, I would not bear it; it would poison the peace between us, and convert our married life into a simple hell!"

He paused; but her only answer was a sob of pain. So he sermonized on:

"Between man and woman, Edith, there should be solemn confidence and trust. When that ceases, love is sure to cease. Why, look at me ! My trust in you is so absolute that no action of yours could shake it ; no matter how peculiar were the circumstances, I should be certain of your faith, your goodness. That is true love — absolute, implicit faith in the beloved object. I wish I could persuade you to imitate it."

"You know that you can trust me," sobbed the poor child, "because I have *proved* my love."

" Have I not proved mine ? " he cried, with irritation. " Have I not made sacrifice upon sacrifice for your sake ? Have I not remained here, in this wretched country place, when I could have been promoted to other and greater spheres of action ? Have I not made you my companion, my confidante, my nearest and dearest friend ? Edith, why do you persist in such accusations? What must I do to signify our attachment? Shall I marry you at once? Speak the word, and although, as you know, it would involve the ruin of all my worldly projects, I will do as you desire."

I had heard enough to convince me that the affair under discussion was no affair of mine, and that I had no right to continue playing the spy; so I was drawing back as gently as possible, and about to return the way I came, when I was suddenly arrested by the next words spoken.

"Give up Mrs. Haldane!"

The nymph was the speaker. She stood with her wild eyes fixed upon the other's face, which did not improve in beauty of expression. For myself, I started, stung to the quick; then I returned, trembling, to my place of espionage.

"Give up Mrs. Haldane!" repeated the girl. " I ask nothing more than that. I will not force you to marry me, Charles, till it is for your good ; indeed, if I did, I know that we should be unhappy, and that you would never forgive me. But you can at least cease to be so familiar with Mrs. Haldane."

He had discovered by this time, I suppose, that the pleading mood availed him little ; at all events, he suddenly changed his tone, and with a cry of angry indignation, he exclaimed—

" Edith, take care ! I have told you that I will not suffer it ! How dare you suspect that lady ! How dare you ! "

And he stood towering over her (the satyr !) in the fulness of his snowy shirt-front and the whiteness of his moral indignation.

"It is no use being angry," she returned, with a certain stubbornness, though I could see that she was cowed, in the manner of gentle women, by his violent physical passion. "After what you have told me, after what I have seen—— "

"Edith, again, take care!"

"You are always with her," she continued, "night-time and day-time. I am amazed that Mr. Haldane does not notice it. It is the talk of the place."

With another exclamation, he turned his back and walked rapidly away.

"Come back!" she cried hysterically. "If you leave like that, I will drown myself in the river."

He returned and faced her.

" You will drive me mad ! " he said. " I am sick of it. I am more like a slave than a free man. You will not suffer me even to have a friend."

" She is more than a friend. You have told me yourself, that you loved her."

"And so I did," he answered, "though of course she is nothing to me *now*."

" Why are you always with her ? "

" I am interested in her, deeply interested. She is unhappy with her husband, and as a minister of the gospel—— "

With her tearful, truthful eyes, fixed so earnestly upon him, no wonder he paused and blushed.

" Charles, do not be a hypocrite ! At least be honest. She is more to you than a friend."

He raised his hands heavenward, in pulpit fashion, and protested.

"Edith, I swear to you before God, that there is nothing whatever between us. She is a stainless lady, her husband does not understand her, I am her spiritual friend and guide."

"Yes, Charles ; I understand," she said, still earnestly watching him. *"Just as you were mine!"*

I think it worth while to put that little sentence in italics. It was a home stroke, and took away the satyr's breath.

"Edith, for shame!" he cried. "You know you do not mean what you say. If I thought you meant it, I should break with you for ever. I tell you again, Mrs. Haldane is above reproach, and it is simply disgraceful to couple her name, in such a manner, with mine. And you would infer, now, that I have influenced your own life for evil; you would mock at my spiritual pretensions, and brand me as a base, unworthy creature. Well, Edith, perhaps you are right. Perhaps I have given you cause. I have shown you that I love you, beyond position, beyond the world, beyond even my own self-respect, and this is my return."

I could have sprung out and strangled the fellow, he was so cruel and yet so plausible, so superbly selfish and yet so completely self-deceiving; and I saw that with every word he uttered he gained a fresh hold over the heart of the pretty fool who was listening. While he spoke, she sobbed as if her little heart was ready to break; and when he ceased, she eagerly held out her arms.

"Oh, Charles, don't say that! Don't say that my love has been a curse to you!"

"You drive me to say it," he answered moodily; "you make me miserable with your jealousy, ycur suspicion."

"Don't say that I make you miserable—don't!" she sobbed.

"You used to be so different," he continued, still preserving his tone of moral injury; "you used to be so interested in my work, my daily duties. Now, you do nothing but reproach me; and why? Because I have found an old friend, who happens to be of your own sex, but who is far above the folly of a meaningless flirtation, and who little deserves the cruel slur you cast upon her. Am I, then, to have no friends, no acquaintances? Is every step I take to be measured by the unreasoning suspicion of a jealous woman?"

By this time she had put her arms

about his neck, and was sobbing on his breast.

" Oh, Charles, don't be so hard with me ! It is all because I love you— ah, so much ! "

" But you should conquer these wicked feelings—— "

" I try ! I try ! "

" You should have more confidence, more faith. You know how much I care for you."

" Yes ; but sometimes I feel afraid. Mrs. Haldane is so much cleverer, so much more beautiful, than I am, and she was your first love. They say men never love twice."

" That is nonsense, Edith."

" But you do love me, dear ? you do ? "

Ugh, the satyr ! He answered her with kisses, straining her to his heart ;

and she, sobbing and clinging round him, was quite conquered. I felt sick to see her at his mercy. Then their voices sank, and he whispered, and I saw the bright blood mount to her cheek and brow. But, alas! she did not shrink away any more.

Thus whispering and kissing, with eyes of passion fixed upon one another, they moved away, taking a lonely path into the woods beyond me. My first impulse was to follow them, and to tear them asunder. But after all, I reflected it was no affair of mine, and I knew now, moreover, that nothing in the world would save her from him—or from herself.

END OF VOL. II.

PRINTED BY WILLIAM CLOWES AND SONS, LIMITED,
LONDON AND BECCLES.

FOXGLOVE MANOR

FOXGLOVE MANOR

A Novel

BY

ROBERT BUCHANAN

AUTHOR OF

"GOD AND THE MAN," "THE SHADOW OF THE SWORD,"
"THE NEW ABELARD," ETC.

IN THREE VOLUMES

VOL. III.

London

CHATTO AND WINDUS, PICCADILLY

1884

CONTENTS OF VOL. III.

FOXGLOVE MANOR.

CHAPTER XXVIII.

A MONKISH TALE (FROM THE NOTE-BOOK).

Sunday, Sept. 19.—My wife has gone to church.

I can hear the bells ringing in the distance as I write. . . . Now they cease, and at this very moment the clergyman, " snowy-banded, delicate-handed," is ascending the pulpit stairs, amid the reverent hush of his congregation.

Though several times of late she has suggested that a little church-going would do me good, Ellen did not ask me to accompany her on this occasion; indeed, I thought at first that she was going to stay at home herself. At breakfast she was irritable and absent-minded, and she did not dress or order the carriage until the last moment. There was evidently a hard struggle in her mind whether she should go to church or not. Ultimately, she decided to go.

Out of this and other unpleasant indications, I have made a discovery. My wife, despite her purity, despite her lofty sense of honour, is *jealous* of the clergyman.

The day after my fishing expedition, I quietly told her what I had seen in the woodland. It was not without due deliberation that I determined to do so. One portion of the truth, however, I carefully concealed : namely, the references made by the lovers to herself. For the same reason, I showed no sign of personal suspicion, but treated the affair lightly, as a thing of indifference.

I began the conversation in this way, while beating the shell of my second egg at breakfast—

" By the way, my dear Nell, I have made a discovery."

She looked up and smiled unsuspiciously. " Something terrible, I suppose ; like Dr. Dupré's elixir ? "

" Oh dear no, nothing nearly so scientific ; a mere social discovery, my dear. I have found out that I was right ; that if your pet parson is not married, he ought to be."

I saw her change colour ; but, bending her head over her teacup, she forced a laugh.

" What nonsense you're talking ! "

" Don't call it nonsense till you hear my story. It will interest you, being quite piscatorial and idyllic. Conceive to yourself, first, the primæval woodland ; then two figures, a nymph in a frock and a satyr in a clerical coat. The nymph, your friend Miss Dove ; the satyr, your other friend, Mr. Santley. She was crying ; he consoling. I heard their conversation ; I saw them quarrel, make it up, embrace, kiss, and disappear. I think you will agree with me that so pretty a pastoral should have, in a moral country, but one sequel—marriage."

How white and strange she seemed ! How nervously she fought with her agitation !

" I don't believe a word of what you say ! " she cried. " You saw all this, but how ? "

I told her how, and she uttered a cry of virtuous indignation.

"It is shameful!" she exclaimed. "I will never speak to him again— never!"

"On the contrary, I think you *should* speak to him, and, like a true match-maker, produce the *dénouement*. You need not tell him that I played Peeping Tom; but, without doing so, you can act on the information I have given you. After all, if he really loves the girl—— "

"But he does *not* love her!"

She paused, trembling and flushing, conscious of her blunder.

"Then is he a greater scoundrel than even I suspected!"

"There must be some mistake. I am sure Mr. Santley would do nothing dishonourable. As to marrying, his

ideas are those of the High Church.
He does not think that a priest has any
right to marry."

I looked at her in amazement. After
what I had told her, could she possibly
be attempting to justify him ? If so, the
case was worse than I had foreseen,
and her moral sense had already been
effectually poisoned. She continued
rapidly and eagerly, as if contending
in argument with her own thoughts.

" A clergyman's position is very difficult. If he is unmarried, as a true priest
should be, he is persecuted by all the
marriageable girls of his parish. His
slightest attentions are misconstrued, his
most innocent acts exaggerated ; and
if he shows a friendly interest in any
young person, he is sure to be misunder-
stood. I have no doubt, after all, that
what you saw could be easily explained :

and that, in any case, Miss Dove is the person really to blame."

I was right, then : justification, and —jealousy.

"You forget," I answered quickly, "that I heard the whole conversation. Besides, though the language of words may be distorted, that of kisses and embraces is unmistakable."

"He did not kiss her; he did not embrace her ! I will never believe it."

"Then, you simply assume that I am stating an untruth ?"

"I know how glad you are," she cried passionately, "to put this slur upon him."

With some difficulty I mastered my indignation. Sick of the discussion, I rose and prepared to leave the room ; but before leaving I spoke, with cold decision, to the following effect :—

" I have told you precisely what I saw; it is for you to impeach my motives, if you please, and to think, in your infatuation, that I dislike Mr. Santley because of the cloth he wears. If you doubt me, question the girl; you can possibly get the truth from her. In any case, remember that, from this moment, I forbid you to entertain that man in my house."

So I left her, leaving my words to work.

The next day, *i.e.* yesterday, Santley called. She did not see him, but sent out a message that she was engaged. I saw him creeping, pale and crestfallen, past my laboratory door.

Since the conversation recorded above, Ellen and I have not alluded to the subject ; indeed, we have seen little of each other, and spoken still less. Possibly our temporary estrangement might account for the fixed pallor, the cold look of sorrow and reproach, on my wife's face; but I am inclined to fear otherwise. At all events, the thing had gone so far, and I knew so much, that the overtures to reconciliation could not come from me. I had to conquer my struggling tenderness, and watch.

The great struggle came this morning. I observed it with sickening suspense. Had honest indignation conquered, had Ellen held to her first decision of not returning into that man's church, I think I should have taken her into my arms and begged her pardon for suspecting her. But no! she has gone; not, I am sure, to pray. Surely I am a model husband, to sit so tamely here!

Sunday Evening.—She drove home immediately after morning service, and

I saw by the expression of her face that she was greatly agitated. We lunched in silence, and afterwards she took a volume of sermons and sat reading on the terrace. Later on in the afternoon, while I sat writing alone, she came in behind me, and before I could speak, put her arms around my neck and kissed me.

"Forgive me," she cried, with her beautiful eyes full of tears. "Oh, George, I am so unhappy! I cannot bear to quarrel."

And she knelt by my side, looking pitifully up into my face.

I returned her kiss, and for the time being, in her soft embrace, forgot my suspicions. It was a happy hour! Neither of us spoke of the subject of our disagreement.

Tuesday.—After a temporary calm,

the storm has again broken, and the weather is still charged with thunder. Let me try to record calmly what has taken place.

This afternoon, as I sat at work, Baptisto entered quietly.

" I think you are wanted, señor ; there is some one here."

" What do you mean ?   Who is it ? "

" The clergyman, señor.   He is with my lady."

I started angrily ; then, conquering myself, I demanded—

" Did they send you for me ? "

" No, señor," replied Baptisto, with his mysterious look; " but I thought you would like to know."

I could have struck the fellow, for I saw that he had been playing the spy. Nevertheless, I remembered that I had forbidden Ellen to entertain Santley again at the Manor, and I felt my indignation rapidly rising at the thought of her disobedience. Angry and humiliated, I rose to my feet.

"Where are they?" I asked.

"In the drawing-room, señor."

I at once went thither, uncertain what to say or do; for I was determined, if possible, not to make a scene. Now, the great drawing-rooms of the Manor house consist of two old-fashioned apartments, communicating with a curtained archway, where there was once a folding-door. The inner room opens on a lobby communicating with the house; the outer opens on the terrace. I approached from within, and finding the door open, entered softly. No one was visible; but I heard voices whispering in the outer room.

After a moment's hesitation, I sat

down in an armchair, and took up a book from the table. My back was to the curtained archway, and facing me was a large mirror, in which the archway and the dimly lighted, rose-coloured chamber beyond were clearly reflected.

The whispering continued.

I could bear the suspense no longer, and was about to rise and make my presence known, when the voices were raised, and I heard the clergyman exclaim—

"Ellen, for God's sake! I can explain everything!"

Ellen! My satyr was familiar. I crouched in my armchair, listening, as my wife replied—

"Why should you explain to me? I have no wish to listen, Mr. Santley. Only I am shocked and indignant at what I have heard."

" But there is not one word of truth in it. Who is your informant? I demand to know his name."

I strained my ears in suspense, wondering how she would reply, for I already guessed the bearings of the conversation. To my surprise, she replied parabolically—

" It is the common talk of the place."

" Then it is a simple scandal!"

" You are not engaged to Miss Dove?"

" Certainly not. She herself can tell you that there is nothing of the kind between us. I will admit freely that she has a great esteem for me—that, in short, she is attached to me; and that possibly, if I desired it, she would marry me."

There was a silence. Then I heard Ellen say, quietly and firmly—

" Will you answer me a question?"

"Certainly."

"Did you meet Miss Dove alone, last Thursday?"

I felt that her eyes were fixed upon his face as she put the question, and I guessed how it startled and amazed him; but he was unabashed, and replied instantly—

"Where?"

She waited a moment, like one pausing to give the *coup de grâce*, before she said—

"Close to the river-side, among Lord ——'s plantations."

Greatly to my astonishment, for I naturally expected a denial, the answer came at once, in a clear, decided voice.

"Yes, I did meet her."

I could imagine, though I could not see, my wife's start of virtuous indignation. Almost instantly, I saw her image in the mirror before me, as she

rapidly crossed the room beyond; then
he followed, black-suited, like the devil.
In the dim distance of the mirror, I now
saw their two figures reflected, floating
faintly in the rose-coloured light beyond
the curtains.   Their backs were turned
to me, their faces were looking out upon
the terrace.

"I have nothing to conceal," he continued passionately.   "Some enemy has
been spying upon me; but I repeat, I
have nothing to conceal.   Only, I wished
to spare Miss Dove.   Now that you
have made reserve impossible, I will
admit, frankly, that she has misconstrued
certain harmless attentions, and that, on
the day you mention, she came upon me
by accident, and reproached me for my
coldness, my want of sympathy.   She
even went further, and asked me to
marry her.   I tell you this in sacred

confidence, for I have no right to inform others of the young lady's indiscretion."

"Was that all that passed ?"

"All, I assure you."

Ellen gave a peculiar laugh, the sound of which I did not like at all. There is nothing more significant than a woman's light laugh—nothing, sometimes, more horrible.

"She was reproachful, and you—consoled her ?"

"Consoled her ?"

"As a true lover should,—with kisses and embraces ? You see, I know everything!"

"It is a calumny," cried the clergyman, with seeming indignation. "True, I was gentle with her, for I felt very sorry. I reasoned and remonstrated with the foolish child : after all, she is a child only. Oh, Ellen, how could you listen to such an accusation? You who know that there is but one woman in the world who has my love, my life's devotion, and that *you* are that woman."

Did my eyes deceive me, or had he stretched out an arm to embrace her? No, I was right!

"Take away your arm!" she cried. "I will not suffer it!"

She did suffer it, notwithstanding.

"Ellen! dearest Ellen!"

He drew her towards him, and I thought she was going to yield to his embrace; but she shook herself free, and in a moment, before he knew her purpose, had opened the window and glided out upon the terrace. He followed her with a cry, and so—my mirror was empty. I rose to my feet, sick and dazed with what I had seen, and prepared to follow.

What should I do? Should I at once avow my knowledge of what had taken place, and seize my satyr by the throat; or, smiting him in the face, fling him from my door? Should I stand by tamely, and see my hearth violated, my wife tempted, by a common snake of the parish? If I had been less angry with my wife herself, I am sure I should have taken the violent course. But I saw now, to my horror, that she was neither adamantine nor marble. She had allowed him to know his evil power upon her, and to see that the knowledge of his power over another woman, so far from shocking and repulsing her, had increased the fascination. If I denounced him openly, it would be to admit his rivalry, and, by inference, to complete her degradation.

Fortunately, I have been accustomed,

from youth upward, to control my strongest feelings, whether of tenderness or anger; and though I am capable enough of strong passion, I have generally the power to disguise it. In the present emergency, I found my habit of self-restraint stand me in good stead. I advanced into the outer room. By the time I had reached it, I was calm and cool to all outward appearances.

Quite quietly, I approached the window, and gazed out upon the terrace.

There they stood, he talking eagerly, she with face averted from him, and looking my way. She saw me in a moment, and started in agitation. I nodded grimly, and opening the folding windows, looked out. Then, all at once, I drew back apologetically.

"Ah, there you are!" I said to my wife. "I was looking for you."

She stepped over to the window, looking strangely pale and scared. I had not even looked at, much less addressed, her companion; but he approached, with a ghastly smile.

"I'm afraid I interrupt you," I continued. "Some religious business, I suppose? Shall I retire till it is settled?"

He looked at me doubtfully; but Ellen immediately replied—

"Do not go away. Mr. Santley is just leaving."

Still preserving my *sang froid*, I sat down in one of the garden seats on the terrace, and opened the book which I had lifted at random from the drawing-room table. Curiously enough, it was a work which is rather a favourite of mine, one of Sebastiano's "Tales in Verse." I knew the thing, particularly the passage on which the page had opened, and which, strange to say, had a certain reference to the present situation.

"Pray proceed with your talk," I said. "I have something here to amuse me, till you have done."

So I sat reading, or pretending to read. I did not even glance up, but I felt that they were looking uneasily at one another. There was a long pause. At last I lifted my eyes.

"I'm sure I'm in the way," I said; and rose as if to go.

"No, no!" cried Ellen, more and more uneasy at my manner, which I'm afraid was ominous. "We were only discussing some foolish village matters, on which Mr. Santley wished to have my advice."

"Very well," I replied. Then, turning to Santley, I inquired quietly, "Do you read Spanish?"

He shook his head.

"That's a pity," I continued. "Otherwise, you might have been much amused by this little work, written by a priest like yourself, though not quite of your persuasion."

"Is it a tale?" asked Ellen, bending over me.

"Yes; one of old Sebastiano's 'Tales in Verse.' Its author, I may tell you, was a Castilian monk, who abandoned the Church for the heretical pursuit of story-writing, and took 'Sebastiano' as a pseudonym. The story I am reading here is considered, by many, his masterpiece. The verse is assonantic throughout, the subject——"

Here my satyr could not forbear a gesture of impatience and irritation.

"I'm afraid I bore you, sir," I said, smiling. "Your tastes are not literary, I fear?"

"I seldom read fiction," he answered. "I consider it too trivial, and a waste of time."

"Do you really think so? I grant you, if the work is not of a truly moral nature, like the present. As I was going to tell you, the subject of this story, or tragedy in narrative, is edifying in the extreme. There was once in Castile a parish priest, an exceedingly handsome fellow, who, in a moment of impulse, fell deeply in love with a Spanish lady."

There was no need to look up now. I felt that they were both fascinated, not knowing what was to come. Ellen's hand was on my chair, which vibrated with the violent beating of her heart.

"Very prettily does Sebastiano describe the course of this amour. The priest's first struggles to resist temptation, his frequent fastings and spiritual

purgings, his growing desperation, his
final yielding to the spell. To be brief,
he at last spoke to her, avowed his
passion, and flung himself, despairing
and imploring, at her feet."

" And she ? " asked Ellen, in a voice
so low that I scarcely heard her.

" Oh, the story says but little of her
answer, though doubtless it was to the
purpose, as the sequel proves. They
understood one another, and might
doubtless have been happy, but for one
unfortunate impediment, which both had
forgotten. The lady had—a *husband !* "

Ah, that frightened, beating heart !
how it leapt and struggled, as the little
hand still clutched my chair ! I just
glanced up, and meeting my gaze, she
made an appealing gesture ; for she
began to understand. As for him, he
stood pale and sullen, scowling at me

with his seraphic face, and as yet imperfectly comprehending.

"A husband!" I repeated, turning over a leaf. "He, poor devil, was an alchemist, a dreary, doting seeker for the elixir of immortal life, and they thought him—blind. In this they were mistaken. As the poor flat flounder on the bottom of the sea, lying half buried and invisible in the sand and mud, still with its watery jelly of an eye surveys the liquid welkin overhead, so he, our alchemist, was marking much in silence. Well, sir, the thing grew, till at last, out of that obscure laboratory where the dreamer toiled there came a thunderbolt. One fine morning the lady was found—dead!"

"Dead!"

They both echoed the word involuntarily.

"Yes; but the curious part of the affair has yet to be told. They found her lying, as if sleeping, in her bed; so sweet, so quiet, so peaceful, no one in the world would have dreamed that she had been destroyed by a malignant poison. Such, however, was the case."

Santley buttoned his coat, and moved nervously towards the door.

"A horrible story!" he said. "I detest these tales of violence and murder. Besides, though I am not a Roman Catholic, I look upon such rubbish as a calumny upon the Christian Church."

I smiled.

"The Church's history, I am afraid, offers endless corroborations."

"I do not believe it; and I hold that the Church should be saved from such attacks."

" Pardon me," I persisted ; while Ellen's hand was softly laid upon my shoulder, as if beseeching me to cease, " the Church may be sacred, but so, you will admit, is the marriage tie. For myself, I am old-fashioned enough to sympathize with that poor alchemist, and applaud his rough-and-ready mode of vengeance."

" Then you justify a cowardly murder ? " he returned, trembling violently. " But, there, I must really go."

" Pardon me, I don't call it murder at all."

" Not murder ? " he ejaculated.

" No, sir ; righteous vengeance. Were such a state of things possible *now*— though, of course, wives are now all pure, and priests all immaculate — I should recommend the same remedy. What, *must* you go ? Well, good day ;

and pray excuse a scholar's warmth. Actually, as I discussed that old monkish nonsense, I almost thought it *real*."

He forced a feeble laugh, and then, with one long look at my wife, and a murmured "Good afternoon" to us both, retreated through the drawing-room doors. I sat still, as if intent on my book.

The moment he had gone, Ellen caught me wildly by the arm.

"George! look at me—speak to me!"

"Well?" I said, looking up quietly.

"What does it mean? Why did you tell that wild tale? You did not do it without a purpose."

"Certainly not."

She stood pale as death, clasping her hands together.

"You did not think—you could not, dare not—that—— "

"That what, pray?" I demanded coldly, seeing that she paused.

"That you suspect — that you can believe—that——"

She paused again; then she added pleadingly—

"Oh, George, you would never do me such a wrong!"

"I have done you no wrong," I replied. "You, on the other hand, have disobeyed me?"

"How?"

"I forbade you to entertain that man in my house."

"He came unexpectedly. Indeed, indeed, I wish he had not come."

She looked so pretty and so despairing, that I should have straightway forgiven her, had I not suddenly called to mind the conversation in the drawing-room. Women are strange creatures.

At that moment, I am certain she fervently believed that she was innocent, and I cruel. And yet . . . I knew, by her humility and by her sorrow, that she partially reproached herself for having awakened my anger.

"Let there be an end to this," I said. "You must never speak to that man again."

"Never speak to him!" she repeated imploringly. "But he is our clergyman, and if I break with him there will be a scandal. Indeed, George, he is not as bad as you think him. He is very earnest and impetuous, but he is good and noble."

"What! do you defend him?"

She did not reply.

"You must choose between him and me; between the man whom you know to be a hypocrite, and the man who is your husband.   If he comes here again, I shall deal with him in my own fashion ; remember that!   I spared him to-day, because I thought him too contemptible for any kind of violence.   But I know his character, and you know it ; that is enough.   I shall not warn you again."

With these words, I walked to my den.   There, once alone, I gave way to my overmastering agitation.   I found myself trembling like a leaf ; looking in a mirror, I saw that I was pale as a ghost.

An hour passed thus.   Then I heard a knock at the door.

Enter Baptisto.

"Well, what do you want ? " I cried, angrily enough.

Before I knew it he was on his knees, seizing and kissing my hand.

"Señor,   I   know   everything ! "   he

cried. " I have known it all along. That was why I remained at home when you were away—to watch, to play the spy. Señor, give me leave ! Let me avenge you ! "

I shook him off with an oath, for I hated the fellow's sympathy.

" You fool," I said, " I want no one to play the spy for me. Stop, though ! What do you mean ? What would you like to do ? "

In a moment he had sprung to his feet, and flashed before my eyes one of those long knives that Spaniards carry. His eyes flashed with homicidal fire.

" I would plunge *this* into his heart ! "

I could not help laughing,—a little furiously.

" Put up that knife, you idiot ! Put it up, I say ! This is England, not

Spain, and here we manage matters very differently. And now, let me have no more of this nonsense. Be good enough to go about your business."

He yielded almost instantly to my old mastery over him, and, with a respectful bow, withdrew. So ended the curious events of the day. I have set them down in their order as they occurred. I wonder if this is the last act of my little domestic drama? If not, what is to happen next? Well, we shall soon see.

CHAPTER XXIX.

HUSH-MONEY.

MRS. HALDANE had not exaggerated when, in her cross-examination of the vicar, she had described his intimate friendship to Miss Dove as the common talk of the parish. There beats about the life of an English clergyman a light as fierce, in its small way, as that other light which, according to the poet,

> " . . . beats about the throne,
> And blackens every blot ! "

Charles Santley was very much mistaken if he imagined that his doings altogether escaped scandal. As usual, however, the darkest suspicions and ugliest innuendoes were reserved for the lady ; and before very long Edith Dove was the subject of as pretty a piece of scandal as ever exercised the gossips of even an English village.

Now, the thing was a long time in the air before it reached the ears of the person most concerned. Tongues wagged, fingers pointed, all the machinery of gossip was set in motion for months before poor Edith had any suspicion whatever. Gradually, however, there came upon her the consciousness of a certain social change. Several families with which she had been on intimate terms showed, by signs unmistakable, their desire to avoid her visits, and their determination not to return them. One virtuous spinster, on whom she had expended a large amount of sympathy, not to speak of tea and sugar, openly cut her one morning at the post-office ; and even the paupers of the village showed in their bearing a certain lessening of that servility which, in the mind of a properly constituted British pauper, indicates respect. Things were becoming ominous, when, late one evening, her aunt boldly broached the subject.

Edith had taken her hat and cloak, and was going out, when the old lady spoke.

"Where are you going so late ? I hope—not down to the Vicarage ? "

Edith turned in astonishment.

"Yes, I am going there," she replied.

"Then listen to my advice : take off your things and stay at home."

The tone was so decided, the manner so peculiar, that Edith was startled in

spite of herself.   Before she could make
any remark, her aunt continued—

"Sit down and listen to me.   I mean
to talk to you, for no one has a better
right; and if I can put a stop to your
folly, I will.   Do you know the whole
place is talking of you—that it has been
talking of you for months?   Yes, Edith,
it is the truth; and I am bound to say
you yourself are the very person to
blame."

Almost mechanically, Edith took off
her hat and threw it on the table.   Then
she looked eagerly at her aunt.

"What do they say about me?" she
cried.

"They say you are making a fool of
yourself; but that is not all.   They say
worse—horrible things.   Of course I
know they are untrue, for you were
always a good girl; but you are some-

times so indiscreet. When a young girl is always in the company of a young man, even a clergyman, and nothing comes of it, people will talk. Take my advice, dear, and put an end to it at once !"

Edith smiled—a curious, far-off, bitter smile. She was not surprised at her aunt's warning ; for she had expected it a long time, and had been rather surprised that it had not come before.

" Put an end to what ? " she said quietly. " I don't know what you mean."

" You know well enough, Edith."

" Indeed I do not. If people talk, that is their affair ; but I shall do as I please."

And she took up her hat again, as if to go.

" Edith, I insist ! You shall *not* go

out to-night. It is shameful for Mr.
Santley to encourage you! If you only
knew how people talk! You are not
engaged to Mr. Santley, and I tell you
it is a scandal!"

Edith flushed nervously, as she replied—

"There is no scandal, aunt! Mr.
Santley——"

"I have no patience with him. In
a minister of the gospel, it is disgraceful."

"What is disgraceful?"

"The encouragement he gives you,
when he knows he has no intention of
marrying you."

"How do you know that?" said Edith
again, with that far-off curious smile.

"He has not even proposed; you are
not engaged? If you were, it would
be different."

With a quiet impulse of tenderness, Edith bent over her aunt and kissed her. The old lady looked up in surprise, and saw that her niece's eyes were full of tears.

" Edith, what is it? What do you mean ? "

" That we have been engaged a long time."

" And you did not tell me ? "

" He did not want it known, and even now it is a secret. You must promise to tell no one."

" But why ? There is nothing to be ashamed of."

" It is his wish," said the girl, gently.

Then kissing her aunt again, and leaving her much relieved in mind, she went away, strolling quietly in the direction of the Vicarage. As she walked, her tears continued to fall, and her face was very sorrowful; for there lay upon her spirit a heavy shadow of terror and distrust. With how different an emotion had she, only a year before, flown to meet the man she loved! How eagerly and gladly, *then*, he had awaited her coming! And *now*? Alas, she did not even know if she would find him at all. Sometimes he seemed to avoid her, to be weary of her company. All was so changed, she reflected, since the Haldanes came home to the Manor. He was no longer the same, and she herself was different. Would it ever end? Would she ever be happy again?

The shadows of night were falling as she walked through the lanes, with her eyes sadly fixed on the dim spire of the village church. Close to a plantation on the roadside, she encountered a woman and a man in conversation. She recog-

nized the woman at a glance, as Sal
Bexley, the black sheep of the parish,
who got her living by singing from one
public-house to another; and she had
passed by without a word, when a voice
called her.

" Here, mistress ! "

She turned, and encountered a pair of
bold black eyes. Sal, the pariah, stood
facing her, swinging her old guitar and
grinning mischievously.

" I'm afraid you're growing proud,
mistress. You didn't seem to know
me."

There was something sinister in the
girl's manner. Edith drew aside, and
would have passed on without any reply,
but the other ran before her and blocked
the way.

" No, you don't go like that. I want
a word with thee, my fine lady. Ah,

you may toss your head, but you'd best bide a bit, and listen."

"What do you want? I cannot stay."

"No call to hurry," cried Sal, with a coarse laugh. "Thy man's out, and don't expect thee. Belike he's gone courting some one else. Ah, he's a rum chap, the minister, though he do set up for a saint."

Edith shuddered and shrank back.

"Go away," she said. "How dare you speak to me like that?"

"Dare? That's a good one! No, you shan't pass till I've done wi' thee."

Edith was getting positively frightened, for the girl's manner was so rude and threatening, when she saw a tall figure approaching, and in a moment recognized the clergyman. He was close to them, and paused in astonishment at seeing the two together.

"Miss Dove! Is anything the matter? Why are you here, so late, and in such company?"

He paused, looking suspiciously at Sal, who laughed impudently.

"I was passing by, and she stopped me. Do send her away!"

"Send me away?" cried the pariah. "I'll come when I please, and I'll go when I please. I'm as good as she."

Mr. Santley stepped forward, and placed his hand on her arm.

"What are you doing here? I thought you were far away."

"So I were; but I've come back. Well?"

"Remember what I told you. I will not have my parish disgraced any longer by your conduct. I have warned you repeatedly before. Where are you staying?"

" Down by the river-side, master. I've joined the gipsies, d'ye see."

"Always an outcast," said Santley, with a certain gloomy pity. " Will nothing reform you ?"

" No, master," answered the girl, grinning. " I'm a bad lot."

" I'm afraid you are."

" But mind this," she continued, with some vehemence, " there's others, fine ladies too, as bad as me. Though I like a chap, and ain't afraid to own it, and though I gets my living anyhow, I'm no worse than my betters, master. You've no cause to bully *me*, so don't try it on, master. I can speak when I like, and I can hold my tongue when I like. Gi' me a guinea, and I'll hold my tongue."

She held out her brown hand, leering up into his face.

"What do you mean ? " he exclaimed. "I shall give you no money."

She looked round at Edith, who stood by trembling.

"Tell him he'd best, mistress—for *thy* sake! Come, it's worth a guinea! There's many a folk hereabouts would gi' five, to see what I saw t'other day, down to Omberley wood."

Edith started in a new terror, while her face flushed scarlet and her head swam round. Santley winced, but preserving his composure, looked fixedly and sternly at the outcast.

"You're a bold hussy," he said, between his set teeth, "as bold as bad. But take care! Do you know that if I only say one word, I can have you up before the magistrates and sent back to prison?"

"What for?" snarled the girl.

" For vagrancy, begging, and threatening a lady on the roadside ! "

" A pretty lady.   And I bean't begging, neither.   Well, send me to prison, and when I'm up before the magistrates, I'll tell 'em why you were down upon me.   Come ! "

Santley was about to reply angrily, when Edith interposed.   Trembling and almost fainting, she had taken out her purse.

" Here is some   money," she cried ; " give it to her and let her go ! "

" She does not deserve a farthing," exclaimed Santley.   " Still, if you wish it——"

" Yes, yes !   I—I am sorry for her."

Santley opened the purse, and took out a sovereign.

" If I give you this, will you promise to go out of the parish ? "

" Maybe."

" And to conduct yourself properly—
to turn over a new leaf ? "

Sal grinned viciously from ear to
ear.

" I take example by you, master, and
your young lady there ! Leastways, if I
do go a-larking I'll be like you gentry,
and say naught about it. There, gi'
me the guinea ! Stop, though, make it
two, and I'll go away out o' Omberley
this very night."

Santley and Edith rapidly exchanged
a look, and a second piece of gold was
at once added to the first. Then, after
giving Sal a few words of solemn warning, in his priestly character, Santley
walked away with Edith. The pariah
girl watched them until they disappeared ; then, with a low laugh, she
rejoined her companion, a one-eyed and

middle-aged gipsy, who, during the preceding scene, had phlegmatically stretched himself on his back, along the roadside.

CHAPTER XXX.

"AND LO! WITHIN HER, SOMETHING LEAPT!"

SANTLEY and Edith walked along for some time without a word. At last, after looking round nervously to see that they were not observed or followed, the clergyman broke the silence.

"It is horrible! It is insufferable!" he cried. "I shall be ruined by your indiscretion."

She looked at him in amazement. It was too dark to see his face, but his whole frame, as well as his voice, trembled with anger.

"My indiscretion!" she echoed.

"Yes."

"But I have done nothing."

"I found you talking to that creature, and it is evident that she knows our secret. I shall be ruined through you. What have you told her?"

"Nothing. I met her by accident, and she spoke to me; that is all."

There was a pause. Then Santley stopped short, saying in a whisper—

"Go home now. After to-day we must not be seen together."

But she clung to his arm, weeping.

"Charles, for God's sake, do not be so unkind!"

"I am not unkind," he said; "but I am thinking of your good name, as well as of my own reputation. What that woman knows others must know. It will be the talk of the place. Edith, think of it. We shall both be lost. Go home, I entreat you."

"Charles, listen to me!" exclaimed the weeping girl. "If there is any scandal it will kill me. But there need to be none. You have only to keep your word, as you have promised, and then—— "

"What? and marry you?"

"Yes."

"I cannot—at least, not yet."

"Why not? Oh, Charles, have I not been patient? There is nothing but your own will to come between us. Make me your wife, as you have promised, before it is too late. Even my aunt begins to suspect something. My life is miserable—a daily falsehood. I have loved you next to God. For your sake I have even forgotten Him. I thought there was no sin; you yourself

told me there was no sin—that we were
man and wife in God's sight. But now
I am terrified. I cannot sleep, I cannot
pray. Sometimes I feel as if God had
cast me out. And you——"

She ceased, choked with tears, and,
placing her head upon his shoulder,
sobbed wildly. He shrank from her
touch, and sought to disengage himself,
gazing round on every side and searching
the darkness in dread of being watched.

"Control yourself. If we should be
seen!"

But she did not seem to hear, and his
anger increased in proportion to her
terror.

"Do you want to compromise me?"
he cried. "I begin to think you have
no discretion, no respect for yourself.
I hate these scenes. They make me
wish that we had never met."

"If I thought you wished that from your heart," she sobbed, "I would not live another day."

"There, again. You are so unreasonable, so violent. When I attempt to reason, you talk of suicide or some such mad thing. If you really loved me, as you say, you would be willing to make some sacrifice for my sake. But no; you have only one cry—marriage, marriage!—till I am sick of the very word. Cease crying. Dry your eyes, and listen to me. Go home tonight, and I will think it over. Yes, I will do what I can —anything, rather than be so tormented."

She obeyed him passively, and tried to stifle her deep sorrow. Child as she was, and loving him as she did, she could not bear his words of blame ; and her soul shuddered at the strange tones

of the voice that had once been so kind.
For it was as she had said. She had
made an idol of this man, next to God.
She had offered up to him, at his passionate request, her young life, her purity
of heart, her very soul. He had been
God's voice and very presence to her;
ah! so beautiful! She had been content
to lie at his feet, to obey him like a
slave, to accept his will as law, even
when the law seemed evil. And now
he was so changed. Not base—ah! no,
she could not bear to think him base;
not base—still good, but cruel. Was
she losing him? Was she destined to
lose him for ever, and, with him, surely
her immortal soul?

"Good night," she moaned "I will
go home."

And she held up her face for his kiss;
then, as he kissed her, she yielded again

to her emotion, and clung, wildly crying, about his neck.

"Oh, Charles, be true to me! I have no one in the world but you."

With that fond appeal she left him, turning her tearful face homeward. On reaching the cottage she found the door ajar, stole quietly up to her room, and locked herself in. A few minutes afterwards her aunt knocked.

"Are you there, Edith? Supper is ready."

"I have a headache, and am going to bed," she replied, stifling her sobs.

"May I not come in?" said the old lady. "I want to speak to you."

"Not to-night. I am so tired."

She heard the feeble feet descending the stairs, and again resigned herself to sorrow. Presently, when she had grown a little calmer, she arose, lit a candle, and

proceeded to undress.   The moon, which
had newly risen, shone through the
cottage window, with its white blinds,
and the faint rays, creeping in, mingled
with the yellow candle-light.   The room
was like a white rose, all pale and pure ;
and the girl herself, when she was un-
dressed and clad in her night-dress,
seemed the purest thing there.   But the
night-dress felt like a shroud, and she felt
ready for the grave.

She knelt by the bed to say her
prayers.

How long she remained on her knees
she knew not.   While her lips repeated,
half aloud, the prayers she had learned
as a child, and those which, in later
years, she had framed to include the
name of the man she loved, her tears
still fell, and with her long hair streaming
over her shoulders, and her little hands

clasped together, she sobbed and sobbed. The moonlight crept further into the room, and touched her like a silver hand —not tenderly, not pityingly ; nay, it might have been the very hand of the Madonna herself, bidding her arise to face her fate.

She arose shivering ; and at that very instant there came to her a warning, an omen, full of nameless terror. It seemed to her as if faces were flashing before her eyes, voices shrieking in her ears ; her heart leapt, her head went round, and at the same moment she felt her whole being miraculously thrilled by the quickening of a new life within her own.

With a loud moan, she fainted away upon the floor.

When she returned to consciousness, she was lying, nearly naked, by the bedside, and the moonlight was flooding the little room. She arose, dazed, stupefied, and appalled. Her limbs shook beneath her, and she had to clutch the bedstead for support. Then she tottered to the dressing-table, and holding the candle, looked into the mirror.

Reflected there was a face of ghastly whiteness, with two great despairing eyes, wildly gazing into her own.

CHAPTER XXXI.

A LAST APPEAL.

THE night had passed away, and the chilly light of dawn creeping into Edith's room, found her quietly sleeping. During that night, when the full horror of her situation had flashed for the first time upon her, she had passed through hours of agony similar to those which have turned pretty brown hair grey; then, overcome by a sense of thorough mental exhaustion, she had laid her head upon the pillow and slept.

She slept long and soundly.

When she opened her eyes she saw

that it was broad daylight; indeed, the
day was well spent, for her aunt, after
tapping gently at her door and receiving
no reply, had determined not to disturb
her rest.

Her first feeling on opening her eyes
was one of pleasure, such pleasure as is
felt by a young matron, when the knowledge of approaching maternity first
dawns upon her; but this feeling was
only momentary, and was succeeded in
this case by one of intense mental pain.

She lay for a time, thinking of the
past, and trying to penetrate the future.
She recalled her interviews with Santley;
the last interview which had taken place
only the night before. She remembered
with pleasure the promise he had made,
and she tried to think that all would yet
be well. Yes, even when he knew
nothing, he had yielded to her solici-

tations; and as soon as he *knew*—
for of course at their next meeting
she must tell him—he would not
hesitate for a single day. He had a
double duty now : not only had he to
save her reputation, he had to think of
the future of his child. He had said
that he would think it over ; that the
next day, this very day, she should hear
from him. He would appoint a meeting,
then when she saw him, if he still hesitated, she would tell him, and he would
hesitate no longer.

All that day Edith remained in the
house, pale, silent, but expectant. At
every sound she started and looked
anxiously towards the door ; but Mr.
Santley made no sign. At last, disappointed and heart-broken, she went up
to bed.

Several days passed thus. Edith

fearing to cross the threshold, shrinking in horror at the thought of meeting any of her fellow-creatures, moved about the house in pale, sad silence; expectant sometimes, at others crying her heart out in sickening despair. The suspense was terrible; and terrible too was the thought of having to bear her secret sorrow entirely alone. If she could only see him, tell him, feel his passionate kiss, and hear his whispered words of comfort, her trouble, she thought, would be lightened by one half. Never had she needed him so much; yet never, she thought, had she seemed so utterly alone.

And with this hopeless dread upon her, this sense of mental agony which seemed to be wearing her very life away, she waited and waited for the words which never came.

At last she felt she could wait no longer. Since it was evident he did not intend to send to her, she determined to send to him. So she wrote—

" For Heaven's sake come to me. I must see you at once. Charles, for both our sakes, do not neglect my request.

" EDITH."

It was a mad letter to write, and at another time Edith would not have written it; but now her trouble seemed to be turning her brain. She determined to trust it to no hands but her own; so, having written and sealed it, she put on her hat and cloak to take it to the post.

It was the first time she had been out since that night when she had fainted upon her bedroom floor, and nothing but a sense of utter desperation would have forced her from the house even now. For she felt as if her secret was known to all the world ; that curious eyes looked questioningly into hers, and honest faces turned from her ; and that by one and all she was left to walk along her troubled path alone.

It was not late in the afternoon, but the time for long bright evenings had long since passed away. Though the church clock had not long struck five, darkness was coming on, and a keen north wind was blowing. Edith, who was thickly veiled and well wrapped up in a large fur cloak, walked quickly as if to keep herself warm. She reached the village, slipped her letter into the post, then hurriedly turned to retrace her steps homewards. She had accomplished about half the distance, and was walking very hurriedly, when suddenly she stopped, and her heart gave a great bound. There in the road, quietly walking towards her, was Mr. Santley.

Edith stood for a moment, feeling almost suffocated through the quick beating of her heart ; then, with the wild impetuosity of a child, she ran forward and, seizing his hand, exclaimed—

" Oh, I am glad, so very, very glad that I have met you ! Oh, Charles ! Charles ! how could you leave me so long alone ? "

Santley, utterly taken aback by this wild exhibition of feeling, stared at the girl in calm amazement ; then he said impatiently, shaking her hands away—

" Edith, how many more times am I to tell you that these violent scenes of yours will be my ruin ! "

But this time Edith was not to be cowed. She said—

" I cannot help it, Charles. You bring it on yourself by breaking every promise that you make to me."

" Every promise ? What promise ? What have I done now ? "

Edith looked up at him, her tearful eyes full of amazement as she said—

" Do you not remember ? Have you really forgotten, dear, the last time we were together I asked you to do me justice—to reward my long patience by making me your wife ? You said, ' I will think of it. Yes, I think I will do as you wish, and I will let you know to-morrow.' Well, Charles, to-morrow never came. I waited and waited, and you never sent a word. At last I could wait no longer. I have just been down to the village to post a letter, asking you to come to me."

The clergyman's brow darkened ominously, and a very angry light shone in his handsome eyes.

" It is ridiculous ! " he exclaimed. " Edith, you have no more reasoning power than a child. Why could you not have waited ? A matter like that required serious deliberation ; it could not be decided in a day."

In point of fact, he had never once deliberated over the matter at all. Having comfortably got rid of Edith that night, he had dismissed both the girl and the subject of their conversation entirely from his mind. It was not necessary to tell her this, however. So when, after waiting to hear more from him, she asked quietly, " Have you considered, Charles ? Have you decided ? " he answered—

" Yes. After thinking of it very

deeply, and after having considered it from every point of view, I have decided it would be much better for us both—-to wait !"

She started, and the hand which lay on his arm trembled violently.

" No ; you have not decided—that ! " she exclaimed in a sort of gasp.

" I am not in the habit of lying to you, Edith."

The girl clung piteously to his arm.

" No, no ; I did not mean that," she exclaimed. " But if you have decided so, you will change your mind, dear, will you not?   I have been very patient. I have waited and waited, because you wished it, dear ; but now it is different. I can wait no longer ! "

" I tell you, Edith, it will be better for us both ! "

" Charles,   Charles ! " exclaimed the

girl piteously, trembling more and more, "we have others besides ourselves to think of. We must not, dare not, injure an innocent life which never injured us. If you will not repair the wrong which you have done to me, you must think of—of—the child!"

She lowered her head as she spoke, and hid her face on his bosom.

There was silence. Then Santley spoke.

"Is this so, Edith?"

"Yes, dear; it is so!"

Again there was silence. Edith, trembling and almost happy, with her blushing face still hidden on his bosom, was waiting for him to bring her comfort, by gathering her fondly to his heart. But she waited in vain. The cold hands scarcely touched her shoulder; and the lovely eyes, gazing over her head, were

fixed on vacancy. He was not thinking
of her. Indeed, for the moment, he
seemed scarcely conscious of her presence. As usual, he was thinking of
himself, wondering what, in this ex-
tremely unpleasant emergency, it would
be better for him to do. The news was
not altogether startling to him. It was
an event which, under existing circumstances, might reasonably have been
expected; but hitherto it had not been
of sufficient importance to trouble the
clergyman's thoughts. "Sufficient for
the day is the evil thereof," had hitherto
been his motto; consequently, for the
moment he felt as if a mine had suddenly sprung beneath his feet. So when
Edith raised her head, and asked tear-
fully, "Are you very angry, Charles?"
he answered coldly, almost irritably—

"You cannot expect me to be pleased,

Edith. But there is no use in talking about that. What we must discuss is, what is the next thing to be done ? "

What was best to be done ? It seemed to Edith there was only one thing that could be done, and she said so, quietly and firmly. But Santley, frowning ominously, positively shook her in his irritable impatience.

" Always harping on the one string ! " he exclaimed angrily ; " and yet I tell you it is impossible."

" But why is it impossible ? "

" There are a dozen reasons why I cannot marry you just now."

" Then what am I to do ? Am I to be publicly disgraced and brought to shame ? Is my whole life to be ruined because of my love for you ? Oh, it is cruel, and piteously unjust ! "

" Edith, will you listen to reason ?
Will you have patience ? "

"Will I have patience ? " repeated
the poor girl. "Have I not had patience ?
And my forbearance is well-nigh gone ;
I cannot bear it. Charles, think for
a moment of what all this means to
me, and have some pity."

" Edith, will you listen to me ? "

" Yes. Speak ; I will listen," she returned wearily, trying to stifle the sobs
which almost choked her.

" If you will only control your violence
and be guided by me, there need be
no disgrace in the matter—either to you
or to me. No one knows of this ; no
one need know. All you have to do
is to remain quietly at home until a
further concealment of the truth would
be impossible ; then you will leave home,
as you have done before, to visit your

friends. Once free of the village, you will go to a place which I shall have found for you; and, afterwards, return home."

She listened quietly while he spoke. When he ceased, she said nothing. Presently he said—

"Edith, have you been listening?"

"Yes; I have heard."

"And what do you think?"

"I think," returned the girl, in a voice of utter and hopeless despair—a voice which would have rent the heart of any man but this one, "I think, Charles, that your love for me, if it ever existed, is dead and buried. I think, nay, I am quite sure, that you have decided never to make me your wife."

"This is folly."

"Charles, it is the truth. If you had

any love, any feeling for me, you would not, could not, speak as you have done to-night. If you meant to make me your wife, you would not subject me to such utter shame."

The clergyman entirely lost his self-command. He uttered an exclamation, and impatiently freed himself from her touch.

"Your shame," he said; "your disgrace—it is always that. But what of me? Have I no caste to lose? You talk of my love, but what of yours? If it exists, does it fill you with the least consideration for me? If you talk like this, you will make me wish that we had never met."

"How much better it would have been for me!"

"You think so? Thank God, it is not too late to part."

" But it is too late ! " cried the girl, wildly. " I tell you, it is too late for me ! "

" But it is not too late for me," said Santley, between his set teeth.

"Charles, what do you mean ? Answer me, for God's sake. Will you not make me your wife ? "

" No."

Without a moment's hesitation, without a tremor of the voice, the pitiless word was spoken. The girl staggered back, and clasped her hands to her head. It was as if a bullet had entered her brain. With a wild cry, she stretched forth her hands towards him, but he pushed her roughly away.

" You heard what I said. I mean it. You yourself have opened my eyes, and I see. If I can help you as—as your pastor, I will do so ; but I cannot, I will not, make a sacrifice of my whole life. You always know where to find me. I repeat, I shall always be glad to give you such assistance as a clergy-man can give."

CHAPTER XXXII.

"'FLIEH'! AUF'! HINAUS ! IN'S WEITE LAND!"

FOR several days after that meeting, it seemed to Mrs. Russell that Edith was sickening for a fever. Edith herself was afraid that the terrible trial through which she had passed, was likely to have serious results. In her agony, the girl prayed to die ; but for her there was no such mercy. At the end of a few days the ominous symptoms had passed away, and Edith was almost herself again. No doctor had been sent for. Mrs. Russell in her anxiety, was eager for him to see her niece ; but Edith, driven almost dis-

tracted at the thought, had refused so
decidedly to see him that her Aunt had
yielded, and had promised to put off
sending to him for a few days. At the
end of a few days Edith was better, so
no message was sent, and the doctor
never came.

So the time wore on. Winter had
fairly set in, and everybody in the village
was making preparations for Christmas,
Mrs. Russell following the fashion of all
the rest. From morning till night she
was herself employed with the maid in
the kitchen, chopping up mincemeat, and
preparing various other dainties for
Christmas fare. But her kindly face
was troubled ; she was always thinking of
Edith, who was so sadly changed. The
illness which had been so much dreaded
had passed away, it is true, but something almost as pitiable had been left in

its place. The girl looked pale and worn, and old before her time. She never crossed the threshold, but sat at home day after day, shivering over the fire, and when questioned by her aunt, she merely said—

"I don't feel very well. But don't notice me, aunt dear ; go on with your preparations for Christmas. I like to think that you will make the house bright, for I am sure I shall be better, so much better, when Christmas comes."

Mrs. Russell, according to her usual custom, wanted to have company, since it was dull, she said, for two lonely women to spend their Christmas together. So she proposed to her niece that she should write to Mrs. Hetherington, asking her to come, with her son, and eat her Christmas dinner at the cottage. But this idea was opposed by

Edith as vehemently as the doctor's visit had been ; and in this case, as in the other, the aunt had yielded.

"Well, Edith, shall I ask them for the New Year ? " she asked ; and the girl, eagerly seizing the respite, had answered—

"Yes, aunt ; for the New Year. For this once, you and I will spend our Christmas alone."

So the time passed on, until one morning Edith opened her eyes, and lay listening to the Christmas bells.

"Peace on earth, good will towards men ! "

That was the message they were chiming forth ; that was the doctrine *he* must preach to-day. *He*, through whose cruelty she, who only last Christmas had been a happy, contented girl, now lay there a very sorrowful, weary woman.

Would he think of her when he stood
in his pulpit, gazing into the enraptured
faces of his flock, and preaching to them
the gospel of faith and love? Would
he think for one moment of this poor
girl, whom he had made an outcast?

When mother and daughter sat at
breakfast, Edith announced her determination to stay at home as usual; so
Mrs. Russell went alone through the
snow to hear the vicar's sermon. She
was sorry Edith was not with her, she
said to herself again and again, as she sat
in the church, listening in rapt attention
to the benevolent gospel which Mr.
Santley preached. He had never been
known to have spoken so well before,
and when he had finished, one half of
the congregation had been reduced to
tears.

Mrs. Russell told Edith all about it at

dinner, and again expressed her sorrow
that Edith had not been there to hear.
To this the girl said nothing, but there
passed over her face a look it was well
the aunt did not see.

Thus the day passed—a day so full of
joy to some, so full of sadness to others.
Well, joy and sadness were ended. Mrs.
Russell, following her usual custom,
reached down the old family Bible, and
read from it ; then, taking her niece's
hand in hers, she knelt down to say a
prayer. When they rose from their
knees, Edith put her arms round her
aunt's neck, and kissed her fondly.

" Aunt dear," she said, " I have
often been a great trouble to you—I
have often caused you disappointment
and a deal of unnecessary pain ; but to-
night, on Christmas night, when we
should all forgive and love one another,

you will tell me, will you not, that you
forgive me ?"

With strange, wondering eyes, the old
lady looked at her niece, so pale and
sadly changed ; then she kissed her, as
she said—

"My darling, what there is to forgive
I forgive. We cannot all do as we
ought, Edith—we are poor creatures at
the best of times—but you are a good
girl, Edith ; and perhaps, after all, things
have shaped themselves for the best."

The old lady, all unconscious of the
real state of things, was thinking of the
collapse of the pet scheme she had had
of making Walter Hetherington her son.

"Dear aunt," said Edith, fondly,
"it was impossible."

"Yes, yes ; I know that now, my
dear : and perhaps, after all, as I said
before, it is for the best. There, don't

think of it again to-night, dear, but go to bed and rest !"

So Edith went to her room; and while the rest of the household were falling into blessed, tranquil slumber, she sat, dressed as she was, upon the bed and stared vacantly before her. She did not weep; her time for that had passed away, even as the greatness of her sorrow grew. Her face was fixed and determined; her heart seemed to have hardened to stone. For days and days she had waited for she knew not what; but a vague kind of hopefulness had taken possession of her heart, and she had allowed it to remain. Perhaps, during those terrible days of agonizing suspense, she had thought that she might have received some word or sign from him. It had been a vague, almost a hopeless, hope; nevertheless, it had

been that one spark which had kept
life within her. But now that hope was
gone : he had made no sign. And with
the knowledge that she could no longer
conceal her shame, came also the assurance that the man for whose sake
she had sinned, had pitilessly abandoned
her.

Edith, sitting at home by the fire that
day, had thought over all this, while her
aunt had been at church listening to
the vicar's touching sermon ; and, after
having forced herself to accept and
acknowledge the truth, she had finally
decided what she must do. She had
decided ; it but remained for her to
act. She had determined to leave her
home that night ; to walk whither her
wandering footsteps might lead her, and
leave no trace behind.

So, having reached her room, she sat

until the house was quiet; then she rose, and began to make her preparations for departure. She went to a drawer, and took from it what money still remained there—some bank-notes and gold—and stitched it firmly in a fold of her dress; then she put on her hat and warm winter cloak, and stood ready.

The village clocks were striking twelve.

She opened her door and listened. All was still; so she passed quietly onwards, after securely locking her bedroom door—passed noiselessly down the stairs, out of the house, and stood in the darkness alone.

It was a bitter night. The snow lay thick all round her, and the cruel wind which blew seemed to turn the life-blood in her veins to ice.

Edith stood for a moment, chilled to the heart. She gave one look at the home she was leaving; then, as if fearing the strength of her own resolution, she turned and quickly pursued her way.

Whither she went she knew not, nor did she care to know; she only knew that every step was taking her further and further from her home, and from the man who had broken her heart. So she walked on quickly, with her cloak wrapped well about her, and bending her head to shelter her face from the bitter breath of the wind.

She walked on and on, while the darkness gathered above her and the snow lay thick all around. Sometimes she sat down to rest, and then the thought came to her, that perhaps it would be better if she could end it all;

if she could but lie down on the frozen
earth, with the snow wrapped like a
mantle around her, and sink to her
eternal sleep.   Henceforth there would
be no more sorrow and no more pain.
The idea having occurred to her, took
possession of her mind, and held to it
tenaciously.   Oh, if she could only die !
—close her eyes in the darkness, and
feel for a moment that blessed peace
which had passed from her for ever !
Yes, Edith knew it would be better;
though, with the instinct implanted in
all human things, she shrank from death,
she knew that his presence would be
merciful.   Henceforth, what would life
be to her—an outcast, a thing to be
spoken of with pitiless contempt, to be
hidden for ever from the sight of all
her fellow-men ?   Then she asked herself, "Would it be a sin to take the

life which God had given her, and yield
it up to Him ? " No ; she believed it
would be no sin.

She walked on and on. Then once
more, in the bitter anguish of her heart,
she cried on God to be merciful to her.
For, weary with travelling, cold and
sick at heart, she cast herself down
upon the snow, and sobbed—

" Oh, if I could only die ! "

But death did not come. The snow
closed all round her as she lay fainting
and cold ; but she did not die. Its icy
touch, lying on her parched lips and
brow, revived her. With wild, wandering eyes, she looked around.

The night was well-nigh spent, and
the sky gave tokens of quickly approaching dawn. As every hour passed on,
the air grew colder, and now its touch
chilled her to the very bone ; she

shivered, yet her brow, her lips, and hands were burning. She tried to think, but could not; even the events of the past were becoming strangely blurred and dim.

Where was she? She hardly knew; yet she must have wandered many, many miles from home, since she was footsore, and growing very faint for lack of food. She listened feverishly, and her ear caught the murmuring of a running stream.

She rose; but her limbs were feeble, for she staggered and fell again upon the ground. Then she cried from very weakness, and a sense of utter helplessness and loneliness.

After a while she rose again. How her hands and lips burned! Her brain was in wild confusion, and everything about her seemed fading into the mystery of a dream. Was it coming, that death for which she had prayed?

Suddenly a wild fear seized her. If she fell and lay here on the snow, she might be recognized by some passing traveller and taken home! That must not be. She must never be found, and then no one would ever know.

As this new terror seized her, she heard again the rippling of the stream. It seemed to lure her on. She thrust a handful of snow into her mouth, and staggered forward. The sweet sound of the running water came nearer and nearer. She stood now on the banks of the stream—a stream deep and rapid, flowing between banks now laden with snow. Edith looked down into the dark, cold water, and thought, " If I lay there, quiet and cold, no one would ever find me, and no one would ever know." " Yes, yes ; it would be better,' she cried. " The water called me, and I have come !" And, with a wild sob, she sprang forward, and sank beneath the swiftly flowing waters of the stream.

When Edith opened her eyes, she found herself lying upon a bed of straw. She was dressed in dry clothes, sheltered by a canvas roof, warmed by a fire, and watched by a woman. Her eyes, after having carelessly noted these things, remained fixed on the face of the woman, for she had recognized the bold black eyes of Sal Blexley.

Edith remained dumb, but Sal broke the silence with a loud laugh.

" Yes, it's me, my lady," she said. " I said we should meet again, and so we have, you see. I thought it would come to this."

" Where am I ? " asked Edith, faintly.

"Where are ye ? Why, in a gipsy tent, with me and my pals. I was out on the rampage with my chap, when we saw ye throw yourself in the river. I got him to fish you out—more dead than alive, I bet—and between us we brought ye here. There, don't shrink away, and don't look afeard. I ain't agoin' to harm ye. Your man's deserted ye, I reckon. Well, ye despised me once, ye know, and so did he ; but I mean to let ye see that 'tain't only gentlefolks and clergy that can do a good turn to them as wants it."

CHAPTER XXXIII.

THE NOTE-BOOK AGAIN.

December 15.—The first snow fell yesterday. As I write, the air is still
darkened with the falling flakes. From
here to the village is spread a soft
white carpet, ankle-deep. I am more
than usually interested in this common
phenomenon, as I can tell, by the deep
footprints, exactly who is coming and
going. One track interests me especially
—that of a shapely foot, clad in an
elegant, tightly fitting boot. Its holy
owner came as far as the lodge gate, no
further. To make certain that I was not

mistaken, I inquired of the lodge-keeper, and found that the clergyman *had* passed this morning.

As matters stand now, I can arrange everything with coolness and *sang froid*, for I am really the master of the situation. I hold this man, as it were, in the hollow of my hand. I know his life, his comings and goings, his offences against social propriety, against his own conscience ; there is not a step of that poor instrument, his soul, of which I am not master. Despite all this, he is still absolutely blind to his danger. He thinks me sleeping sound, when I am wide awake. Imbecile !

Well, I mean to have my revenge, somehow or other ; how and when, I have not exactly determined. I should like to read my satyr such a lesson as would last him for a lifetime ; and of course, without any kind of *public* scandal. I have thought once or twice of a way, but it would, perhaps, be playing with fire to attempt it; nor is it easy to carry out without my wife's co-operation.

As for Ellen, she remains restless and bewildered; certain of the man's unworthiness, yet fascinated by his pertinacity. She goes to church, as usual; otherwise, she avoids Santley as much as possible. What would she say, if I were to tell her all I know? I am afraid, after all, it would not facilitate her cure; for, strange to say, women love a scoundrel of the amorous kind.

> " That we should call these delicate creatures ours,
>   And not their —— sentiments ! "

Yes, it is nothing but sentiment, I know. She is as pure as crystal, but she cannot quite forget that she was

once a foolish maid, and this man an
impassioned boy ; and he comes to her,
moreover, in the shining vestments of a
beautiful, though lying, creed. I shall
have to be cruel, I am afraid, very cruel,
before I can quite cure her. . . . Pshaw!
what am I thinking, writing ? Folly,
folly! I am trying to survey Ellen
Haldane philosophically, to assume a
calmness, though I have it not—though
all the time my spirit is in arms against
her. I am jealous, damnably jealous,
that is all.

To talk about the crystal purity of a
woman who has a moral *cancer*, which
must kill her if it is not killed! To
describe her folly as mere sentiment,
when I know, more than most men, that
such sentiment as that is simple con-
science-poisoning! If I did not save
her, if I were not by with my protecting

hand, she would assuredly be lost. Well, I shall cure her, as I said, or kill her in the attempt. Once, when a boy, in a Parisian hospital, I saw an *ouvreuse* operated upon, for a tumorous deposit, which necessitated the excision of the whole of the right breast. It was before the days of chloroform, and the patient's agony was terrible to witness. But she was saved. For the moral cancer also, the knife may be the only remedy; and it will be, as in the other case, kill or cure.

Meantime, our domestic life goes on with characteristic monotony. We have no quarrels, and no confidences. We eat, drink, and sleep like comfortable wedded people. The greater part of my day is spent among my books; the greater part of hers in simple domestic duties, in music, in wanderings about the gardens. She seldom visits in the parish now; but the poor come to her on stated days, and she is, as ever, charitable. At least once every Sunday she goes to church.

A sombre, sultry state of the atmosphere, with gathering thunder!

December 20.—I have been reading, to-day, Naquet's curious pamphlet on "Divorce," a subject which is just now greatly exercising our neighbours across the Channel. This study, combined with that of two new attempts in Zolaesque (which a French friend has been good enough to send me), has left me with a certain sense of nausea. Gradually, but surely, I am afraid, I am losing that fine British faith in the feminine ideal, which was among the legacies left me by a perfect mother. It is dawning upon me, at middle age, as it dawns upon a Parisian at twenty-one, that women are, at best, only the highest, or among the highest, of *animals*, and that sanitary precautions of the State must be taken —to keep them cleanly. It is this discovery which, perpetuated in Art, makes the whole literature of the Second Empire so repulsive to an English Philistine. "And smell so—faugh!" Are the days of chivalry, then, over? Is the ideal of pure maidenhood, of perfect womanhood, utterly overthrown? Is the modern woman—not Imogen, not Portia, not the lily maid of Ascolat, not Romola, not even Helen Pendennis?— but Messalina, Lucretia — nay, even Berthe Rougon, or the shamble-haunting wife of Claude, or the utterable Madame Bovary? Surely, surely, there cannot be all this literary smoke without some little social fire. Thank God, therefore, that the wise Republic has taken to the

drastic remedy of crushing those vipers,
the Christian priests, and of abolishing
the solemn farce of the marriage ceremony. Marriage is a simple contract,
not an arrangement made in heaven ; it
is social and sanitary, not religious and
ideal ;—and when any of the conditions
are broken by either of the contracting
parties, the contract is at an end.

Yes, I suppose it is so ; I suppose
that women are not angels, and that
married life is an arrangement. And
yet how much sweeter was that old-
fashioned belief which pictured the
wedded life as a divine communion of
souls, a golden ladder beginning at the
altar, and reaching—through many dark
shadows, perhaps, but surely reaching—
up to heaven ! Ah, my hymeneal Jacob's
Ladder, with angels for ever descending
and ascending, you have vanished from

the world, with Noah's Dove of Peace, and Christ's Rainbow of Promise! All faiths have gone, and the faith in Love is the last to go.

I find that I am philosophizing—prosing, in other words — instead of setting down events as they occur. But indeed, there are no events to set down. I am in the position of the needy knife-grinder of the Anti-Jacobin:

"Story? God bless you, I have none to tell, sir!"

So, to ease my mind, I pour out my bile on paper.

December 21.—I have made a discovery. During the last few days my wife and Santley have been in correspondence. At any rate, he has written to her; and I suspect she has replied.

Baptisto has been my informant. Despite my command that he should

cease to play the spy, he has persisted
in keeping his eyes and ears open, and
has managed to convey to me, in one
way or another, exactly what he has
seen or heard. This morning, when
hanging about the lodge (still fascinated,
I suspect, by the little widow), he discovered that there was a letter there
addressed to his mistress, and he asked
me, quite innocently, if he should fetch
and take it to her. I showed no sign
of anger or surprise, but bade him mind
his own business. In the forenoon, I
saw Ellen emerge from the house, and
stroll carelessly in the direction of the
lodge gates. I followed her at a distance, and saw her enter the lodge, and
emerge directly afterwards with a letter,
which she read hastily and thrust into
her bosom.

When she returned up the avenue, I

was standing outside my den, waiting for her.

She came up smiling, with her air of perfect innocence. Wrapped from head to foot in furs, and wearing the prettiest of fur caps *à la Russe*, she looked her very best and brightest. The sun was shining clearly on the snow, and, as she came, she left soft footprints behind her.

"What is my Bear doing," she cried, "out in the cold, and without his great coat, too?"

"The day looked so bright that I was tempted out. Where have you been?"

"Only for a little stroll," she replied; "it is so pleasant out of doors. By-the-bye, dear, they are skating down on Omberley Pond. I think I shall drive over. Will you come?"

"Not to-day, Nell."

She did not look sorry, I thought, at my refusal.

" Is there a party ? " I asked carelessly.

" I don't know ; but I heard the Armstrongs were going, and some of the people from the Abbey."

" And Mr. Santley, I suppose ? "

She flushed slightly, but answered without hesitation—

" Perhaps he will be there ; but I need not speak to him, if you forbid it. I will stay at home if you wish it, dear."

" I don't wish it," I said. " Go and amuse yourself."

" *Won't* you come ? " she murmured, hesitating.

I shook my head, and turned back to my den. She looked after me, and sighed ; then walked slowly towards the house. What a sullen beast she must have thought me! But I was irritated beyond measure by what I had seen at the lodge. Not a word of the letter!

Half an hour afterwards I saw the pony-carriage waiting for her, and presently she drove off, looking (as I thought) bright and happy enough. No sooner had she gone than I was mad with myself for not having accompanied her. Was it a *rendezvous?* Had she gone, of set purpose, to meet *him?* I cursed my stupidity, my sullenness. At a word from me she would have remained. I had almost made up my mind to walk over, when in came Baptisto. He was wrapped up to the chin in an old travelling cloak, and his nose was blue with cold.

" Have you any message in the village, señor ? " he asked. " I am going there."

I could not resist the temptation,

though I hated myself for setting a spy upon her.

" No, I have no message. Stay, though! While you are there, pass by the skating-pond, and see if any of our friends are there."

He understood me perfectly, and went away, well satisfied at the commission. More and more, as the days go on, the rascal intrudes himself into my confidence, with silent looks of sympathy, dumb signs of devotion. He says nothing, but his looks are ever significant. Sometimes I long, in my irritation, to get rid of him for ever; but no, I may find him useful. I know he would go through fire and water for my sake.

In about two hours he returned with his report.

" Well ? " I said, scowling at him.

" The pond is covered, señor, with gentlemen and ladies. His lordship is there, and they are very gay. It is pretty to see them gliding about the ice, the ladies and the gentlemen hand in hand. Sometimes the ladies slip, and the gentlemen catch them in their arms, and then all laugh! It is a pity that you are not there; you would be amused."

" Is this all you have to tell me ? "

"Yes, señor, except that my mistress is among them. She bade me tell you—— "

" Yes! yes ! "

" That she was enjoying herself so much, and would not be home for lunch."

He stood with head bent gently, respectful and submissive, but his face wore the expression which had often irritated me before—an expression which

said, as plainly as words, " How far will
you let them go ? Cannot you perceive
what is going on ? It is no affair of
mine, but is it possible that you will
endure so much and so long ? " I read
all this, I say, in the fellow's face.

"Very well," I said sternly, dismissing
him with a wave of the hand.

He went lingeringly, knowing I would
be certain to call him back. As I did.

" Was Mr. Santley there ? "

Baptisto smiled—darkly, malignantly.

" Oh yes, señor, *of course !* "

I could have struck him.

Damn him ! does he think I am
already ornamented, like Falstaff, with
an ugly pair of horns ? I shall have to
get rid of him, after all. He saw the
expression on my face, and was gone in
a moment ; but he had left his poison to
work.

All the devil was awake within me.
I could not work, I could not read, I
could not rest in any place. When the
lunch-bell sounded, I went in, and drank
a couple of glasses of wine, but ate
nothing. Then for some hours I flitted
about like a ghost, from room to room,
from the house to the laboratory, upstairs and down. I went into her
boudoir. The rosy curtains were drawn,
and the air was still sweet with perfumes, with the very breath of her body.
I am afraid I was mean enough to play
the spy—to open drawers, to look into
her work-basket; nay, I even went so
far as to inspect her wardrobe, and
examine the pocket of the dress she had
worn that morning.

I wanted that letter.

If I could have found it, and read in
it any confirmation of my suspicions, I

would have taken instant action. But I could not find it.

In the drawer of the work-table, however, I found something.

A sheet of paper, carefully folded up. I opened it, and found it covered with writing in a man's hand. At the top was written—"*I think these are the verses you wanted? I have transcribed them for you.—C. S.*" The verses followed—some twaddle about the meeting in heaven of those who have lived on earth ; with incredible images of cherubs sitting on clouds (blowing their own trumpets, I suppose, with angelic self-satisfaction) ; descriptions of impossible habitations, with roofs of gold and silver, and inspired rhymes of "love" and "dove," "eyes" and "paradise." The paper was the pinkest of pinks, and delicately perfumed ; the writing beautiful, with ethereal curves and upsweeps, exquisite punctuation, and a liberal supply of points of exclamation. I put the rubbish back in its place. It had obviously been lying there for some time, and was not at all the sort of document of which I was in search. So I quitted the boudoir, not much wiser than when I entered it, and resumed my uneasy ramblings about the house.

About four in the afternoon, I heard wheels coming up the avenue. I looked out, and was just in time to see the pony-carriage pass. What was my amazement, however, when I beheld, calmly driving the carriage, with my wife seated at his side, the clergyman himself.

My head went round, and I felt positively bloodthirsty. Seizing my hat, I hastened round, and arrived just as Santley was carrying Ellen up the steps into the house. Yes, actually carrying her in his arms! I could scarcely believe my eyes; but, coming up close, I saw that she was ghastly pale, and that something unusual must have occurred.

He had placed her on a chair in the lobby, and was bending over her just as I followed. I am afraid that the expression of my face was sinister and agitated enough; I stood glaring at the two, like one gasping for breath.

"Don't be alarmed," he said, meeting my eyes. "There has been a slight accident, that is all. Mrs. Haldane slipped on the ice, and, falling, sprained her ankle."

Ellen, who seemed in great pain, looked up at me with a beseeching expression ; for she at least read my suspicion in my face.

" It was so stupid of me ! " she murmured, forcing a faint smile, and reaching out her hand.   " I could not come home alone—I was in such pain—and Mr. Santley kindly volunteered to bring me."

What could I do ?   I could not knock a man down for having performed what appeared a simple act of courtesy.   I could not exhibit any anger, without looking like an idiot or a boor.   Santley had merely done what any other gentleman would have done under the circumstances.   For all that, I had an uneasy sense of being humbugged.

" Let me look at your foot," I said gruffly.

She pushed it from underneath her dress.   The boot had been taken off, and a white silk handkerchief tightly wrapped about the ankle.

"Mr. Santley bound it up," she explained.

I took the foot in my hand, and in my secret fury, I think I was a little rough, for she uttered a cry.

"Take care!" cried the clergyman. "It is very tender."

I looked up at him with a scowl, but said nothing.

"Shall I carry you into the drawing-room?" he said, with tender solicitude.

"No; I am better now, and George will give me his arm. Pray do not stay."

She rose with difficulty, and, resting all her weight upon her left foot, leant upon me. In this manner she managed to limp into the drawing-room, and to place herself upon a couch. Her pallor

still continued, and I felt sorry, for I
hate to see a woman suffer. Santley,
who had followed us, and was watching
her with extraordinary sympathy, now
bent softly over her.

"Are you still in pain ?" he murmured.

"A little ; but——"

"Shall I send Doctor Spruce over ?
I shall be passing the surgery on my
way back. If he is not at home, I will
procure some remedies, and bring them
on myself."

Here I interposed.

"Pray do not trouble yourself," I said.
with a sneer. "A sprained ankle is a
trifle, and I can attend to it. Unless
my wife is in need of *religious* ministra-
tion, you need not remain."

I spoke brutally, as I felt ; and, meeting the man's pale, sad, astonished gaze,

I became secretly humiliated. A husband, I perceive, is a ridiculous animal, and always at a disadvantage. I begin to understand how the poets, from Molière downwards, have made married men their shuttlecocks. A jealous lover has dignity ; a jealous husband, none. Nobody sympathizes with my lord of Rimini, while all the world weeps for Lancelot and Francesca. Even Ford, ere he turns the tables on Sir John, poses as an ass. All the right was on my side, all the offended dignity, all the outraged honesty ; yet somehow I felt, at that moment, like an ill-conditioned cur.

"I am not here in a religious capacity," he replied courteously, " so your sneer is hardly fair. However, since I can be of no further service, I will go."

He turned softly to Ellen, holding out his hand.

"Good-bye. I hope you will be better to-morrow."

"Good-bye, and thank you," she replied. "It was so good of you to bring me home."

And so, with a courteous bow to me, which I returned with a nod, he retired victoriously. Yes, he had the best of it for the time being. For some minutes after he left, and while the scent of his perfumed handkerchief still filled the air, I stood moodily waiting. At last Ellen spoke.

"I hope you are not angry. What could I do? I could not come home in such pain, and no one else offered to escort me."

"I did not ask you to excuse yourself," I said coldly.

I saw the tears standing in her eyes. Her voice trembled as she murmured—

" I did not think you could have been so unkind ! "

As I did not answer, she continued—

" Of late you have not been like yourself. You used to trust me; we used to be so happy ! If this is to go on, we had better separate ; it makes my life a misery."

She had touched the wrong chord, if she thought to move my pity. My jealous brain was at work at once. She was thinking of a separation, then ? Perhaps she wished it; and perhaps the true reason was her love for that man ?

I spoke out in the heat of the moment—

" If you wish to separate, it can be arranged."

She looked at me so pleadingly, so piteously, that I had to turn my eyes away. In encounters of this kind the man has no chance against the woman, especially if he is magnanimous. What are all his arguments, all his indignation, against her battery of woeful looks, her tears, her pseudo-innocence, and real helplessness? One feels like a coward, too, in such an encounter. I did, I know.

Nevertheless, I was ready to give her the *coup de grace.*

"Show me that letter," I said suddenly.

"What letter?" she asked, as if she did not comprehend.

"The letter you received from that man this morning."

For a moment her cheeks went scarlet, then became deadly pale again.

"Pray do not attempt any subterfuge," I continued. "I know that you have been in correspondence. Where

is that last letter? I demand to
see it."

She replied without hesitation.

"You cannot see it."

"Why?"

"Because I have burned it."

At this admission I lost my self-
command, and uttered an execration.

"There was nothing in it," she said
sorrowfully; "it was a mere request for
an interview. You have no right to be
so violent."

"No right, woman!" I cried.

"There is nothing between us to
make me ashamed. If I were the most
guilty woman in the world, you could
not treat me more cruelly. You have
no pity, none. It is my fault, my
punishment, to have married a man
without sympathy, without religion."

Religion again! How I hated the

word! It stung me into retorting fiercely—

"It is my misfortune, rather, to have married a sentimental hypocrite!"

I had gone too far. Her proud spirit rose against me. Pale and indignant, she tried to rise to her feet. But she had forgotten her sprained ankle. Her face was contracted with sudden torture, and, with a low cry of pain, she fainted away upon the floor.

December 23.—In two more days the Christmas bells will ring, with their merry tidings of peace, good will, and plum-pudding to all the world. Well, mine is likely to be a cheerful Christmas Day. The snow is still on the ground, and more is falling; and outside the Manor, as I write, the dreariest of dreary winds is wailing. Here, inside, there is even greater gloom. A cheerless hearth, a husband and wife estranged. Bah ! the old story.

Things have come to a crisis at last between us. I know now that I must either strike a cruel blow, or lose my wife for ever. Any mere armistice is impossible. Either I must assault my enemy's camp, get him by the throat, and cover him with punishment and confusion ; or haul down my matrimonial flag, capitulate, and let the Church and the devil come in to take possession.

CHAPTER XXXIV.

BAITING A MOUSE-TRAP (FROM THE NOTE-BOOK).

LET me write down, as calmly as I can, exactly what has taken place.

Yesterday, after that little scene, I carried my swooning wife up to her room, placed her on the bed, and sent her maid to attend to her. Then I walked off to my den, to have my dark hour alone; for I was thoroughly miserable. So far, I felt, I had been beaten with my own weapons. Ellen was going to pose as a Christian martyr, and I had committed the indiscretion of showing the full extent of my jealousy. It would have been far better, on the whole, if, instead of storming and grumbling, I had quietly kicked the clergyman out of my house ; but then, I could hardly deal in that way with a man who had simply, on the face of it, performed an act of common civility. The time for kicking had gone past ; I had stupidly let it slip. If, when I caught him in the act of trying to embrace my Ellen, and of addressing her softly by her Christian name, I had calmly and decisively thrashed him, he could hardly have accused me of impoliteness ; nor would he have been able, without exposing his own fatuity, to noise the affair about.

Now, I was not only angry with my wife for her indiscretion, I was in a rage with myself for having behaved with so much brutality. The picture of her pale, suffering face followed me to my den, and haunted me reproachfully. She had really met with an accident, and was in sharp physical pain ; and I, who at another time would have cut off my right hand to prevent her little finger from aching, had chosen the time of her suffering to come · upon her like a woman-eating tiger. Just the husband's luck again—always at a disadvantage ; for precisely to the degree in which she felt herself treated unkindly and ungently by me, would rise her sympathy for the man who had been so zealous and so tender. Damn him, again !

The night passed wretchedly enough. I sat up working till nearly daybreak. When I went upstairs, and entered my dressing-room, I felt guilty and ashamed, yet angry still. But she was asleep—I could hear her soft breathing from the adjoining bedchamber. Lamp in hand, I crept in. Yes, there she lay, soundly slumbering, her eyes red with weeping, her dark hair falling wildly around her pallid face, her neck and throat bare, her arms outside the coverlid, which rose and fell with her breathing. As I bent over her, my shadow crossed her soul in sleep, and she moaned and stirred. Poor child! I longed to kiss her, but I was ashamed.

I think we men, the strongest and coldest of us even, are weak as water, where a woman is concerned. I used to fancy once that, if a wife of mine failed in faith, or fell away from me in sin, I could strike her dead without pity; or if I suffered her to live, pass an eternity with no thought but loathing and detestation. But as I bent over that sad bed, I seemed to understand how it was that husbands, in the fulness of time, had pardoned even *that*, the foulest and deadliest of infidelities ; how, with a love stronger than sin, and a hope stronger than death, they had welcomed back the penitent, in forgiveness, sorrow, and despair—even as a father would take back an erring child, part of the very blood and life within his veins. Weakness, I know ; but weak as water, in virtue of its very strength, is Love.

It was horrible, horrible, this falling away from each other. I wished, just then, that I had had religion ; perhaps then we might have been happier together. Women love a sort of matrimonial Village Blacksmith, who asks no questions, works hard all the week, and goes three times to church, in an irreproachably white shirt, on Sunday. They cannot bear revolt in any shape. They were the last to cling to the old gods, and they will be last to cling to the dead Christ. Does the law which works for righteousness, somehow or other, justify them? Was my dear wife's alienation a curse upon me for dealing in occult scientific mysteries, like an old necromancer, and forgetting, if I ever learned, the sweet religion of the heart? Somehow, last night, I felt as if it were so. There she lay, white as snow. I knew she had prayed to God before sleeping; and I—I could not pray. I was an outcast, an unbeliever; "atheist! atheist!" said the preacher. I crept away to my own solitary bed, feeling more sad and lonely than I had ever done in all my life.

Till midday to-day, she kept her

room ; but after lunch, she managed to get downstairs.   I had returned to my den, and we did not meet ; nor was I in the mood for meeting, for the gentle impulses of overnight had passed away, and the morning had found me gloomy, quarrelsome, and atrabilious.   She did not send for me, though I secretly hoped that she might do so.   I learned from Baptisto that she was stretched upon the drawing-room sofa, which was drawn close to the window, and was reading some religious book.

Restless and wretched, I took my hat and walked out into the snow.   The great fir trees, loaded with the leaden whiteness, were ranged like grim sentinels on each side of the dreary avenue, and beyond these the leafless woods stretched white and cold.   The sun had gone in, and the air was full of a heavy lowering sadness—a sort of darkness visible. It was cheerless weather; and as I thought of my domestic misery, and of the clouded world, with all its sins and sorrows, I was more miserable than ever.

Nevertheless, I walked on rapidly, till I came out among the frozen fields of the open country. How desolate looked the snowy meadows, with broad patches of green, thaw-like mildew, and the fallow fields, with snow thick in the furrows and wretched low-lying hedges on every side! Here and there a few miserable small birds were fluttering, starved robins for the most part; and a kestrel was hunting the furrow, hovering in a slow, dejected way, as if field-mice were scarce, and his whole occupation, like the weather, cruelly forlorn.

Before four o'clock it was quite dark.

Through the windy darkness I made my way back to the Manor. By that time I had thought it all over. Conquered by the utter desolation within and without me, I had said to myself, " Life like this is worse than death. I will try one way more ; I will go to her, I will take her to my heart, I will beg her to love and trust me, and to accept my tender forgiveness. Perhaps I have been too hard, too taciturn and sullen. She has mistaken my sorrow for coldness, my pride for cruelty and pertinacity. There shall be an end to this. She shall understand the full tenderness of my love, once and for ever." With these thoughts struggling wildly within me, I hastened home.

Then, as the devil would have it, I saw Baptisto, waiting on the threshold of my den. The moment I appeared he crept up to me, and clutched my arm.

"Señor, señor! where have you been? I have been waiting for you."

"What is it, man?" I asked, startled by his manner.

"Come and see!"

He led me towards the house. I walked a few steps, then paused nervously.

"What has happened?" I asked.

"Nothing, señor; but the clergyman is here again, with my lady."

That was enough. It turned my tenderness into anger, my lethargy into passion. Shaking off the fellow's touch, I hastened to the house. As I went I saw lights in the drawing-room; and, instead of entering the house door, I ascended the flight of iron steps which leads to the terrace. Then, with the

cunning of jealousy, cold enough to
subdue the fever of rage, I crept along
the terrace till I reached the folding
doors of the drawing-room. The doors
were closed, the curtains and blinds were
drawn, but there was one small space
through which I could see into the
room.

I looked in.

For a moment my eyes, clouded by
the darkness, were dazzled by the light
of the room within ; but despite the loud
crying of the wind around me, I heard a
murmur of voices. Then I distinguished
the form of my wife on a sofa drawn up
before the fire, and, bending over her, the
form of the minister. Her back was
turned to me, but I saw *his* face, noticed
the burning eyes fixed eagerly on
hers.

What were they saying—doing ? I

strained my eyes, my ears. At last I caught a sound.

" Go now!" she was saying; "go now, I beseech you!"

Even as she spoke, he flung himself wildly on his knees, placing his arms around her.

"Oh, you are mad, mad!" she cried.

"Not mad, but desperate," he answered. "I have thought it all over; I have struggled and struggled, but it is in vain. Ellen, have pity! There is no peace or happiness for me, in this world or the next, without your love. My darling! my angel!"

"Silence, for God's sake! Oh, if you should be heard——"

"I do not care who hears me. I am beyond fear. As for that man, your husband, he is busy, no doubt, with his blasphemous books, his sinful investiga-

tions. Oh, my darling, that you should
be linked to such a man! A man
without religion—a man without God!
It was that which first made me pity
you, and pity is akin to love. You owe
him no duty. He is a heretic—an
atheist, as you know."

As he clung to her and embraced
her, she struggled nervously. Carried
beyond himself, he covered her hands
with kisses, and would have kissed her
lips, but she drew back.

"Go, go!" she moaned. "Hark! I
hear footsteps. If you do not go now,
I will never speak to you again."

He rose to his feet, hot, flushed, and
trembling like a leaf.

"I will go, since you wish it," he said.
"Good night, my darling!"

He stooped over, and—kissed her?
Yes, I was sure he kissed her, though

I think she shrunk away, with her face nervously turned to the door, dreading a surprise. Then I saw his shadow cross the room, and vanish through the door, which was closed behind him.

I was about to force open the French windows and enter, when a curious impulse possessed me to delay a little, and see what she would do when left alone. So I watched her. She sat trembling on her seat ; then, reaching to the table, took a flask of eau-de-cologne, poured some upon her hand-kerchief, and bathed her face. Then, with momentary glances at the door, she smoothed down her straggling hair, and adjusted the bosom of her dress. Finally, she contrived, though not without pain, to rise to her feet, and, leaning on the marble mantelpiece, to look at her face in the mirror. I could see her face reflected, all flushed and warm, and her eyes gleaming with unusual brightness. After again smoothing her hair, she got back to the sofa, posed herself prettily, and, not without another glance at the door, took up a book and pretended to read.

By this time I was diabolically cool; so cool that I could have killed her just then in cold blood. Entering into the spirit of her hypocrisy, I refrained from entering by the terrace, but, passing round to the hall door, entered there. A few minutes afterwards, I entered the drawing-room, with as unconcerned an air as I could possibly command.

There she sat, quite calm and self-possessed, her robe arranged decently over her feet, her face pale, her hair smoothed down Madonna-like over her temples, her eyes fixed upon a book.

As I entered, she looked up with a sweet smile, just as if there had never been any quarrel between us.

"Well, dear? You see, I have got down."

I nodded, and sank into a chair.

"You don't ask me if my ankle is better? Well, it is nearly all right. But, George, I hope you are not angry with me still for what occurred yesterday. Do forgive me, dear!"

"Oh, I'm not angry," I replied; "only—— "

"Only we both lost our tempers; I with my stupid sprained ankle, you with your stupid books. I was so sorry you let Mr. Santley see you were annoyed. He must have thought it so odd."

How light and free of heart she seemed! how bright and languishing her eyes were! She could laugh, too,

and she was not much given to laughter
I looked at her with amazement, so
little did I, or do I, understand women.
There seemed to be an ugliness, a
guiltiness, about her tender coquetry
that evening, coming so close upon what
I had seen.

"By the way," she continued, after
a few minutes' pause, "I hope you will
not scold me again, but I think I ought
to tell you—that Mr. Santley has just
called. There, now you are angry ; but
I thought it right to tell you."

"Thank you," I said drily. "I was
aware that he had called. What brought
him, pray ? "

"He wished to ascertain if I had
recovered from the effects of my fall,"
she replied, with a little more nervous-
ness than before.

"Oh, a mere visit of politeness !"

" Yes," she answered, faltering.

I rose quietly, and stood on the hearthrug, looking down upon her.

"Would it surprise you to hear," I asked grimly, "that I know exactly what took place between you ? "

Her face flushed scarlet, the book fell from her hands.

"Oh, George! what do you mean ? " she murmured somewhat irrelevantly.

" Precisely what I say. He made hot love to you—embraced you—kissed you, madam. He informed you that your husband was a heretic, and that to make him a cuckold would be a certain way of getting an express pass right through to paradise. Very polite indeed, you will agree ! "

She saw that I knew everything, and wrung her hands in protestation and despair.

"George, if you know so much—and some one has been playing the spy— you know that it was all against my will ; you know that I tried to silence him, to thrust him from me, but, being ill and helpless, sick, and in pain——"

Here her self-pity, coming sharp upon her consternation, quite conquered her, and she fell into hysterical tears.

"O God ! God !" she sobbed.

What kaleidoscopes are women ! From light to shade, from brightness to dimness, and back again to brightness ; from one colour to another, from the tints of the thunder-cloud to the hues of the rainbow, how suddenly they can flit and change ! Ellen, who had just before been so gay and smiling, seemed now liked a broken woman. I watched her gloomily, almost despairingly. I knew that ten minutes afterwards, she might change again, scattering away her tears as the sunshine scatters the drops of dew.

Midnight.—I have just left my wife's bedside. Ellen has promised me, if I spare the man and avoid any scandal, that she will never speak to him again, or even enter his church. Can I trust her? I believe *not.* However, we shall see.

Christmas Eve.—My mind is now made up. To-day I intercepted a letter from Santley to Ellen, left as usual at the lodge gate. It ran as follows:—

" To-morrow is Christmas Day, and I have not a moment to spare. I will call, however, next day, on *the business about which we spoke yesterday.* Pray for me till then, as I pray for you.—C. S."

The italics are the satyr's own.

This letter, then, has decided me. My scheme of revenge is now perfectly complete, and I shall no longer hesitate to carry it out. To make all certain, I shall send a verbal message by Baptisto to-morrow to the effect that Mrs. Haldane " will be glad to see Mr. Santley as arranged, the day after Christmas Day." In the mean time I shall make my preparations. All the servants but two have been given a holiday for that day—I have taken care of that ; and as they purpose going into the neighbouring town, they will not return till very late. The two remaining are the kitchen-maid, who is an idiot and notices nothing ; and Baptisto, who is for once to combine two functions—that of cook (he cooks like an angel) and waiter at table. Ellen is quite satisfied with this arrangement. She knows nothing of Santley's letter.

We see little or nothing of each other, and a shadow as of death hangs over the entire house.

Christmas Day.—I astonished Ellen very much this morning, by expressing my intention of accompanying her to church ; but, instead of rejoicing, as she would have done a little time ago, she seemed rather frightened and startled. We drove over to the old church at Hamleigh, seven miles off, and heard a drowsy sermon by the drowsiest of octogenarians—the right sort of preacher, in my opinion, for a creed so worn out, mildewy, and old-fashioned. Ellen did not seem to share my appreciation of the old fellow's antiquated twaddle. She sat like a marble woman. We drove home without a word.

A pretty Christmas ! But, never mind, I am going to have my revenge.

Everything lends itself to my purpose. To begin with, Foxglove Manor is miles away from any other habitation ; and no one ever comes near the "uncanny" place, except on special business. All the servants, but the idiot of a kitchen-maid, leave early for their holiday. For a day at least I can do as I please ; and my intentions are simply murderous. In the course of twelve hours a human creature may be disposed of, and buried out of sight, if necessary, in these grounds. Baptisto knows my terrible purpose, and approves it, with his usual bloodthirstiness, to the full.

"To-morrow, and to-morrow, and to-morrow!" Come, then, my satyr, my wolf in sheep's clothing, and I shall be ready for you—

> " And all our yesterdays have lighted fools
> The way to dusty Death ! "

CHAPTER XXXV

THE ASSIGNATION.

ON the morning after Christmas Day, 18—, the Rev. Charles Santley, vicar of Omberley, rose early from that sweet slumber which only the righteous enjoy, and from those nightly visions of celestial bliss which only the pure of heart are suffered to behold. Although, infant-like, he had been "talking with angels in his sleep" all night, he looked pale, careworn, and anxious. He dressed himself with unusual care, surveyed himself again and again in the mirror, sighed softly, and descended to the sitting-room, where his· sister was

already awaiting him at the breakfast-
table.

To his surprise, she looked unusually
agitated, and addressed him eagerly the
moment he appeared.

" I am so glad you are come down.
Rachel has just been here from the
cottage, where they are in a terrible
state of alarm."

Rachel was the name of Miss Russell's
maidservant.

" But what is the matter ? "

" Edith went out early yesterday
evening, and she has not returned.
They cannot guess what has become of
her.   Oh, Charles, go over at once !   If
anything has happened to her ! "

The clergyman listened in no little
agitation.

" Did she leave no message ? " he
asked.

" None. She is such a strange girl ; and lately, I am afraid, she has been unhappy. I am going down to the station to make inquiries, and they fancy she may have taken the train to London."

" It is very strange ! "

"Strange ? It is horrible ! Oh, Charles, she has never been quite the same since her cousin came down here visiting. I thought that you were her choice, and I hoped you would some day marry her ; but since young Hetherington was here—— "

Santley, who had broken a little bread and drunk a cup of tea, rose impatiently.

" You women think of nothing but marrying and giving in marriage," he said. " Well, I will go over and speak to Miss Russell. I cannot think that any harm has happened to Edith."

"I hope and pray not. But to be away all night—it is unaccountable."

"Perhaps," suggested Santley, more troubled than he cared to show, "she has gone to London."

"But why go without a word?"

"I really cannot tell. Young ladies take strange fancies; and if, as you suggest, there is anything between young Hetherington and herself——"

"I did not suggest anything of the kind."

"Excuse me, Mary, you did."

"I am sure she cares nothing for her cousin," returned Miss Santley.

Her brother shrugged his shoulders, and, putting on his hat and overcoat, walked out of the Vicarage. On reaching the open air, where all looked dark and cold, he trembled like a leaf. What could it mean? What last freak had

come over the infatuated girl? Could
it be possible that she had carried out
her wild threat to leave the place, and
take her secret with her—perhaps to
some nameless grave? He remembered
their last conversation, when she had
first told him of her condition, and
beseeched him at once to make her his
wife. He remembered how wild she
had seemed, how despairing, and of how
little avail, to calm her, his words had
been. If any harm had come to her,
the evil lay at his door. It was horrible
to think of! Although another woman
had come between them, although he no
longer loved her with that wild frenzy
which had first urged him to evil, he
had still a conscience, and he could not
bear to think that any harm had come
to her. Then, again, he shuddered at
the thought of any exposure. He had

meant to marry her, sooner or later ; and he had already made arrangements to hide from the world any knowledge of her condition. She was to have gone away to a secret place; and then, when her travail was over, he had meant to act honourably by her. And now, by some act of madness, she had perhaps put it out of his power ! Surely, if she had gone away in accordance with the plan they had made together, she would have sent him some intimation of her purpose. It was extraordinary, altogether.

On reaching the cottage, he found Miss Russell in violent grief, and quite bewildered what to do. He tried to console her, pointing out that perhaps some little lover's quarrel with her cousin had taken her niece up to town ; and the old lady listened eagerly, hoping against hope.

"Of late she has been so strange," sobbed the old lady, "so unlike herself. Often, listening at her door o' nights, I have heard her crying as if her heart was like to break ; and she would never tell me what was the matter. Do you think—do you really think, sir, it was her cousin Walter ? "

"I am almost certain of it," said the good shepherd. "Did they correspond ? "

"I think so—sometimes ; but latterly they were estranged. Oh dear ! Oh dear ! "

"Depend upon it, she has gone to London to see him. You will no doubt have a letter from her in the course of the day. Keep up your spirits ! Miss Dove is a good young lady, and I am sure God will protect her. Is there anything more that I can do for you ? "

"It was so kind of you to come," said the poor soul. "Your words are indeed a comfort."

"I am glad to hear you say so. Your dear niece was always a favourite of mine."

"Oh, sir, I know that; and sometimes I thought—— But there, it's no time to talk of that *now*. If she had only gone to you for advice, you would have guided her for her good, and this would never have happened. She was always pious-minded, but latterly, I'm afraid, she didn't go to church as often as she ought."

"Don't say that, Miss Russell. She was most regular in her religious duties —a pattern, indeed, to all my flock. There, there! I feel satisfied there is no cause for alarm. I will go myself and make every inquiry."

"Oh, sir, you are an angel!" cried the old lady, looking at him in admiration. And she really meant what she said.

"Alas! no," he answered, shaking his head solemnly—"only a poor miserable sinner. We are all miserable sinners. *Good* morning. Put your trust in God."

"I do indeed, sir. But, sir, before you go, may I ask you a favour?"

"Certainly."

"If you would kindly kneel down with me a moment, and say a prayer for my poor girl, I think it might help to bring her back. The Lord hears the prayers of the righteous, Mr. Santley."

Thus entreated, Santley could not refuse. To do him justice, he felt no little moral nausea at the proposal; but he was helpless under the circumstances. So they knelt down in the parlour together, and the good man extemporized a short but eloquent prayer for the occasion, entreating the Lord to bring back the stray lamb to the fold, and beseeching a blessing then and for ever on all that house. Miss Russell wept profusely. His words were so beautiful, his voice so musical, his manner so seraphic. At last he rose to his feet, looking pale and almost scared at a proceeding which (to his own conscience) looked something like blasphemy; and then, amidst profuse blessings from the distracted old lady, he respectfully took his leave.

While on his way to make inquiries in the village, he met his sister returning. She had discovered nothing, save that several persons had gone on to London by the midnight train the previous night, and that one of them was a lady who

might have been Miss Dove. There
was nothing for it but to wait out the
day, and see if any communication came.
In the mean time Miss Santley said she
would hasten up to the cottage, to
condole and consult with Mrs. Dove.

"Shall you be in to lunch?" she asked,
as they parted on the roadside.

"No; not till evening. I think I
shall walk over to Lewstone, to see about
some books. I will make inquiries on
the way, in case Edith has gone in that
direction."

Lewstone was a small county town,
seven miles off, where there was a
library, a newspaper, and a great
brewery. The way to it lay past Foxglove Manor. Santley did not care to
tell his sister that he had an appointment with Mrs. Haldane for that
morning. He knew that Miss Santley

regarded with some anxiety her brother's relations with the handsome lady of the Manor. Much as she admired him, and great as was her faith in his spiritual purity, she knew him sufficiently well to be aware that his weak point was his admiration for beauty in the opposite sex. Not for a moment did she dream —indeed, she would have supposed the idea as almost blasphemous—that that admiration was not perfectly harmless and honourable; but it led' him, she thought, to take delight in feminine society generally, and to overlook the attractions of the woman she wanted him to marry. He would marry some day—it was inevitable; and she had made up her mind that he was to marry Edith, who was her friend, and would doubtless allow her to keep her place at the Vicarage, whereas another woman a stranger, might take possession of him and resent all sisterly interference.

" Shall you call at the Manor as you pass ? " she inquired.

" I think so ; I am not quite sure."

" Perhaps it will be better," she said, thoughtfully. " They may know something about Edith."

The sun was now high up in the heavens, but deeply veiled in wintry cloud. It was a dark, dismal day— darkness in the sky and whiteness on the ground. The road which led to the Manor was unusually cheerless and dismal, and few people were abroad. Before long Santley came into the shadow of the Manor woods, which skirted one side of the highway for several miles. It was a gloomy walk.

Nevertheless, Santley soon forgot his anxiety, in the prospect of a meeting .

with Ellen Haldane. He had been greatly troubled the previous Christmas Day, by the fact that she had not put in an appearance at church ; but her message, making the appointment, which had been duly conveyed to him by Baptisto had filled him with eager expectation. It was the first time she had actually desired him to come to her, and his hopes rose high. Perhaps his devotion had at last moved her heart ; perhaps she had at last discovered that true happiness was only to be found, not with her heretic husband, but with the man whom she had loved when a girl. In the eyes of the world, there might be wickedness in tempting her from her wifely duty ; but surely, in the eyes of heaven, there was no great sin. By living on with an unbeliever, she was in danger of losing her soul alive. The man was admittedly an atheist, an enemy of the Church, and she was wretched in his society, without sympathy, without conservation, without religion. And on one point the clergyman's mind was now made up. If Ellen was willing, he would take her with him to some foreign land, where he might labour in some way useful to the Lord, and forget all the petty humiliations of an English village. There might be, there would be, a scandal; but what need they care, when they were far away? In any case, scandal was likely to come, now that Edith Dove was in so sad a predicament. No; after all, he would not marry Edith. She was a foolish girl, and would soon find a more suitable husband; and whether or not, he had long ago discovered that they were not at all suited to each other.

Thus musing, Santley drew nearer and nearer to the Manor gates.

From the glimpse we have given of his thoughts, it may be gathered that the man's moral deterioration was at last complete. What had been at first a mere religious amorousness, a soft sensuous delight in female sympathy and female beauty, much the same as that which filled him when the organ played, and the scented incense rose, and the dainty congregation fluttered and flushed beneath him, had gradually developed, through self-indulgence, into a determined and uncontrollable sensuality. The devil, with a bait of warm nakedness, had hooked him fast. And already, in his own heart, he knew that he was lost; and so long as he reached the summit of his desires, he did not care. One sign of his degeneration was

unmistakable : he had lost for ever his
old faith in the chastity and purity of
women. He could remember the time,
not long past, when a beautiful woman
was to him a spiritual thing, something
sanctified, to be approached with awe—
such as fills the worshipper who gazes
on the Madonna of some great painter.
Now he often found himself gazing on
the Madonnas in his own study, with
a satyr's delight in their plumpness,
their naked arms, their swelling breasts.
His nature was subdued to what it
worked in, like the dyer's hand. His
easy conquest over Edith Dove, whose
sin was in loving so madly and so
much, had degraded his whole nature.
Once having snapped the chain of con-
ventional morality, which is the only
band to bind such men as this, he was
reckless and exultant ; and to possess

Ellen Haldane, in her superb beauty and glowing womanhood, was his daily thought and his nightly dream.

This is speaking plainly, but it is a simple statement of the fact. As for the ultimate consequence of his acts, he was quite unable to realize them, having lost the power of reason and self-control.

He approached the lodge. How cold and chill it looked, in the darkness of the overhanging, snow-clad boughs! He put on his stereotyped smile, expecting to see little Mrs. Ferne step out, as was her custom, and drop him a country curtsey. But the lodge seemed empty that morning.

He passed through the side gate, which was unfastened, and stepped into the avenue—the long, dreary colonade of trees, a mile long, winding up to the steps of the Manor house. Glancing up it, he fancied he saw in the distance the figure of a man, looking his way ; but in another moment it was gone.

Bleak, lonely, and inexpressibly dismal looked the avenue, with its white road of snow between the dark trees, and the one dark figure of the clergyman slowly advancing. The gloom of the place seemed to settle upon his spirit, and to dispel it he quickened his footsteps.

Suddenly, he heard from the distance a low, deep sound, like the tolling of a church bell.

He started, listening, and at first he could not believe the evidence of his ears. There was no church near, and the sound seemed unaccountable and strangely ominous. After a pause, slow as the drawing of a deep, long breath, it was repeated.

Toll ! toll !

Santley was by nature a superstitious man, and, though no coward, he was terrified. What could it mean ? It was like a funeral bell, tolling for the dead. Listening attentively, he found that the sound came down the avenue, and that at every step he took it was more plainly heard. He hastened on, with increasing wonder and alarm.

Toll ! toll ! toll !

Yes, there could be no mistake—it was the tolling of a bell. Hollow and faint, yet filling the dark silence, it fell upon the wintry air. There was no stir in the shrouded woods, which closed dismally on every side ; no answer from the dull, leaden, brooding sky—only the dull, dreadful, dreary peal, like a chime from the very gates of the tomb.

It was horrible.

He advanced, coming ever nearer to the sound, and at last, to his amazement, he discovered from whence it came. At a turning of the avenue, he came in full view of the ruined chapel, and, looking up to the naked belfry, he saw the old bell slowly swinging, while giving forth that solemn, melancholy peal.

Toll! toll! toll! with measured intervals, just as those which are counted when the bell rings for the dead.

Shocked and surprised, Santley hurried up to the chapel door, and looked in. Standing in the doorway was Baptisto, dressed from head to foot in solemn black, holding the rope, and with face turned upward leisurely ringing the bell.

CHAPTER XXXVI.

A FUNERAL PEAL.

Toll ! toll ! toll ! toll ! toll !

Heard from just underneath, the
sound was hideous ; for the bell was
rusty and old, and jangled with dull
vibrations long after each peal had
ceased. The minister looked and listened with horror. Knowing as he did
that the place had been turned to unholy
uses, and retained none of its sacred character, he felt the whole proceeding to
be diabolic.

He called to Baptisto, but the
Spaniard, still keeping his sallow face

turned upward, and monotonously continuing his work, did not seem to hear.

Toll ! toll ! toll ! toll !—a sound to set the soul, as well as the teeth, on edge ; a peal worthy of Satan himself.

All at once it ceased, with a last quivering jangle of moribund moaning notes.

Baptisto released the rope, took off his hat, and taking out his handkerchief, quietly wiped his brow ; then, turning his dark eyes as if by accident towards the door, he perceived the minister.

He did not seem at all surprised, but sighed heavily, and turned up the whites of his eyes ; then with a bow of profound respect, he advanced. In his suit of deep black, bound up with crape, and his high hat, crape-bound also, he looked like a highly respectable English undertaker. The resemblance was complete

when he put his snow-white handkerchief to his mouth, and coughed solemnly
behind it.

"In Heaven's name, man, what are
you about?" cried Santley, aghast.

Baptisto sighed again, turned up his
eyes, and shook his head dismally.

"Señor," he replied in a low voice, "I
was ringing the chapel bell."

"So I heard.   But why?" the clergyman demanded. ·

"Hush! not so loud, señor," he said,
sinking his voice still lower.   "Respect
our sorrow!"

Santley's astonishment increased, and
he gazed wildly at Baptisto.

"Have you gone mad?" he returned,
unconsciously obeying the request and
sinking his voice.   "Your sorrow?   What
sorrow?   Be good enough to explain
this mystery."

"Will you step into the house, señor, and speak to my master. He will explain to you, I do not doubt; oh yes, he will explain."

And Baptisto sighed again.

"He is at home, then?"

"Yes, señor!"

"And Mrs. Haldane?"

Baptisto groaned, and shook his head from side to side.

"You know I have an appointment with your mistress to-day?"

"Yes, señor, I know that," answered Baptisto; then, as if greatly affected he turned away and put his handkerchief to his eyes.

"In the name of God," cried Santley, "what does it all mean?"

Baptisto turned, and fixed his great black eyes on those of the clergyman.

"Señor, what do they say in your own

church ? ' In the midst of life, we are in death !' "

As he spoke, he pointed upward solemnly. Santley started as if stabbed. Then for the first time he began to understand. The dreary bell, the servant's suit of black, the man's unaccountably solemn and mysterious manner, all seemed to point to some horrible fatality.

" Good heavens !" he exclaimed. " Is any one dead ? Who is it ? Speak—tell me—— "

Baptisto paused, still fixing his eyes on Santley, and preparing to watch the full effect of his words.

" Alas, señor, my mistress ! my poor mistress !"

Santley staggered back, and his face, which had before been very pale, became livid.

"Not dead! no, no!" he moaned.

"Señor," replied the Spaniard, "it is true. She died last night."

Alas, the blackness of the wintry sky! That dreary darkness of the earth, the snow-wrapt woods! Before that woeful message, delivered so sadly yet so impressively by the Spaniard, the last brightness of the light seemed to fade away! Though the bell had ceased to toll, its dull vibration seemed still to ring on the air! The clergyman staggered back, his heart stopped; for a moment he seemed about to faint, and he had to clutch the doorway of the chapel for support. Baptisto saw the movement, but made no sign; even if the other had been falling to the earth, indeed, he would have offered him no assistance.

With one hand upon his heart, as if

some sharp pain was there, the clergyman struggled for speech.   At last it
came.

"It is a lie," he panted : "it *must* be
a lie.   No, no !   She is not dead ; it is
impossible.   Speak, man !   If you have
any mercy, say it is a lie !   She lives !"

The Spaniard, who with a very ugly
expression had heard himself accused of
falsehood, and whose black eyes had
gleamed very balefully, almost smiled—
the faint, wicked, inner smile peculiar to
him.

"Yes, you are right, señor ; she
lives !"

Santley drew a quick breath of relief,
and, coming closer, clutched the
Spaniard's arm.

"I knew it—I was sure of it.   What
did you mean by telling me that falsehood ? "

Quietly, but firmly, Baptisto took the other's hand and displaced it from his arm. His air of cold respect did not change, but the expression of his eyes and mouth was malignant.

" I did not lie, señor."

" What ! and yet you said—— "

" I said my lady lived, señor, and it is true. We Spaniards do not lie. She lives indeed—not here, but *yonder*, señor, among the angels of the sky. Ah yes, she is there ! Her body is at rest ; her soul, señor, lives still for ever."

" Dead ! O God ! . . . When did she die ? "

" Last night, señor, as I said."

It was true, then, though so inconceivable. There was no mistaking the words, the manner of the man ; and yet beneath them both, there was a sinister appearance of horrible satisfaction. The grief seemed simulated, the solemnity strangely false and treacherous. The cruel black eyes, which shone so balefully, seemed to express a malignant pleasure in the torture the tongue was inflicting. And yet, all the while, Baptisto's manner was perfectly polite—the manner of a servant to a superior, stately in the manner of his race, but characteristically calm and respectful.

"Since you doubt me, señor," continued the Spaniard, "speak to my master. He himself will tell you of his sorrow, and you will know from him that, after all, I do not lie."

As the man spoke, he fixed his eyes on something beyond the doorway, and bowed profoundly. Santley turned, and saw, standing close to him, the master of Foxglove Manor.

CHAPTER XXXVII.

THE DEATH-BED.

HALDANE, like Baptisto, was clad funereally. A long black travelling cloak was wrapped around him, and a Spanish sombrero, also black, was drawn over his forehead. He was ghastly pale. He stood with knitted brows, gazing quietly at the clergyman.

Santley tried to speak, but could not. Again his left hand clutched his heart, and he seemed about to fall. Then he heard, as if in a dream—for the voice seemed far away —these words :

" I see, reverend sir, that Baptisto has

told you everything. Yes, it is quite
true, and yet so sudden, that even I can
scarce realize my loss."

"It is incredible," cried Santley.
"Only a few hours since, I know, she
was alive and well ; and now——"

"And now," returned Haldane, in the
same cold, clear voice, "the end has
come. It is strange that you, with your
religious views, should be so surprised
at what is sadly common. We mortals
are like men travelling in ships upon a
great sea ; we eat, drink, and are merry
—too often forgetting that there is only
a mere plank between us and the
grave."

Santley listened in wonder, less at the
words than at the calmness, the perfect
self-control, with which they were
uttered. He had always thought
Haldane hard and callous, but now he

seemed to him a very monster of cold-bloodedness.

"I cannot believe it," he cried; "and you—you seem so calm. Surely, if she were dead, indeed——"

"What would you have me do?" interrupted Haldane. "Weep, wring my hands? Will wailing and gnashing of teeth buy back the lost? If it would do so, reverend sir, then I might rave and tear my hair? But no; philosophy has taught me to contemplate the inevitable with resignation."

"But she was so young! So—so beautiful!"

"Alas! the young too often die first, and the prettiest flowers are the first to fade away. She was always delicate, and latterly, I fear, the spirit was too strong for the frail body. It is comfort to reflect, now all is done, that she had at least the consolations of your holy faith. Death comes to all. Life is but the business of a day. One dies at dawn, another not till afternoon ; another creeps wearily on till evening, when the stars of the eternity twinkle down upon his sad grey hairs. She died in her prime, and was at least spared the sorrows and infirmities that attend the lingering decay of nature. So peace be with her !"

"It is too horrible !" cried Santley. "If this is true, life is a hideous nightmare—a waking curse. She was too young, too good, to die !"

"It is strange," returned Haldane thoughtfully, "that you, with your beautiful faith in immortality, should fear death so much. I have often noticed this inconsistency in men of your religion. Strong as is your belief in another life—a life, moreover, of eternal delight and happiness—you cling with curious tenacity to this life, which, at the same time, you admit to be miserable. We men of science, on the other hand, who believe death to be the final disso- lution of the creature into his component element, can contemplate the change with equanimity."

Santley looked at him in positive horror. Cold as ice, the man discussed his loss as if it were a mere matter for intellectual argument, a question in which he felt merely the interest of a dispassionate spectator of human affairs. And this, with the very shadow of death upon him ; with his wife lying dead in the house, struck down, as it were, by the very thunderbolt of God. So far, then, he, Santley, was justified. He had not wronged the man, when he thought him a creature devoid of common tenderness and feeling, warmed out of his humanity by his frightful creed of negation. Such a being was beyond the pale of Christian brotherhood. He had done right; he had not sinned, when he had sought to lead Mrs. Haldane from the martyrdom of an evil wedlock, to the shining heights of a happier and more spiritual life.

"How did she die? It must have been very sudden. Tell me, for pity's sake!"

"Calm yourself, reverend sir. Ah! you must have a tender disposition to feel another's loss so much. You could not feel it more deeply, if you had lost a person very dear to you—a wife of your own bosom, so to speak."

"I—I esteemed the lady," stammered the clergyman, shrinking before the other's cold, scrutinizing gaze. " She was so good, so noble ! "

" Ah ! was she not ? But you asked me how she died ? I think it was some obscure affection of the *heart.* She was always so emotional, so impulsive ; and latterly, I fear, she was under great excitement. You will be grieved to hear she passed away in bitter mental pain."

Santley started. Haldane continued, in the same cold voice, always keeping his eyes fixed steadily on those of the clergyman.

" There was something on her mind —some load, some trouble, some cruel self-reproach. I gathered from her fragmentary words that she was unhappy, that she sought my forgiveness for some fault of which she considered herself guilty. Whatever that fault was, it preyed upon her life, and hastened her end."

"Why did not you send for me? It is horrible to think she died without the last offices of religion. I would have comforted her, prayed with her; I—— "

He paused in confusion, shrinking before the other's steady gaze.

" There was no time," answered Haldane ; "and besides, to be honest, I did not care to have a clergyman."

"It was not an outrage ! " cried Santley. " It was blasphemous !"

" Pardon me. I don't believe in confession, even at the extreme moment; and I thought that, if she had anything to reveal, it had better be told to the person most interested, namely, her husband."

" Anything to reveal !" exclaimed

Santley, shuddering. "What do you mean?"

"What I say. I am aware you are not a Roman Catholic, but I am afraid your sentiments lean dangerously to the offices of that pertinacious priesthood. You would doubtless have asked her to pour her secret into your ears, with a view to absolution. I preferred to keep her dying message sacred to myself. If she had erred and was penitent, as I suppose, no priest, Catholic or Protestant, lay or clerical, could absolve her?"

Utterly bewildered and aghast, the unfortunate clergyman listened on. Surely hell had opened, and the thick sulphurous fumes were rising up to cover and darken the wholesome earth. That cold, grim figure, talking so calmly and watching him so keenly; that other dark figure of the Spaniard, still

crouching near them in the doorway ;
surely, too, these were not men, but
devils, sent to torture him and drive
him mad.   He looked around him.   The
snow-clad wood stretched on every
side, save where the white lawns opened,
marked with damp black spots of thaw,
and stretching up to the doors of the
gloomy mansion ; but overhead the
dark heavens had opened for a moment,
and one sickly beam, falling aslant from
the vaporous sky, was gleaming on the
mansion's roof.   Unconsciously he fixed
his eyes on that spot of brightness, in
wonder and in terror, for he was thinking of the piteous sight within the house.

Dull as his faculties seemed, paralyzed
by the extraordinary shock he had
received, he had not failed to understand
Haldane's statement that his wife had
suffered mental agony, and had made, or

tried to make, some kind of confession. After a long pause, still fixing his eyes on the sunbeam upon the roof, he murmured, almost vacantly—

"I am not quite myself, and do not seem to comprehend. Did you say that Mrs. Haldane asked for a clergyman before she died?"

"Certainly. She asked—for *you!*"

Had his eyes not been turned away, he would have been startled by the expression on Haldane's face—so full of cold satisfaction and contempt.

"For me?" he murmured; "for me?"

"Yes. You had great influence over her—a singular influence. Perhaps, having been her spiritual adviser and knowing her thoughts so intimately, you could help me to discover the cause of the sorrow, the self-reproach, of which I have spoken."

" I—I do not understand. She always seemed so bright, so happy."

" She had no cause for secret grief? None, you think? "

" None."

Unconsciously, as he spoke, he turned and met the gaze of his cross-questioner. He flushed nervously, and turned his eyes away. Did Haldane suspect the secret of his love? Had Ellen, before she died, spoken anything to incriminate him? Surely not; else his reception would have been different. Yet in her husband's manner and look, despite his frigid politeness, there seemed a strange suspicion. The cold, cruel eyes never ceased to scrutinize him; they seemed to read his very soul.

" I see, reverend sir, that you cannot realize what has taken place."

" I cannot realize it ! "

" You will at least believe the evidence of your own eyes. Step with me to the house, and look upon her ! "

As he spoke, Haldane moved towards the house. After a moment's hesitation, Santley followed. Yes, he would look upon her for the last time ; he would kneel and pray beside her. As he walked, he staggered like à drunken man.

They passed from the dismal shadow of the trees, crossed the snowy lawn, and ascended the steps leading to the house door. How dark and funereal looked the old mansion as they entered ! All was silent ; not a soul stirred ; their footsteps sounded hollow on the paven floor of the open hall.

Haldane led the way into the drawing-room. The blinds were drawn, there was no fire, and the chamber seemed like a tomb.

"Wait here one moment," said Haldane; and he retired, closing the door.

Santley sat and waited. His very life seemed ebbing away within him, but the low, deep thud of his overburdened heart kept time like a clock, and his ears were full of a sound like low thunder. His lips were dry as dust, and he moistened them vainly with his trembling tongue. Even then, as he sat shivering, he heard again from the distance the faint chime of the desolate chapel bell.

Toll! toll! toll! toll!

The door opened.

Haldane, bareheaded, appeared on the threshold.

"Come this way," he said in a whisper.

Santley rose and tremulously followed. Through the dark lobbies, up the broad staircase, he went in terror, till Haldane paused at the closed door of the room on the first story, and, placing his finger solemnly on his lips, turned a key and entered.

Santley followed, and found himself at last in the chamber of death.

It was a large bedchamber, dimly lighted by the faint rays that crept through the blind, and scented, or so it seemed, with some sickly perfume. In one corner stood the white, cold bed, snowy sheeted, snowy curtained ; and there, stretched out chill and stark, lay something whiter and colder — the marble bust of what had once been a living creature.

Yes, it was she, beautiful even in death. Her eyes were closed, her hair was smoothed softly over her brows, her face was fixed like marble in ghastly pallor, her waxen hands were folded on the sheet which covered her from feet to chin. She almost seemed to be sleeping, not dead, she was so calm, peaceful, and lovely, in that last repose.

On a small table beside the bed lay her Bible (Santley knew it well ; it was a present from himself, with his own name written on the flyleaf), and a waxen taper, unlighted. Lying on the coverlet, close to her fingers, was a wreath of immortelles.

And through the window, which was left open at the top to admit the pure air, came again, wafted by the wind, the low, dreadful tolling of the chapel bell.

Toll ! toll !

Haldane stood close by the bedside, not looking at his wife, but always keeping his stern eyes fixed upon the clergyman. Step by step, horrified yet fascinated, Santley crept nearer and nearer to the bed, his eyes dilated, his face even more ghastly than the face on which he gazed. He noticed everything —the marble features, the folded hands, the closed eyes beneath their waxen lids; he felt in his nostrils the sick perfume of death.

Then, overmastered by the piteous sight, he raised his arms wildly in the air, uttered a cry of anguish and despair, and fell, moaning and sobbing, on his knees by the bedside.

CHAPTER XXXVIII.

TORTURE—AND CONFESSION.

FOR some minutes he remained kneeling, his strong frame shaken by deep sobs, his lips murmuring some incoherent prayer. Then he felt a touch upon the shoulder. He looked up, shuddering.

"Come!" said Haldane, looking darkly down upon him.

"No, no!" he cried, in the extremity of his agitation. "Let me stay here! Let me pray by her side a little while!"

"Come away!" answered Haldane, more sternly. "This is no place for you."

Santley rose trembling to his feet, and gazed again upon the cold sleeping face and form.

" Leave me ! leave me !" he exclaimed, turning wildly towards his torturer. " Leave me alone with her !"

The face of the master of the house became terrible in its sternness, as he responded—

" Command yourself, man, and follow me ! You forget yourself. This place is sacred. '

" My office is sacred. I desire you to leave me alone with the dead."

" And I refuse. I do not want your prayers, nor does she need them. Come !"

With a low moan, Santley turned again towards the bed, stretching out his arms ; but this time Haldane interposed, with angry determination—

"Are you mad? I command you to come away."

"O God! God!"

"Do not blaspheme. She who sleeps there is nothing, or should be nothing, to you. Leave the room, or, by Heaven, I shall have to make you!"

Beside himself with excitement, Santley glared at Haldane, and clenched his hands, as if he would have struck him; but, remembering the place in which he stood, and the solemnity of the occasion, he conquered his insane impulse, and tottered to the door. Haldane followed, and as he turned on the threshold, put out his hand and pushed him into the lobby; then followed, and turned the key in the lock.

"Come with me," he said, in a voice of command.

Santley obeyed, and the two descended

the stairs. On the way down they met Baptisto ascending, with whom Haldane whispered hurriedly for a moment. Then they made their way through the dark lobbies, and again entered the gloomy drawing-room. With a groan Santley threw himself on a chair, and hid his face in his hands.

"You are strangely moved," said Haldane, coldly. "What was my wife to you, that you should exhibit this unseemly grief?"

Santley drew his hands from his face and looked up wildly.

"What was she to me?" he cried. "More than life—the light of all the world. Now that light is gone, and I am desolate."

"Strange words," said Haldane quietly, "to come from so holy a man! You are not in your sane mind."

"God knows I am not," returned the clergyman, "and yet . . . I am sane enough to know what I am saying. Yes, you may stare! I am sick of disguise. I'll wear the mask no more. I loved your wife."

Still perfectly retaining his composure, and almost smiling, Haldane said, with a dark sneer—

"Most reverend sir, I knew it."

"You know it *now !* "

"Pardon me, I have known it all along."

"You may have guessed something, but not all. I loved your wife. You were unworthy of her. I sought to win her from you, and I succeeded—yes, for she hated you, and loved me. God was on my side, for you were an unbeliever, a blasphemer. I tried to make her leave the shelter of your roof for mine. She was my first love. I tried, do you hear, day and night, to make her my own— my own in this world, and in the next."

Again that calm reply—

" Most sainted sir, I knew it."

" And I tell you, I succeeded. She loved me. She would have followed me to the world's end. This house was hell to her, because you had no religion. Her soul was mine."

" And *now ?* " said the other coldly. " And *now*, most holy and reverend sir ? "

" And *now*, though she has passed away in her beauty and her holiness, I love her still. She is dead, and I shall die. In heaven, at least, we shall be together ! "

" Are you so sure that she is *there ?* " said Haldane, still very calmly. " Are you so sure that *you* will follow her ? *I*

am not so sure. If there be the heaven
you speak of, it was never made for the
guilty. The door of your paradise is
wide, but it is too narrow, I have heard,
for the sinner who dies without repentance."

"The sinner? Who is the sinner?"

"She who sleeps upstairs?"

"It is a falsehood," said Santley,
rising to his feet. "She was an angel,
without a stain, and you—you made her
wretched. Yes, wretched! She was
too good for you—too holy and spiritual.
A saint! a martyr! God will cherish
and justify her!"

"Saints have fallen; and she fell."

"Fell? You dare not accuse her!"

"I do accuse her; I accuse you both!
. . . Ah! my man of God, there was no
need to throw aside the mask at all; I
knew the face behind it from the first.

She is punished as she deserves. Now it is your turn."

His manner had changed, from one of cold self-control to one of concentrated passion. With voice raised and hand pointing, he advanced towards the clergyman. They stood close together, face to face.

But Santley fell back, horrified.

"Whatever I am, she was pure—too pure and good for this black world. Speak reverently of her! Although I loved her—and I tell you my love is justified—she was not guilty of any sin. She was only too faithful to her wifely vow—faithful in thought and deed. Again I tell you, speak reverently of her!"

"No hypocrisy can save her now," said Haldane, sternly. "You have thrown aside the mask, as you say ; it is useless to assume it again. I know everything —her guilt, and yours!"

"She was not guilty. You cannot believe it!"

"Why should I doubt it? The thing was a thousand times stronger than your proofs of Holy Writ. Now, if I said to you that she had confessed her guilt, what would you say?"

"I should say that it was not true!"

"Not true!"

"A lie—the wickedest of lies."

"Then, if she was innocent, your guilt is trebled, and you are her murderer."

"Her murderer? her murderer?"

"Yes. You have been liberal in confession; I will follow your example. You saw her lying yonder? Calm, cold, and beautiful, was she not?—yes, as a sleeping infant. Shall I tell you how she died ? By poison. By the deadliest of all poisons."

" Poisoned ? " cried the clergyman, raising his voice to a scream.

" Precisely. A painless death, though sure and sudden. You see, although I kept within my right, I was merciful. Death was better than disgrace, and so —I killed her ! "

Santley clutched at Haldane—then, with a moan, sank swooning upon the floor.

When he recovered, he staggered to his feet, and looked around him. He was still there, in the room, which was now quite dark, but he was alone. He awoke as from death, with the cold sweat upon his forehead, his form shaking like a leaf. What a change the experience of the last hour had made in him ! He felt as if he had been mad for years. As the sick horror of his position spread over his bewildered senses, he groaned aloud.

Then remembering where he was, and fearing the surrounding darkness, he groped towards the door.

Suddenly it opened, and Haldane himself, holding a lamp in his hand, appeared upon the threshold. As the light flashed upon the minister's form, it showed a face horrible in its anguish and despair. With his hair wild and dishevelled, his neckcloth disarranged, his black frock suit disordered, Santley seemed transformed. His beauty was turned into ugliness, his elegance into coarseness; his head, no longer erect and proud, drooped between his shoulders like an old man's.

"Where are you going?" said Haldane, interposing, and placing down the lamp he carried.

"Up yonder, to see if it is true. It is surely a frightful dream! Let me pass!"

"Stay where you are! Your presence shall not outrage the dead again."

"She *is* dead, then?"

"What you have seen, you have seen."

"And—you—you killed her? Is it true?"

"Perfectly."

With a wild cry, Santley clutched Haldane; but his hold was so weak, so tremulous, that the other's strong frame scarcely shook.

"You shall not escape," cried the minister. "Coward! murderer! I will deliver you up to justice!"

"Pshaw!"

With a powerful movement, Haldane

disengaged himself, and his opponent fell back into the room. Santley was not a strong man, and just then he seemed positively helpless; nor would he at any time have been a match for the square-built, broad-shouldered master of Foxglove Manor.

"Hands off, if you please," said Haldane. "If it comes to a trial of strength, I shall crush your reverend carcase like an egg. Another man, in my position, would have wrung your neck long ago. Do you know why I have been so gentle with you?"

Santley gazed at him vacantly, and did not speak.

"Because I prefer to prolong your agony as long as possible, and to let the world know of what stuff its priests are made."

"You are a murderer," gasped Santley

again, clutching at him, but with the feeble grasp of a sick child. " You are a murderer, on your own confession. I tell you, I will give you up."

" *Après ?* " said Haldane, coolly.

" You have destroyed your wife—the purest and best woman God ever made. She was innocent of all wrong. She was an angel married to a devil, that was all."

· " Will you swear to me, before the God you worship, that there was nothing between you ? "

" Yes, I will swear it. I loved her, but she was pure. If there was any sin, it was on my shoulders, for I tempted her. Yet you destroyed the innocent, and let the guilty live."

Overcome by his emotion, Santley sank into a chair, sobbing. Haldane watched him for a short space in silence ;

then approached him and placed a hand on his shoulder. He tried to shake off the touch, with a shiver of loathing.

"I am glad that you perceive your own guilt; that is something. Under the mask of friendship—worse, under cover of your holy calling, you came to this house. I welcomed you, entertained you. I gave you my hand freely, as man to man; trusted you, even respected you, despite your superstitions. How did you reward this hospitality? By seducing, or seeking to seduce, the wife of the man who welcomed you without suspicion. This was your religion—this was your sense of Christian brotherhood. My man of God was a hypocrite—an adulterer. I tell you, a dog would have more honour, more purity. You made my house a hell. In return, I have put hell into your heart. You hear? Into your heart, if you have a heart, which would seem doubtful. Another would have killed you; I preferred to let you live."

The clergyman looked up piteously. His force seemed broken, his eyes streamed with tears.

"You should have killed me," he returned. "I was to blame, not she. You may kill me now. I shall then be at rest with *her*."

Haldane's face blackened.

"Do not couple your names together. The guilt of her death is yours, not mine."

"Mine?"

"Yes. I was only the instrument, you were the cause. The seed of all this sorrow was sown in your black heart. Had you never tempted her, had you never filled her mind with the poison bred in your own, she would be living now, a happy, honoured wife. You see, my man of God, that you are the murderer; you have killed her, not I."

"O God! God!" moaned Santley, hiding his face in horror.

"It is too late to call on God. If *that* is true," pursued the other, "this also is true—that you have lost her eternally. Your God is a God of justice. He does not, either in hell or heaven, bring the murderer and his victim together. You murdered her soul first; then, since you made it inevitable, I destroyed its mortal dwelling. Since you believe in hell, surely this is enough to damn you. Say she is innocent. The better for her; the worse for you. She is among the angels; your place is elsewhere, eternally; *there* you may wail and gnash your teeth in vain. You see, reverend sir, I am comforting you with your own beautiful creed. Your faith in it was great ; through your faith in it, you are lost for ever."

With a cry, almost an imprecation, Santley staggered to his feet, unable to listen any longer. Sorrow, shame, terror, horror, contended within him. Already it seemed as if the earth was opened to swallow him, the forked tongues of fire shooting up to envelop and consume him.

He rushed towards the door. This time the other did not interpose.

"Where are you going, pray?" he demanded quietly.

Santley turned round upon him, livid, glaring like a madman.

"To fetch the police," he answered. "I shall denounce you. Whatever becomes of me, you shall die, upon the gallows."

"Permit me to light you to the door," answered the philosopher, smiling. "You could not go upon a better errand. Sound the alarm, fetch the police hither; the sooner the better. When they come, they shall be acquainted with the truth. They shall know, all the world shall know, that I killed my wife; and *why?* Because a clergyman, a man of God, honoured by many, respected by all, had come to my house like a satyr, and made it a nest of pollution. I shall stand in the dock, and the chief witness against me will be yourself—the Rev. Charles Santley, Vicar of Omberley, a living light, a pillar of the Church, self-convicted as hypocrite, liar, adulterer, seducer, satyr—filthy from the soul to the finger-tips. How the sweet maids of your congregation will stare ! It will be a *cause célèbre*—a nine-days' wonder. And on the next Sabbath, perhaps, you will preach the gospel of love and purity, as usual ! "

Santley clung to the doorway, limp and crushed, a picture of mingled fury and desolation.

" By the way, I shall call witnesses in my own defence. First, Miss Dove, —you see, I know her—one of the many who have ornamented slippers for the holy man's feet, and cloths for his altar. She will tell them of meetings by night, of holy trysts, of Eden, and—of the fall. Oh, it will be a famous affair, and greatly to the honour of the Church. But why are you lingering so long ? Go at once, reverend sir, and proclaim the murder. You see, I am quite ready."

He pointed to the hall door. With a wild cry, Santley passed along the lobby, opened the door, and rushed out into the air.

CHAPTER XXXIX.

GETHSEMANE.

By this time darkness had fallen, though it was still early in the afternoon.

There was a high wind, moaning around among the leafless trees ; and, from time to time, flakes of snow were falling—large, and far apart. As he descended the snow-clad steps, he stumbled and fell among the drift, but rose again immediately, covered with patches of whiteness, and pursued his way.

Was it the wind shrieking, or something in his own troubled brain ? He

looked wildly around him, plunging this
way and that, like a blind man. The
darkness frothed before his eyes, and
burst into spangled stars, as when one
receives a violent blow, or as when one
is sinking in deep water and choking
for breath.

Presently he turned and looked back
from the centre of the frozen lawn.
Behind him, blacker than the blackness
of the night, lay the great shadow of the
Manor house; but from one window
above the entrance came a feeble light.
He knew the window well. It was that
of the chamber wherein he had looked
upon the dead.

Alone in the darkness, he threw up
his arms and uttered a wail of despair.
As his voice rose upon the wind, other
voices seemed to echo him with sounds
of mocking laughter. Haldane had told

him that he had lost his soul alive.
Indeed it seemed so, and hell was
already around, and in him.

But he remembered his purpose, and
hastened on. Whatever the issue might
be, he was determined to hand over that
man to the law, to make him expiate
on the gallows his act of cowardly,
treacherous vengeance. He had not
spared *her*, and he should, at least, pay
the penalty. *Then*, when he had
avenged her death, he cared not what
became of himself. He could die, too ;
yes, and would.

Ah ! but the man was right, when
he had torn his soul open and showed
the cancerous sore within it. He had
broken the laws of God, and he had lost
eternally what he loved. There was no
justification for him—none. He had
been an adulterer in thought, if not in

deed—a hypocrite, hiding a loathsome lust under the garment of religion. Why had he not been warned in time? He might have known that the man he had to deal with—a man who believed in nothing—would pause at nothing. He remembered, too late, that monkish tale of jealousy and murder, which might have told him, had he not been so mad, what was lurking so pitilessly in the man's mind. It was little comfort now, to reflect that he was innocent in act. The consequences had been the same, as horrible, as irrevocable, as if he had sinned seventy times and seven. By his abominable solicitation, he had betrayed the woman he adored. Yes, he had killed her! What hope could there be for him, in this world or another, after that?

Nevertheless, he hastened on, fighting

with his own thoughts in the darkness, stumbling through the drifted snow. He found the avenue and entered it—passing into deeper darkness, hearing the wind shriek more loudly on every side. The police barrack was at Omberley, five miles distant. He would hasten there without delay, tell what had taken place, and return with the officers that night. He would not rest until he had the murderer bound and captured ; for even yet, if he did come back quickly, he might escape.

Then he thought of all the shame, the scandal, which must assuredly come with the revelation of the truth. The women who had thought him almost a sainted creature, the villagers who had watched him with simple reverence—all who had respected him and heard the gospel of love from his lips, would point at him as a shameless creature, a scandal to his holy office. He could never mount the pulpit again, or walk in the sun. They would strip the priestly raiment from his back, and hound him away into the world. Even his own sister, who thought him the purest and best of men, would, shrink from him with loathing ; nay, how could he look her, or any pure creature, in the face ?

All that, and more, he thought, could have been borne, could he only have restored the dead to life. His own fall and degradation would have been a trifle, if he had not sacrificed that sainted being —the woman of his early love, the creature of his idolatry, the object of his insane and fatal passion. She had suffered for his guilt, but she had not atoned for it. Nothing could atone, nothing. How gladly that night would he have died, if by death he could have restored her to the sunshine of the world !

Then, in his despair, he reproached her God—the God who had made her so beautiful, and him so weak. Why had God ever brought them together ? Why, having once separated them, had He ever caused them to meet again ? It was cruel, unmerciful, to tempt a man so much ! He had only asked for a little love, and without love life was so dark. And before temptation came, had he not done God good service ? More than one doubting heart had been turned, by his persuasion, back to the faith of Christ ; more than one erring sinner had, through him, been led back, penitent and weeping, to the Church's fold ! All men had respected him for his blameless life, for his good deeds.

He had been kind to the suffering, generous to the poor. He had been an example of Christian charity to his fellows. He had reflected honour on the university which gave him to the Church, and on the Church which had accepted him into her bosom. Though so young, he had risen high, by his own talents, his intelligence, his own blameless character. And now he had lost everything, because he had pined for a little sympathy, a little love.

As these thoughts passed through his brain, his eyes were blinded with tears, and, in utter self-pity, he sobbed aloud.

How dark it was! how miserably dark and cold! He could not see an inch before him, could not even perceive the white ground beneath his feet; but the wind wailed louder and louder on every side.

He remembered how gladly, the previous day, he had proclaimed the good tidings of the birth of Christ. The bells had rung, and from every side, over the white landscape, cold, but cheerful and light with sunshine, the people had come gathering in—rich and poor, old and young, all gaily clad for Christmas-tide. He had stood away—stoled in the pulpit, and had seen the shining faces upturned reverently to his, and had heard the clear voices ring out in happiness and praise. Ah, it had been a beautiful time! Only yesterday, and already it seemed so far away!

In his misery, he quite forgot how much and how often he had fretted under the yoke of his priestly duties; how he had despised the ignoble natures of his flock; how he had panted again and again for a freer life and for more

eventful days! What he had lost for
ever now seemed strangely dear. As
he reviewed his life in the village, he
remembered none of its cares, none of
its indignities; it seemed all peaceful,
all beautiful, *now!* Yes, it was heaven,
though he had not known it; heaven,
though he had fallen from it. And he
could never return to it again; never
preach in the church, never minister to
man or woman, never know the blessing
and the peace of a divine vocation any
more!

Suddenly he paused, stumbling in be-
wilderment and terror. He had stepped
into a deep snowdrift, which rose nearly
to his knees. He looked wildly round,
but could discern nothing. He pressed
his way forward, and stumbled against
the frozen root of a great tree. He
turned and groped another way; again

something interposed. Gradually, straining his eyes through the darkness, he discerned that he was surrounded by trees on every side.

He had wandered from the avenue, and was long among the plantations— he could not tell in what direction.

How long he wandered among the dreary woods he could not tell.

A mortal fever was upon him, and he struggled confusedly this way and that, sometimes stumbling and falling amid the snow, sometimes coming violently against the frozen tree-trunks, sometimes rushing among briers and tangled underwoods which clutched him like fingers, and rent his clothing as he tore himself away.

He shouted, thinking he might be heard. His shout rose faintly on the

wind, and was echoed by unearthly
voices.

Then he seemed to see sheeted shapes
passing before him; ghostly faces flashing into his own, and fading away. He
saw *her* face, marble-white as he had
seen it in death, and with horrible re-
buking eyes.

Ah, that night! that night! He
passed an eternity of agony, in a few
hours!

At last he fell, half fainting, on the
stump of a tree, and rested, afraid to
venture further. Pausing there, he
clasped his hands together and prayed.

For her; for himself. He prayed
to Heaven for help and mercy. In his
abject fear and humiliation, he prostrated
his soul before his God. His strength
seemed failing him, and he felt as if he
were dying. Ah, the horrible darkness!

the nameless terror! Would he ever live to see the light again?

The snow thickened and fell upon him; he shook it off again and again, but still it fell, blinding and covering him. He became very cold, despite the fever in his veins—cold as death. Afraid to perish that way, he rose to his feet and struggled on.

At last, after wandering on and on for an indefinite space of time, he saw a light breaking through the trees. He shouted, and ran forward.

The light came from the windows of some building, and streamed brightly out into the darkness, lighting up the snowy ground, revealing the trees and branches in silhouette. Wild and despairing, he approached nearer, and saw a door, through the hinges of which shone a faint radiance. Then he recognized the place. It was the ruined chapel of Foxglove Manor.

He did not hesitate, but pushed open the door. He found himself in the building which George Haldane had turned from a temple of God into a laboratory of science. In the centre of it, surrounded by books, papers, and scientific implements of divers kinds, a man sat, calmly writing by the light of a brilliant oil-lamp.

As Santley entered, he looked up. The master of Foxglove Manor.

Spectral and ghastly, his hair dishevelled, his dress torn and disordered, covered with mud, the minister staggered into the chapel. Who, in that frenzied apparition, would have recognized the sometime spruce and comely Vicar of Omberley? In one of his falls he had cut his forehead on a tree or stone, and blood was oozing from the wound. He was a horrible sight—horrible and pitiable.

Haldane looked up, and nodded.

"So, it is *you!*" he said, pushing his papers aside.

A large meerschaum pipe lay on the table beside him, with a box of lucifers. He struck a light, and quietly began to smoke, as he continued—

"You have returned quickly. Pray, have you brought the police with you?"

Without answering him directly, Santley approached the table, and, fixing his wild eyes upon him, demanded in a hollow voice—

"What are you doing?"

The philosopher leant back in his chair, and blew a cloud of smoke into the air.

"Writing, as you see."

"Writing!" echoed Santley.

"Yes; at my history.   To-night's experience has furnished me with material for a new chapter—on 'Spiritual Vivisection.'"

The man was inconceivable, even satanic.   Santley was again dominated by his supernatural *sang froid*, his supreme self-control.

"Have you a heart, man?" he cried, gazing in horror upon him.

Haldane smiled diabolically.

"A reference to the most rudimentary system of physiology," he replied, "would convince you that I could not exist without one."

"Death in your house, murder in your heart, you can sit here so calmly, still busy with your blasphemies?   You cannot be human."

"On the contrary, I am particularly human."

"No, no ; you are a devil ! a devil !"

"If you were a philosopher, you would know that devils do not exist ; even your own not too intellectual Church has rejected demonology. I am simply a physician ; yours."

"Mine ! my physician."

"I have opened your heart, to show you the canker existing within it. I have shown you, in an interesting experiment, that the disease of supersensuous desire, which with you is constitutional and inherited, culminates in moral scrofula, imbecility, hysterical mania, and death. It is, moreover, capable of spreading contagion—a sort of cancerous cell, which, inhaled by the lips or from the polluted atmosphere, must inevitably bring disease and death to others.   The kiss of the leper, reverend sir! For the future, I should recommend you to carry a clapper with you, as they do in the East, to warn off the unwary."

The comparison was a hideous one; but indeed, at that moment, it did not seem inappropriate.   Wild, ghastly, dishevelled, bloody, and degraded, Santley looked a creature to be avoided and even feared. He listened to the cold periods of his torturer, fixed his pale eyeballs, which seemed vacant of all light, upon his face; then suddenly, with a spasmodic scream, he leapt upon him and seized him by the throat.

The attack was so unexpected and so sudden, that Haldane was taken by surprise.   He sprang to his feet, while the other clung around him like a wild cat.   But the struggle was only brief.

In another minute he had gripped the vicar with his powerful arms, and pinned him against the wall of the chapel. There he writhed and wrestled, impotent, furious, foaming at the mouth.

" If you don't control yourself better," said the philosopher, between his set teeth, " you will soon want a strait-waistcoat. Be quiet, will you ? "

And he shook him as a wiry terrier shakes a rat.

" Let me go ! "

" I have a good mind to give you your *coup de grâce*," returned Haldane, with a little less composure than before. " Why, I could strangle you if I pleased."

"Strangle me, then ! "

" Bah ! you are not worth the trouble," said the other, throwing him off. " Tell me again, where are your police-officers ? Why did you not bring them ? "

Utterly conquered and helpless, Santley did not reply. Haldane pointed to the door.

"At any rate, get out of this. I am going to close my studies and go to bed."

And he proceeded to turn down the lamp, previous to blowing it out.

Santley moved towards the door. As he did so, the lamp was extinguished, and the chapel left in pitch darkness. He groped his way out, and stood waiting on the threshold. The philosopher followed, and they stood together in the open darkness. Then Haldane closed the door and turned the key.

"Your way lies yonder, reverend sir," he said, pointing towards the avenue. "Take my advice and sleep upon it, before you return to arrest me. I will keep your secret, if you will keep mine."

" I will make no terms with you," cried the vicar. " I will return, and have you dragged to justice."

"As you please," was the reply.

Haldane walked slowly in the direction of the house. Santley, after a minute's wild hesitation, rushed away again into the night.

By this time the snow had ceased falling, and the air was a little clearer. With little difficulty, Santley found the avenue, and, running rather than walking, followed it till he reached the lodge. As he did so, he heard voices singing in merry chorus. He waited, and presently a light cart drove up, turning into the avenue. He called out, and it stopped. He came close, and found that it contained five persons, two men and three women.

"Who are you?" he demanded. "Where are you going?"

Mrs. Ferne, the lodge-keeper, who was one of the party, informed him that they were Mr. Haldane's servants, returning from their holiday excursion to the neighbouring town.

"Go up to the house at once!" he cried. "Seize your master, detain him till I return. Your mistress has been murdered!"

They cried out in terror and astonishment, asking for particulars.

"I cannot stay," he answered wildly. "Go on, and watch till I return. It is as I say; he has murdered your mistress. I am going for the police."

Then he fled on in the direction of the village. But as he went, his pace seemed to fail him, and his head to go round and round.

At last he reached the village, where all was dark and desolate, and, passing by the shadow of his own church, reached the Vicarage gate. Here he paused, almost spent. He could not go any further. He would go in and get a little brandy, then he would hasten on for assistance.

He staggered in through the gate, and across the garden. There was a light in the window, for Miss Santley was sitting up for her brother, wondering what had kept him so late. He crept close to the window and tapped upon it.

" Mary ! Mary !" he moaned.

She heard him, looked out, and then opened the door, standing on the threshold with a lighted candle in her hand.

At the sight of his blood-stained face and disordered dress, she uttered a cry of fear.

As she did so, he stretched out his hands, and fell like a corpse across the threshold.

CHAPTER XL.

THREE LETTERS.

THEY carried him into the house and
laid him on a bed ; then, seeing him still
speechless, and to all appearance sense-
less, Miss Santley sent for Dr. Spruce,
who lived close by. By the time that
the doctor, a homely old country practi-
tioner, with much professional skill and
worldly wisdom, entered the chamber,
Santley was sitting up and talking incoherently. He tried to leave his bed
and fly forth upon some wild errand, and
his speech was a confused medley, in

which the words " murder," " poison," and " Ellen Haldane," were constantly repeated. He did not seem to recognize any one, and his whole appearance was alarming in the extreme.

Miss Santley told how she had found him, and in what condition. The doctor shook his head.

" I'm afraid it's brain fever," he muttered. "You must keep him very quiet."

Before morning, the doctor's prediction proved to be right. Brain fever of the most violent kind had set in. He lay as if at death's door, incoherently raving.

Alarmed by the constant references to the one subject of " murder," and the constant repetitions of Mrs. Haldane's name, Miss Santley next day sent a messenger up to Foxglove Manor to make inquiries. Her messenger ascertained from Mrs. Ferne, the lodge-keeper, that the vicar had been seen by the servants the previous night, in a state resembling mania, and had told them some wild story of Mrs. Haldane's death by violence. For the rest, Mrs. Ferne said, nothing of an extraordinary nature had occurred at the Manor, and her mistress, though slightly indisposed, was up and about.

So Miss Santley kept watch by the delirious man's bedside, while he lay and fought for life.

The crisis passed. One morning the vicar opened his eyes, and saw his sister sitting silently close to his bed. The fever had almost left him, and he recognized his own room in the Vicarage.

" Is it you, Mary ? " he asked, reaching out his hand, now worn almost to a skeleton.

" Yes, it is I. But you must not speak."

" Have I been ill, Mary ? "

"Yes ; very, very ill."

He closed his eyes, and seemed to fall into a sleep, which lasted for some hours. Suddenly he started up, as if listening, and seemed about to spring from the bed.

" What is it, dear ? " asked his sister, softly soothing him.

He recognized her, and became calm in a moment.

" I was dreaming. I thought I was up at the Manor. Mary, quick—speak to me ! Have they buried her ? "

She looked at him in wonder and terror.

" Hush, dear ! The doctor says you are to keep very quiet."

" But I must know. Tell me, or you will kill me ! What has happened ? How long have I been lying here ? "

" Many days. But you are better now."

" Do you know what has taken place?" he whispered. " Ellen Haldane is dead —murdered ! He killed her."

She shook her head pityingly.

" No, no ! Do not distress yourself. dear, or you will be ill again. Mrs. Haldane is quite well."

" Quite well ? No, no ! "

" You have been dreaming, that is all."

" Only dreaming ? " he repeated, vacantly. " But I tell you I saw her, dead, shrouded for her grave. Mary, it must be true ! "

She succeeded at last, after repeated assurances, in soothing his distracted spirit, and he fell asleep again, moaning to himself.

It was quite true, as his sister told him, that Mrs. Haldane lived. She did not tell him, however, that she had left the Manor, with her husband, and gone away back to Spain.

Was it all a dream, then, after all ?

A week later, when Santley was convalescent, but still horribly overshadowed and perplexed, his sister gave him a letter, which (she said) had been left for him by the master of Foxglove Manor. It was marked "strictly private." Santley waited until he was alone, and then, tearing it open with tremulous fingers, read as follows :—

" SIR,

"I hear that you have been ill. Before leaving for Spain, I have left this with your sister, with instructions that it is to be given you when you are strong enough to read and understand. What it contains, observe, is strictly between you and me; and if you keep your own counsel, no one will know the secret of your indisposition but ourselves.

" In the first place, be comforted by my assurance that my wife is in excellent health. If, in your delirium, you have been under delusions concerning her, dispel them; all that has passed. She lives; and you will live. If you have thought otherwise (and we know sick men have wild fancies), consider that you have merely had an extraordinary dream. Yet, remembering that men have often ere now been warned by visions of calamities to ensue as the consequence of their own mad acts, accept the dream as a sort of divine admonition—an inspiration to lead you towards a better and calmer life. In your dream, sir, you have had your own heart vivisected, and have thus been made conscious of its disease; you have suffered terribly, as all patients must suffer, under the knife. But you will be healed. You will begin the world afresh, and, God willing, become a new man, thanking God, every day you live, that it was only a dream.

"By the time you read this we shall be far away. With my sincere hopes for your perfect recovery, I am, sir, yours truly,

" George Haldane.

"P.S.—My wife knows nothing of your

dream, in any of its phenomena. Some day, perhaps, I shall enlighten her, but not yet. She sends you her best wishes."

That was all Santley read and re-read in amazement, not quite comprehending, yet dimly guessing that there had been some strange mystery. At last, relieved by the thought that all his guilty agony had perhaps been a dream indeed, he sunk back upon the pillow of his armchair, and wept aloud.

That same afternoon, as he sat looking at his loving nurse, he questioned her concerning Edith. It was the first time, since his recovery, that he had mentioned her name.

"Where is she? Have they heard from her? Is she well?"

"She is well, I believe," replied Miss Santley. "Just after you fell ill, her aunt heard from her, and went away to join her in London. They are there together now."

" Do you know their address ? "

" Yes ; I heard from Rachel that they are staying at the Golden Cross Hotel, near the station."

In the evening, Santley insisted on having pen, ink, and paper. His sister begged him not to fatigue himself by writing, but he was determined.

"Charles," she said softly, as she brought him what he wanted, " is it to Edith you are going to write ? "

"Yes," he replied ; and she stooped and kissed him approvingly. Then she left him alone, and he wrote as follows :—

" DEAREST EDITH,

        "Come to me ; come back to Omberley. I have had a dangerous

illness, but through it, God has opened my eyes. I love you, darling. We will be married at once in the dear old church. Yours till death,

"CHARLES SANTLEY."

Two days afterwards, the reply came, in Ellen's own handwriting, thus :

" I, too, have had an illness, in which, also, God has been pleased to open my eyes. I know, now, that it is all over between us. I shall never marry you ; I shall never return to Omberley. I am going abroad with my aunt, who knows all I have suffered, and approves an eternal separation.

"EDITH DOVE."

Some months later, the vicar resigned his living in the parish, and disappeared from the scene of his early labours. The year following, it was publicly stated in the religious newspapers that the Rev. Charles Santley, sometime Vicar of Omberley, had entered the Church of Rome.

THE END.

PRINTED BY WILLIAM CLOWES AND SONS, LIMITED,
LONDON AND BECCLES.